Just One Night...

MIRA LYN KELLY
LUCY KING
SHOMA NARAYANAN

First Published in Great Britain 2016
By Mills & Boon, an imprint of HarperCollins*Publishers*
1 London Bridge Street, London, SE1 9GF

JUST ONCE MORE. . . © 2016 Harlequin Books S. A.

Once Is Never Enough, One More Sleepless Night and *The One She Was Warned About* were first published in Great Britain by Harlequin (UK) Limited.

Once Is Never Enough © 2013 Mira Lyn Sperl
One More Sleepless Night © 2013 Lucy King
The One She Was Warned About © 2013 Shoma Narayanan

ISBN: 978-0-263-92072-7

05-0716

Our policy is to use papers that are natural, renewable and recyclable products and made from wood grown in sustainable forests.The logging and manufacturing processes conform to the legal environmental regulations of the country of origin.

Printed and bound in Spain
by CPI, Barcelona

ONCE IS
NEVER ENOUGH

BY
MIRA LYN KELLY

Mira Lynn Kelly grew up in the Chicago area and earned her degree in Fine Arts from Loyola University. She met the love of her life while studying abroad in Rome, Italy, only to discover he'd been living right around the corner from her for the previous two years. Having spent her twenties working and playing in the Windy City, she's now settled with her husband in rural Minnesota, where their four beautiful children provide an excess of action, adventure and entertainment.

With writing as her passion, and inspiration striking at the most unpredictable times, Mira can always be found with a notebook at the ready. (More than once the neighbours have caught her, covered in grass clippings, scribbling away atop the compost container!)

When she isn't reading, writing or running to keep up with the kids, she loves watching movies, blabbing with the girls and cooking with her husband and friends. Check out her website, www.miralynkelly.com, for the latest dish!

To my brilliant, hilarious, talented, sweet,
beautiful and more-fun-than-fiction children.
You are my real-life Happily-Ever-Afters. I love you.

PROLOGUE

"So you take your reckless adventuring like you take your coffee: lukewarm and watered down?"

Nichole Daniels stared first at the *shu mai* being jabbed in dumpling accusation from across their small table, and then at the gleaming blue eyes centering her best friend's face beyond. "*Hypothetical* reckless adventuring. And, for clarification, I want to enjoy my coffee. Not get hurt by it. So I take it hot, but not scalding. I like it brewed strong, but cut with something creamy to avoid heartburn."

Maeve snorted. "You cut it with skim milk. Cripes! The whole point of this was to embrace the no-consequences element of a fantasy we weren't planning to live out. I mean, seriously, I don't want to be trapped on a deserted island at all. And if I actually was, I'd hope it would be with some kind of mechanical genius who played survival games of the non-cannibal variety in his spare time. But for the purpose of this chatty lunchtime game girlfriends play…in a context *separate* from reality…for one single night without consequences maybe you'd want something *robust*…rich… Oh, my God…something topped with whipped cream!"

"Enough, enough." Nichole laughed, cutting into Maeve's ramping excitement before the whole restaurant started staring at them. "I get the concept. Honestly, I'm just not interested."

Maeve narrowed her eyes. "It's a *fantasy*. How can you not be interested?"

Echoes of a distant conversation teased through Nichole's mind—accusations and blame, heartbreak and humiliation, and the fantasy she'd bet her future on revealed for the nightmare it was. Everything she'd lost. *Everyone*.

She'd been down that road. Twice already. No thanks for a third.

It didn't pay to pretend. Not even over a *dim sum* lunch with her best friend.

"I'm just not," she managed through a stiff smile.

"Hence your overnight-on-a-deserted-island order for a male of unspecified looks who's safe, honest and can keep up his end of a conversation." Another jab of the chopsticks. *"Lame."*

"Not lame. Maybe my reality is everything I want it to be. How about that? I've got a kickass career, a button-cute place in a cool neighborhood and the greatest friends in the world," she said, batting her eyes at the best of them. "What more could a girl ask for?"

"Do you want me to start down at the toes or up at the head… Or should I just start in the middle, 'cause that region might make my point a little faster."

"None of the above! Now, stop taunting me with your dumpling or I'm going to eat it."

Maeve snapped her chopsticks back, popping the shrimp bundle into her mouth with a grin. On finishing the bite, though, her look became more contemplative than teasing. "I'm serious, Nikki. It's been three years. Don't you ever get lonely?"

Nichole stared back, the word *no* poised on her tongue. Only as the seconds stretched, the single word that was the lie she'd been telling herself for all too long suddenly wouldn't form. Her life was so *right*—in all the ways that mattered—she hadn't let herself think too much about those times when the stillness of her apartment left a sort of hollow feeling deep in her chest. Or when the empty chair across her table kept her from using the bay window breakfast nook that was half the reason she'd signed the lease in the first place. But they were there, nonetheless, apparently lying in wait for the right opportunity to glare at her.

Maeve slumped back in her chair. "I should have given you the last *shu mai*."

"Please, it's not so dire as that," she assured her, starting to stack the plates cluttering the table. "I'm just not interested in another relationship."

"But what about—?"

The strains of Van Halen's "Hot for Teacher" cut in, signaling a call from Maeve's brother.

Hallelujah.

With Maeve scheduled to leave town for business the next day, Garrett Carter would probably keep her on the line for the next twenty minutes, reassuring himself she wouldn't leave the coffeepot on, let anyone—*anyone*—into her hotel room, or accept candy from strangers in general. Only the reprieve proved short-lived when Maeve thumbed the call through to voicemail.

Nichole reached for her wine as an unholy gleam lit her friend's eyes.

"I should set you up with Garrett."

The crisp, fruity vintage burned like acid as it hit her sinuses. Napkin to her mouth, lungs wrestling to expel the alcohol in exchange for oxygen, she choked out a strangled, "What?" Then, wheezing, "I *thought* you were my friend."

"I was thinking maybe you could learn something from him."

"Like what? The most effective antibiotics for treating—?"

"Hey." Maeve cut her off with a stern glance. "Uncalled for. He's not so bad."

Nichole cocked a brow at her. "They call him *The Panty Whisperer.* I've seen his name on the ladies' room wall. And my mother warned me about men like him."

Maeve chuckled, a sisterly combination of worship and irritation filling her eyes. "You could be dating Attila the Hun and your mother would be delirious with the whole breathless 'he's so powerful' business. Trust me, she'd take Garrett with open arms."

Nichole shook her head, knowing it was true.

"And, between you and me, Mary Newton wrote that on the wall to get even with him for putting her off when she offered up the goods. I know you've never met him, but Garrett's actually a pretty decent guy."

"'Domineering, hypocritical, arrogant, womanizing, workaholic control freak.' Gee, where did I hear that from, I wonder?"

Maeve shook her head. "Okay, take it easy. I'm not serious about setting you up. And even if I were he wouldn't go out with you. He's got a rule about dating his sisters' friends."

Handy. Because Nichole had a similar rule. She'd lost enough friends because of broken relationships. People she'd already considered family—

Fingers snapped in front of her face. "Chill! I told you I was kidding."

The muscles down her back relaxed. "Your point, then?"

"Just this. Maybe it's time to dip a toe back into the

dating pool. Test the waters and see how it goes. I know in the past your relationships have always been…serious. But they don't have to be. Look, Garrett's the only guy I know as commitment-phobic as you. But you can bet *he* isn't lonely. He's proof positive a couple of dates for the sake of some non-platonic company can be just that—a couple of dates. Simple. No big deal."

Yeah, except the last time Nichole had gone on "a couple of dates" she ended up with a white dress she'd never worn, thousands blown on non-refundable deposits, the very fabric of her life torn asunder and an aversion to fantasies and forever powerful enough to keep her out of romance for three years running.

As it turned out, that fateful "it's not me, it's you" speech had been the best thing ever to happen to her.

She'd been lucky to escape a marriage that, despite what she'd believed at the time, would have been a train wreck. Lucky to have chosen Chicago as the city to clean slate her life in. And luckiest of all to have picked the open treadmill next to Maeve's that Friday that had, in essence, been the first day of the rest of Nichole's new life.

She hadn't been tempted to even the merest flirtation since. Not once. And she honestly couldn't imagine that changing anytime soon.

But, seeing Maeve about to come at her from another angle, Nichole held up a staying hand. "How about this. If I happen to meet someone who actually makes it hard to say no, I promise I'll give Garrett a call to talk me through The Panty Whisperer's six-step guide to keeping it casual—"

"Ha-ha. Very funny," Maeve grumbled, flagging the waitress for their check.

"But until then I'm not dipping my toe in anything."

CHAPTER ONE

GOOD LORD, WAS THAT a tongue?

Nichole Daniels ripped her attention from the kiss deepening at exponential rates less than fifty feet away and dragged it back to where Chicago's cityscape reflected the molten hues of the western sky.

Having arrived early to help her friend Sam set up for his rooftop bash to welcome his older brother home from Europe, she'd been stocking wash pails with beer, wine and a myriad other pre-packaged cocktails when the lovebirds had pushed out the door, their breathless laughter dying at the sight of her. With the party scheduled to start—well, right then, for the few minutes before the guests migrated up to the terrace she'd figured the roof would be big enough for the three of them. Only now the evening breeze had picked up, carrying with it whispers not meant for her ears. Private words and promises of the kind of forever she'd stopped dreaming about years ago. The intimacy of their exchange had her feeling like some kind of creepy voyeur.

Boxing up the last packaging to recycle, she eyed the door. Anytime now...

People always showed up early for Sam's parties. The view from his roof was one of the best in the city for watching the sunset.

A muffled groan.

Awkward.

Tipping the longneck that hung from her fingers for a small draw of the lemony draft, she glanced down at her phone for the hundredth time. She saw a text from her mother, who was checking to see if she had any *special* plans for the night, so she pushed it aside on the picnic tabletop, making a mental note to call her the next day.

Tonight she wasn't in the mood for a diatribe on beggars versus choosers, ticking clocks and doing the work to make her dreams a reality. No matter how well-intentioned her mother might be, a guilt-flavored pep-talk wasn't on the evening's agenda.

Another gasp. This one edged with unmistakable need—and she hazarded a sidelong glance—

Whoa! Mistake!

She *hadn't* just seen…and the hands…and the legs…

Jumping clumsily from the picnic table, Nichole stumbled back and made a beeline for the stairway access.

Eyes on the ground. Eyes. On. The. Ground.

She was halfway down the narrow flight, ready to text Maeve her first report from the party, when she stopped, staring blankly at her open, empty palm.

She'd left her phone.

Her stomach turned to lead as she hesitantly looked back up to the roof. The sunset she could live without. But that phone was her lifeline. All her contacts… appointments…shopping lists…music…*Maeve.*

She had to go back. Only she *really* didn't want to.

Maybe if she gave it a minute or two they'd be done and she'd be able to collect her phone without feeling like she needed to boil her eyes in bleach or start therapy seven days a week to scrub the memory from her mind.

How long had it been already? She didn't even know.

So accustomed to her pretty little pink-rubber-clad smartphone, who needed a watch?

Okay, this was ridiculous. She was an adult, and her phone was a critical part of her existence. She turned toward the roof, bottom lip parked between her teeth, foot poised to advance—

The door below opened and she glanced back, hoping against hope it was Sam so she could make *him* get the darned phone for her. Only this wasn't her five-foot-ten-if-she-looked-up-just-right, whipcord-thin blond bud, come to rescue her phone, but rather a six-foot-something stranger in worn jeans and a white Oxford rolled back at the arms, shouldering through a doorway made too small by his frame.

Head bowed, he called back to someone within the apartment, "Yeah, see you up there in a few."

Maybe she should warn the guy about the rooftop action. Only before she could figure quite how to phrase it, the head topped with short, disheveled, dark curls tipped back, revealing a set of electric blue eyes that sent a shock straight through the center of her. Her mind whirled and stalled as recognition washed over her in a wave, receding just as quickly.

She'd have sworn she knew him.

"Looks like we had the same idea to catch the sunset," he offered with an easy smile and a jut of his chin toward the roof as he took the steps at a loose jog, meeting her at the midpoint of the stairwell. "You going up?"

"I think I have to," she answered weakly, her eyes tracking nervously to the rectangle of open sky at the top of the stairs. "I left my phone when I ran...."

Her phone would be fine. It wasn't like she'd left it balancing on the rail.

Was it possible they were finished?

"Ran?"

Of course it was possible. Probable? Who knew?

"Did something happen up there?"

"Yeah," she answered with a shudder as she covered her eyes with her hands. The way they'd started going at it—she'd never seen...never done....

Heat penetrated the fog of her embarrassed shock, radiating from a concentrated point where his hand, wide and heavy, covered her shoulder in a reassuring squeeze. "Go down to Sam. Stay with him."

And then he was bypassing her on the narrow stairwell, somehow managing to keep all that brawn from doing more than warming the scant space between them. The proximity was unnerving, distracting her even more than the scene she'd witnessed on the rooftop...where this guy was heading...his every step landing like an increasing threat.

Wait. *Did something happen?*

Oh...*no.*

Her breath caught.

Oh, no.

"Oh, no! Wait," she gasped, realizing too late what he'd been asking her.

The eyes that looked back at her as his steps continued were anything but laughing. "Go downstairs. I'll take care of this guy."

Take care of—? She watched his retreating back expand impossibly, blotting out the light of the evening sky beyond. "No, really," she yelped, scrambling up the steps behind him. "You—um—blue-eyed guy—wait!"

But he just held a staying hand behind him as he hit the open access to the rooftop. At best this was about to get extremely embarrassing for both of them. She had to do something—and fast.

"Sex!"

Oh, God, that hadn't come out right either. Except the guy's steps slowed and his head cranked around, revealing all that deep blue intensity replaced with confusion. "Excuse me?"

She raced up the stairs behind him, heart pounding—though not due to any sort of exertion from the short flight. Heck, she and Maeve could run a half-marathon on the treadmill if they had a season of *Game of Thrones* playing in front of them. Her heart had hit double-time due to embarrassment and a desperate need to stop this really protective guy before he tossed someone off the side of the roof.

Swallowing hard, one hand waving around, she looked for a salvation that wasn't coming. Finally she looked at him apologetically. "They were sort of having sex up there. That's what happened. I'm sorry…and…um…thank you too—I think."

She'd never seen eyes change in so many ways in such a short span of time. But this guy's were like a visual aid for defining "window to the soul." Everything was right there within them. Shock, relief, amusement, and then a slow-growing interest that tugged at some long-forgotten place inside her.

Something she shook off without more than a second's consideration.

A fractured cry of the climactic variety split the air between them, setting her cheeks to blaze like the sky beyond.

"Damn," was his only response, and something about the smacked look on his face struck her as ridiculously funny within the awkwardness of the moment.

"Yeah." She laughed, covering her ears. "You're telling me. I think we ought to give them some privacy…

but I really need my phone. I'll bake you a cake if you'll get it for me."

Maeve would bake the cake. If she'd been here, none of this would have happened.

"Cake?"

"Please?"

"I'm a tough customer when it comes to cake. My sisters have spoiled me pretty bad. How about this? You go grab your phone and I'll take care of Team Romance behind us."

This guy didn't know what he was missing. But if Blue Eyes didn't want Maeve's baking…? Fine with her. This way she got her sunset, her phone and a cake too. Because, now that she was thinking about it, Maeve was *definitely* going to make her one when she got back in town. "Deal."

An awkward moment, many murmured apologies and some quiet shuffling later, her defender of public decency stepped up to the rail beside her, resting his forearms over the worn wood as he squinted into the sinking sun. "I'll admit I was half tempted to pull out a pencil and start taking notes."

Nichole shook her head, unable to fight the pull at the corner of her mouth.

"What? I would have given you a copy. Though maybe too early for that kind of kink in our relationship?"

Coughing out a laugh, she leaned back, forcibly resisting the draw to lean closer. "Yeah, you're probably right."

"Based on that pretty blush, I'd say definitely. So how about it, Red? Sun's going down fast."

"Red?" she asked, mildly disappointed by the moniker that had followed her around half her life. For some unaccountable reason she'd thought—hoped?—no, that couldn't be right—this guy might be different.

"Blue-eyed guy?" he challenged back, then tapped a finger to his cheek while nodding at hers. "Red."

For her blush, not her hair.

Such a small distinction, and yet big enough to push a smile to her lips as she followed his gaze to the burned amber glow of the pooling sun. It was beautiful. And, with the mellow notes of Jack Johnson filtering the rush of city traffic rising from the streets below, peaceful.

For long moments they watched, remaining quiet until the last molten drop bled beneath the horizon.

Forearms resting over the rail, muscular back rounded beneath the pull of his shirt, the familiar stranger beside her let out a long, deeply contented breath.

"Wow. That good, huh?" she asked teasingly, anxious to relieve the unsettling intimacy of the moment.

Casting her a sidelong glance, he considered. Then, pushing back to straighten, he shoved his hands into his pockets and met her gaze in earnest. "Yeah, it was."

"Not a lot of time for sunsets?"

His mouth pulled to the side and his broad shoulders hunched forward. "You know, it's not that I haven't seen them. More a matter of being too caught up in everything else going on—where I've got to be next, how much needs to get done, what all's about to get away from me." He shook his head, a frown darkening his gaze as it held hers. "Been a long time since I've been able to slow down and just…enjoy the simple stuff. Too long."

A few plainly spoken words. Nothing particularly deep. And yet the way he'd said them—as though making a reluctant admission—gave them power enough to penetrate the superficial and resonate within her.

"I get it. The little things have a way of passing you by pretty quickly if you aren't paying attention. And then, when you finally notice, sometimes all you've missed doesn't exactly feel so small."

"Yeah, that's about it." He laughed then—a brusque, dismissive sound—but even as he did so those deep blue eyes held hers with an almost questioning intensity. "So what's been passing you by?"

Maybe just this.

She should have looked away. Made light of the two of them standing there. Thrown out a joke or an excuse to put some space between them. Only for the first time in three years she didn't want the space or the buffer of meaningless banter. She wanted to stretch the moment and all the simplicity it offered—make it last for the both of them.

That was crazy. She didn't know this guy. Didn't know anything more than that he'd made some vague reference to a busy life and the desire not to miss out on the simple stuff. And yet there was something about him— an odd sense of familiarity, connection—that made her feel like she did. Made her think about her own life and the simple things she avoided out of fear for the complications they could bring.

"That much, huh?" he asked, breaking into her thoughts with a reminder she hadn't answered. Laugh lines creased the skin around his eyes as he cocked his head to the side. "Looks like we could both use a few more sunsets."

"Looks like," she agreed, all too grateful for the simple reprieve.

Damn, there it was again. That hot red rising to the surface of her skin. Betraying the woman beneath in all the best ways. He couldn't get enough, and it was taking the bulk of his restraint not to work her pretty blush for everything it was worth.

But he hadn't come to Jesse's welcome-home party to pick someone up. In fact finding a woman had been the last thing on his mind.

He'd wanted to go out. Reconnect with friends. Watch a sunset.

After six years of walking through his front door with half his takeout already consumed and heading straight to his back office—where, on a good day, he'd be able to set aside one kind of work for another—he was done. And now, degree in hand, he wanted the straightforward simplicity of knowing he'd put his day to bed and the night was his…finally…to do with as he pleased.

But there she'd been. Looking lost. And, damn, he hadn't known what. Having raised his four sisters through their teens, he found his mind had a way of going to dark places pretty fast when he didn't understand what was happening. Thank God he'd been wrong. Only by the time he'd understood where all that vulnerability was coming from—the mad make-out scene which even *he* had to admit had been pretty intense— she'd made his radar. Registered as more than a collection of pleasing physical attributes falling under the category of female.

And then she'd been standing there, backlit by the cooling sky, looking into his eyes with that thoughtful kind of amazement in hers telling him she *got* him. Making him wonder if maybe she did.

"Well, would you look what the cat dragged in?" came the first of several raucous calls, derailing his train of thought as a group of the old crew jogged up to the rooftop.

"Sam said you were here, man, but I didn't dare believe."

"Dude! No way."

Laughing brown eyes peered up at him. "All this is for you?"

"So it would seem," he answered, with a wide grin at seeing so many of the old faces he'd lost touch with. "It's been a while."

"Too long?" she asked, a mirthful smile playing across her lips.

"Definitely too long."

Just then her phone sounded and, holding it up with a little wave, she started to back away. "I'll let you catch up, then."

He reached for her elbow. Followed her gaze as it slipped to the point of contact between them, lingered and then returned almost tentatively to his.

"Thanks for the sunset, Red."

"You too, Blue Eyes," she offered quietly, backing away as he withdrew his hand, before she took the stairs down to Sam's apartment.

A solid clap on his shoulder pulled him back to the guys, the laughter, greetings and jibes.

"Damn, Garrett. What are you? Here fifteen minutes and already you've got the next victim cued up and ready to go. I bow to you, dude."

Garrett Carter looked back at the guys he'd gone to high school with and shook his head.

Aw, hell. Not this again.

CHAPTER TWO

PHONE CLUTCHED to her ear, Nichole stopped in the quiet alcove at the bottom of the stairwell, her heart thumping in her chest. "I think I dipped a toe back in the pool."

"Wait—what? You think—" Maeve's distracted voice was cut off as her breath was sucked in. "Shut it! You didn't… Oh, my God—tell. *Tell!*"

Nichole hadn't gotten more than a few sentences in when Maeve interrupted.

"Stop, stop, stop. Set the stage, for crying out loud. Details. And, so you don't waste my time with a lot of trash about the temperature or the number of cigarette butts around the roof, I'm talking about the guy. Hotness ranking. The good kind of dirty or clean-cut? Build and bulk. Distinguishing features. Height. You get the idea. Don't skimp. Then get to the good toe-dipping stuff… Damn it, *why* am I in Denver?"

Nichole pulled the phone from her ear and looked at it, suddenly wishing she'd thought to Skype. Maeve sounded like she hadn't slept in two days and Nichole figured the look on her face as she shot off her rapid fire laundry list of must-know information would be priceless.

"Easy, Maeve." She laughed into the phone, stepping

clear as a large group edged past her, heading for the roof. "How are negotiations on the deal going?"

"The guy, Nikki. Don't make me beg."

"Okay, okay. So he's definitely one of those men who draws the eye. Kind of magnetic. Over six feet. More rugged than pretty. And there was something about his eyes… When this guy looks at you…I don't even know how to describe it."

"Mmhmm…mmhmm. I like it. Keep going."

Nichole shook her head and chuckled, leaning back against the wall as she laid down what physical details she could before recounting the few minutes they'd shared. When she'd finished, Maeve let out an indelicate cough.

"That's *it?* What part of that had your toe anywhere near the pool? It doesn't sound like you got wet at all."

Feeling slightly miffed, Nichole ignored the snicker and subtle pun to counter, "I didn't say I jumped him! It was just a really nice quiet moment that had a very different feel than when I'm hanging out with Sam or you or any of the usual crowd, for example. It wasn't going anywhere. But there was a kind of sizzly thing in the air, and it definitely had a toe-dipping feel."

Maeve was quiet a moment, then asked. "So, if there was sizzle, why wouldn't it go anywhere?"

"Hold on a sec." Nichole pressed further into the wall behind her, waving quick hellos to a stream of partygoers heading up to the roof. After the stairwell was cleared, she answered, "I don't think he's even from around here. I've never seen him before. But he knows a bunch of guys I think must be Jesse's friends. I kind of got the feeling he was visiting from out of town."

"Hmm… So let's recap. You've got an aversion to commitment. You've met a ruggedly hot hunk with whom you share 'sizzle' and you think he's just in town for a visit. It feels like there ought to be an obvious solution here. Like maybe you could have your hunk and eat hi—"

"That's enough," she cut in, feeling a renewed burn in her cheeks. "I get what you're saying. But, no. Seriously, just no."

Maeve's sigh was long suffering, and even longer drawn out, but Nichole could hear the smile behind it.

"Fine. Waste this perfectly good opportunity for what sounds like some simple fun without a whole lot of strings."

Nichole's brows drew down and her gaze slid up to the rooftop doorway.

No. It had been a couple of minutes. A fleeting kind of connection. That was all.

Another larger group filed past. Following them up, she wrapped her call with Maeve, promising more gossip and snaps from the party as available.

On the roof, Nichole glanced around at what had become a dense crowd. With the way people were pouring into the place now she probably wouldn't even see him again. Which was good. Because she really wasn't interested.

Though even as she thought it, she realized she was scanning faces. Her gaze slipping past friends and acquaintances without stopping in an absent-minded search for the stranger who was making a liar out of her even as she stood there.

And then she found him. Nearly a head taller than most everyone around him. That vivid blue gaze locked steadily with hers.

A loud cheer sounded and all attention shifted to the doorway. Jesse had jogged up and was standing with a stunned grin on his face. She'd only met him once before he'd left, two years ago, but she remembered him to be as cool as his brother, who was now pulling him in for a solid hug.

She looked back to where her blue-eyed hero had been a moment before, but within the shifting crowd she'd lost him.

The party was in full swing, the roof packed to capacity, the atmosphere as welcoming as Jesse and Sam's ever-expanding social network. Garrett had managed to get a couple of minutes with his oldest friend and to secure plans for later in the week before letting the next eager guest at him. He hadn't been two feet out of the crush before finding *her* again.

Nichole. That was her name. It had taken him the better part of an hour to pick it out from a nearby conversation, roll it around in his mind and connect it to the woman with the glittering almond eyes and fiery spill of curls, the long legs in dark jeans and the strappy little top with the tiny bow.

Standing within a loose grouping of friends and acquaintances of whom they both seemed to know some, but not all, they'd been talking around each other for hours now. Much as they'd been circling throughout the night. Picking up hints through rapid banter interspersed with old stories and private jokes. Exchanging looks that, within their lifespan of a scant handful of seconds, said more than all the words they'd shared combined…and then moving on.

Only now all those hints, bits and pieces had begun to take shape in his mind, forming the image of a woman he liked. A woman who laughed easily, spoke intelligently and didn't take herself too seriously. A woman who liked to joke and tease. Who gave as good as she got. And whose unconscious smile did something to him he couldn't quite put a name to.

He wanted her.

Not the way he usually wanted his dates. Not for some superficial conversation and perfunctory dinner or drinks that were the means to an end he'd been limiting himself to for as long as he could remember. All he'd had time for. All he could afford. Because he'd spent every spare minute he had on making his construction company top in the city, earning his degree and keeping his four sisters from doing all the things he didn't want them to do.

Nichole made him want more. She made him curious. Made him want to linger. To take his time and find out if maybe they could have something…uncomplicated. Casual, but real. For a while.

He wanted the rest too. The parts where he pushed that pretty blush to see how deep and dark and far it could spread. The parts where he had her beneath him, all that fiery red hair wrapped around his fists and spilling over his pillow as he pushed inside her body. But when those parts were over, and before they even began, he wanted more. And he wanted it soon.

Laughter subsiding, Nichole sighed, her dark gaze finding his beneath the ashy fringe of her lashes. It wasn't coy or contrived. Nor the blatant invitation he'd lost interest in back in his twenties. It was contemplative. Heated, but questioning. Enticing in its hint of uncertainty.

Damn, if that didn't make her all the better.

Around them the conversation had somehow found its way to movies filmed in Chicago and who could name the most. Beneath the titles volleying back and forth,

Garrett gave a subtle nod of his head toward the quiet corner of the rooftop where they'd watched the sunset.

Nichole's slender brows drew together, her teeth setting into her lush bottom lip in the ultimate expression of uncertainty.

It shouldn't have gone straight to his groin, but it did. At least until he saw her fooling with that phone she carried around. One thumb brushed the smooth screen and—was she...*texting?*

Immediately he thought of his sister, "using a lifeline" to make some inane decision she didn't trust him enough to help her with. Was that what this was? Indecision over whether to step over to a corner and *talk* with him?

Sure, he had every intention of taking it further, but for now—

Wait... What the hell...? She was *not* holding that phone up to take his picture.

Eyes on the screen, only half listening to an escalating debate over whether the outlying suburbs and thus the John Hughes classics counted, Nichole had been trying to frame the shot when her subject was suddenly front and center—closer than he'd been edging past her down in the access stairwell.

Oh, God. She'd been busted taking his picture to send to Maeve. This was an all-time low.

Her gaze crawling up the towering expanse of Oxford cloth and then creeping over the tantalizing stretch of bare masculine skin at the base of his neck, she forced herself to keep going until she reached the now steely blue of his eyes. Her stomach tumbled into free fall.

"What're you doing, Red?"

Swallowing past the tight knot in her throat, she shook her head.

What *was* she doing? Trying to snap a picture of some
virtual stranger because she couldn't account for the
reaction she was having to him? Because she couldn't
keep her eyes off him for more than three seconds at a
stretch and she needed the judgment of a reliable outside source? Someone who knew her just about as well
as she knew herself. Maeve.

So, basically, she was acting like a complete nut-job.

And yet a part of her still twitched with the need to
get a photo and hit "send." It must have been obvious
too, because seconds later a hand firmed around her
wrist—loose, but uncompromising—and pushed the
phone down to her side.

The skin beneath his grasp warmed as though a low
charge ran from his hand up through hers. It felt good.
Too good. And suddenly all she could think about was
how long it had been since anyone had touched her for
more than the briefest instant. What a simple pleasure
that heated, lingering contact was. And how she hadn't
even realized she missed it.

He was bending close to her ear and his breath washed
warm across skin that seemed to come alive beneath it.
"Red?"

The air went thin around her as the slow tingle behind
her ear began to spread, sliding down her neck, shoulder
and arm until it came to mingle with the charge emanating from her wrist.

"I don't know what I'm doing. Men don't usually—
I mean, I don't—" Trying to find the words, she licked
her lips, watched his eyes darken at the sight. "There's
something about you."

Maybe it was the way he hadn't hesitated to protect
a woman he didn't know. Or how he was built like he
pounded rocks for a living but could argue international

economics as easily as the merits of Leia over Uhura. How he savored opportunities to stop and enjoy the simple stuff. Or how his offbeat jokes made her laugh like she'd known him forever.

Or maybe it was just that when his gaze drifted to her hair, she could *feel* his fingers tightening in it.

Could it be so simple? He made her feel like a woman and made her notice him as a man...when for so long no one else had.

A gravel-rough laugh rumbled from low in his chest and the hand at her wrist loosened, easing into a slow up and down caress over the bare skin of her arm. "There's something about you too. So what do you say to getting out of here and figuring out just what it is?"

Getting out of here? Her heart slammed to a stop.

That was no toe in the pool. No testing the waters or even taking a tentative dip. It was a full-on, feel-the-rush blast down a water slide—total body immersion into the deep end. And the most frightening thing about it was...as she peered into those brilliant blues...it was tempting as hell.

Where was Maeve when she needed her most?

When she wanted someone skilled in the art of justification and adventurous enough to—?

And then it struck her. She didn't need Maeve at all. Not only did she know with one-hundred-percent certainty what her friend would want her to do...she knew herself.

This guy was the simple pleasure she'd been missing. He had a connection to and was obviously liked by nearly half the people at the party—so chances were good he wasn't a serial killer. This was the first time she'd met him, and from what she'd gathered he didn't live in the area but up north somewhere—so chances were even better this could be something brief. Something quick.

Something in the moment.

Something she wanted more with every second that passed.

A slow smile spread to her lips.

"Okay, Blue Eyes. Let's go."

CHAPTER THREE

"Let's go."

Garrett had known even before the words left her mouth. He'd seen the way those soft brown eyes steadied, sensed the change in the air between them, and had felt his own body respond to the first victory.

A quick scan of the rooftop confirmed at least half a dozen sets of eyes on them. Not what he would have preferred, but there was nothing to be done about it now.

"Yeah, let's go." Taking her hand, he kept his eyes on hers as they headed toward the stairwell. If she was looking at him she wouldn't notice the raised brows, wouldn't worry about the quiet snickers, wouldn't think about anything but finding a place where they could talk. *To* each other instead of *around* each other. There'd used to be a coffee house in the neighborhood he'd heard was pretty popular for the late-night crowd. Perhaps it was time to find out for himself.

At the bottom of the stairs Nichole stopped. "Do you need to say goodbye to anyone?"

"Nah, I'm good." He'd call Jesse tomorrow. The rest of the guys he'd see soon enough. "You?"

Her mouth pulled to the side as she shook her head and glanced away.

"Are you worried about people seeing us leave to-gether?" He hoped like hell that wasn't it. While his re-turning to the party alone would possibly minimize it, most likely the damage was already done.

"I'm twenty-six, not sixteen." She laughed, sounding more nervous, he was sure, than she'd intended. "It's just that I'm acting a little out of character here and I don't want to lose my nerve."

Damn, she was cute. He rubbed his thumb in a light circle over her knuckle and leaned in conspiratorially. "Lose your nerve for what?"

He'd asked it as a taunt, finding her all too easy to tease and loving the fast rise of red to her cheeks. Only when she turned, head tipping back as her gaze lifted to his, the wild blush he'd been hoping for wasn't any-where to be found. Instead a sort of uncertain determi-nation lit her face, making him wonder just what she was struggling with.

Brushing a stray curl from her brow, he caught the quick dart of a pink tongue across the swell of her bot-tom lip, felt the pull of this thing between them tugging him closer, making him want to take advantage of the empty stairwell, the dim lighting and the mouth that was driving him to distraction.

He needed to get her out of there. Into his b—

No. Not yet. This one was different.

Those soulful brown eyes searched his, the lingering intimacy fraying the tether of his restraint. The soft press of her body against his, unraveling his control.

"My nerve for this," she murmured, her breath a flut-tery rush against his skin an instant before she kissed him—pressed her mouth to his and tasted his lips with the barest flick of her tongue, demolishing the man he'd wanted to be for her and giving rise to the man she'd invited in.

Hell.

Tucking the hand still holding hers at the small of her back, he drew a slow breath at that most enticing spot just below a woman's ear. Let her quiet shudder and sweet scent flood his senses and wreak havoc on his body.

"That's what you want?" he asked in a low growl, knowing it was but wanting to hear her say it just the same.

"I've been worried about avoiding complications so long I think maybe I've been missing a lot of the simple stuff too." She swallowed, heat pouring off her as she finished, "I don't want to miss this."

She couldn't get any better. "Then you won't."

Ten minutes later, amid gasps of laughter and lust, Garrett turned the key and Nichole's front door swung open under the combined weight of their bodies. Spilling into her front hall, Garrett righted them both, kicked the door closed with a sweep of his leg and threw the lock. She backed across the open hardwood, barely a step ahead of him, eyes glittering, lips curved and parted as her breath came in shallow pants.

Her gaze swept the length of him and the now persistent flush of her cheeks deepened, driving the blood hard and fast to his already aching groin. Reaching for him, her slender fingers curved around his belt, pulling until he allowed her to tow him closer. Close enough that he could reach around her, cover the firm curves of her ass with his hands, slide lower still to the backs of her thighs and hoist her up against him.

Her breath caught as her ankles locked behind his

back, the soft brown of her eyes going nearly black as her pupils pushed wide.

"God, you're beautiful," he groaned, fighting the urge to take her there against the wall.

Nodding distractedly, she went to work on the buttons down the front of his shirt, pushing at the panels like she was revealing Superman's emblem beneath. And when she answered, "You too," her eyes glazing at the sight of him, taking a building in a single bound didn't seem so impossible.

The door to her room was open ahead, and the sight of her neat bed with its delicate lilac print spread made him harder than he could ever remember being. Hell, yes, he was hungry for the sex. For her body. For the pretty pink that tinged her skin and the sounds she'd make when he took her over the edge. He wanted all of that. But this— this anticipation burning through his veins—was for what would come after. For the part that was going to be different. The part he would wait for until he'd wrung every moan and gasp Nichole's body had to offer out of her.

At her bed, he set her back on the mattress, supporting himself on one arm.

Legs still wrapped around his hips, she looked up at him. "I don't even know your name."

He'd opened his mouth to tell her when something in the depths of those deep dark eyes gave him pause. Something excited.

The corner of his mouth kicked up. Lowering his voice to a taunting growl, he asked, "So the question is, do you like it better that way?"

The half-moan, half-gasp that escaped her slender throat was answer enough to just about push him over the edge.

Had he actually thought she couldn't get any better?

* * *

Perfect. This hot, hard, mouthwatering male specimen was her sunset. Her uncomplicated simple pleasure. This was the fantasy she could finally afford to play out. The reckless adventure she hadn't dared to dream. And, more, it was safe.

Because she didn't even know his name.

Women didn't plan forevers around nameless men. They didn't get the wrong idea. Misinterpret intentions. Or get caught up in dreams that would take them nowhere.

They got a single night *sans* complications.

This was the one night of wild abandon she'd been unconsciously saving up for for three years. Longer than that if she was willing to look back. But she wasn't. Not tonight. Not when this moment, right now—as the familiar stranger above her lowered his mouth to the hollow between her breasts—was too good to miss even one second of.

Those blue eyes peered up at her as the corner of his mouth twisted into a mischievous smile. "This little bow here," he murmured gruffly, "has been begging me to play with it all night." Then, catching one loose string between his teeth, he tugged until the knot slipped free, taking Nichole's next breath with it.

She hadn't thought of the peach cami as particularly sexy, hadn't consciously drawn attention to herself for years. But at the rough sound of appreciation scraping from his throat as he used his hand to part the tiny expanse of soft cotton between her breasts just that much further, she flushed with the pleasure of knowing it was.

His tongue swirled deep in the hollow there, wetting the skin first and then blowing a cool breath across it after, making her belly turn and twist.

There wasn't enough contact between them. Not for the way her body was beginning to ache. To heat. To need. He was above her on the bed, his weight supported on one arm and the knees that straddled her thigh.

His tongue made another wet foray across the swell of her breast and then stopped within a warm, teasing breath of her nipple. So close.

Arching into him, she offered the straining bud to his kiss, begging him to push her bra aside and take. But just as quickly he eased back, drawing another wet trail up to her collarbone, her neck and then to the decadent spot behind her ear that had never felt quite so sensitive as this.

"I want you naked, Nichole," he growled against the spot, making her heart skitter and pound.

"You know my name," she gasped as his palm smoothed over her belly to the hem of her shirt and pushed it up.

Pulling the gathered fabric over her head, he tossed the shirt aside and stared down at her breasts, covered in a plain cream demi-cup. "And you don't know mine."

She swallowed hard.

It shouldn't have been exciting. She only wanted to think of it as a safeguard, a defense against this man who'd stirred the first response her body had known in three years, and quite possibly the strongest ever. But there was no mistaking the playful taunt in his tone. This was sexy gameplay. Or maybe a second cousin to it. It had to be some relation based on the way the words alone and all their suggestive implications licked at the needy, achy places within her. Places she hadn't thought existed.

A flick of his finger and the front clasp opened. Another and she was bared to him. The peaks of her nipples tight and straining for a touch only he could give her. And now, watching the way that electric blue glaze zeroed in on them, she didn't think she'd manage her next breath if he didn't ease them.

"Naked, Nichole."

CHAPTER FOUR

BACKING OFF THE BED he helped her out of her jeans and panties. Staring in blatant appreciation at her naked form spread out before him, he shed his shirt with a few efficient jerks and went to work on his belt.

Nichole's mouth went dry, her eyes wide. And then she was on her knees at the edge of the bed, pushing his hands from the wide length of leather and running her own up the steep plains of his chest. She'd felt the power in his shoulders when he carried her, seen the definition across his pecs when she'd opened his shirt, but this— nothing had prepared her for the hard-cut terrain of his shirtless form.

He was like a work of art. A Greek god. A veritable playground of muscle and man. And he was only *half* undressed.

"Naked," she murmured, her fingers jumping the crest of each abdominal ridge as they descended back to his belt, tugged the stiff leather until the buckle freed, before moving on to his straining fly.

He stood patient before her as she opened his zipper with trembling fingers. As if he sensed her need to be an active participant rather than a passive player. But still he touched her all the while, never breaking contact, his hands always moving, coasting over her bare shoulders, her neck and back as she pushed the denim low on his hips. His thumbs brushed the line of her jaw, the swell of her bottom lip, the hollow at the base of her throat as she eased the stretchy waistband of his white cotton boxer briefs over the thick head of his erection and saw for the first time his actual size.

Big. Like everything else about him.

Different. Than anything she'd experienced before.

Exciting. In a way she'd never known.

Unable to resist, she closed a hand over him, testing the steely length.

"Nichole."

At the gruff sound of her name she lifted her gaze up, up, up until she met the blue burn of his. Intense. Barely contained. A shocking contrast to the light touch he'd treated her to. The look in his eyes said he wanted to throw her back on the bed and take her hard. Let the weight of his body hold her down.

Wow. Okay. She was pretty sure she wanted that too.

She gave him the space to toe off his shoes and discard his jeans, retrieving his wallet and the condom within in the process.

Breathless with mounting anticipation, she waited for him to rip it open and roll it on…frowned as he tossed it onto the bed instead.

Please don't let him be one of those guys who only wants to wear protection at the very end. She was so excited, so caught up in the magic of what was happening, the wet blanket of a conversation about risks and necessity and protection really wasn't one she wanted to need to have.

At her questioning stare, his brow quirked.

Okay—so, yes. She was going to have to have the

conversation. "Umm, you're going to wear that? The whole time, right?"

The eyes above her looked briefly confused, then cleared completely. "I would never take that kind of risk, Nichole. Not with your life. Not with mine."

The conviction in his words was unmistakable, and left her with no doubt about his sincerity or commitment to their mutual protection. Which was incredibly sexy.

Almost as much as when his mouth tipped in a way that suggested a secret lingered behind his crooked smile. One he looked forward to sharing with her.

"What? You didn't think the fun and games were over yet, did you?"

She swallowed, unwilling to admit that in her experience the bulk sum of "fun and games" took place between the time the condom went on and came off. "I—I don't know."

He leaned in closer, and then closer still, so the light pressure of his mouth against her ear and his bare chest at her shoulder guided her down to the bed. "Not even close."

Nervous laughter escaped her even as her inner walls clenched with unmet need.

His hand moved between her legs, cupping her sex as he held her gaze. A single thick finger slid between her swollen folds and then inside her. Deep and deeper. Slow and steady. He withdrew to paint a light circle around that throbbing bundle of nerves—the callused pad of a workman's finger adding sensation when she was already beyond what she'd believed she could take—his gentle, rough touch a decadent sensual contrast.

Different.

Every single thing about him.

About this night.

Another slow thrust of his finger and her hips rocked to meet him. Her back arched and the desire pooling warm and thick through her belly spilled free, making her slick, making her beg. "Please. I need—"

"You need more?" A second finger joined the first, this one pushing a gasp from her lungs instead of words.

Want coiled tight within her, making her pulse around his slow thrusts. Making her skin heat and her center burn. "I need you—"

"To make you wait? Make you so hot and ready…" the strong draw of his mouth on her nipple stole conscious thought "…that when you finally fall over the edge it'll feel like forever?"

"Oh, God." Her body seized, liquid heat scorching through her veins, pushing her fast toward the very edge he'd threatened to pull her back from. "I— I'm so close. Please—it's been so long. Please."

His touch far inside her, he met her gaze. "How long?"

Another deep thrust, this one slower, so she felt the curl of his fingers stroking, teasing some wicked spot that promised to make her its slave.

"Years," she admitted on a broken gasp, unable to bear the intensity of his stare a moment longer.

His hand stilled. Withdrew as the bed sagged under his shifting weight.

Her eyes shot open, panic slamming through her. He couldn't stop. Not now. "No, wait—"

Only then she saw he wasn't leaving the bed at all, but rather moving between her legs. His wide hands spread them apart in a way that with any other man would have left her feeling vulnerable, exposed. Not with him. Not when his big hands slid beneath her bottom and wide shoulders braced her thighs. Not when he looked into her eyes and said, "No more waiting."

And then his mouth was covering her, his tongue mimicking the actions of his fingers and hands only moments ago…only it was different. So very, incredibly different. So much more…intense. Stimulating. Hard and soft and wet and strong. Everything. He was delving inside her and then licking a path to her most sensitive spot.

Stroking.

Nibbling.

Circling with the wet velvet point of his tongue.

Making her gasp and cry and beg and scream.

And then he closed over her…drawing deep against the throbbing, needy ache. Pulling sensation from every tingling extremity…centering it all…at that one…concentrated…spot.

She was falling.

So hard. So good. So long.

Finding her release had never been so incredible. Not even close.

Maybe it was the anonymity. Or semi-anonymity anyway, since he'd made it clear he knew her name, saying it again and again in a deep, rumbling voice that stroked her every nerve like the wet tongue that spoke it.

And then he was crawling over her, giving her a taste of his body atop hers.

His lips grazed her neck. Tender. Lingering. He was going for the condom, but not in any rush. And she realized he was savoring her as he'd savored their sunset.

Oh, no. That fluttery sort of ache in her chest, making her want to link her arms around his neck and pull him closer, didn't belong there. Or maybe it did. Maybe it was just a normal side effect of endorphins being released and not her reckless heart getting ahead of her. She didn't know. What she needed was an expert. Someone with a point of reference when it came to "casual."

She couldn't even believe she was thinking it—and while she was still in bed with her blue-eyed stranger. But maybe Maeve was right and she should talk to—

"Garrett," came the gruff, deeply masculine voice from above her.

Her eyes blinked wide as the flutter in her chest dropped into her belly, turning leaden and still.

"I can feel you getting tense."

The decadent weight she'd been basking under eased as he shifted to his elbows and peered down into her eyes. *Familiar eyes.*

Oh, God.

"It's fun to play and all, but I didn't want you to wonder or worry about who you were with. My name's Garrett."

"Garrett…Carter?" Her throat closed over the name, fighting what she knew deep in the pit of her stomach to be true.

His muscles tensed. "You know me?"

Oh, yeah. She knew him. And her face must have said as much because Garrett flinched, looking pained and then…resigned. Moving to a chair in the corner, he grabbed the light quilt from the back and tossed it to her.

Shoving one leg into his jeans, and then the other, he pulled them over his hips before he turned back. "I don't know what you heard, but this—tonight, Nichole—it's not—"

He stood immobile, his gaze searing over her skin, her hair—sweeping across her bedroom until it settled at the ladder-style bookshelf at the opposite side of the room. His body seemed to lock tight. She knew what he'd see there. The photo Maeve had given her for Christmas last year. The one where their grinning faces filled the frame.

He took a halting step forward, his features hardening.

His eyes slammed shut. "Nichole?"

Pulling the quilt around her breasts, she tried to ignore the sensitivity of her nipples and the knowledge *Garrett* had made them that way. With his mouth. His teeth. Tongue—

"Nikki Daniels?"

Garrett Carter. Maeve's brother. *The Panty Whisperer.*

Yeah, she couldn't quite believe it either.

Stalking across the room as he raked his fingers through his hair, Garrett—because, as clumsy as it felt tumbling around her thoughts, that's what his name was—looked as dismayed as she felt. One thing was certain. She didn't have to worry about the night turning into anything more complicated than—well, *this*.

Granted, *this* was messy. But the makings of some emotional train wreck it wasn't.

Maeve would laugh about this. Nichole knew she would. She had to.

There wasn't any risk to their relationship—not over one innocuous little slip she hadn't seen coming.

"What is that?" demanded the voice that had been growling her name in her ear mere minutes before.

Her head snapped up and then followed Garrett's pointed gaze back to her hand and the slim rectangle of technology she'd unconsciously reached for. "My phone."

Her lifeline to sorting out the mess in her head. To Maeve reassuring her their friendship was as strong as ever. There wouldn't be any awkwardness. Not this time. Not like with—

"No kidding. A phone, Nikki?"

Jerked back from the brink of one of the worst memories of her life, Nichole refocused on the man glowering down at her.

Her brow pushed up a degree. So now she was *Nikki?* Like *Garrett* thought he knew her or something? But before she could call him on his presumption he was back at her.

"What are you doing with it?"

Nothing yet. But the intent was obvious. Even if it had taken a moment for her head to catch up to her thumbs. "Texting Maeve."

He'd crossed to the bed in two strides.

"Like hell you are." Paling, he grabbed her hand and turned it over in his. "If you snapped a picture of me on this thing, so help me—"

"What? Are you insane? You think I took photos of you when you were…were…doing *that?*"

Arms folded over his chest, Garrett pulled back. "No. I hadn't actually thought—" Another, deeper growl. "But you tried to take a picture of me at the party."

"And you said no, so I didn't. Though in retrospect I'm fairly certain both of us would have preferred I had."

What Garrett had given her was beyond anything she could have imagined. But regardless of how good it had felt—how much she might have needed it—nothing was worth risking her relationship with Maeve.

Brows drawn, he asked, "You think Maeve would have warned you off me?"

Seriously? "Don't you?"

Granted it would have been for reasons different than Nichole's, but, yes, she was fairly certain Maeve would have wanted her to know who she was about to take a dip with.

One dark brow cocked in amusement. "I think she'd have been laughing too hard to hit 'send.' But for you, she'd have tried."

Nichole felt her lips twitching at the thought, along

with relief flooding through her at hearing Garrett too believed Maeve would have a good sense of humor about this. "You could be right."

Garrett sat at the foot of the bed—not close enough to touch, but not a total snub either. Just maintaining the distance between them.

Snaking a leg out from beneath the blanket's overlap, she stretched, trying to reach the panties lying three feet from the bed without actually leaving it.

There was something significantly different about being naked in front of Garrett now that she knew who he was. What he was.

At risk of severe cramp, she strained further, extending her leg until finally she was able to snare the little heap of lace-edged cotton with her toes. Only just as she had them Garrett turned, one arm braced on the bed, muscles bunched thick from the weight of his torso, and cocked a curious brow at her. "What are you doing?"

"Panties."

His brow drew down as his gaze flickered over the length of her barely concealed form, making her pull and pluck at the corners of the blanket to try and hide further beneath it.

"You really didn't know who I was?" he asked, pushing to his feet.

"I would have run the other way. No offense," she offered belatedly, wondering whether it was possible *not* to take offense.

But apparently he hadn't. "No, that's good."

"Why?"

"I just didn't like the idea of what happened tonight being some kind of conquest thing."

She sat up straighter. "This from The Panty Whisperer?"

Garrett froze where he was, jeans pulled over his hips but the fly left open. Bare feet, bare chest, the short dark waves of his hair a tousled mess... It would have been a calendar-hot snapshot in time if not for the hard set of his jaw and narrowed eyes. "You did *not* just call me that."

"Well, I mean..."

He paced the room and back. Coming to stop in front of her.

"What?" he demanded, thumbs hooked into the front pockets of his jeans—a position that pushed them down just that extra inch in front, showing off a nearly scandalous stretch of skin. "You're not suggesting I 'whispered' *you* out of anything?"

With a noncommittal wave she tried to bat away the question. In three years she hadn't even been tempted by another man. And in less than one night she'd fallen flat on her back and practically begged him to follow her down. If that wasn't some kind of freakish sexual panty magic she didn't know what was.

CHAPTER FIVE

Fighting the string of obscenities rioting on the tip of his tongue, Garrett ground his molars together and pinched the bridge of his nose.

It didn't get worse than this.

Well, that wasn't true. It did get worse. It *had* been worse. Back when he'd been eighteen and his older sister's friends had been trying to hook up with him intentionally. That had been way worse.

This, at least, was an accident.

Nikki. Hell, no wonder he'd had that bizarre sense of connection. He'd been listening to Maeve talk about her for years. He knew she'd grown up in Milwaukee, worked insane hours as an accountant at some big downtown firm, liked action movies over chick-flicks, read everything from sci-fi to biographies and that her favorite snack was peanut butter cups and corn chips. She sang along to the radio, badly, when she thought no one was listening and she didn't date—ever.

So what the hell was she doing tumbling into bed with him? Bringing some *stranger* into her home?

Garrett's stomach dropped as his feet stilled on the carpet.

It was all that talk about appreciating the simple stuff. *Aw, hell.* Maybe he *had* "whispered" her.

"Um…Garrett?"

The muscles along his spine tightened as he turned to look back and found her clutching that damn phone to her chest like some kind of security blanket.

"Look, I'm sorry, but I'm not going to lie to Maeve about this."

She thought he was worried about Maeve finding out? Not even close.

"If she teases you, you'll just have to man up and take it."

Man up? He laughed out loud. Nikki was definitely one of his sister's friends, because no one else on the planet would have the gall to talk to him like that.

"I'm not worried about a little teasing." Though he knew full well there wouldn't be anything *little* about it. The teasing would be merciless, carried out by a seasoned professional he'd trained himself. But teasing he could take. It was part of the deal. *You dish it, you better be able to take it.*

"So what's the problem, then?" she asked, working the thin cover until it was wrapped around her, pulled up tight to her neck.

And that was the first thing. The sight of a woman who had been so completely open to him not twenty minutes ago—bare and beautiful and unselfconscious as she panted for more, urged him on with the dig of her heels at his back and begged him not to stop. That woman—his little sister's best friend—who hadn't had sex in three years and for some insane reason had brought *him* back to her bed—was hiding awkwardly behind a blanket. That was the problem. He hated it.

Clearing his throat, he answered, "You deserve better."

The second thing. Maybe a part of him was disappointed. Felt short-changed.

He'd thought for a moment they could have *something*. Obviously he wasn't after a deep commitment or extended obligation. He needed another responsibility like he needed a hole in his head. But something light. Fun.

She'd seemed really fun. And intelligent. And just… *easy* in a way that had nothing to do with the kind of women he'd been scratching his itch with the past fifteen years. The kind who knew the score and weren't after anything more than he was. A few hours. Once in a while.

Nichole had made him think about things like movies and conversation and walks and all the stuff an average joe had tried on for size back in high school or college. Not that he'd tell her all that. She didn't need to know. Probably wouldn't believe him anyway, considering how easily that Panty Whisperer business had rolled off her tongue.

Damn, he could only imagine all the preconceived notions she must have about him. And the truth of it was, letting her hold on to them would serve his purpose better than any of the clarifications he could make. Because she was Maeve's best friend. Which meant all the concerns he'd never had with other women were suddenly there, front and center.

He couldn't attempt something casual with her because he'd worry about the implications his relationship *with her* would have on the one *she had with Maeve*. On *his* relationship with Maeve. And even though he was looking for more than some single night score, the relationship he was ready for was about taking in the occasional sunset…not riding off into one. It was about enjoying some pleasurable company for a while…not forever.

It was about *dating*. Casually—his eyes cut back to Nichole—but exclusively.

"Look, Nikki, you're an amazing girl, but I don't date my sisters' friends. It's a rule I've got."

Her expression cleared and she was leaning toward him then, the blanket draping more provocatively than she could have realized, based on the shy way she'd been covering up just moments before. He tried not to let his eye linger on the seductive gaps and tantalizing glimpses of the flesh he'd had full access to and could still feel beneath his fingers and lips, but were now completely off-limits. Round. Soft. Succulent. The kind of tempting swells that begged to be nipped and nibbled. Licked and suckled.

The sound of a throat clearing in a pointed, eyes-up-here-mister kind of way had Garrett yanked out of that land of forbidden territory and rubbing a hand along the tightening muscles of his neck.

"Okay, I know you're freaking out a little right now."

The hand stilled as he arched a brow at the woman who'd just uttered the impossible. "Excuse me?"

Those bare shoulders were pulled up into a delicate shrug as she waved a hand around in his direction. "But you honestly don't need to be. I didn't have any misconceptions about what was happening tonight. Where it could go or what it could mean. *Really*."

Uh-huh. "You don't need to pretend with me, Nikki. I think we both know—"

"No, Garrett. I don't know what you *think* you know about me. But—"

"I know it's been three years. And before that dry spell you'd gone out with precisely two guys. Both of whom you ended up engaged to. So I'd say, yeah, you probably were serious." Too serious for a guy like him.

"So, I'm going to pretend it doesn't creep me out that you know that. And I'll wait until you leave to have my discussion with your sister about privacy, trust and boundaries—"

Oh, man. This was going downhill fast. Holding out a staying hand, he tried not to get caught up in all the ways the bit of red rushing to the skin at Nichole's neck and shoulders was different than what he'd sampled earlier.

"What?" she snapped.

"Don't get pissed at Maeve about this." And already with the complications a simple exchange of names might have avoided. "Please. She was just giving me some re-assurance about the crowd she hung around with. Making sure I knew you weren't trouble. That you were… you know…into commitment…a 'nice girl.'" There was something about the slow upward push of her brows that warned of danger, had him backtracking as he tried an-other tack. "Not that I don't think you're nice now."

"You should probably just stop, Garrett."

Yeah, he probably should. Get out of there and get started on figuring out what it was going to take to ap-pease his little sister when she found out he'd gotten her into hot water with her closest girlfriend. Only the way things were right now—hell, less than a single night and already he felt the press of new responsibility settling on his shoulders—he needed to know she was okay.

She'd trusted him. Let him into her bed. "Nikki—"

"Here's the thing." Shaking her head, Nichole tucked a wild curl neatly behind her ear. "Tonight was an ac-cident. An error in judgment on both our parts. So why don't we both agree to put it behind us? I mean, it's not like we've been tripping over each other these last few years. I'm guessing it's a pretty safe bet our paths won't cross again anytime soon. And, believe me, I'm okay with that. This wasn't supposed to be more than a single night anyway."

He blinked. No way. She was just being tough to protect her pride.

Except those almond eyes were steady, clear as they held his. And wasn't that an ironic twist? The first woman he'd pursued with the intent of having something "more" didn't see him as anything more than the kind of one-night stand he'd been ready to leave behind.

It shouldn't have rubbed—but, *man*.

Shaking it off, because he knew it was for the best, Garrett nodded his acceptance. Walked back to the bed and, catching the soft line of her jaw in his palm, tipped her face to drop a kiss at her temple. "I'm sorry about this, Nikki."

She blinked at him, the corner of her mouth tipping the barest amount. "Don't be. I'm not."

Two hours later and Nichole had given up on the idea of sleep altogether. And if ever there was a time for a BFF to step up it was after she'd been busted selling out the details of her friend's nonexistent sex-life to The Panty Whisperer. Which was why Nichole was parked in front of her laptop, staring down the video feed as—across the country—Maeve paced in a knee length T-shirt in front of her own laptop.

"It's not like I was detailing the chronicles of your personal *Red Shoe Diaries* on Twitter, for God's sake."

Nichole balled her hands on her hips, glaring through cyberspace as she waited Maeve out.

It didn't take long before her friend gave under the pressure, her entire form signaling defeat as the arms crossed defiantly over her chest went spaghetti-loose along with the rest of her body and she spilled into the couch behind her. "Okay, I'm sorry! I shouldn't have told anyone about your personal business and I don't even know why exactly I did—except Garrett isn't like a real person. He's just got this knack for extracting information from people. He's patient. Unrelenting. And when he wants to know something…nothing gets in his way."

This she'd heard before. But it didn't change one simple fact. "My sexual experience is none of his business."

None.

God, the way he'd looked at her so apologetically as he'd nailed her with the "commitment" tag and "nice girl" nonsense. This guy she'd brought home without even knowing his name had wrapped her up in all the labels she'd spent three years trying to shed. She wasn't looking to get married. Didn't want—*anything*. Especially not from him, and so it didn't matter what he thought.

With that reminder, Nichole blew out a stiff breath.

Sliding the arm flung across her eyes up to her brow, Maeve frowned at her. "I know. I know. And I really am sorry. But now that you've met him, how can you even wonder about his ability to get what he wants?"

Nichole shook her head. "The guy lives in town. If he's so worried about your lifestyle why doesn't he meet your friends?"

Maeve stared up at the ceiling. "When it comes to my dates, given the opportunity, you better believe he's all over them. But girlfriends not so much. You know that saying about having to beat women off with a stick? That's what it was like for him with Bethany's, Carla's and Erin's friends. Mine to a lesser extent. But he avoids our girlfriends pretty much like the plague. Besides, the last few years he's been so tied up with building the company and working to get his degree there hasn't been a whole lot of time for anything else. I barely see him."

Nichole blinked as another piece of the puzzle fell into place. She'd forgotten about the school thing. A detail Maeve had shared with her. Garrett had put all of his sisters through school and only started himself when everyone else had been paid for and finished.

"So that's what he meant by saying he was trying to get back to living a little."

Maeve, casting all dramatics aside, sat upright, leaning forward. "Really? What else did he say?"

Suddenly Nichole felt unsure about the lines in this family dynamic she'd somehow gotten tangled in. Rather than try to sort them out, she opted to put the conversation back on track. "Okay, I know you would never be careless with my privacy or indifferent to my feelings—it just took me by surprise." Like so many things that evening. "But from now on can we agree—?"

Maeve waved her off with a shake of her head. "I swear. Never again. Not another word about your sexual experience to him."

Nichole arched a brow. "How about you just leave me out of the conversation completely?"

Maeve's mouth squinched up and she cocked her head. "Yeah, that's probably not entirely realistic. This is Garrett we're talking about. And now that you're on his radar I imagine he's going to feel a little protective of you. Which means I'm probably going to be answering some questions from time to time."

Nichole's mouth popped open, but Maeve just shrugged. "He kind of can't help himself. So…welcome to my world!"

"Maeve!"

Her friend sprang up from her slump at the couch and hustled right up in front of her laptop, resting her chin in the vee of her palms. "So now that we're back to being besties again…on a scale of skim milk to heavy whipping cream…."

Garrett pried one eyelid open, scowling hard as the screeching of a tiny banshee emanating from down the hall reached his ears.

"I know you're there, Garrett Carter. You pick up this phone right now or so help me…."

So help her, what? She was going to fly home and jab her little finger at his chest? Scowl up at him with those eyes that said he'd betrayed her in the most fundamental way and she was both hurt and disappointed?

Garrett's other eye was open and his feet were swinging over the side of the bed in a second flat. Reaching for the extension at his nightstand with one hand, he rubbed at his morning stubble with the other.

"A little early, isn't it, Maeve?"

"You're alone?"

He blew his breath out with a good deal of his patience. "It's only been…" squinting at the clock, he noted it was just after five "…a few hours since I left her apartment. Do you really think I'd stop and pick up someone else on the way back?"

The answering silence said she wouldn't put it past him.

"Geez, yes, I'm alone. And, for what it's worth, I had no idea who she was."

A little hiss sounded through the line. "Yeah, but everyone else did. What were you even doing at Sam's party?"

"It was a party for his brother. You know Jesse? My

oldest friend? Artist? Touring for the past two years? Any of this ringing a bell? So, Nikki's close with Sam?"

"We're out with him, like, once a week at least. He's part of the core crowd."

Garrett's brows dropped down, the fog of sleep clearing faster now. "Wait. He hangs out with that old crowd from my class—"

"Give me a break, Garrett. I see Sam and the guys all the time. These days they're more my friends than yours."

What the—?

"I'm not surprised you don't know. Aside from the fact you've been AWOL for the last few years, doing your twenty-two-hours-a-day summa-cum-look-at-Superman-earning-top-honors-while-running-his-company thing, you've got a reputation as kind of a psycho when it comes to your sisters. I wasn't about to tell you, and it doesn't surprise me no one else had the guts to do it either."

This time the deafening silence was booming out of his corner as he let that little gem sink in.

Maeve.

Hanging out with *his* friends.

A pack of low-life scum who thought the nickname Panty Whisperer bad-ass enough to *ooh* and *aah* at its inception, giving high-fives and back-slaps as though going home with whomever it had been back then hadn't simply been some callow escape, but a conquest worth celebration.

They'd been hanging out with his little sister.

And lying to him about it.

"Oh, wait. Before you flip. I'm not talking about Joey and those guys. Mostly Sam. Once in a while Rafe and Mitch show up. And, to be clear, I don't date any of them. Ever."

A relieved breath hissed through his teeth and a few seconds later his jaw unlocked too.

"Helloo? Earth to Panty Whisperer, betrayer of sisters' trust everywhere."

Wow. Little Maeve with the one-two punch. The girl knew how to drop a bomb and then turn the tables in a heartbeat. God help the guy who landed *her*.

"Maeve, just give me a minute to catch up. To wake up, okay?"

He could hear her tongue clucking through the line. Could practically see that impatient posture and pouty scowl. The same one she'd been pulling since she was six years old. Of course back then it wouldn't have been directed at him. Back then he'd been her hero. The one to intervene on her behalf with older sisters who didn't want clumsy hands breaking their stuff.

"Ready yet?"

"Yeah, why not? Go ahead and give it to me." He pushed up from the bed, figuring there wouldn't be any getting back to it after this, and headed in search of sustenance of the coffee-and-cookies variety.

"I can't believe you told Nikki you knew how long it had been since she had sex. I can't *believe,* after you figured out who she was, you would be so thoughtless as to violate my trust like that. And you didn't just stop at…."

Pushing the start button on the coffeepot, he grunted his acknowledgment of wrongdoing, knowing it would be a move just short of suicide to interrupt the rant in progress for the petty satisfaction of pointing out that *she'd* broken Nichole's trust first.

Garrett was halfway through his first cup of coffee when the quiet from the other end of the line hit a point where it was clear this wasn't just Maeve taking a breath, but she was waiting for a response.

Setting the mug aside, Garrett rubbed a palm over the smooth finish of his kitchen table. "So, aside from being pissed you'd told me about her dating history, did she sound okay?"

There was another silence from across the miles, though this one Garrett wasn't quite sure how to read.

Then, "She was fine. Why wouldn't she be?"

"You know. Because she's a commitment girl." He still didn't know how they'd gotten their lines crossed so badly. In all these years he'd never made such a mess—

"Oh, that. Yeah. Get over yourself, Garrett. She wasn't looking for serious with you. Which I'm pretty sure she actually told you already."

Yeah, she had. But maybe he just hadn't liked the sound of it. Or maybe he hadn't wanted to believe it was true because for some reason he didn't like the idea of it in the context of her…with him.

"Okay, I can practically hear you worrying over there. But you're going to have to take my word for it. Nikki is fine. This was exactly what she needed. Except the part about it being *you* and all."

Thank you, Maeve.

"She wanted to prove to herself she could have a little fun without it having to turn into some white-dress event. And she did. So no biggie." Maeve let out a giggle in the background. "Though next time I'm guessing she'll get the guy's name first."

Next time.

Garrett closed his eyes against the words. Figured out it only facilitated the mental peep show—Nichole leaning back on her bed with those big brown eyes peering up at…*not him.* Hell.

Walking over to the counter, he refilled his mug and

threw half of it back at once. Time to wake up and get on with the new day.

"Yeah. Hopefully."

CHAPTER SIX

NICHOLE SANK THE SIX and watched the cue ball come to rest neatly behind the four. Nice.

Across the felt landscape Maeve tapped her foot impatiently against the leg of her stool, watching as Nichole adjusted her stance and lined up her shot.

"Wow, your form's really improved."

Nichole paused, glanced up. "Huh?"

"No, really." All nonchalance, Maeve waved toward the pool cue, the twitch at the corner of her mouth a warning of what was to come.

Hard to believe it had only been a week with the amount of ribbing she'd taken. But there it was. A week since she'd had the hot press of Garrett's mouth against hers, the weight of his body—

"You've got a firm grasp on that *butt*...while the *shaft* just glides through your fingers. I don't know...it's almost like you've had some practice with the *wood* lately."

Mouth hanging open, Nichole fought the slow burn spreading across her cheeks and neck...and lost. "Seriously?"

Maeve smirked. "Ohh, shoot! Your alignment just went to hell."

"You wish."

Leaning over the table she straightened out the shot, drew back, focused—

"Gentle with the tip."

—and scratched. "Maeve!"

Her friend looked less than chagrined. "What? This is pool. I was working the lingo. Whatever your depraved mind does with it is on you." Jumping from the stool, she winked. "Plus, I really want to win!"

Nichole waited until Maeve was all lined up before settling a hip at the side of the table. "You know, Maeve, there's more to the game than your stroke. *The stick you choose,* for example."

An expression of horror crept over Maeve's face. "You wouldn't."

No, she wouldn't.

Well, maybe just a little. "I recently had my hands on a nice hard *wood.* I think I'll tell you about it. In detail. Let's start with—"

"Enough!" Maeve's frantic squeak was punctuated by the one-two thud of the eight and the cue sinking in short order. "You win! Oh, my God, I feel dirty."

Nichole tossed her hair over her shoulder, reveling in the victory. "As you should, cheater."

"Yeah, yeah," Maeve grumbled, too competitive to let any loss go without at least a brief sulk and most likely one more go at retaliation. Only she seemed to shake it off in a blink, her smile returning to full blast. "So, what do you want from the bar?"

"Whatever. You pick."

Maeve leaned in and craned her neck in an exaggerated manner. "Garrett? You want something too?"

Nichole froze in her spot as the skin across her back began to tingle and burn.

"Hey, Nikki, maybe Garrett would like to hear what

you thought about that stick you were using? How much you liked the feel of that hard wood and all? Heck, maybe he could even help you perfect your hold!" And with that she darted off for the bar.

He wasn't there. He couldn't be.

And yet even as she turned she knew.

Her gaze started at the floor and the size-twelve boots planted in a wide stance less than a handful of feet away, crawled up the saddle-brown twill of cargo-style pants and followed the gray long-sleeve tee stretched to perfection over his torso before making the unsettling jump to firm lips slanted in an off-kilter smile and the single raised brow demanding clarification.

"Maeve just being Maeve?" he asked, and the breath Nichole hadn't realized she'd been holding rushed out in relief.

No lie necessary. "Exactly."

Only those too intense blue eyes narrowed the slightest bit. "So the *wood* you guys were talking about was really…wood?"

She hadn't believed it was possible to choke on words that weren't her own, but there she was, sputtering as though she'd swallowed a string of oversized letters cut from rough stone. They blocked the pathway from her lungs to her mouth, making the intake of breath an impossible thing.

Lie. Simple. Just lie now and everything would be fine.

Except she could already feel his gaze following the hot path of her heated skin over her cheeks, down her neck…lower.

Clearing her throat, she dug in the front pocket of her jeans, pulling out a couple of quarters. "We were talking about pool. Sticks. Cues."

The corner of his mouth twitched and his eyes flashed back to hers. "Shafts and butts?"

"Technical terms."

Garrett stepped closer, resting his hand at her waist as he bowed his head toward her ear, close enough so she could smell the clean masculine scent of him. Soap and skin and the barest hint of lingering sawdust. Close enough so fingers of warmth from his body could reach out and touch hers. Close enough to send her senses reeling as his breath washed over her ear, carrying his gruff, taunting words. "Yeah? Why don't you tell me about it?"

Nichole's eyes flew wide with her mouth. "No— nothing," she managed, stumbling back only to be steadied by Garrett's strong hand.

"Liar, liar, pants on fire," he laughed in challenge. Then, with a conspiratorial wink, added, "Red."

And with a word she was back to that night.

To the flirtation, the slow pulling need, the fast-rising hunger. Dim hallways and dark shadows. His mouth, his hands, his body…his name.

Garrett.

Her eyes pinched shut as she cleared her mind and drew a cleansing breath. "What are you doing here?"

"Jesse." He nodded toward the table across the bar where she and Maeve had been sitting with the guys before starting their game of pool. "I didn't expect to see you."

And, though he hadn't tried to avoid her, it was pretty clear if he had known, he wouldn't have come. She got it. That was how one-nighters went. *One night.*

"I didn't know you were coming either." If she had she might have glanced at her hair before she left home. Gone for the cherry ChapStick instead of the original. She might have worn a skirt.

And not with the expectation that those big hands would find their way under it. No!

She cleared her head with a stern shake.

"It was a last-minute thing. Deciding to come out. But…" His jaw cocked to one side as his gaze slid over the second-floor bar before returning to search her eyes. "I don't have to stay if this is uncomfortable for you."

Nichole was already shaking her head when a tall glass of what was probably rum and Coke cut between them, followed by Maeve's disgusted voice. "Didn't I tell you to get over yourself? Nikki couldn't care less about you showing up here."

Not exactly true, but at least it was Maeve saying it instead of her. And, judging from the glint of amusement in Garrett's eyes, his little sister's biting words didn't faze him.

His focus shifted to Maeve. "How'd that job in Denver work out?"

"Same ol', same ol'." Maeve shrugged, snaking an arm around her brother's waist for a quick hug. "I'm scheduled to go back next week."

Nichole watched the two fall into the conversation she knew one side of by heart, and wondered how it was possible she hadn't recognized Garrett for who he was.

Only on some level she had. She'd seen his face at least a hundred times in photos in Maeve's old albums. And, though most of those pictures were of a kid rather than a man, some of them had been recent. Which had to be the reason for that sense of connection. The immediate *click*.

Watching them together now, though, there was one thing she couldn't miss. Being around Garrett wasn't going to be a problem in any sense. His focus on Maeve was utterly complete.

There wasn't any lingering tension—at least not from his side. He'd showed up, said hello when he saw her, been friendly and then moved on as though nothing had happened between them at all.

Maeve had been right about her brother being the expert in keeping relationships simple. And lucky Nichole to have the Panty Whisperer for her mentor.

Garrett stood with his back to the bar, his eyes focused on the pool table across the room where Nichole was lining up her shot, his tongue lodged somewhere halfway down his throat.

She moved from one spot to another, bending at the waist, bracing her weight with a hand on the table, widening her stance until—

Until every damn guy in the bar was leering as she took her shot. Just like him. The only thing setting him apart from the rest of the hounds panting after her was *he* knew just exactly what he was missing. He knew what it felt like to kneel between those legs. He knew what it felt like to spread his palm over the flat of her belly. To run his tongue the length of her.

Which meant, right then, he envied them. At least they could tell themselves it probably wouldn't be as good as their imagination was making it.

Nichole let out a whoop, high-fiving Maeve as two guys he didn't know took losing with dopey grins and an offer of more drinks.

Garrett's eyes narrowed as he started sizing them up. They looked harmless, but guys put on a lot of façades.

His gaze shot over to his sister, who seemed to be handling the attention fine, passing on the drinks—good girl—and whatever else the guys were offering. Same as Nichole. Only there was something different about the way the two women handled it. Maeve leaned into the conversation, taking the flattery with grace even as she rejected it, while Nichole simply didn't seem to register it at all. She was smiling freely at the guys, but without any kind of sexual recognition whatsoever.

Even when one of the guys reached for her hand, trying to angle in for some eye contact, she just wrapped her free hand around his fingers and basically handed them back to him...with a smile.

She was *friendly.*

Like he'd never seen "friendly" done before. Some girls played at it. Used it like a kind of game of push-and-pull. But Nichole...she was completely open and available only in one clearly identifiable way that said "not a chance" without ever having to say it at all.

"What's up, man?"

Garrett shot a look over his shoulder to where Jesse was moving in beside him, his brother Sam a step behind.

"Just wondering how in the hell I ever got past that," he answered with a nod in Nichole's direction.

Jesse's hands came up with the corners of his mouth. "Don't look at me. I thought about asking her out back before I left, but she 'friended' me so fast there was no point in even trying."

Jesse was one of the few friends Garrett had maintained regular interaction with over the years. He'd been a mellow, genuine guy from as far back as Garrett could remember. And through those first years after losing his dad, when it had seemed like the world was going to collapse around his shoulders and there was no way he'd be able to *be everything* he needed to be for everyone who needed it, Jesse had unrelentingly been there for him, refusing to let Garrett be alone no matter that the life he'd been a part of—the one with sports and chicks and hanging out—was gone. He'd been the guy to get his twenty-four-year-old sister to babysit once a month so Garrett could go out for a couple hours. The one who hadn't crowed about cheap conquests. The one who'd understood. Maybe his artist's mentality gave him more insight than the other meatheads. Whatever. He was a good friend—one of the only ones he truly felt comfortable confiding in.

An hour later Garrett was having to put significantly more effort into not feeling like a stalker than he generally cared to. But, honest to God, he just couldn't keep his eyes from working their way back to that auburn tumble of hair and contagious laugh.

"She like this with everyone?" he asked Sam, watching as she yucked it up with yet another group of what he'd bet good money had been strangers until just that night. It seemed like she could talk to anyone about anything.

"What do you mean—friendly, easygoing?" Sam flagged the bartender for another round. Then, at Garrett's nod, he shrugged. "Pretty much. But she can take care of herself. With one recent exception, nobody gets past her 'friend' zone. Some jack-off burned her pretty bad a few years ago and she's been avoiding the flames ever since. So you don't really need to worry about looking out for her. Aside from doing a damn good job of it herself, she's got a lot of people who care about how she gets treated."

There was an edge in those last words that had Garrett's head cranking around to where Sam was watching him, a matter-of-fact look in his eyes. "You talking about me?"

Jesse covered his mouth with his hand, but a low laugh escaped regardless.

There was no way Jesse's little brother was warning *him* off of Nichole? But, sure enough, he was.

"Relax, man. I'm not going anywhere near her."

"You've already been near her. And the way you've been watching her all night…."

Garrett was about to tell Sam he was nuts when that same sort of gravitational pull had him turning around again…and locking eyes with Nichole. Who'd been watching him.

Her lips parted, and from across the room he could actually feel the catch of *her* breath in *his* chest.

And then there it was—that blaze of heat working up her neck and cheeks. The one that made him wonder if he would feel the change it brought against his lips if they were positioned in just the right spot.

The corner of his mouth edged up as he tapped his cheek, mouthing the word *red* to the woman he was suddenly alone with across the expanse of this crowded bar.

Her answering smile was too many kinds of different to count from what she'd been giving to every other guy there tonight, and it hit him like a pile-driver to the gut, effectively knocking the wind out of him as he turned back to his closest friend and shook his head in genuine bewilderment.

Jesse let out a low chuckle. "I'm starting to wonder if the real question isn't how you got past her, but how *she* got past *you*."

CHAPTER SEVEN

"YOU AGAIN?" Nichole cocked a brow at Garrett as he slid into an empty seat across the narrow table running the length of the trendy downtown gastropub. Not that she was surprised. After three weeks of bumping into the guy most every time she went out, these rendezvous were becoming the rule rather than the exception.

At first they'd both been surprised. Accepting. Maybe even amused.

When it had become obvious that the crossing of their paths wasn't simply a fluke but a consequence of the overlap of their friends, they'd found a few minutes to talk away from everyone else, both wanting to ensure the other was comfortable.

And they were. Mostly.

The conversation always came easily. Naturally. So much so that by the end of an evening more often than not she and Garrett would discover they'd been so caught up in their own interaction they'd lost the rest of the group along the way. Which was when things became the littlest bit less comfortable.

The laughter would die down between them, the break between one topic and the next filling with an awareness of the things they didn't want. They'd look around for another conversation to dive into, but they'd be alone.

Which would lead to the moment when her focus would drop to his mouth, the open collar of his shirt, a button or two even lower...

And then she'd realize how late it was. Or he'd remember the early call he had to get up for. Or they'd both catch sight of someone and quickly return to the group, going on as they had before, figuring it would get easier along the way.

Eventually.

Only as Garrett's long legs brushed hers beneath the polished benchtop, and her breath sucked in with the unwilling image of their legs caught together in a tangle of heat and skin, she realized *eventually* couldn't happen soon enough.

"Red," came the gruff observation from across the table. Quiet enough the rest of the group, chatting in their usual animated fashion, didn't seem to catch it.

But if anyone had bothered to look up as she had, no one would have missed the heat in Garrett's eyes.

"It'll go away," she murmured, flipping her menu open in the hopes of shielding herself to some degree.

Only then the contact that had been inadvertent just the moment before was back. This time blatant and intentional. The press of his leg along hers, holding until she met his eyes.

"I'm starting to wonder."

Garrett glared into the men's room mirror after trying to stop the low simmer running through his veins with a cold splash of water. It wasn't working.

So much for thinking this coffee shop concert would keep him out of trouble just because they wouldn't be able to talk. He'd seen her. Seen when her eyes met his. And he didn't need words because already he knew too

much about her. And every damn time he went out…
whether Nichole was actually there are or not…he found
out more.

And, God help him, he liked it all.

She was cool and funny and clever and thoughtful and
generous and loyal…and, *damn it,* he knew just exactly
how good she tasted on his tongue.

And he couldn't have her. Because he didn't want her.
And she didn't want him.

They'd talked about it. More than once. Probably more
than they needed to. Except for some reason it was one of
those topics that seemed to require excessive amounts of
reinforcement. He was starting to think maybe this girly
splash of cold water wasn't the way to go. He needed the
reason hammered into his head.

Handy that he owned his own construction company.
He ought to be able to find someone to do it for him.

With a hard shake of his head, he stalked out of the
men's room into the back hallway and came up short at
the sight of Nichole at the far end.

This was the problem. The pull. With words or without, it was like there was some kind of force drawing
them together…and it wouldn't stop until they were as
close as two bodies could be.

Yeah.

Echoes of the classical guitar they'd come to the coffee house to hear filled the otherwise deserted space as
he closed the distance between them. Watched with the
kind of satisfaction that should have made him ashamed
as Nichole's eyes went wide with understanding and she
looked for a means of escape. Only in the end they both
knew she didn't want to get away any more than he
wanted her to.

And then he had her. He hooked a finger through the

belt loop of her jeans, giving himself mad props for refraining from sliding that finger between the denim and the bare skin of her belly the way he wanted to.

Tugging gently, he pulled her down the hall, away from where the intimate concert was being held toward a flight of stairs that led to a second floor.

"What's up there?" Nichole asked, craning a bit to try and see around the bend as Garrett led the way.

"No idea. But we need to talk."

A quick shake of her head. "I just came to say goodbye. I've— I think— I need to take off early tonight."

Because the tension between them was growing thicker with every encounter. Every exchange. Every accidental or even not so accidental brush.

And she'd wised up.

Only too late.

"You can't just—just corral me like this, Garrett," she laughed nervously, working her way up the steps backward even when she had to know the only escape was from the other direction.

Of course he could. And unless she actually used the magic word *no,* he would. "That first night, Nichole… why did you let me take you home?"

Nichole stopped, caught in the dark pull of eyes she never should have looked into.

They'd talked about this. To a degree. But neither of them had been able to move past it. Get free of what had happened and the lingering connection that kept pulling them back to it.

"Because when I met you it was the first time in as long as I could remember I wanted more than friendship." Another backward step and she nearly tripped on the stair. But Garrett was there, his hand at her elbow, steadying her even as he crowded her back.

What was he doing? Being this close, asking her about that night…it was a mistake. They couldn't go on like this. At first it had been all fun and games. The lingering tension and chemistry between them almost a joke. A dirty secret they shared. Something amusing. A challenge to overcome.

But as the weeks moved past, as the tension and temptations grew, having to say no to something she wanted with more urgency every time they met had ceased being funny.

Nichole *wanted* this man.

So much more than she should.

"I brought you home with me because I thought it would be safe. There wouldn't be any risk of getting involved, of things getting too complicated, of me—" She swallowed, closed her eyes and forced herself to say the rest of it. "Of me getting ahead of myself. Because I didn't even know your name."

She'd been so wrong. Because now not only did she know just exactly who she'd been with and precisely how to find him…she had to see him all the time.

"So, about that…." His fingers curved around her waist, ending her retreat where she stood, balanced on the third stair from the top of the landing in a space she had no right occupying.

Garrett took the next step, closing the distance between them until his chest brushed against hers and their breath mingled warm and wet together.

Her lashes fluttered as better judgment warred against *want*. "What are you doing?"

"Reminiscing. It was very hot."

She shouldn't have liked the sound of that so much.

Not when there was no place to go with it. But the part of her that had never been entirely confident in the sexual arena…the part that even after years remained just the littlest bit bruised over the way her last relationship had ended…*needed* to know. Needed to hear. "My not wanting to know your name was hot?"

"No, that was just kinky fun."

It was everything she could do not to purr.

Kinky…*her?*

Oh, that was a first. One she'd savor.

"What was hot…" his voice dropped lower as he leaned closer toward her ear "…were the soft, throaty little moans you made and the way you gave your whole body over to me when I pulled you close."

Her mouth went dry and even the nervous butterflies batting about her stomach stilled…waited. "You're whispering me again."

Those eyes.

"Maybe I am."

His mouth.

"I thought we were friends. I thought we agreed."

The *heat.*

He nodded. "We did."

"Then why?"

Her jeans were snug with the tightening of Garrett's fists at her sides, adding to the sensation of his touch, his hold, extending beyond just his fingers to everywhere the fabric touched her. Around her hips, her bottom, between her legs and down her thighs.

"The strings are already there, Nichole. The lines have already been crossed. And if you really want to know, I cross them more every damn time I look at you. I can't stop thinking about hearing you make those sounds again. Only this time I want to hear them when you're saying my name."

"Garrett—"

"Hell, *yes.*"

And then the space between them that was all potential and unmet need and *why* and *why not* was gone. Replaced by contact. Hot and concentrated. The mind-blowing sensation of Garrett's chest moving up against her own as he took that final step. Hard-packed muscle and cotton created a teasing friction against her nipples that left her breathless, lips still parted on a broken gasp when his head bowed to hers.

"Just like that." His words were a kiss against her lips. The soft brush before the bruising crush. The taste that warned it would never be enough.

Garrett.

His mouth moved against hers like an unspoken demand, rubbing slowly, telling her what he wanted, what she wanted to give him. He parted her lips beneath the insistent pressure of his own, working back and forth without giving her the "more" she ached for, stroking her need until it surpassed his own and she was wordlessly begging: with her hands—one clutching and releasing and then clutching again at the fabric of his shirt, the other flexed against all that contained strength, riding the peaks and valleys of a musculature she'd only believed existed in the land of airbrush and fiction. Begging with her body—bowed forward in an arch that was needy and shameless; with the same throaty whimper that had brought them to this point in the first place. The one that apparently did the trick, because in the next second she had what she wanted—Garrett's tongue thrusting past her parted lips, rolling against her own, delivering a deeper, more potent version of the moan he'd been talking about in the process, ensuring they were in fact together in this desperation.

And that was the most intoxicating part of it all. They were *together*.

Another thrust and the hands gripping her hips tightened. And then she was sucking lightly over his tongue, gasping at the flick of it against her bottom lip, getting lost in all the places only this man had been able to take her—in the physical sensations unique to being with him, in the slide of his arms around her back so one hand came to rest across her bottom and thigh and the other wound into her hair and tightened there so she felt his hold against a thousand points of contact within her skin.

Oh, and she knew what he was going to do next—whimpered in anticipation of a repeat of the move that had haunted her nights so relentlessly.

Garrett's lips curled against her own. "Say it."

"Garrett."

The tension at her scalp tightened incrementally as he used her hair to guide her head back, extending her neck further, opening her mouth to him so the kiss that came next was one he took. One he controlled. One he gave. One that made her groan and melt beneath it.

Made her ache through every point of contact yet to be made.

The hand across her bottom pulled her closer. Held her firm against the straining ridge of his erection.

Another whimper. Another reckless pant of his name.

Another thrust of his tongue into her waiting mouth.

All that mattered was this. More. Easing the almost painful clench of need so deep inside her.

And then the hand in her hair slipped free. Her head came up and in a daze she met the blue flame of Garrett's eyes…tried to close the distance between them he had opened. She reached for his shoulder, his hair. Leaned in to his kiss, getting less than a taste before he broke away again.

Too much. She'd gone too far again. Gotten carried away—

Except he had her hand in his. The muscle in his jaw was jumping as he raked his other hand through the hair that was standing up in a guilty mess. "There's got to be a back way out of here. Let's go. I think I can make it to my car."

The haze of arousal cleared further and Nichole looked around, stunned to find herself in this state of reckless abandon in the back hall of a coffee house. Oh, God. *Mistake!*

"Garrett, I can't."

He nodded, shoved his hand through his hair again and then grabbed her hips and lifted her up against him in a move so swift and deft she had her legs wrapped around his waist before she'd even realized what was happening.

No, this she had to stop—and fast. Because Garrett was carrying her up the last stairs, groaning some kind of agreement that neither could he. And then her back was against the wall and his hips were rocking against the needy spot between her legs that made her stupid in ways she could never have imagined prior to meeting him.

"Garrett," she gasped when his mouth closed over her neck.

And that totally hadn't come out the way it had been supposed to. But before she could even think about where she'd gone wrong with that one single critical word, the sensual, disorienting fog was descending again. Rolling in thicker with each flick of his tongue, every rock of his hips and brush of his thumb against the straining peak of her nipple.

Because, yes, this guy was plenty strong enough to hold her against the wall with one hand. And, God, wasn't that the hottest thing? Next to all the other billion hot things about him. She was a little ashamed to admit his being so worked up enough to do her against the back wall of a public place was one of them.

But it had to stop.

She needed to check her libido and her ego and—

"Garrrrett..."

What...how...that was...would he do it again?

Then his mouth was back at her ear. His breath a hot rush against the tender tissue. His low growl a rough stroke against all the places where she ached for him. "Are you wet, Nichole?"

She opened her mouth, trying to form words—only her mind had blanked of coherent thought. And apparently Garrett didn't need an answer anyway, because somewhere along the way he'd gotten her fly undone, loosened the denim enough to skim his hand down the back.

"Aww, baby, you're *so*—"

"Stop."

She didn't know where she'd found the resolve to say it, or how Garrett had even heard, the word was so small. So not at all what she wanted. But there it was. And he had heard, because that marauding hand of his was working a steady retreat back to her hip, where he continued to hold her against him.

So maybe unlocking her ankles from the small of his back and letting go of his shirt and hair should be her next step.

Reluctantly, she did so. And, sure enough, Garrett

eased her down to her feet from there. Let his forehead rest against hers and, with a pained groan, refastened her jeans. Because he was just that kind of guy.

Which made her want him all the more.

And that was a problem. Because Nichole wasn't ready for this.

Thanks to her deadbeat dad's underwhelming commitment to fatherhood she'd always been skittish about getting involved. The two guys she'd risked her heart with in the past had been more about building relationships than scoring bases. She'd known them for years, trusted them and made plans with them. With Paul… they'd been so young. When he'd ended things, she'd understood and recovered with only a few scars. But with Joel she'd been so hurt. So humiliated by what had happened it had taken her three years to brave up enough to dip just her toe back in.

Okay, fine. She'd done the full-on skinny-dip. But still… What she'd done she'd done believing it would be a one-time isolated incident with a guy who wouldn't be around twenty-four-seven, tempting her to invest more of her heart than she should.

Garrett murmured, "Nichole, this thing between us isn't going away."

No, it wasn't. "I'm not sure we're giving it much of a chance to."

"Maybe not." Pulling back, Garrett looked around them, as if just realizing exactly where they were, and swore. "I'm sorry about this. I don't know what I was—"

"Yeah, neither do I." With a quiet laugh, Nichole added, "You are *really* going to get the wrong idea about what kind of girl I am."

Garrett caught her chin with his finger and brought her gaze to his. "No, I won't."

Then, leading her down the flight, he stopped at the bottom stair and pulled her down to sit beside him. The guitarist had moved on to a new piece—something slow and soulful. Each pluck of the strings seemed weighted with a melancholy that resonated inside her.

Forearms resting over his widespread knees, Garrett scrubbed a palm over his face. "I know I'm the one who said this wouldn't work. That I didn't want it. But it sort of feels like we already have it, whether we meant to or not... Nichole, I can handle the part about Maeve."

"But I'm not sure I can." Maeve was her best friend. Her rock. The person she couldn't live without. The person she'd need to turn to if her heart ever got trampled again. "Let's just say you aren't the only one with a protective streak when it comes to your family."

Garrett's brows shot skyward, as though the thought had never occurred to him. "Are you worried you're going to break my heart and Maeve's going to hold it against you?"

"Well, no." While something told her Garrett's heart was immune to breaking, there were no guarantees when it came to hard feelings. "But she didn't take too kindly to an off-the-cuff remark I made last month. And that was before I'd actually even met you."

His expression closed down as he asked, "What kind of remark?"

Why had she brought it up? She didn't want to tell him what she'd said. Didn't want to risk his feelings or insult him. But he was staring at her, waiting. "Something about antibiotics. It was stupid and totally off-base and I apologize."

A nod. "The Panty Whisperer garbage. I get it. I've earned it."

Something about those last words and the weary resignation in them cut at her.

"Garrett, I didn't know anything about you. But I do now—"

At that, his mouth curved into a wry smile. "Yeah, and I'm betting what just happened at the top of these stairs pretty well backs up every rumor you've ever heard."

It might have if this connection she'd somehow formed with Garrett hadn't given her a deeper insight into who he was. Into what he valued. But he seemed as genuinely undone by the attraction between them as she was. Fighting it and trying to push it aside so they could enjoy a friendship regardless.

She didn't want her careless words to hurt him or undermine all there was to respect.

If ever she needed a lifeline it was now. She wanted Maeve to tell her what to say. Although now that she thought about it...

"I do have to admit I'm pretty impressed. I always sort of assumed the rumors were exaggerated. But, *damn*, Garrett."

He was a Carter, after all. And teasing was their foremost means of affection.

His sudden stunned bark of laughter was everything she'd wanted to hear. And then he leaned back and studied her, his gaze tracking from her eyes to her mouth and back. "Okay, Red. Tell me again why this isn't going to work."

"Because neither of us wants to risk jeopardizing our relationship with Maeve over...anything. We both know better than to think we could keep our relationship with each other separate from our relationship with her. And I've lost people after relationships ended before—people I really cared about."

She'd never forget what it had been like to go from being embraced as the daughter Paul's mother never had, to realizing the same woman was walking out of the market without her groceries to avoid having to talk to her. The friends who suddenly hadn't seen her when they passed. That feeling of being cast adrift from everything she'd thought was safe and secure.

When she'd transferred to Chicago for a fresh start Maeve had been the one to give it to her. Maeve's had been the open heart she'd so desperately needed after having so many others shut against her.

When it looked like Garrett might be ready to argue Nichole held up a staying finger. "And because I think you're a very good guy. I know too much about the part of you that has nothing to do with whispering panties and everything to do with the care and protection of your family. I know about the guy who drives around Chicago at five in the morning after a big snow to dig out his sisters' cars so they can drive to work. The guy who puts his own needs last every time. And the guy who knows the value of a simple sunset."

"Are you whispering *me* right now?"

Nichole shook her head, half wishing she was. "No, I'm telling you why this won't work. It's because you're too good of a guy for me not to fall for. I'm not ready for something serious and I don't know how to do casual. Believe it or not, that's actually how your name came up with Maeve. She'd been joking around about you giving me lessons on keeping it light. She even threatened to set us up. Ironic, huh?"

When Nichole looked up from the neat stack of her hands on her knees Garrett was watching her, his brows drawn down so his shadowed eyes left her guessing at his reaction.

"So what are we going to do about this...*thing* between us?"

"What we planned from the start. Ignore it." She let out a soft laugh. "Find a distraction until it goes away. Because us getting together would be a mistake and I think we both know it."

"Okay, Nichole. I get it." Garrett pushed to his feet and, taking her hand, pulled her to her own.

Looking down at where their fingers had intertwined, she asked, "No more whispering?"

One last rough stroke of his thumb across her knuckles and he let her go. "Not tonight."

CHAPTER EIGHT

GARRETT GRIPPED THE WHEEL, ten and two, his knuckles going white as his most beloved baby sister rambled on, heedless of how close she was to being dumped by the side of a road and left to hoof it the rest of the way to Carla's in the next burb over.

"...all I'm saying is you don't have to be such a hard-ass about everything all the time—sorry, Aunt Gloria."

Their great-aunt waved a papery hand, her focus on the passing houses more than on the fight Maeve had picked with him the moment she'd slid into the backseat.

"You think I like this? That I enjoy always being the heavy? Come on, Maeve. If I don't tell Erin to turn her head on and open her eyes about this guy then who the hell will? You? Beth? Carla? I don't think so. You girls are so caught up in all the romance B.S. you don't even register the impracticality of a guy who literally weaves baskets for a living."

"He's an artist," she sniped back.

"Oh, he *is*. Everyone was talking about how beauti-ful his work was at the Acres."

The seniors' living facility where his latest works were on sale.

Maeve's eyes narrowed and she crossed her arms over

her chest. "It doesn't matter what he does, Garrett. Erin loves him."

At his scoff, she grumbled from the back, "And to think I'd been looking forward to seeing you. Where have you been anyway?"

He made some noise about work and scowled at the road ahead, not wanting to get into it. But Maeve was… *Maeve*.

"Cripes, it's either feast or famine with you. Years of you only pulling your head out of your business and books long enough to bitch about whatever we're doing wrong, and then suddenly you're like a plague. Everywhere." Her eyes rolled as she let out a dramatic huff. "And just when I start thinking it was kind of fun having you around, you drop off the face of the earth again."

Teeth gritting down, he glanced in the mirror at her. "You've managed fine in the past."

"Yeah, but I always had Nichole around. And she's been suspiciously absent these last couple weeks. Tired. Busy. Working late."

Garrett's hands tightened on the wheel as the implication hung in the air.

Damn it.

"Anything you want to own up to?"

Not even close. "No."

The silence stretched between them until finally he shot a demanding look into the rearview mirror. "What?"

"I thought you liked her."

"I do." More than he should, considering what he had to offer.

"You know, Garrett, I've always wanted a sister."

Wonderful. And now she was playing with him for sport. Because that was what demon sisters did.

Breathe. Don't start looking for a ditch. "You have three."

"But not a *little* sister. You know Nikki is two months younger than I am?"

"It's not like that, Maeve."

Gloria's frail hand reached up through the seats to pinch his cheek. "It's wonderful, dear. All your wild-oat sowing has to stop sometime. Nikki's a darling girl."

Another reminder that Nichole was in with his entire family. Including his great-aunt.

"It's not like that," he said again, though why he bothered he had no idea.

"So what's it like, then, Big Brother?"

Did he really want to have this conversation? Only a glance into the back showed that both women, despite their respective teasing and maternal pats, were intent on getting the scoop. And maybe saying it out loud would help it finally sink in.

"I don't want to marry her."

Maeve barked out an indignant cough. "Geez, I didn't realize she'd asked."

Snide. Nice.

"She didn't. Obviously. But—" Damn it, he'd wanted to get that critical tidbit out first, because it seemed important. But the way it landed he sounded like an ass. For more than one reason. Cue the clarifications. "I'm just trying to explain. It isn't because she isn't good enough. She is. I mean, I can't believe either of those schmucks she was engaged to let her get away. Any guy would be lucky to have her. Trust me when I tell you I *want* to have her. Just not in the way she deserves."

"It's okay," Maeve offered from the backseat. "You've had an overfull plate for a long time. And after Mom and

Dad you have a hard time letting people in. Getting close. You aren't ready to think about marriage yet."

He bristled, not for the first time cursing Maeve's freshman-year psychology class.

It wasn't about letting people get close. Or what had happened with his parents.

True, he didn't have a lot of people outside Jesse and his sisters he shared much of a bond with. But that had more to do with what his life had been like these last years than any avoidance on his part. And the connection with Nichole had been immediate. She was the person he'd become *most* comfortable talking to.

It was about things like this damn recurring conversation about Erin's boyfriend. He'd been playing the "hardass" and making tough calls for over half his life already, and what he wanted out of a relationship was something where those kinds of responsibilities didn't apply. Where the consequences of his actions and choices didn't impact the rest of another person's life.

Hell, just thinking about it had the muscles in his gut starting to knot.

"It's not just *yet*. I don't know if I'm going to want it *ever*. Which makes me a bum deal for a woman with 'someday' in mind." His fingers tightened around the wheel. "Nichole's been engaged twice. She's a woman with a white picket fence dream just waiting to be realized."

Maeve sat back in her seat, arms crossed in a contemplative pose. "I don't know, Garrett. Yeah, she's going to want to get married eventually. But I think for now Nikki just needs to learn how to have a little fun again. And from what I hear…you're a pretty fun guy."

He let out a humorless laugh, not feeling like much fun at all. "But not the guy for Nichole."

They'd decided already. They weren't going to pursue it. And the problem wasn't just an off alignment of goals...it was also the little lady sitting in the seat behind him. It was the strings.

Maeve's lips pursed as she stared him down.

"And you're cool with that?"

"Yep." No. But he'd get there.

"Just as well. There are a lot of fun guys out there. And her dance card is filling up anyway."

Sure...right...wait— "What?"

Only Maeve seemed to have lost interest in him and turned to Gloria.

"So, yesterday two guys from her office asked her out. Within an hour of each other..."

Of course they had. Because she was gorgeous. And she'd probably had that smile going—the one that stuck with a guy for days after he'd seen it. The kind of smile that made a guy want to get to the bottom of what exactly put it there and make sure—

"And you know Nikki—she's always with the flat-out forget it, but in that really smooth way she's got. Probably because she doesn't even realize it's going on most of the time. But this time—"

A horn blared and Garrett jerked the wheel. Hell.

"Geez, Garrett. Take it easy. Precious cargo back here."

"Sorry, girls." He needed to get his head together. But, damn, Maeve needed to knock off the dish...or get to the point a hell of a lot faster.

Only now his great-aunt Gloria was tapping at the window. "Oh, would you look at this house?"

Maeve nodded her approval. "I love the landscaping."

Garrett did a mental ten count, willing his heart rate to slow, his blood to cool. There was no way Maeve was going to leave them hanging, was there? And even if she'd seriously lost her train of thought how was it his aunt wasn't demanding resolution?

"My roses never bloom like that. I've added eggshells, coffee grounds."

"Maybe it's got to do with the sun or how much water they get."

"Nichole," Garrett barked out, fast on his way to losing his cool. "What did she do?"

Silence from the back of the car. He checked the mirror and found both Maeve and Gloria staring at him. One looking quietly amused, the other looking...satisfied.

"What did she do when, Garrett?"

Molars grinding down, he shot a look at his baby sister he hadn't been forced to use since she was sixteen. A look that seemed to have lost its mojo, based on the way she crossed her arms and jutted her chin at him.

"You mean with all the guys asking her out?"

Now it was *all the guys?* The steering wheel creaked within his grasp and he forced his grip looser. "Yes."

Maeve checked her nails. "She hadn't decided when I talked to her. But she did say a date might be just the distraction she needed."

The car slammed to a stop and he stared out the windshield at his sister's driveway. The front door opened and relatives streamed out to greet them, but Garrett just cranked around in his seat. "A distraction?"

Maeve blanched, leaning back in her seat as Gloria shuffled out of the car.

"I'm sure she didn't mean it...however it is you're taking it."

Except Garrett was damn sure she did. Which meant she was still as hung up as he was.

And she was about to look to another guy to distract her.

"Out of the car, Maeve."

CHAPTER NINE

KNOCK, KNOCK, KNOCK. Knock, knock.

Nichole swallowed hard, her heart beating like the fist at her door.

Garrett.

Maeve's single cryptic text had been the only warning. No explanation of what he wanted. No response when she'd texted back. And now, after two weeks of avoiding him, of lying awake at night thinking about the hard crush of his mouth and the low rumble of his voice, of telling herself just a few more days and she'd get past this physio-emotional chaos she'd never expected herself to be a part of, he was here.

She didn't have to answer. She could walk back to her room. Turn out the lights and lie in bed until the sun came up the next day. It didn't matter that Garrett had seen the light in her windows and knew she was home. It wasn't as though he wouldn't understand what she was doing. He might not even blame her.

So why wasn't she turning around and walking back down the hall? Why wasn't she flipping off the lights and climbing into her bed alone?

Because it would be rude? Because he'd spent the last forty minutes driving back from a family party he hadn't even made it inside for to see her? Because maybe they needed to talk around an issue they'd already beaten to death?

No.

The answer lay in the nervous flutter deep in her belly. In the almost painful thump of her heart. In the eager ache that had permeated her body as a whole.

She *wanted* him.

Like she couldn't remember wanting anything before.

Fingers trembling, she reached for the door. Felt the pull of him like a loose charge in the air even as she grounded herself against the knob. And then the door was swinging open and there was Garrett with those deep blue whirlpool eyes coming up to meet hers as his lips slanted into a grin.

This was such a mistake.

One solid arm was braced against the frame above her head as he reached for the back of her neck and leaned in, stopping only a breath away. "I hear you need a *distraction*."

Ah-ha.

Now she understood. Maeve had repeated something only Garrett could fully understand. And he hadn't liked what he'd heard.

Heat rushed her cheeks and, wetting her lips, she tried to think of something to say. Only the rough growl of approval as his eyes followed the movement blanked her mind of anything beyond how glad she was to see him… and how wrong that was.

She looked up into his eyes. "I keep thinking about you."

A nod. She could feel his breath swirling over the side of her face.

"Same here."

"I thought—" She swallowed, tried not to lean into all

the heat of a body too close to ignore. "Giving someone else a chance might help."

The fingers at the back of her neck stroked, soft and gentle. "So you've got a date?"

And yet there was no mistaking the firm hold for anything but the possessive claim it was.

"No. I backed out." It wouldn't be fair to go out with one man solely in the hopes of his distracting her from another. Especially when the likelihood of it working was so slim.

"Good."

God, those eyes. The feel of him so close. Her body hummed in response to his proximity. What were they going to do about this?

"So I've got an idea."

Nichole nodded. She was starting to get an idea as well. One night. The night they never should have left unfinished all those weeks ago. Finally out of their systems. And then they'd never get within fifty feet of each other again. It wouldn't interfere with her relationship with Maeve. It wouldn't threaten anything.

"I like it," she murmured, pressing her palms into the broad chest too temptingly close to ignore.

Garrett let out a gruff laugh, then tipped her head back to bring her attention up to his eyes. "I'm glad. But how about you hear it first, then agree?"

Was she really going to do this?

A look into those eyes burning with a need that matched her own—yes. Definitely.

One night. It was all she needed.

"Tell me." Her palms skimmed downward, riding the dips and valleys of his abdomen.

"We give Maeve's plan a go."

That caught her attention. Chin pulling back, she

shook off the haze of need and focused on the man before her. "What?"

"You say you don't know how to do casual. And I
don't know how to do anything else. So we meet in the
middle. Find some safe place that feels good. That's
about having some fun instead of forever. I'm thinking,
for a while, we could be friends and lovers. We'd trust
each other not to let it go too far and just…learn to date."

For a while. Not one night.

She let out a heavy breath.

"Garrett, I don't think you're the right guy to practice dating with. You were right about the strings. Those
complications matter."

"I'm the perfect guy. And the only string I see is the
one Maeve keeps dangling in front of me—the one with
you on the end. She's not going to flip when this is over.
She's a big girl. And she's your best friend, so give her
some credit."

Nichole's mouth dropped open in shock. *Garrett* was
telling *her* to give Maeve some credit?

"You've got to be kidding?"

Garrett shook his head, brought his thumb around to
stroke across her bottom lip.

Oh, God. Such slight contact…but with an earth-
shattering impact.

"Not even close. And, to underscore my point, I'm
going to give you your first lesson in keeping it casual."
Those deep blue pools were pulling her deeper. The
gravel-rough voice was like a siren song, luring her to
depths she shouldn't go. "Don't make things more complicated than they need to be. Neither one of us wants
this to get too serious. So it won't. Simple."

"Easy for The Panty Whisperer to say." His thumb

was still at her lip, offering that tantalizing sensation with every word.

"Easy for anyone on the same page to say." He ducked down so his eyes were level with hers. "And you're the perfect woman for me because I need more, Nichole. More than the kind of meaningless that's been on tap for longer than I want to remember. But my *more* has a pretty hard limit when it comes to the future. And you might be the only woman I trust not to try and change that. Don't you see? Right now, at this place in our lives, we're a perfect fit."

She wanted to believe him. Wanted it to be that easy. But sometimes things didn't go the way people planned. Sometimes the best intentions led to the worst kinds of hurt. And she was afraid.

He leaned closer then, so his words slid around her ear in warm rush. "*Trust me,* Nichole."

Trust. He was asking her to trust him. To trust Maeve. To trust herself.

Could she do it?

If she ever wanted a full life she had to learn how.

And this man she wanted so desperately understood so much about her.

Knuckles coasting down the length of her neck, Garrett murmured, "Trust me to take care of you."

Her breath caught as he pulled back to look down at her, the dark promise in his eyes enough to make her belly twist in on itself.

Her lips parted on what might have a warning to herself, or maybe just his name because she loved the feel of it on her tongue—but he was already there. Closing those last scant inches between them and catching her mouth with his kiss.

She was lost. No more denials. No more waiting.

Arms snaked around her back, he pulled her close, taking her weight as he took her self-control. He carried her inside and kicked the door closed behind them.

Feet dangling above the floor, she reveled in the strength of his embrace, the power of his need. The ever-tightening hold that roared they'd waited too long already and threatened nothing short of *everything* would be enough.

Her arms laced around his neck, pulling him closer, because after telling herself no for so long this was finally *yes*.

He walked them down the hall toward her room, deepening the kiss as they went. Taking the access she offered and thrusting inside. Retreating and then sliding past her lips again, slow and steady. Telling her what he wanted to do to her without words. Filling her mouth with the rough stroke of his tongue, the taste of him. Decadent and delicious.

Yes!

He thrust again and she closed around him, sucking softly in an urgent, needy plea. Begging him for more. For all.

He pressed into her hips, so the steely thick ridge of his erection nudged firm against her belly. It was a hint. A taunt. A tease that left her whimpering as she tried to squirm closer. Take what she needed.

And then her back was against the wall and his hands were sliding across her bottom, strong fingers splaying wide as they pushed down the backs of her thighs past the hem of her sundress. Each point of contact became a bruising demand as they guided her legs around him, positioning her so his hot length met her center with a rolling pressure just exactly right.

"Garrett—oh, God, like that," she gasped, her words

taking on an insistent quality, warning of a total loss of control.

Garrett did it again and again until desire lanced her core.

Her legs tightened with her fists in his hair, and the low growl vibrating between them was his. "I need to get inside you, baby."

His hands released their hold on her hips, letting her legs slip down the heavy slabs of his thighs until her feet touched the floor.

"Yes, please." Her eyes were trailing up and down his body, her mind plotting the fastest way to rid him of his clothes, working justifications on which ones weren't critical in the removal process. Because really all she needed was him sitting on that bed, his fly open and boxers pushed down. *Oh, God.*

A shudder ripped through her at the mental image alone.

Glancing over her shoulder, she saw they were mere feet from her room. Her bed. From her half-clothed, full-penetration, hard-and-fast-and-finally fantasy.

Dragging her eyes back to his, she whispered, "I can't wait anymore."

She pulled at Garrett's belt with greedy, shaking hands and, unbuckling it, used the tongue to lead him the rest of the way.

At her bed, she caught the sides of her skirt in each hand and pulled the dress over her head, tossing it to the floor.

Garrett froze, his own shirt caught over one shoulder as he stared down at her, naked but for white cotton bikini panties.

Her thumbs pushed into the delicate waistband, pushing them down.

Fabric ripped and buttons bounced across the floor, followed by the tattered remnants of Garrett's shirt. The denim of his jeans put up a better defense, but soon it too was piled in a heap and her back was hitting the mattress as Garrett followed her down, kissing her hard all the way, his body covering hers in a tease of flesh against flesh before he broke away to sheath himself.

And then his thick head was nudging at her opening as his blue eyes held with hers. All the urgency and frantic need slipped away as, slowly, he pushed inside. Easing in and out by incremental degrees as her body stretched to accommodate the greater size of his. The cost of his restraint and his care was etched in all the lines of his face until, at last, he sank deep, filling the snug hold of her body.

Her lips parted on a fragile gasp that was decadent torture and supreme satisfaction all in one. So totally, incomparably worth the wait.

She wanted to stay like that forever, with him buried so thick and deep within her that she felt his every breath and heartbeat in the most intimate, erotic way— something Garrett seemed to be in agreement with as he held himself on straightened arms, staring down into her eyes with a look that made her feel like the sunset he'd waited years to see.

Without thought her hands went to his face, the light stubble a tender scrape beneath her fingers. "You're every fantasy I never dared to dream."

Garrett's smile was satisfied and wanting all at once. "I don't think you have enough fantasies, sweetheart."

"Then maybe you'll give me some more."

His hips began to move and his eyes took on an intensity she never could have fathomed. "Starting now, Nichole."

* * *

Nichole collapsed on the bed. Her limbs weak and useless. Her mind spinning over the events of the last few hours.

Even now her belly curled in and on to itself at the memory. So. Unbelievably. Good.

The kind of *good* a girl could get used to. Spoiled by. Caught up in.

Summoning all her strength, she turned her head on her pillow to look at Garrett, who'd collapsed beside her. He was staring at the ceiling, his breath working in and out of his chest in ragged draws.

He really *had* done most of the work.

She thought back to the chair. Maybe seventy-five percent.

The hallway. Okay, eighty-five. God, that had been so good.

And she must have purred her approval too, because Garrett's brows edged up as he looked over at her, that arrogantly satisfied smile stamped across his mouth. "Something on your mind?"

No sense in denying it. "The hall."

His lids went to half-mast. His voice even lower. *"The hall."*

And then he was reaching for her, pulling her in with arms so big and strong she felt as though she were thin as a wisp and lighter than air rather than the flesh-and-blood real woman she was. Another decadent sensation.

Leaning in to taste her lips once, then once more, but this time slow and lingering with a low, rumbling groan finish, Garrett looked deeply into her eyes.

"So there's something I'd like to try, if you're up for it. You know—feeling…experimental and all." His gaze dropped to her mouth. "It's something I've never done before."

Nichole blinked, thoughts of the last handful of hours running through her mind like a PowerPoint presentation for Experimental 101.

Something even *Garrett* hadn't tried?

Her heart skipped and a flutter of genuine nerves pulled her too-loose limbs back into working order. "Um…I'm not saying no…yet. But…um…Garrett, what exactly are you talking about…*exactly?*"

He pulled her closer still, so she ended up lying on top of him, and let out a long breath. "Seriously, only if you're into it, Nichole. Only if you really think you can handle it."

She swallowed. "Just tell me."

Garrett drew her head toward his and whispered in her ear, "I'd like to spend the night. Stay. Sleep here with you."

Nichole reared back, planting her hands over his wide chest and tucking her knees at either side of his ribs.

"You!" She laughed on a rush of breath. "I can't believe you—you know what—" But then all she could do was laugh, looking down into Mr. All-Innocence's smirking face. "You're bad."

Hands coasting up her bare legs, over her hips and back down again, he answered, "Like there was ever any question… But maybe not quite as bad as you assumed."

"No. Not at all." The teasing fell away and reality settled around her. He was asking her for something serious, disguising it behind laughter and games.

"You've really never slept over at a woman's place before?"

"No."

This time it wasn't nerves running through her but

something else. Something warmer. Something she was certain was still just this side of okay in terms of the whole caring-while-keeping-it-casual deal they'd struck.

Leaning forward, so this time she was the one whispering in his ear, she said, "Don't worry. Since this is your first time I promise to be gentle."

CHAPTER TEN

GARRETT LEANED BACK against Nichole's kitchen counter, the sound and smell of brewing coffee filling the air around him. He'd woken at five, like he normally did, only to discover there was nothing normal about this morning.

He wasn't in his apartment. And not crashed out on one of his sisters' couches or spare beds either. But still in the delectable Nichole's bed and completely wrapped around her.

And, damn, if that hadn't felt good.

A little too good, based on the way he'd been pressed hard against her back.

He'd entertained a handful of fun-and-games kind of wake-up scenarios, most of which involved getting his tongue all over her before she quite knew what was doing. But they'd only actually gone to sleep about three hours before. And, while *his* internal alarm wouldn't cut him any slack, if Nichole could catch the extra Zs she should.

He didn't want her nodding off at the wheel or letting her body wear down.

Figuring he'd pass on worrying about all the what-ifs of Nichole not getting enough rest, he'd climbed out of bed—mindful of the woman still sleeping there.

Now he was milling around her kitchen, waiting for the coffee to brew…making a mental list of repairs the place needed. The hinge on the cabinet door. The track on the silverware drawer.

He'd be willing to bet she'd like a new counter. One of those granite slabs to replace the tile she had.

And then there was the fact that he didn't need to be taking over the maintenance of Nichole's place. What was he *doing?*

She didn't need this from him. And he didn't need—

"Hey."

Garrett turned around and all thoughts about replacing a segment of the baseboard or not were temporarily shelved as he looked to where Nichole stood on the threshold of the kitchen, wrapped up in one of those stretchy thin robes that didn't actually look all that warm…and, so far as he could tell, nothing else.

"Hey, yourself. Hope you don't mind I started a pot?"

Her mouth pulled to one side as she finger-combed a few wild curls from her face. "You're asking me if I mind that you made coffee, but not that you've pried up a piece of my floor?"

He looked down at where his Swiss Army knife was wedged between the wall and—and *hell*. Looking back at Nichole, he offered the only defense he had. "I'm good at fixing things. And it's just the baseboard. The floor beneath looks fine."

Shuffling into the kitchen, Nichole just nodded at him, looking adorably exhausted as she folded herself into a kitchen chair and then tried to cover an enormous yawn with her small hand.

"Okay, but your kind is notorious for taking things apart and leaving them that way. Indefinitely. Anything you touch in this place gets put back to rights within the week." She slanted a look at him. "Regardless of whether this thing with us has run its course."

Giving them less than a week to run their course? Grumpy, grumpy. She didn't need to worry about his taking her place apart piece by piece. It was a habit, but one he intended to kick. With Nichole, he didn't want to be the guy who had to fix everything.

Okay, he'd fix the baseboard...because now that he'd seen it, the damn thing would nag at the back of his mind until he knew it was taken care of. But that was it.

Garrett looked between Nichole and the coffee. After the baseboard, the only thing he'd fix for Nichole was a hot cup of joe. Grabbing a mug from the tree beside the pot, he poured her a cup. "Cream? Sugar?"

A smile flickered at the corner of her mouth as she looked him up and down. "Whipped cream."

With a shrug, he turned for the fridge, but Nichole was already up and walking over. "Thank you, Garrett, but I'll get it dressed up. I'm kind of particular."

"Sure." Even better.

He watched her navigating her space, seeing a routine he never would have thought to imagine, liking the look of her in the morning in this environment that so few would have the opportunity to experience.

Possessive satisfaction swelled within him at the thought, urging him into closer contact. His fingers played through her hair as she topped off her coffee with skim milk, swirled a spoon through the pale brew and then clinked it at the side of the mug twice.

Another sideways glance and she was looking very amused. "So, was it...*good for you?*"

The overnight.

Giving in to the laugh Nichole always seemed to pull from him, he nodded. "Very."

"Seriously, how is it you've never spent the night with a woman before?"

Garrett took her hand and led her over to the breakfast nook by the bay window and, setting down his own coffee rather than giving up the loose hold he had on her fingers, pulled out her chair. "It just always seemed more of a complication than it would be worth."

But then, he hadn't exactly known what he was missing.

Parking it across the table, he threw back half his own mug—more about the infusion of caffeine than the lingering warmth he'd take his time over on the next cup.

"Really?" she asked, pulling her feet up beneath her as she settled in. "I guess I would have thought in some ways making a getaway would be more complicated."

Nichole brought the mug to her lips and took a long swallow, her satisfaction all too distracting. But she'd asked a question. And, though the answer wasn't exactly simple, he trusted her with it.

"Not really. I mean, at first it just wasn't an option. I didn't go off to college at eighteen like most of the other guys did, so it wasn't like I could just sneak some co-ed into my dorm. I was living at home with my four sisters. Basically raising them."

"Wait—Bethany's a year older than you, and wasn't your mom still around? I mean weren't there times you could have got away if you'd wanted to? Weren't there co-eds trying to sneak you into their dorms?"

Sure there were. Truth be told, there had been for years. "Yeah, but there was a lot going on. Our situation at home was pretty precarious for a number of reasons. My parents hadn't done a lot of contingency planning. There was a small policy that got us through the first couple years, but my mom didn't work, and I didn't want the girls' futures to die with my dad. Bethany was smart as hell. Always making those gifted programs at school. A hell of a lot more going on than I ever had, that's for sure. And with the earning potential in the house pretty well limited to what I could eke out, her grades were her ticket into college. So that was her job and she nailed it. Free ride right through."

Nichole was smiling at him then, and he knew she'd seen the pride he couldn't contain when it came to his older sister.

"Which was great, but it meant she was basically gone by the time I was seventeen." He'd never been a senior in high school, because by then he'd dropped out to work full-time. Everyone had helped out in the day-to-day— but the money, the bills, keeping the house fixed up had fallen to Garrett.

"My mom had always been kind of fragile. I have no idea how she managed to have five kids, but even before Dad died we'd all become pretty adept at chipping in. Which is probably the only reason we were able to make it the way we did. She never really recovered from losing him."

"Garrett, that must have been so hard."

He nodded, closing his eyes. And for a moment he was back in his kitchen that day, with some textbook open in front of him, his dad blowing through the room with all his endless energy, trailing a bunch of little girls clamoring for a last kiss before he took off for work. He'd leaned over Garrett and looked at the page, shaking his head in that bewildered way he'd had when it came to school.

He'd been blue-collar to the core. Working in construction from his teens. No higher education. Just a salt-of-the-earth, meat-and-potatoes man's man who'd loved his family.

He'd clapped Garrett on the shoulder and nodded toward his wife over at the counter, cleaning up breakfast. "You're the man of the house while I'm gone, son. Make me proud."

Same words every day. And Garrett had grinned, rolling his eyes at the idea. Still, he always gave his dad his everyday commitment—"Yes, sir"—earning that last, "Good kid," as he left for work.

Thirty minutes later his father had been dead. And all Garrett had had to honor the man he'd worshipped was that last promise he'd made.

Clearing his throat, he looked back at Nichole. "Mom tried. She got meals on the table and held it together enough so, for a while, the relatives weren't asking questions. But even as kids we had a sort of instinctual understanding of her limitations. She cried a lot. Spent more and more time in her room. Less and less time doing the things a capable parent did. If there was a crisis in the middle of the night she wasn't the one the girls went to. It was me. And by the end—when I was eighteen—it got to where she needed the kind of help she couldn't get at home. Hell, she should have had help before then, but we— I just didn't understand."

The guilt inexorably tied to thoughts of his mother pushed at him, weighing in his gut and chest. The question that never went away… If he'd gotten her help earlier would she have had a chance?

"My God, Garrett, I'm so sorry. I didn't realize your mother— Maeve doesn't talk a lot about her."

It didn't surprise him. "Maeve missed out on the most Mom had to give. She was just a little kid. And it was tough to lose so much at once. It was tough on all of them, but we got through it. And, long story short, someone needed to be around. I sure as hell didn't like the idea of my sisters being alone overnight, you know?"

There were just too many things that could happen... and he'd thought about *all* of them.

Nichole's brow pushed up. "That being the case, how in the world did you ever get this Panty Whisperer reputation?"

"I was a teenager." He laughed. "With *needs*. No privacy at home. And a *very* short window of free time every other week or so to take care of them. Thank God I had a few friends with older sisters who were willing to be the responsible party and babysit once in a while."

"So you're citing your libido as an example of necessity being the mother of invention?"

"Exactly." Then he held up a hand. "Only I don't want it to sound like I was one of those guys who'd say anything to get into a girl's pants. I wasn't."

She laughed, shaking her head. "I'm guessing you probably wouldn't need to, Garrett."

But then her eyes found his again and they were still serious. Still waiting.

"What about later, though? After you got Maeve and the rest through school and out on their own? What about then?"

"By then I'd taken over running the construction company and I was going after my own degree. Still not a lot of free time. But, yeah, obviously I could have spent some of it crashed out overnight in a woman's bed. It just seemed smarter not to."

"Afraid they'd get ideas?"

"Yes." It sounded bad. But all he had was the truth. "It was important to me that the women I took out didn't get the wrong idea about what was happening. About what *could* happen."

He hadn't had the time to get to know them well enough to figure out if he could trust them to take his word for the kinds of limits a relationship with him would have. And so his romantic interactions had always been sort of stunted, shallow exercises that served a specific need.

Until Nichole.

Because not only did he finally have the time, but she already knew the score. She already knew him better than any other woman he'd ever taken out. They had honesty and communication on their side.

And the freedom in that—just to be together and enjoy what they were doing—was incredible.

There was only one problem. He hadn't actually taken Nichole *out* at all.

If ever there was a woman who deserved a solid date from him it was this one. But so far he'd picked her up at a party, literally picked her up in the back of a coffee shop and backed her into her place with no intention of letting her out until he'd gotten her to...well, where he'd gotten her. Several times, he mentally amended, giving into a satisfied grin.

"What's that look about?" Nichole asked, cuddling her coffee mug to her chest.

"I was just thinking about where I should take you for our first date."

CHAPTER ELEVEN

"YOU CAN'T BE SERIOUS." Nichole laughed, trying to keep up as Garrett half-towed her through a parking lot toward what appeared to be some kind of two-dimensional enchanted castle ahead.

"Why not? This is our first date—*official* first date. Because the weeknight dinners don't count and I actually *called* you in advance to set this one up—so it seemed appropriate."

God, she loved that he was so into giving them a first date. Even if they *had* spent five of the last six nights together, with Garrett proving to her time and time again what a stellar decision it had been going forward with a relationship.

Giving her hand a squeeze, he added, "And it's on my bucket list."

Nichole ground to a stop, thinking she'd never get used to the things that came out of this man's mouth. "Your bucket list?"

"Yeah." He brushed a strand of flyaway hair back from her face, tucking it behind her ear. "The stuff you want to do before you die."

"I know what it is. I'm just surprised to learn miniature golf makes yours." The idea of him trying to navigate that big body through a tiny maze of six-foot fairways was just too much.

"Why? Because it's such good clean fun?" Leaning in, he let his voice take on a conspiratorial tone. "If helping me live out one of my adolescent fantasies is too wholesome for you we could always make it a little more *interesting*..."

Her heart skipped a beat as she met his hot gaze. "You want to wager?"

"Why not? We could come up with some creative terms." Wrapping that powerful arm around her shoulders, he guided them toward the main entrance. "And I've never played before...so your chances of winning are about as good as they're going to get."

She'd been hearing Maeve talk about this guy for years. He was relentlessly competitive. And a natural at most everything he put his mind to trying. Which meant, regardless of his experience, there was a good chance she wasn't going to win. "What kind of terms?"

The hot glint in Garrett's eyes had her belly tightening and nervous excitement zinging across the surface of her skin.

Five minutes later Nichole was intimately acquainted with the business end of Garrett's brawn. The side of him that had made him the perfect candidate to move out of heavy lifting and take over his mentor's construction company. He was a guy who liked to negotiate, and he wasn't above a little hardball when it came to getting his outrageous terms laid down in lead on the back of the scorecard. And she liked that side of him too.

Who was she kidding? She liked everything about him.

The way he took her by surprise and caught her off guard. His first dates. His soulful reflections. His naughty wish-lists. He was just so much more than she'd expected. More than she'd been prepared for.

So much more…that there were moments when quiet alarms began to sound in the back of her mind. But then she'd catch his eye and see all that steady confidence shining out at her, and she'd remember they knew what they were doing. That this was safe. And she'd just give in to all the incredible feel-good that was being with Garrett.

She trusted him.

Or at least she *had*.

One mini-golf slaughter later, Nichole was flopped over the wide slab of Garrett's shoulder, one hand fisted around his belt, the other clinging to his back pocket, as the hard, cold truth washed over her.

She'd been hustled.

Outraged, incensed and entirely too charmed by his betrayal, she charged, "You told me you'd never played before!"

"I haven't," he answered, those long legs striding through the now mostly empty parking lot. "But I've got a knack for picking new things up. Especially when there's an incentive on the line."

Then, in typical Garrett fashion, with a hand behind her head to ensure she didn't bump it, he set her into the car.

"And the backseat is on your bucket list too?"

He at least had the good sense to look chagrined. "No. But having to work my way into your panties is."

"I think you know just exactly how willing I am. How willing we've *all* been."

He hushed her with a warm breath at her ear. "Come on. I won. You've got to play hard-to-get."

She backed further across the bench seat, heat pouring through her center as it did every other time Garrett looked at her the way he was looking at her right then.

He wanted to have to work for her, did he?

"I'm not sure I should let you anywhere near me after the stunt you just pulled."

The satisfaction shining out of those half-lidded blues was almost enough for her to throw down any pretense at resistance and haul him into the seat beside her. Better yet, on top of her.

But he wanted to play. And playing was something she'd never had enough practice with. So here, in the far corner of a darkened parking lot, Nichole was ready to prioritize fun.

As Garrett wrapped one strong hand around the seat-back beside her, hefting himself into a space too small to accommodate him, she offered the most skeptical, resistant look she could muster. "I'm not sure about this, Garrett."

His answering deep-chested groan promised her feigned hard-to-get was hitting the right note. That and the hell-yes glint in his eyes.

"Oh, come on, Nichole," he cajoled. "I promise. I just want to talk. That's all."

Yeah, her too. Right. "Maybe…just for a minute."

Nichole had been prepared for the questions. She was out with Maeve, Bethany and Erin for their usual girls' night dinner…and she'd been dating their brother in an official public capacity for three weeks now.

Sure, Maeve had been giving her a good grilling on and off since the very first night. But apparently she'd been holding back. Storing up for tonight.

It was almost laughable—except there was something way too serious in the three sets of eyes watching her from across the mostly cleared table. And she was getting a very one-against-three vibe.

"But you guys got arrested together!"

Shaking her head, she shot Maeve a murderous look. "I told you—they didn't even take us in."

Maeve did the whole shoulders-around-her-ears thing while she dabbed at the corner of her mouth with her napkin. "And I told you I wouldn't say anything. But apparently you didn't secure the same blood oath from Officer Klinsky...who happened to be in Carla's class. And ran into one of her girlfriends at the video store yesterday. Sordid tales travel fast, honey."

Bethany grinned from behind her wineglass. "But thank you for confirming a story I hadn't believed."

Perfect.

Erin's mouth was doing one of those weird twitchy things that happened when someone was trying exceptionally hard to keep a straight face. Not happening. Not even close.

Leaning an elbow on the table, Nichole laid her napkin to the side of her plate. "Just spit it out. I can see you've got something good."

Wicked laughter that was totally Carter family burst past her lips as she glanced from one sister to the other and then back to Nichole. "Can you see the invitations? Embossed with bars? A pair of handcuffs between their names?"

All three Carter girls broke into gales of laughter, but suddenly Nichole didn't feel like laughing. Invitations. *Wedding* invitations.

Just the kind of place she didn't want her mind to go.

And then, to make matters worse, she had the sudden certain sense they weren't alone. Sure enough, within seconds a wide hand was warming her shoulder and another Carter's deeper, darker and yet just as playful voice was joining in with the rest. "I thought I recognized those cackles."

A chorus of delighted welcome sounded around the table as Garrett made the rounds, dropping a kiss at each sister's cheek as he went. An endearing habit which had Nichole smiling despite the fact her number-one taboo topic had been introduced mere seconds before.

Had Garrett heard?

Everything was going so well between them. The relationship was staying neatly within the lines they'd drawn. And it all felt so good. She didn't want anything…anyone…to jeopardize it. But one glance around the table and she knew without a shadow of a doubt there was no way Garrett wasn't going to get an earful about their brush with the law and what a special theme it would make, come marriage-time.

She almost wanted to drag him away to the nearest back hall for one last walk on the *Garrett side* before she had to let him go.

"What are you doing, crashing our girls' night out?" Bethany asked, clearly delighted to see her brother.

Garrett nodded toward the plate-glass window across the dining room. "Had a dinner meeting at the place down the street. Was heading to catch a cab when I happened to look in and see this table of lovely ladies. Don't worry, I won't stay. Just wanted to say hello and make sure you were all getting enough to eat."

At that moment the waiter arrived, hefting a tray laden with every dessert on the menu. None of which they'd ordered. "Compliments of the gentleman."

"Dinner's on me, girls." He grinned as his sisters chirped out delighted thank-yous and then started staking claims on which decadent tart, chocolate pot or indulgent wedge of cake they wanted to try first.

Nichole took his hand and, when he met her eyes, mouthed a thank-you of her own.

He winked, giving her a squeeze. "Enjoy the evening and don't do anything rumor suggests I might do."

At that, Bethany threatened tears if he didn't join them, and when everyone joined in he happily relented, taking a seat beside Nichole.

"So—having a good night, girls?"

There was really no way to warn him.

"The best, Garrett," Erin assured him. "But not as good a night as it sounds like *you* had two weeks ago."

Nichole had to give him credit. The guy didn't bat an eye or let on in any way he was squirming. And if she hadn't caught the ever so slight darkening across his cheekbones she might not have known at all. But there it was. *Red.*

And for once it wasn't her.

"Apparently the cop knows Carla," she offered helpfully.

And then Erin dropped the bomb, sharing her fabulous ideas on an arrest-themed wedding.

Nichole had expected Garrett's reaction to be something along the lines of a sudden silence. A cool withdrawal. Or maybe just the stiffening of his body.

What she hadn't expected was his bark of laughter, or the way he took her hand and grinned, stage whispering to her, "I thought those plans were going to be a surprise!"

A few more ideas for the "wedding" got thrown around, including horizontally striped black-and-white bridesmaid dresses and "get out of jail free" seating cards, followed by a handful of jabs at Garrett for fooling around in the backseat of a car in a parking lot. And then the conversation shifted again and they were talking about Bethany's upcoming trip to Disney with the family, and Maeve's less entertaining travel plans for work.

And through it all Nichole sat somewhat shell-shocked by the ease with which they'd sailed through what she'd honestly expected to be the beginning of the end. Stunned to see her hand still the object of Garrett's idle touch. Startled by the revelation that this man at her side had just given her yet another lesson in the art of not taking things too seriously.

A tension she hadn't been aware of eased from her shoulders and spine, allowing her to relax back into her seat, her night and the incredible ride she was taking.

Garrett stayed the remainder of the evening, which lasted far beyond the last bite of crème brulée and through all the coffees and cappuccinos. He knew wedding talk—even in jest—was a hot button for Nichole. One that, when pushed, got her head spinning in all the directions neither of them needed it to go.

He didn't want her to worry he was running off freaked out about the mere mention of the "M" word, and he didn't want to give her the opportunity to go there herself. And once the conversation had moved on, he'd had a damn good time listening to the girls gabbing about their lives. Listening to talk spanning the spectrum from reality dating shows to mortgages to the rocky state of a mutual friend's marriage. It reminded him of when they'd all still been under one roof and he'd been privy to every inane and profound thought to cross their minds. And it was even better tonight, because intermixed with the ringing laughter he'd been hearing his whole life were the rich notes of Nichole's phenomenal laugh.

It was something he could definitely get used to, but if he wanted the chance, a little damage control was in order. And it started within a half-block of the restaurant as they walked down Randolph for some air before catching a cab.

Slanting a look at the woman tucked beneath his arm, he brought up the topic he knew had never fully left her thoughts. "That made you pretty uncomfortable tonight? The jokes about getting married?"

She glanced up at him, the relief in her eyes suggesting she'd been revving up to broach the subject herself. "It's awkward. I mean, isn't it awkward for you?"

It might have been if he wasn't with someone he knew was on the same page. "It's not a big deal. I mean, it's just talk. From my sisters. I'm used to it. But then, I've never been engaged. So I'm probably not so sensitive as you are."

There was a subtle tensing of her shoulders and Garrett knew he'd touched a nerve. "You don't have to tell me about it if you don't want to, but I'd like to know what happened."

They continued to walk another quarter of a block in silence. Only a few cars were passing so late on a weeknight downtown.

"With Paul, I was really young and very stupid," she started. "We'd been friends since grade school and started to date at fifteen. He was the nicest boy I knew and, because we were such good friends first, when we hit the next level…the relationship kind of *took*."

Garrett nodded his understanding. Though he hadn't done much legitimate dating in high school himself, he remembered what it had been like with his friends. Oftentimes there'd been an attraction and not much else, which meant a fair amount of turnover when it came to young love. But not so for Nichole.

Because in this, like in everything else, she'd been different. Ahead of the curve.

And she'd paid for it.

"A lot of girls sort of had that wandering-eye thing. New crushes every month or so. But I liked having something steady in my life. I *liked* Paul as much as I loved him, and pretty soon we were graduating, and we'd been together for three years, and we were going to the same college. Everyone thought it was so romantic and kept asking us about whether we were going to get married. I think maybe we simply got used to the idea. Like, *Yeah, of course we will. We love each other. Why not?*" She was shaking her head then, with a quiet laugh. "Of course, the *why not* answer should have been, we were basically kids. Only no one seemed to notice."

Garrett couldn't even imagine. "What about your parents? Didn't they try to talk you out of it? I mean what were you? Eighteen?"

"His parents thought we were a great match. His mom told me how I was like the daughter she'd never had. And my mom. *Sheesh.*" She opened her mouth, tried to find the words and seemed to fail. Then, pulling a guilty face, she tried again. "My mom is wonderful, but her priorities...her sense...sometimes it's not what it should be. She got pregnant with me when she was seventeen and my dad never married her. He basically took off when he found out about me and sent a check once or twice a year for a while. So in her book, me getting married— and to a guy she'd known forever, with us both so close at Marquette University—it was about the best news she'd ever heard."

He'd known her father wasn't around. But it wasn't

until this moment he understood the extent of that absence. No father. No brother. Just a mother who'd wanted a commitment for her girl even if she was too young to make one.

Clearing his throat, he prompted her for more. "But it didn't work out?"

She shrugged. "Paul came to his senses about six months before the wedding. He was so apologetic. So genuinely sorry. He was looking around him, seeing everyone else in the world just starting their lives and figuring out who they were. What they wanted. And there we were, ready to call it done. He thought we both deserved a chance to figure ourselves out a little more. And deep down I knew he was right. So we called off the wedding and went our separate ways. He transferred to a school out east and I got on with my life."

She didn't seem bitter. But he knew from talking with Maeve—and from the hints he'd picked up from her, her heart had been badly abused.

"And you met someone else?"

The way her features tightened up told him this schmuck was someone he never wanted to meet. Contrary to popular belief, and with a very few exceptions, Garrett wasn't generally a violent guy. But the pain that flashed across Nichole's face had him wanting to do physical harm before he'd even heard the story.

"Joel was…" She let out a sigh. "He was a few years older. And when I met him he just struck me as so confident. Like he totally knew what he wanted—which appealed to me, I'm sure, for very obvious reasons."

"You thought he'd be safe." Garrett gave her shoulder a rub and then stopped to take her hand in his. He wanted to know what had happened. Wanted to see her face when she told him.

"I'd had a couple of years to lick my wounds over Paul, and when Joel finally asked me out I was excited to go. Ready for something new." She slanted a glance at him. "Ready for my mother to stop with the heavy sighs every time I talked to her and the subtle nudges that I should apologize to Paul—"

"What?" he barked out, but she waved him off.

"For pressuring him, or letting him go, or whatever it was that day. Anyway, she was probably more excited than I was when things got serious with Joel. And I guess I didn't have enough experience to see what was real and what wasn't. Maybe I didn't want to see it because I was so hungry to build myself the family I'd wanted as a kid. Or maybe my heart just didn't have any breaks on it. Who knows? But it never should have gone as far as it did."

Garrett listened, his temper escalating as Nichole tried to explain what had gone wrong. The actions and events she'd misinterpreted. The off-the-cuff remarks she'd taken to heart. She was trying to tell him what had happened with this chump had been as much her fault as her ex's, but all Garrett could see was some spineless jackass unwilling to take responsibility for his words and actions.

"*He asked you to marry him.* After two years. How is *that* rushing or your fault?"

Nichole's skin looked pale beneath the fading light as she looked away, shame haunting her eyes. Making his gut twist for asking her.

"He said being with me was like being caught in a riptide. He didn't realize how dangerous I was until it was almost too late."

Dangerous.

Garrett's teeth ground down as he struggled for patience. Told himself not to try to look this guy up so he could pay him a visit. Have a few words.

But, damn it, what a piece of work.

When she spoke again it was so quietly he almost missed it.

"I thought we wanted the same things. That we were in it together. But I was wrong."

And though she didn't say the word he knew it was there in her head. *Again.*

Garrett gripped her shoulders, pulling her into his chest so his words would fall from his lips to her ears. "There's nothing wrong with wanting those things, Nichole. In the past, you just wanted them with the wrong guys. But you're a different woman now. With more life experience. You won't make the same mistakes. You won't get burned again."

Catching the delicate turn of her jaw in his palm, he met her eyes.

"When you meet the right guy—one who actually deserves you—you won't be too young. You won't be caught up in a bunch of empty promises. You'll be ready and so will he."

And maybe Garrett would get invited to the wedding, because even though he'd been with her like this, he couldn't imagine their not being friends when the rest was over. Couldn't imagine not being able to talk and laugh with her.

Okay, right now he couldn't imagine not being able to put his hands on her or move inside her body, but that part would go away when this thing between them finally ran its course.

Someday some guy was going to get everything he'd ever wanted in this woman. But in the here and now, at least for a little while, Nichole was his. And he was going to make every minute they had together count. Starting right now, with getting her mind off the past by distracting her with a short-term future he'd been thinking about for a few weeks now.

"Until then…" He leaned closer to her ear, so his mouth played around the delicate shell as he spoke, effectively changing the tone of their communication within a few choice words.

Nichole's hands tightened against his chest. So sensitive.

"I've got a spectacular idea…"

CHAPTER TWELVE

"YOU CAN'T JUST SAY *bucket list* and assume it's the end of the discussion."

Nichole was walking a step ahead of him now, laughing over her shoulder as they approached the intersection.

"Sure I can," he answered, watching with satisfaction as she turned an arched brow on him, her mind about as far from the two guys who'd torn up her life as possible. This…now…it was about *them*.

"Sure I can?" she demanded, that one betraying curve at the corner of her mouth spurring him on.

"Uh-huh." Reaching the corner, he moved into her space, wrapping an arm around her waist to pull her against him as he reached around her to flag a cab a block down. "You know you can't resist this face."

"Garrett," she growled at him, in a way that was more laughter than anything else.

"Nichole," he rumbled back against her ear, loving how her body almost melted into his as a result. "It's Crush, Napa Valley. A single weekend a few months from now. I want to take you."

They'd have fun. Hit a handful of wineries. Get drunk on each other for a few nights out of town.

"Trust me, Nichole. It'll be amazing."

"I do trust you. Trusting *you* isn't the problem. It's just—"

"What? It's just a weekend. Two like-minded adults, on the same page, getting away for a little not-so-serious fun." He nuzzled her ear, catching the shell in the light grasp of his teeth for barely a second and then pulling away. "Say yes."

Her breath was soft and warm against his neck.

"I'll think about it, Garrett," she whispered as a cab slowed to a stop behind them. "How about that?"

"Perfect."

For now. He had plenty of time to convince her.

Nichole glanced at her nightstand and let out a frustrated sigh. Three a.m. and still her mind wouldn't slow down enough to sleep. And it had nothing to do with the coffee she'd had after dinner. Her thoughts had been ping-ponging around her head for half the night. Working out justifications. Trades. Negotiations with herself to ensure this tightrope of emotional investment she was walking didn't trip her up and cause her to fall.

Garrett had said they were on the same page, in the same place. And maybe if Paul and Joel hadn't come up that evening she wouldn't have thought twice…but, oh, she *really* didn't want to fall. She didn't want to be the one who got swept away. The one who cared too much.

What she wanted was everything to continue on with Garrett the way it was. Her remaining just this side of *in too deep*. The place she already stood. *Without* Garrett taking her on some romantic weekend getaway.

To Napa.

They'd talked about wine a few weeks ago—Garrett's surprise years ago on discovering his appreciation and interest in it, her curiosity about what set one vineyard apart from another, her amazement at the idea of air infused with the scent of fresh picked grapes.

And now he wanted to take her to wine country for Crush.

It would be incredible. Romantic. Fun.

They could find a little bed-and-breakfast. Rent bicycles or take the wine train. They could roll around in bed all night. Laze around through the morning.

Make love…

Sure, it was more than a few hours out with a group of friends and then a night spent getting creative between the sheets. More than laughing on her couch as they talked the night away. More than some quick kiss before darting out the door at the break of dawn to hit an early meeting. It was intimacy on an extended basis. The kind of *romantic* with the potential to rock the status quo…

Garrett understood her fears. Knew what held her back. He'd whispered in her ear that she didn't need to worry about their relationship going too far. That even if she got carried away he'd keep his feet on the ground. That she could count on him.

Closing her eyes against the yawning void of night, she drew a deep long breath and pushed it out. Tried to let her body go lax and find a quiet spot in her mind. Only she couldn't stop thinking.

About the way they talked. Laughed. And played.

About how she felt when they were together.

She knew she could trust Garrett. But she was beginning to wonder if she could trust herself.

Garrett threw an arm over his eyes and let out a feral growl.

It wasn't like he and Nichole spent every night together. They only saw each other three or four nights a week. Okay, sometimes five. But it had become something of a standard when they did get together…they stayed together. And he liked it.

Last night he'd dropped her at home, though, without even an attempt at going in. He'd seen that flash of panic in her eyes at his Napa suggestion and recognized what she needed was a little time to get used to the idea. To let it sink in that they could make plans for a weekend in the future without the worry of it being about *building* a future together. She needed to trust in both of them so she could enjoy what they had to its fullest potential.

She'd come around, he knew. But he'd figured the space would help.

Only now he'd been awake all damn night.

At four forty-five it didn't even make sense to keep trying to sleep.

On a grunt, he jackknifed up from the bed, swinging his legs over the side as he scrubbed a palm over his jaw.

How the hell was he going to make it through the day? He had meetings scheduled back-to-back until six. He'd never make it. Not like this.

If it were just the sleep deprivation he'd be fine. Hell, with the load he'd been carrying these last years he was no stranger to pulling all-nighters. But the lack of sleep coupled with this other problem—this hunger and ache that seemed to have permeated every damn cell in his system…?

Yeah, *that* was going to get in the way.

He had to do something.

Twenty-five minutes later Garrett was standing outside Nichole's door, a tray of espressos in one hand and a bag of Danish in the other. Balanced on one foot, he kicked the door—quietly. Sort of.

If she didn't answer he'd take off. Throw back the jet fuel and chow down the pastry. Head back to his own apartment and get on with the day that would have been a thousand times better if it had involved Nichole from the start.

Nichole sat up in bed, her brow furrowed as she cocked her head, listening. Because someone had just knocked on her door. Reaching for her phone, she checked her messages. Not finding any, she headed down the hall, slipping on her robe as she went.

There was only one person on the planet who would show up unannounced at the ungodly hour of five in the morning. And at that minute Nichole couldn't have been happier for the intrusion.

Maeve was just the woman to talk some sense into her. Assure her this invitation for a weekend away wasn't anything to get her panties in a twist over.

She'd tell her to relax. Settle down. Skip the theatrics and just enjoy the ride, taking it as it came. She'd remind her that neither of them was interested in something serious. So *serious* wouldn't happen.

Only she'd say it in some typically crass Maeve way that would have Nichole nearly weeping with laughter.

Throwing the door open with relief, she'd got as far as, "I love yo—" when her eyes focused on the figure that was most definitely not Maeve standing on her stoop.

Amusement tinged with confusion filled those deep blue eyes as Garrett's head cocked to the side and he asked, "Expecting someone else?"

Hand flying to her mouth, she shook her head, coughed so hard she ended up gasping and then finally wheezed out an emphatic, "Yes!"

Garrett's mouth opened, then closed as he looked off toward the sky before finally returning to her with a totally mystified stare. "Since I dropped you here at eleven last night?"

At which point she realized what she'd said and once again gave in to a fit of sputtering while she shook her head. Only then she saw Garrett was just playing with her, because that glint of mischief said he wasn't concerned at all.

And then he was stepping into her home before she'd thought to invite him, moving into her space like he knew without asking how badly she wanted him to be there. He backed her down the hall toward the kitchen, crowding her as much with the predatory intent in his eyes as the solid mass of his body. Making her come alive in a way five a.m. had never seen before.

"I thought maybe it was—"

"Yeah," he cut in, his eyes working a slow descent from her shoulders to her breasts, waist, hips, legs and toes. "I know exactly who you thought it was. The only person on the planet with the nerve to show up unannounced before the crack of dawn. My sister."

Nichole peered up at him. Sexy was radiating off his form like the rising sun. Warming everything it touched.

Sounding breathless in a way she'd only experienced with Garrett, she teased, "It must run in the family, then?"

"I wouldn't have thought so until today, but here I am."

The small of her back made contact with the island countertop, preventing any further retreat. Garrett set the tray of breakfast down beside her, then slid it away, leaving room for his hands to rest on the counter at either side of her. Caging her in.

"What are you doing here?"

"What does it look like, sweetheart?" Leaning in ever closer, so his breath played around the whorl of her ear, he answered, "I'm here for breakfast."

Taking the stairs two at a time, Garrett left the repetitive sound of hammering, power saws and the shouts of his crew behind as he ducked out in search of some relative quiet. Eyeing the progress from across the street, he dialed back his sister and held the phone to his ear.

"Sorry about that, Bethany. I'm at the Worther site today. Noisy. Everything okay?" he asked, as he always did when one of his sisters called unexpectedly.

After she'd assured him she and the kids were fine, she asked about his plans for the evening, cluing him in to the reason behind her call—though if left to her own devices she probably wouldn't have managed to spit out her actual request for another five minutes at least.

Bethany, who hated to ask anyone for anything, needed a sitter.

"I've got plans to see Nichole tonight, but I'm sure she wouldn't mind a slight change."

Bethany heaved a sigh of relief, thanking him with all the sisterly devotion reserved for sacrificial bailouts, then adding a mandatory, "Are you sure? If it's any inconvenience I'll figure something else out."

Nice offer, but she needed help. And when it came to his sisters he couldn't say no.

Or at least not when he knew they really needed it. No to a new car, to a date with the bass player from a band, a degree in basket weaving appreciation? Another story altogether.

"Not a problem. So, what time do you want us there?"

A silent beat followed and Garrett checked the phone to ensure the call hadn't been disconnected.

"Beth?"

"Um…so you're *both* coming over tonight?" she asked, in a way so the question dragged out to a point where you couldn't miss that there was way more going on than the words actually spoken.

She had a problem. But Nichole had babysat with Maeve before. Maybe even once or twice without Maeve. The kids knew and liked her.

Then he realized it might not be Nichole his sister had a problem with at all.

Just him…*with* Nichole.

Damn it, this was that Panty Whisperer bull again.

He could only imagine the rumors his sisters had heard about him over the years. What they might be spurring her on to think. Surely nothing so wholesome as making out on the living room couch after the kids went to bed? No. It would probably be some totally depraved act in the kitchen, involving half the cooking utensils. Which wasn't to say there wasn't some appeal in that idea…in his own kitchen…with Nichole the only other person in the house. But Bethany couldn't seriously believe…

"You know nothing would ever happen between us while we were responsible for the boys."

"Oh, no! Garrett, that's not what I was thinking at all. I swear," she answered, so fast and so urgently he wondered exactly how much of the sting he'd revealed in his voice. "Honey, I know you would never be anything but one hundred percent responsible while taking care of your nephews."

Garrett blinked, his mouth curving at the realization

he'd just heard "the big sister voice." Something it had been the better part of two decades since he'd had the privilege of earning. *She* was reassuring *him*. Easing *his* insecurities. The novelty of it was enough to make him laugh.

"What's with that laugh?"

"Don't worry about it, Beth. Something funny from this end." True enough. He never liked to lie to his sisters. Made it a point not to do it. But the occasional dodge...that much he could live with. "So, if you're not worried about me making you an auntie again on your stairwell, what's with the drawn-out hesitation?"

She let out a laugh, again making him feel all kinds of little brother. After all these years it was a bizarre experience, to say the least.

"Well, I guess I'm a little surprised. I mean, I know you're dating, but for you to bring her for something like this...how serious are you?"

"We're not." The words fired out of his mouth, leaving a guilty aftertaste behind.

"Really? Did I just miss all the other women you've brought around to hang out with your family over the past decade or so?"

When she put it that way... Relatively speaking, this relationship with Nichole went far beyond the hookups he'd been making do with until now. But *serious* was the one word he'd had to swear to Nichole not to use. Still, the kinds of clarifications he'd have to make for his sister to understand weren't something he was up to sharing.

"Okay, yeah, I get what you're saying. But don't get too many ideas about Nichole. We're—"

"Friends with benefits?" she offered helpfully.

"No." *More than that.* "I mean, we're definitely

friends too." But it wasn't like they were just a couple of pals using each other to get off. Not even close. They were more than friends, enjoying each other in an honest, open, safe capacity... They both understood, even if they couldn't quite put a name to it. They were at a good place together. A place they could both handle. "Look, don't worry about it. We're not planning to elope. And, while I honestly care about her, the only reason I've been 'bringing her around' is because she already knows you guys. I mean, hell, with this babysitting thing tonight— she's actually watched your kids on her own before. We already had plans. It would be weird not to bring her."

"Sure—no, I totally get that."

Suddenly Garrett was looking at the phone again, sliding a finger into the collar of his shirt and tugging the already open neck for more breathing room. What was with that voice? That sing-songy sort of patronizing amusement?

It was freaking him out.

"I'm serious. Look, it was an accident we even hooked up. I didn't know who she was or it never would have happened. But then it was too late. And she *does* know you. And it doesn't mean anything more than it just makes sense, okay?"

He couldn't remember the last time he'd heard his sister laugh so hard. And the sound would have been music to his ears if it hadn't so very obviously, so totally, been at his expense. To hell with this.

"Enough. Look, Bethany, we'll be there tonight. Text me the details. I've got a building to put up."

Disconnecting the call, he tried to shrug off the uncomfortable sense that despite everything he'd said, his sister hadn't heard a word.

It shouldn't matter what she thought.

It didn't matter.

Not when, for the first time in as long as he could remember, his life was exactly what he wanted.

CHAPTER THIRTEEN

NICHOLE WASN'T SURE what to expect when she walked into Bethany Slovak's home except to say she hadn't expected what she found.

AC/DC blasting at top volume and Garrett mid-jump, guitar twisted to his right as he landed in front of the TV. His nephews were squealing with delight and too focused on their absolutely *insane* uncle to actually follow the TV prompts from whichever one of those video rock band games they were playing. Or at least Garrett was playing. Sort of.

Obviously he needed some work on hitting the right notes, but when it came to flaunting a rocker attitude and entertaining his two charges…the full belly laughs coming from Neil and Norman said it all. He was a star.

Beloved.

The song ended and Garrett swung around in a showy move that ended in a deep bow toward his fellow bandmates.

But by then the kids had caught sight of her and were running across the living room, one talking over the other as they whooped and jumped and went into a nearly impossible-to-follow account of what Garrett had been up to since he'd arrived. The rules he'd broken the last time he'd watched them…inadvertently, of course…and how their mommy had made sure to remind him.

Garrett walked over, an unholy glint in his eyes, his hair standing up in a spiky mess. "You ready to rock?"

Brows shooting skyward, she started to shake her head, but Garrett already had her hand and was pulling her over to the mic.

Nichole took one look at Garrett's tie, cinched around the stand, and laughed helplessly, "As ready as I'll ever be."

God, he was fun.

Too many songs later, her voice had taken on a two-pack-day rasp, suggesting Garrett's declaration it was time to wind down with a story had come at the perfect moment. Heading to the kitchen, she got a glass of water from the tap as Garrett settled in the center of the couch, one boy on either side, and read from *The Chronicles of Narnia*. His voice was low and clear. His audience—all three of them—were held utterly rapt.

It was…beautiful.

When the chapter was through Garrett closed the book, smiling indulgently as the boys pleaded for a few more pages. But Garrett was no lightweight when it came to kids and quickly the boys were helping to put the room to rights. Their uncle reminded them to be responsible for their toys, to respect their mother and not expect her to pick up their things, assuring them they were growing up to be men he was proud of. He shook their hands and they glowed under his praise as he pulled them each in for a hug and secured their promises they would do something silly the next day and not grow up too fast.

It made her heart ache and her throat burn in a way that had nothing to do with belting out eighties rock ballads at the top of her lungs and everything to do with

the man in front of her with his nose in those little boys'
hair and all that incredible, undeniable love filling the
space around them. And that was when the ground beneath her feet began to give. When the world around her
shook. And the status quo didn't just rock, but crumbled
beneath the wave of emotion crashing over it. Catching
her unprepared and dragging her back to sea with it.

Was this the riptide Joel had compared her to?

The current so stealthy and strong that once caught
within it, escape was nearly impossible?

It had to be, because within the span of one man voic-
ing his hopes for two others she'd gone from relative
safety to in way too deep. And despite all Garrett's good
intentions, she was afraid not even he could pull her back
from the depths to which she'd drifted. *She loved him.*

When teeth were brushed, one more drink taken and
the last trips to the bathroom made, Garrett tucked the
boys in while Nichole waited downstairs on the couch.

She was holding it together—because this wasn't the
time or place for a discussion about the state of their relationship or what this latest emotional revelation meant
for it. They would see the night through, talk and joke,
and she would soak up every last minute of this easy
time together before it came to an end and the tough decisions had to be made.

Garrett walked into the living room and sank into the
cushions beside her, letting out a thoroughly whipped
breath as he did.

"I think they're down for the count."

It looked like he might be too.

"You're a very sweet uncle," she offered, wanting
him to know how she saw him. "Those boys are lucky
to have you."

He gave her a lopsided grin that faded as he met her

eyes. "I'm lucky to have them. I didn't always appreciate it."

"But you do now?"

He nodded. "When I first heard Bethany was pregnant and then that she was expecting twins, I was... overwhelmed by their existence. The idea of them alone scared the hell out of me."

"Oh, Garrett."

His head rocked back against the cushions and he closed his eyes. "I look at them now and I'm ashamed to think back to that time. I just... Hell, Nichole. There was already so much. It's no excuse. But I felt like I was drowning. All the time. For years. Forever fighting to get my head back above water, hoping for one more gasp of breath to get me through whatever crisis or crossroads or challenge we were facing. Each night thinking just a couple more years until Maeve's out of school, or Erin's finished with her nursing degree, or Carla's married. I was counting down my list of responsibilities and suddenly there were two more getting added on. They weren't even brand-new yet. Barely more than potential. And all I could think was I wasn't ready to start the clock again with another twenty-two years on it."

Nichole leaned into him, resting her head on his chest, silently telling him she understood. Didn't judge him.

Garrett stroked a hand over her hair, playing with a curl at the end before circling back to stroke again. "It doesn't feel that way anymore. The day the boys were born I went to the hospital to check on Bethany. See the little people she'd created. And all it took was one look. Love at first sight. They were miracles. Those ugly, crinkled-up faces were about the most beautiful things I'd ever seen."

Even with her heart breaking, she couldn't help but smile at the awe behind Garrett's words.

"It was crazy. I mean there they were, completely helpless. Their mother gorked out on whatever pain-killers they'd given her following the C-section and all I could think was they would be fine. Ned was so proud. Such a *dad*. He looked like he could have taken down a hundred of me if I'd gotten in the way of the little family they'd built."

"You didn't feel responsible for them?"

At that Garrett let out a short laugh. "I felt responsible, all right. I mean what if something happened to Ned? To Bethany? Trust me, the *what ifs* are infinite. But I didn't mind. I loved them. Which meant all those things I was going to have to do to feel like they were protected the way I needed them to be…were things I *wanted* to do. Couldn't wait to do."

The steady beat of Garrett's heart sounded beneath her ear. Constant, like the man who housed it.

Once he gave his word, his protection, his love…it was forever. No wonder he guarded each so fiercely.

Nichole blinked, her body going still as a sudden thought whirled through her mind. He hadn't thought he was ready to love those boys…but he did. Without reservation.

What if she hadn't been the only one caught by surprise? What if now that Garrett had had a taste of what their being together was like he could embrace it and make room for one more in his heart? His future?

It was possible.

Yes, they'd agreed not to get serious, and she'd certainly tried to adhere to the plan…but the chemistry, the way they connected.…

He'd promised he wouldn't let her get too deep, but

she was miles from shore. Maybe it was because he'd been caught in the same current and they were truly in this together.

Swallowing past that surge of hope, she tried to stay calm. To rein herself in enough so she wouldn't betray everything she was thinking.

"I know you're still just getting used to your freedom, now that you've finished school and your sisters are all on their own, but when you look ahead do you think you'll ever want a family for yourself?"

Garrett let out a long sigh, then shifted lower on the couch, pulling her with him as he did.

"I don't know, Nichole. A part of me feels like I've already raised four daughters. I've stayed up nights worrying about them. I've been their hero, the bane of their existence and everything in between. I've sweated with them over test scores and been as proud as a guy could be when I got to see each one of them graduate from college. And putting them first was something I was happy to do. But now that they're older... Honestly, the idea of doing it again...*choosing* to make that commitment... *asking* for another responsibility. After all the years of living with the fear that I was going to drop the ball— and it would mean the difference between a future the girls could look forward to and no future at all—I just don't think I want to go through that again."

So much responsibility for one man. "I can't even imagine what it must have been like. You were basically thrust into the role of single parent for four teen and pre-teen girls while you were still a kid yourself. But you did it, Garrett. You kept your family together and every one of you is a success in your own right."

Garrett leaned close to her ear, teasing. "A sign I

should stop while I'm ahead, not get greedy and press my luck, huh?"

He was joking, but Nichole couldn't smile. A desperation was coming alive within her that wouldn't allow her to let the subject drop until there was no question left. No uncertainty surrounding what was *possible*.

"But what if you met someone you didn't want to live without? Someone who could be a partner to you? So you weren't in it alone?"

Her breath held as Garrett seemed to ponder. Finally, he simply answered, "No, Nichole. It's just not what I want."

CHAPTER FOURTEEN

NICHOLE SAT AT the edge of her loveseat, shoes on, ready to walk out the door. As ready as she'd been for the past hour. As ready as she could be when everything inside her was begging and pleading that she reconsider. To give it just a little more time. To pull back, draw a new emotional line in the sand and give herself another week of pretending she could keep her heart in check before giving up to inevitability…there was no coming back from the place she'd gone.

And in that place she was alone. Because Garrett had kept things casual from his end. Staying true to their agreement in that regard at least.

Now she needed to get out before she got hurt any worse than she already was.

Forcing her fingers to open, she pushed slowly to a stand. Put one foot in front of the other until she found herself locking her door. Then stepping into a cab. And finally arriving at the restaurant.

Before she'd even paid the driver Garrett was there on the sidewalk, waiting for her with that big body, easy smile and ready arm.

So considerate.

Attentive.

Lovable.

Stepping into the warmth of him, she felt the first crack in her defenses. And when he pulled her into the hold of his body she almost crumbled.

She drew a deep breath, looking for strength, but found instead the clean scent of Garrett.

She should have broken away. Only knowing this was most likely the last time she'd feel his arms around her, smell the spice of his skin, take the heat of his body within her, she couldn't do it. For one minute she burrowed closer. Drew deeply through her nose and only exhaled with the greatest reluctance.

"Hey, you okay?" came the muffled sound of Garrett's voice as it whispered through the curls atop her head.

He had no idea of the havoc he wreaked within her.

Her palms flattened against his abdomen, absorbing the feel of the ridged muscles beneath even as she turned her face into the center of his chest, whispered a kiss against the spot that protected the part which wouldn't ever be hers and stepped back.

"I'm fine," she said, pushing a smile to her lips. "You want to go inside and we can get a drink?"

Arm still snug around her, because even though he didn't love her he loved the intimacy of contact, he said, "They're holding a table for us—"

"I'd rather just get a drink if you don't mind." She sounded tense even to her own ears, and Garrett picked up on it immediately.

His eyes narrowed, the skin across his cheekbones going taut, but he led her inside regardless.

Moments later they were seated at the end of the bar. A vodka tonic sweating condensation down her glass. She shouldn't have ordered it. Wouldn't have more than a sip or two. But she needed something to occupy her hands while she did what she needed to be done.

* * *

Garrett should have known something was going on. Nichole hadn't spent the night with him after they'd left Bethany's, offering an excuse about early meetings and being exhausted. He'd seen the tension in her face, felt it beneath his hands as he held her close. But he'd accepted it as fatigue, followed her home and kissed her goodnight at her door.

Only now the work day was done but the tension remained, and Nichole wanted a drink rather than dinner. It didn't take a genius or even someone with a shot glass full of relationship experience to recognize that whatever was up was about them.

Damn it.

"Talk to me, Nichole."

On her barstool beside him she closed her eyes and drew a deep breath. And then she was angling toward him, an expression on her face he'd never seen before. One so completely different than anything she'd shown him in the past, if he hadn't been sitting right beside her he might not even have recognized who this woman with the fixed semi-smile and shuttered eyes actually was.

"What we've had together these last few weeks has been incredible. Something I could never have anticipated or recognized was missing from my life. But, Garrett, neither of us were thinking it was going to be forever. And I guess what I'm saying is I think maybe it's time we end things now."

He nodded—but to himself, in a general confirmation of *yes, it's about you, Garrett*—and for a second those emotionless eyes staring boldly at him registered relief. But her relief was to be short-lived, because he wasn't about to agree.

"What's this about, Nichole? Of course I get this isn't forever. But why end it now?"

The rising din of the busy restaurant and bar gave Nichole a short reprieve in which she cleared her throat and searched every corner of the establishment like she was going to find an answer tucked behind a spare chair or potted plant. But Garrett wasn't going anywhere, and when the next lull came and her eyes drifted back to his he was still there, waiting. Holding his mounting frustration in check with the mental assurance this wasn't any big deal. Because there was no reason why something so good as what they had should end.

And he wasn't about to let it.

"Did something happen I don't know about?" Something with his sister? With Nichole's work…? Maybe they'd had a misunderstanding he hadn't even noticed. He was a guy. Apparently that sort of thing happened with them.

"No. It's not any particular thing. No incident. It's… gone on long enough, I think, if we plan to end things on a good note. You know?"

Garrett rubbed a hand over the back of his neck, wondering if more practice in the dating arena would have better prepared him for a conversation like this one. Because as it stood it didn't make sense. "Nichole, so what you're saying is there really isn't any problem. You aren't mad at me for forgetting a somehow significant anniversary or because I didn't call when I said I would. The attraction and connection are still there. This is just about ending 'on a good note'?"

The stiff set of her shoulders said it wasn't.

"It's about this getting more serious than it was supposed to," she said, her tone level and too cool for what was coming out of her mouth. "I care about you, Garrett. Maybe too much. Enough that what we have doesn't feel casual and safe to me anymore. It feels…like more than we agreed on."

She seemed relieved to have the words out, but his heart was starting to pound, the rush of blood was coming loud past his ears. This wasn't what he wanted. What either of them wanted.

She was scared. And with her past, with those guys leading her on and then letting her go, he couldn't blame her. But he wasn't going to do that. He wouldn't give her false expectations or promises he couldn't keep. All they needed to do was… Hell, they needed to get out of here.

With a nod at her glass, he asked, "Are you going to drink that?"

"No."

Garrett pulled a couple bills from his wallet and flagged the bartender before tucking them under his glass. Then, turning to Nichole, he held out his hand. "Come on."

Outside the restaurant he looked up and down the street, trying to get his bearings in a neighborhood he knew like the back of his hand but was too damned frustrated about what was happening with Nichole—scratch that—what *wasn't* going to happen with Nichole—to be able to bring into focus.

"Thank you for understanding, Garrett. Especially because of Maeve, it's important to me that we not let things get tense between us."

Understanding? Not really. And as for tense…seriously?

This was what he'd heard the guys grousing about over the years. This was the kind of *unreasonable* behind those baffled looks he'd never truly understood.

But now he wanted to call up his friends from ten years ago and tell them he felt for them.

Because this sucked.

"Okay, so I'm going to catch this cab…"

A red awning halfway down the block caught his eye and he remembered parking in front of it. Great.

He took her hand.

"Garrett, wait. What are you doing?"

Looking back over his shoulder at Nichole, who he was basically towing behind him, he answered, "I'm taking you home. I get why you wanted to have this conversation in a crowded bar, but I think the least you can do is give me the courtesy of a private conversation. Fair?"

She blanched at the harshness of his tone, but he wanted her to care and he wanted her to know, without question, he did too.

"Fair." The single word came grudgingly, but he'd take it.

"Look, let's save it until we get back to your place. I don't want to do this on the street or while I'm driving."

At his car, Garrett helped Nichole in and then closed the door behind her. Rubbing the back of his neck, he figured he had ten minutes before he got her back to her place. Ten minutes to figure out how the hell he was going to fix what had inexplicably gone wrong.

Twelve and a half minutes later Nichole was ahead of him at her door and Garrett had a plan. He watched as she slid the key into the lock, turned the knob and swung open the door. Waited until she'd stepped inside and turned to him, probably with some sort of invitation he wasn't interested in hearing or willing to limit himself to poised on her tongue.

Moving into her instead of around her, Garrett slid

one hand to her waist and the other into her hair, catching her lips open. Her quiet gasp of surprise was arrested and her body without defense—he kissed her. Angling his mouth over hers and sinking into the kind of contact that had never been in question between them.

Reminding her of just one of the reasons she didn't want to end what they had. The one that, for her, had brought them together in the first place.

And she remembered, because her body was suddenly melting against his, her head falling back to grant him more access to her kiss, her hands caught in his shirt and then moving up to his face.

He wanted to press her hand more firmly to his cheek. Hold her there and just—just *be*. But he couldn't stop. Not yet. He needed her breathless. Desperate. Aching for what she could only get from him.

And then, as he gave it to her, he'd tell her she didn't need to worry. Maybe a little *serious* wasn't so bad. What they had—this kind of connection and fun and feel-good—was something they should hold on to until the very last.

Until Nichole was at a point where she was ready to move on with the white picket fence life she should have been living for years already. Or until it stopped feeling good and being everything that made him wonder how the hell she could be trying to walk away.

Hot tears pushed at her eyes as her throat tightened around all the things she didn't want to say. Everything Garrett didn't want to see…refused to understand.

"Please," she begged, her fingers already curled into his hair.

"I don't want to stop, Nichole. And I can hear it in

your voice, in your breath…you don't want me to stop either."

It was true. She didn't. She wanted him to take her body. Make it his own. She wanted him to break down her defenses with his hands, his mouth and most of all his heart. She wanted him to want more than an affair.

Because *he'd* made her want more.

Only Garrett wasn't interested in the kind of *more* that would put this relationship back into a balance she could live with. Which meant as much as she might *want* the feel of his mouth on her neck, his hands pulling at her clothes, tightening over her hips…she couldn't have it.

So she uncurled her fingers from those silky strands of his hair, worked them between them and pushed.

"No."

It was a word she knew he would respect. Would never press. And, to her relief and heartbreak, in an instant he'd stepped back so the only contact that remained was where his fingers lightly grasped her own.

"Nichole. Don't do this." Dark eyes met with hers, frustrated and intense. "What we have is good. It doesn't have to end."

She shook her head, staring at him as the first tears slipped past her lids. "How can you look at me and even say that?"

"Because it's true! Okay—I get it. You feel like things have gone further than we planned and it scares you. So—fine, we slow down a little and—"

"It didn't work, Garrett. I tried to slow down but it's not enough. You're right about it being good. It's so good between us that it's started making me want more than I have."

His eyes held hers—but she could see the shift in them. "What kind of more?"

It was a different kind of tension from simply not wanting to lose her. Telling.

"More than the promise we *won't* have a future. That you'll *never* look at me and think, *I want her. I want it all.*"

Garrett stared down at her, his expression turning hard. "We talked about this. From the start. You *understood.*"

"I know that!" she answered hotly. "Like we talked about *you* keeping *me* from getting in too deep. But even with our eyes open—" She shook her head. "It's time we take a step back."

The muscle in his jaw flexed and for a moment she thought he would continue to disagree. Maybe it was that she hoped he would.

But there was no revelation on the horizon. No argument or silent assault. Just Garrett's slow nod. "Okay, Nichole. I get it. And…I'm sorry."

Yes. Sorry. So was she.

Dropping a kiss at her cheek, he murmured. "Take care, sweetheart."

CHAPTER FIFTEEN

A WEEK WOULD have been too soon, so Garrett gave it ten days before venturing out with Jesse for a night of laughs at The Second City. Sam had organized the group, and Nichole loved improv, so Garrett figured it was a safe bet she'd be there. He wasn't disappointed. Walking through the doors, he caught sight of her tumble of red-brown curls across the room and let out a breath he hadn't realized he was holding.

The days had been crawling by since he'd walked out of Nichole's apartment. The nights even more so. And, while he understood the romantic element of their relationship was going to have to be over, he was ready to resume their friendship. Because, *damn,* he missed her. Missed the talking and laughing and the having someone who got what he was saying. People went from friends to lovers and back all the time. Without the sex clouding it up they would too.

Waving a greeting across the room, he shrugged out of his coat and started across the floor. Jesse hit him with a nod, and a few others turned around with smiles. But it wasn't until Maeve mouthed his name that the one he'd been waiting for turned, revealing those big brown eyes of hers filled with anxious trepidation.

She didn't need to worry.

It wasn't going to be awkward or tense. He wouldn't let it be.

When he met the group he exchanged a few back-slaps, knuckle-bumps and shoulder-claps before pulling Nichole in for a one-armed hug that lasted just long enough to emphasize genuine caring without pushing past platonic.

Because he was totally on board with them being friends. No matter how good that all too brief instant when her body had pressed soft and sweet into his had felt.

"How've you been, Nichole?" he asked, dropping his arm and taking a step back.

Not weird at all.

She swallowed, her eyes shifting restlessly around the space before meeting up with his. "Good, thanks. I wasn't expecting to see you."

Okay. A little weird.

"Last-minute thing. I've been caught up at the office, hammering out a new contract. Good to be busy, but I'm definitely ready for a break. A few laughs, you know."

"Sure, of course."

It wasn't going the way he'd seen it. Nichole was wound tight and suddenly he felt like a heel having come. With a nod toward the bar he rested a hand at her elbow, leading her a few feet off from the group.

"It's okay that I'm here."

The words hadn't even passed his lips before he realized his phrasing alone had made what should have been a question more of a statement. He didn't want her to say no—apparently enough that he didn't actually give her the option to.

Nichole's eyes went wide. "Oh, no, Garrett. I mean, yes. Of course it's okay for you to be here. I didn't mean—" She broke off, glancing briefly away before turning back to him with an apology in her eyes. "You caught me off guard, is all."

"I should have called to let you know I was coming."

She glanced from Maeve back to him. "We're adults. It's not a big deal."

This time her smile was more genuine and Garrett felt himself relaxing into the idea of this new phase in their relationship. "Great. How about I go grab us a drink?"

"What do you mean, you aren't coming?" Maeve demanded through the line, her voice low as though she were trying not to be overheard.

Which was why Nichole had texted her in the first place with the news that she wasn't going to make it to Bethany's barbecue. She'd been hoping to avoid a discussion altogether, but then thirty-seven seconds after hitting "send" her phone had started its little jitterbug, announcing Maeve's call.

"My car didn't start this morning so I have to take it in."

"You're a liar."

"No." Yes. A total liar. But to Maeve, today, she wasn't about to own up to it. "I'm thinking maybe it's the alternator, or maybe—"

"Or maybe you're bailing because of Garrett. Again."

"Nope."

"You told me it wasn't going to be weird, Nichole. That what happened with you guys wasn't going to get in the way of the rest of our lives."

Guilt twisted through her belly. "It's not. I just…."

What could she even say? She'd believed it at the time. She simply hadn't known.

Nichole stared out the window at the sunshine streaming down for the first time in days. It was perfect weather for a barbecue, and she'd have loved to see everyone there. Everyone except Garrett.

Only that wasn't true. She wanted to see him…no matter how it hurt.

It had been nearly a month since they'd broken up, and she'd seen him five times. That first night had been a shock, to be certain. But after she'd been prepared for the possibility of his showing up. Ready for it. What she *hadn't* been prepared for was how difficult being friends was when her heart wanted so much more.

Garrett only had to enter the room and her body temperature rose, everything within her tuning in to his frequency, subconsciously seeking out any hint that maybe she'd been wrong and he'd changed his mind about the idea of a future.

But nothing had changed. Because, God, she was never enough. Not for Paul. Not for Joel. Not even for her own father. Why would it be any different with this man who had warned her from the first what his limitations were?

Garrett was as comfortable as ever. Casually at ease. Attentive—albeit in a platonic sense. He'd make his way over to where she was, check in, exchange a few words before moving on to catch up with everyone else. And if that was where it had ended she might have been fine. But throughout the evening somehow he always gravitated back to her. Leaning in to share some private joke or quiet insight. Sitting closer than her heart could stand because it wasn't quite close enough. Touching her elbow or the small of her back as he passed, oblivious to the destruction those unconscious intimacies caused her.

"Look, Maeve, I'm going to have to miss today. I

don't have a car, so please give Bethany and everyone
my best."

"You sure you want to stick with that story?"

"Positive."

"Fine. Garrett'll be there in ten minutes to pick you
up."

Garrett turned the key, listening to her car start smoothly
for the fifth time in a row. He'd already been under the
hood. Had her start it while he listened and looked. And
he was getting ready to call his mechanic to come pick
the damn thing up and see if he could figure out what
was wrong.

A prime example of why it never paid to lie.

"It was probably just a fluke. Really, I'm sure the car
will be fine."

Garrett looked out the open door at her. "You're sure?"

Her eyes skating away inevitably shouted all kinds of
guilty, but she couldn't look at him as she flat-out lied
for about the sixtieth time that day.

The door shut behind her and she figured Garrett
would suggest they get a move on if they were heading
out to Bethany's. She'd have to ride with him now. Her
car was "unreliable." And he was here.

They'd be alone together in an intimate, enclosed
space for a minimum of twenty minutes.

Involuntarily her mind wandered to the time they'd
spent in cars before. When he'd pulled over with a gruff
curse after her flirtations had pushed him to the breaking point. The fogged glass. The occasional law enforce-
ment officer's intervention.

With a firm shake of her head she reminded herself
it wasn't going to be that way again.

"There's nothing wrong with your car, is there?"

Time to cut her losses. She shook her head.

He stuffed his hands into his jeans pockets, staring up at the cloudless sky. "Any chance this was some elaborate ruse to get me alone?"

She stared, and after a beat he glanced back at her and then tapped his cheek. "Red."

"I wanted to avoid you."

"You may need to reconsider your approach. I've got this borderline personality disorder when it comes to damsels in distress."

Taking her hand, he rubbed her knuckle with the rough pad of his thumb. "How about you tell me what's going on? I think we're friends enough we can handle the truth between us."

Nichole let her gaze roam his face. Followed the tilt of his smile and the glint in his eyes. All of his features were working in concert to pull her in.

Even now, everything about him made her want to get closer. Made her want more than she could have.

"No," she said, slowly withdrawing her hand from his grasp, refusing to look away as his eyes hardened and the charm went flat. "That's just it, Garrett. I can't be your friend. I know you thought if we took a step back, took a few days off, it would be enough. But your friendship, your smile, your do-gooding over-protective drive are all the things that make me want more than I can have. The conversation and the laughter. The two a.m. debates. The way everything you do and everything you say makes me feel so good I can't defend myself against it."

"So you thought you'd skip Bethany's picnic today, and then what? Only go out when you know I won't be there? Is that how it's going to be? We avoid each other completely?"

The idea of not seeing Garrett anymore hurt her heart,

but a part of her wished it could be so simple. Only those complications, the strings, all the obvious reasons they should have avoided this thing from the start were still there. "I don't think that's realistic or fair."

Garrett rocked back on his heels, his eyes flashing anger and shock as he demanded, "But it's what you want?"

Not even close. But what she wanted wasn't on offer.

"Garrett, there's so much overlap in our social circles our paths continuing to cross is inevitable. I wouldn't ask you to stay away any more than I would want to myself—"

"So what, then?" He raked a hand through his hair, the color in his own cheeks high from the rising temper he'd never shown her before. "What do you want?"

The temper that was spurring her own.

"I want you to stop being so nice to me," she shot back, wondering how this man could refuse to see what was so completely and obviously right in front of his face. "Stop trying to whisper me into a friendship that only makes me ache for something more. Stop killing me with all your kindness. Because this show of caring—I can't take it."

Garrett's eyes were blazing, his voice going low. "I'm not trying to *whisper* you into anything."

She shouldn't have said it. Knew how it got under his skin.

But maybe that was why she'd done it. Maybe the only way to get him to stop playing nice was if she stopped first.

And so, knowing how unfair she was being, she went on, "You haven't been trying to give me much space either."

"How the hell can you say that? The first thing I want

to do when I see you is kiss you. Back you around some corner so I can show you how much I've missed having my hands on you. But I barely even touch you."

She shook her head, firing back, "You don't *get* it! The problem isn't the sex. That part I can handle fine. That part I could handle every night and never get tired of it and not worry about building unrealistic fantasies about any future we could build on how physically compatible we are together. You want to back me against a wall and push my skirt up to my waist? Fine—do it. Just make sure you walk away when you're done. It would be a thousand times easier for me than you being so damned perfect all the time!"

Instant heat flooded his gaze, but along with it came frustration. Resentment.

"What the hell is wrong with you, Nichole? You want me to *use you* and walk away?"

Her breath was coming fast, her skin hot. "Maybe I do."

Garrett's gaze darkened. "I won't."

"Why? Afraid I won't *like* you anymore? That's the point, Garrett. Even if I can't stop *wanting* you, I don't *want* to like you anymore."

His gaze darkened as he leaned closer. Close enough so she could feel the heat pulsing off his body as well. "I don't want to be some jerk who treats you like garbage."

"And I don't want to pine away for some prince who can't stop treating me like gold but doesn't think I'm worth enough to—"

"Damn it. That's not it." Garrett's hands were hot on her shoulders, his face right up in hers as he gave her a firm but gentle shake. "You know that's not how it is!"

Nichole shook him off. "Close enough, Garrett."

CHAPTER SIXTEEN

ACROSS THE GALLERY, Nichole set her empty glass on a passing tray and smoothly picked up another.

She wasn't drunk.

But there was a kind of liquid grace to her movements she hadn't possessed when she'd first arrived, met his eyes for a beat and then turned away—presumably to congratulate Jesse on his latest opening. But he couldn't say for sure as he'd stayed rooted in place at the far side of the gallery.

He hadn't actually exchanged more than a cursory greeting and goodnight with Nichole since that afternoon two weeks before, when she'd basically told him the only thing he could do for her was be a bastard.

He'd been so damned mad he walked away without a word. Skipped out on his family plans and gone home to stare at the wall and swear at the empty space around him for the next three hours. That Nichole would even dare to—

Hell, he wasn't going there again.

"Excuse me...Garrett Carter?"

Garrett shifted his focus to the woman standing in front of him, a direct smile on her lips, invitation in her eyes. He tried to place her face but nothing came to him.

"Yes?"

"I thought I recognized you." She offered her hand. "I'm Fawn Lesley. Walter Lesley's daughter. You probably don't remember me, but we met briefly about five years ago, when—"

"Of course—Fawn." Her father had been putting up some luxury condos and Garrett had bid on the contract before Walter Lesley ended up backing out because of cash flow problems. The daughter must have been at one of the information meetings. "How's your father doing?"

Fawn replied that he was well, then transitioned into some light chit-chat, her hand reaching out to touch his arm in a way that was supposed to suggest an unconscious intimacy but in Garrett's experience had always been fairly rife with intent.

She was an attractive woman, by all means. Nicely built, with a sensual assortment of features. But he wasn't interested. Could barely keep his eyes on her, in fact, because they kept drifting across the room to—to where some guy was pulling Nichole into an embrace that had every muscle in Garrett's body going taut.

Not a hug. No. Not the way those arms closed around her body, almost pulling her up and in. And the extra second or six they lingered, like whoever this guy was didn't want to let her go.

Who was he?

Garrett scanned the gallery for someone to grill, but Maeve wasn't there, he didn't see Sam, and Jesse was talking to a reporter from the *Trib*. He reached for his phone, thinking Maeve did this sort of thing all the time.

He stopped to think, *Maeve did this sort of thing all the time.*

"So, Garrett—I have a confession."

He look back at Fay—no, Fawn—feeling like an ass

for forgetting she was there. Nice guy. "I'm sorry? What was that?"

Lowering her impossibly thick black lashes—truly impossibly thick, because he couldn't begin to imagine what she'd put on them to make them look that way— she went on, "I had a mad crush on you that first time we met. And I know I was too young, but now...."

She let the words trail off, and Garrett pulled his mental faculties together enough to focus on what he was going to say. What he always said. Only across the room Nichole was still blinking up at the yet to be identified hugger, one hand hovering around her throat as though he'd completely caught her off guard and she was still recovering.

Damn it. Walter Lesley's girl—right. Smiling down at her, he shook his head. "I'm flattered, Fawn, but I'm... involved with someone right now."

He'd been about to give her his pat speech about not mixing business with pleasure, ready to use his association with her father as an excuse, when he realized he had a truth at his disposal that was much more straightforward.

Nichole might have ended their relationship, but the fact that he was essentially flipping out about the guy across the room said Garrett was still very much involved. He might have stepped back, but he hadn't let go.

"Give your father my best."

And then Garrett's focus returned to where it had been. To Nichole, with her head tipped back, exposing the delicate line of her neck as she laughed at something the guy said and gestured animatedly in the air between them, pulling him in to some private joke they both seemed to understand.

Another laugh. Open. Genuine.

The riveted focus of Nichole's eyes was on this man's face like she simply couldn't look away.

And Garrett's gut took it like a blow.

Tension laced up his spine, tightening the muscles at the base of his skull, around his jaw and through his temples.

He couldn't watch this—and yet he couldn't look away.

Only he had to. Because if he sat there much longer... if he had to see the inevitable moment when this guy tested the waters with some innocuous touch...

Hell, already he wanted to take the guy's arm off and he hadn't even moved on her yet. But it was coming. Garrett recognized the signs. And God help him if Nichole moved into that touch instead of skirting away. He wouldn't be able to stand it.

And then it happened. The world around him closed in.

The blood tore past his eardrums like a freight train.

Immobilized by that single graze of some chump's fingertips at the bare skin of her elbow, Garrett couldn't do anything but wait. Watch. Stare. Until he saw how Nichole would answer the unspoken question with the language of her body. Would she move in to the touch, inviting more? Hesitate and contemplate, making herself all the more enticing a challenge and target? Or would she step back out of reach, putting up those invisible barriers that had kept her out of most men's reach for the better part of three years?

Her gaze lowered to her arm where the man had touched her. No subtlety about it. Just blatant awareness. And, God damn it, uncertainty. Didn't she know that indecision was like a red flag? A challenge. A reward not every Tom, Dick and Harry got to have.

The fingers at her elbow moved to catch her chin. Lightly, tipping her face.

The knot through Garrett's gut twisted tight. He knew what this guy was going to see in her big brown eyes. Vulnerability. Questions. Warmth and desire.

Everything Garrett saw the minute he closed his own. And now this guy—

Wasn't going to see any of it. At least not directed at *him*.

Oh, it was there in her eyes, all right. Only now her gaze had slid away from the man in front of her, was moving across the room in a slow, steady path, suggesting she knew exactly where her target lay—and had landed on *him*.

Asking if he could really let her go. Asking if he cared.

Whatever relief Garrett had felt was short-lived as frustration and hostility began to crawl up his throat.

Game-play. And he hadn't even realized she was doing it. Hadn't realized she was even capable of it.

She'd let her guard down enough to lure this sorry bastard in just to test his reaction.

See what he would do.

That was a mistake, Nichole.

She must have read his eyes, because her chin pulled back and her eyes went fractionally wider. More wary.

She'd made her point in reminding him he couldn't sleep tight secure in the knowledge that while he wasn't touching her no one else would either.

Only her little plan wouldn't work out the way she'd expected.

Across the room those deep blue eyes began to blaze and Nichole felt her skin flush at the sight of them.

The finger at her chin drifted away, along with whatever questions Nichole had about whether it was possible for her to be attracted to another man. Even a man who'd once been her whole world. Of course looking back, it hardly seemed fair to have burdened Paul that way when he'd been so young at the time. He'd barely been a man at all.

Hence the broken engagement.

Just like Garrett, Paul had needed a chance to live. Be free. But while she couldn't begrudge him the decision now, it would have been nice if he'd recognized it before putting a ring on her finger.

"Who's that?"

Forcing her attention back to the man who, if things had been different, might have become her husband, she answered without pretense, "Garrett Carter."

"Carter who just put up that skyscraper down off Wabash?" At her nod, he asked, "You two have something going on?"

She smiled up at him and, recognizing Paul for the old friend Garrett had wanted to be himself, didn't bother to hide the heartbreak in her eyes. "We did."

Another sidelong glance and Paul's jaw set in obvious disappointment.

"And it's not quite over," he observed. Leaning in, he chucked his knuckles in a light graze beneath her chin. "I know you're tough, Nichole, but if you need a shoulder or an ear…I'd like to be there for you."

As she watched that piece of her past walk away a low heat built at her back and her body took on a subtle charge unique to Garrett.

"Are you done?"

"It wasn't about you." The words were out before they'd even been processed in her mind, and as soon as they passed her lips she realized how untrue they were.

She'd known he was there. Known he'd been watching her. She'd felt it as the hours passed. And though running into Paul had a been a complete surprise, and her curiosity about her reaction to him genuine, just knowing Garrett's eyes were on her throughout had made it about him as much as anything else.

Before she could admit it, Garrett's temper crackled at her ear. "Bull."

She could feel the tension vibrating between them, the hostility and accusation.

"Are you leaving with me," he growled, "or am I going to follow you home?"

She spun around to stare at him. "I don't need you to follow me home, Garrett."

With only inches between them to start, he leaned closer. "You're sure as hell acting like you need something."

Her breath caught, and then very deliberately she took a step back, and another. Turning, she muttered, "Tell Jesse goodnight for me. I'll call him tomorrow."

Returning home, Nichole didn't bother to close the door behind her after letting it swing wide enough to bounce against the far wall when she pushed through. Breath ripping in and out of her lungs, she replayed the events of the night, coloring each scene as it unfolded with what she *should* have said. What she'd wanted to scream.

He had no right!

Slapping her keys atop the bookshelf, she pinched her lips between her teeth.

You're sure as hell acting like you need something.

To hell with him.

The door closed with a hard thud behind her. The lock sounded next, putting every nerve in her body on alert. Tightening her skin, her belly.

She turned, glaring at Garrett from across the distance of her hall.

"What did you think would happen?" he asked, walking toward her as he jerked the tie at his throat until it came free.

"I wasn't—" But her denial fell short when his hands moved to his collar, opening the top button and then the next.

"You were," he answered, his voice too low and controlled to do anything but underscore the hostility surging within him. Hostility and purpose.

Another button and her heart skipped a beat, her feet starting to move in an effort to restore the space between them.

Garrett didn't hesitate to step into her space. To crowd her back into the seldom-used dining room, continuing to close in even when she had no place left to go. The thick lip of the table pressed into her flesh as her hands braced behind her.

She didn't know how far he intended to take this. What he planned to do. All she could say for certain was she couldn't look away. Couldn't say the single word it would take to make him leave. Couldn't give up this interaction that fell on the wrong side of restraint, control and good sense.

Because she was desperate for it. Starved for what she knew she shouldn't have.

"Did you think seeing another man touch you, put his

hands on your body…" his palms shaped her hips and the contact was like a charge detonating deep in her belly, pushing down the line of her leg to fist the fabric and then draw it up "…would make me insane?"

The hem of her skirt rose with his hands, exposing inch after inch of her bare thighs and the pale silk of her panties to the cool air in her apartment.

"Did you think it would drive me to my knees, Nichole?" he asked, dropping to one knee and then the other without ever freeing her from the harsh burn of his stare. Making her wonder if she could ever actually be free of him at all.

It seemed impossible when, in this moment, so totally devoid of the tenderness and joy that had been a part of their every interaction, she still felt as though he owned her.

Releasing the fabric bunched at her waist, he smoothed his fingers beneath the black jersey skirt, catching her panties as he pulled them down.

"What's this about, Garrett?" Her words sounded weak and shaky. Desperate.

Exactly the way she felt.

"It's about you getting what you want," he challenged. "Isn't it?"

Before she could answer, tell him she didn't even know what she wanted, he'd brought his mouth to her, shooting sensation through that critical point of contact. The firm stroke of his tongue was shaking loose whatever fragile grasp she'd maintained on reason, lacing desire through her center, pulling the strings of her need taut and making her ache blindly for more.

Fingers curled over the edge of the table rather than through the silky waves of his dark hair, she greedily took everything Garrett gave her. It didn't matter that this need was fueled in equal parts by anger and desire, each building off the other. Or that there was no love in Garrett's eyes. That he was being cold. Callous. Proving something to her as he proved it to himself.

All that mattered was she could have him. Like this. Right now.

God damn it, Nichole needed to end this. Slap his face and tell him to get the hell out. She needed to stop him, because he sure as hell couldn't stop himself. He hadn't even realized how far gone he was until he had the silk of her skin beneath his palms and the honeyed taste of her on his tongue.

The fact that she knew exactly what was happening between them—knew this wasn't about tender affection and wanted it anyway—was all wrong. It bothered the hell out of him.

So why was he hard as a spike and letting her soft gasps wash over him again and again, hoping they never stopped?

His fingers clenched on her hips as he teased her with his mouth, let the light pressure open her to him. And still she didn't break away from his stare. Those deep brown hungry eyes—the ones he'd been certain would be the first to give—were locked with his, the desire in them obscuring everything else.

Lifting her to rest on the table's edge, he ran his hand up the center of her body and pushed her back with the steady pressure of his palm until her weight rested on her elbows and he could slip her legs over his shoulders. Leaving her open and exposed, laid out to him like a feast for his taking.

His.

Because that was what this was about.

Proving to himself that the only hands on her tonight were his. Nothing mattered beyond that one simple fact. Not game-play. Not pride. Nothing.

It wasn't Garrett's kiss she was receiving. Nothing so tender or affectionate as that. It was something else altogether. Something that had to do with power and control. Both of which she'd already given over.

It was a claim. One she greedily accepted in exchange for the scrape of his evening stubble rubbing rough against her inner thigh. *Heaven.*

His mouth moved over her. Licking. Tasting. Teasing with the barest hint of teeth until she was writhing beneath him, her breath ragged and frayed. Then, covering that achy spot of need, he drew against it with a steady, rhythmic suction more about the destination than the journey getting there. It was so good. But too fast. Too much… Not enough. Already she was coming apart.

"Garrett!"

The last wave of her orgasm subsided and, tugging at his hair, she urged him higher with a breathless, "Please. All of you."

It was only sex. She knew that. But she wanted the completion of union she'd ached for every night. Wanted the heady rush of his body moving within her. She wanted the slickness of his shoulders beneath her palms and the coarse groan of his satisfaction against her neck. The pounding of his heart echoing through her own.

She wanted him to crawl over her and push inside. Take what he needed. What she wanted him to have.

Only he'd turned to stone. Gone rigid. Immovable.

Head down now, he was no longer looking at her. Still, without seeing his eyes, she could sense the tension in him.

"Garrett?" she started, suddenly feeling more vulnerable and exposed than she'd ever been before.

She wanted to cover herself, though she knew Garrett was no longer looking. Didn't want to see her.

"Could we talk—?"

"Goodnight, Nichole."

And though he walked out without another word the message couldn't have been more clear. He'd just given her a lesson in meaningless sex. And the way this felt she'd never need another.

CHAPTER SEVENTEEN

FIRST JEALOUSY. Then shame. And now, as if the past two days hadn't been shaping up to suck enough, Garrett was topping them off with a solid helping of guilt.

"Her fiancé?" A string of hot vulgarities spilled out of his mouth, and even after he'd realized they were pouring straight into his little sister's ear he couldn't manage to curb them.

That explained the familiarity he'd seen. The intimacy. And, hell, even the questions in their eyes.

This was the guy who'd been Nichole's first...*everything.* Her first boyfriend. First kiss. First lover. First fiancé... First broken heart.

And he'd been little more than a kid through it all. Which meant as much as Garrett didn't want to be able to relate to that feeling of having bitten off more than he could chew...he did. He understood how a kid could have someone as incredible as Nichole ready to offer him her forever and not be able to take it.

Only Paul wasn't a kid anymore. And, thinking back to the night at the gallery, Garrett was pretty sure he'd seen all the familiar shades of longing and regret in the guy's eyes as he followed Nichole's every word, laugh and move.

"Ex-fiancé. But, yeah. And F.Y.I. he was asking Sam

about her after you guys left," Maeve sniped. When he didn't offer whatever threat of beat-down she was looking for, she let out an irritable huff. "Maybe you missed the subtext of what I was saying? He's interested in Nikki. The guy she once told me would probably have been the one if she'd met him ten years later. So what are you going to do about it?"

Garrett raked a hand through his hair, looking out the window of his office at the darkening sky.

What *was* he going to do? Get lost in work for a while—like the next month or so—however long it took to get past this situation with Nichole. To stop wondering when he'd be able to see her next. What she'd think of some development at work. How hard she'd laugh at the tasteless jokes he'd picked up at the site. He needed to get past that place where so much of what he looked forward to was tied to her.

Because it wasn't fair to hold on to her when all he could offer was less than she deserved. When she'd *let him* offer her so much less than she deserved.

"I'm not going to do anything. Nichole and I are through. It's up to her if she wants to give this *Paul* another chance."

"You're through?" Another huff—this one edged with a growl. "You're a jackass, Garrett."

Totally. Without question.

But he was through being a bastard. Nichole might have thought it would be easier, but he'd barely been able to stomach himself. He owed Nichole an apology, but every damn time he got near her it seemed he took something he shouldn't. So, rather than using this as another excuse to get into her space, he was going to give her what she'd been asking him for for over a month. He was going to get out of her life for real.

The fact that they'd left things on such a foul note… Well, it just meant it would be easier for her to put him out of her head and move on with the life she was supposed to have.

When Garrett didn't turn up at her door the next day or the day after that Nichole realized he wasn't coming back. That this time it was truly over between them.

She should have been relieved. Maybe she was. Only it was hard to identify much of anything beneath the ache in her heart.

After a couple of weeks of carefully avoiding the topic of her brother, Maeve had let it drop that Garrett hadn't been out since that night at the gallery either. Though her friend had simply meant to let her know it was safe to get back in the water, Nichole had taken no comfort in the assurance.

Garrett had built a life around sacrifice and putting his responsibilities before himself. He'd missed out on so much already. Just when he'd found his way back to his friends, to the kind of full life he'd been missing all these years—she didn't want him to give it up for her.

It was time someone else made the sacrifice so Garrett didn't have to. She'd moved on with her life before… found a new path when she'd needed to. She could do it again.

The twins' birthday was the typical run of insanity Garrett had come to expect over the years. The boys were jacked up on cake and presents and what was probably going on their fourth glass of chocolate milk. Bethany's mother-in-law was in the living room, narrating a digital slideshow chronicling the boys' lives from news of fertilization through their soccer game the week before.

Garrett sat through it each year, but today it was more than he could take.

It had been a month since that last night with Nichole, and instead of it getting easier with the passing of time her absence from his life had become a hole in his chest…growing bigger every day. Numbing all the parts of him that were necessary to live.

This morning he'd woken with the absurd notion he might run into her tonight. He'd shaken the idea off immediately. In all these years she'd never been invited. And, though she'd become closer to all his sisters over the past months—even if Bethany had asked her to come—from the scant intel he'd gathered, she'd gone off the grid completely. Yet somehow he'd retained a shred of hope, because upon arrival the first thing he'd done was walk through the place, scanning each room as he went.

Now, an hour in, he was trying to keep up the façade of easygoing uncle… But the second the boys were distracted by a new guest's arrival it fell away. He needed to get out of there. Needed to walk outside. Get some air. See the sky.

He needed to breathe and it just didn't feel like he could.

Walking through the party, he looked for his sisters—only to discover they were conspicuously absent. What the—?

The laundry room? One of Ned's relatives had probably made a crack about Bethany's nacho dip and the rest of the Carter girls were talking her down from the ledge.

Following the hall behind the kitchen, he saw the door to the little room was closed but an inch gap of light showed at the base. It was quieter here, allowing him to hear the murmur of voices from within.

Busted.

Swinging the door open with an intent to rib his sisters about hiding during a family event, he didn't even make it a step into the room before a single word stopped him in his tracks.

"Pregnant—"

Whispered by Maeve and left hanging when all four of their faces swung around to his, eyes wide in varying degrees of fear and horror.

Pregnant.

Time seemed to stall as a slow burn worked across his chest, pins and needles of sensation spreading through organs that had gone numb but were suddenly alive.

The air whooshed into his lungs as he grabbed Maeve's shoulders with shaking hands.

"She's pregnant?" he demanded, a thousand things running through his head at once. Volvos and car seats, savings bonds and swing sets. A house with a yard and a fence and a back porch where they could watch the kids play while the sun set in the background.

What if something happened to her? What if they made a family and—God—what if she was taken away? If he lost her? What if he had to hold this tiny, precious little life that was Nichole's legacy in his clumsy hands and he was alone?

His gut clenched hard, but then he thought of those big brown eyes looking across the pillow at him each morning.

What if he didn't have to do it alone? What if this time it was Nichole standing beside him through the good times and the bad? Laughing with him. Letting him hold her.

Another gulp of air. This one deeper than the last.

What if this was everything that mattered?

"Garrett, just calm down," Maeve pleaded, her eyes darting nervously back and forth.

She didn't get it. She didn't need to be nervous about him finding out because with lightning clarity it struck him that he was—

"You need to listen. Everything is going to be fine. She's going to marry him and—"

"What?" His vision pushed in, going tunnel. The only thing he could see was Maeve's face, contorting from fear to confusion to...*amusement?*

She thought this was *funny?*

"Oh, my God, no, Garrett. Not *Nichole.*" Maeve was really trying not to laugh now. "I'm sorry. But it's... Erin."

His chin jerked back as another set of feminine hands grabbed at his shirt, tugging him around to face his sister.

"Garrett, please don't do anything crazy. He loves me—and look!" Erin was shoving her left hand in front of his face, showing him the neat cluster of diamonds in the shape of a heart on her third finger. "We're getting married."

Leaning back against the folding counter behind him, he met his sister's eyes. Forced his head around the information in front of him that felt like too much to comprehend. "Do you love him? Really love him? Are you sure you want to get married?"

Erin blinked at him, then turned slowly to her sisters and back. "Umm...yes."

Bethany hissed something from her corner by the dryer and Erin stood a little straighter and smiled.

"Yes. Garrett, we've been talking about getting married for months, before he found out about the baby. I guess he wanted to wait until Christmas—not because he didn't want to have to get me a ring and a present or anything, but because he thought it would be romantic."

Garrett held up a hand, almost too deflated to bear its weight. "Then, honey, I'm happy for you."

He was. It was just that for a minute he'd been happy for himself. He'd thought he had it all. And the realization he didn't had pretty well knocked the wind from his sails.

A second later the laundry room door opened again. George popped his head in, looked down at Erin's hand still held in front of Garrett's eyes, blanched and backed out with a quick slam of the door.

Garrett rolled his eyes as Maeve let out an indelicate snort. The girls started laughing, and him along with them. Looking from one sister to the next, he thought George was going to have to toughen up if he was going to be a parent. It was no walk in the park…but it would be worth it. Garrett thought about all that Erin and George were in for together and it struck him how incredibly lucky they were. How much beauty and awe lay ahead.

Then Bethany, Carla and Erin left the room, leaving Garrett and Maeve behind. His littlest sister cocked a brow at him and asked, "You okay?"

"Not yet," he answered, rubbing at that bruised feeling over his chest.

She stepped into him and gave him one of those very sweet kisses that involved tugging him low even as she stood on her toes to reach his cheek. "You did such a good job with us, Garrett. You protected our family. And, as much as I hate what you had to give up to do it, I'm thankful you did—because you kept us together. But now it's time for you to take care of yourself. I love you, bro."

CHAPTER EIGHTEEN

NICHOLE SHOULDN'T have come. It was stupid and self-destructive. Equivalent to picking at the wound over her heart that already wouldn't heal. But Sam had asked her to come over for dinner, wanting to talk. And when she'd tried to make an excuse, he'd rather effectively guilt-tripped her into it with a reminder about her month-long disappearing act.

He wanted her out of her apartment.

He wanted her to talk.

And so she'd come.

But now she was sitting on the rooftop of her dreams and nightmares. The chilly October air was biting her cheeks as Sam ran downstairs to grab them a couple of mulled ciders he'd whipped up.

The sun was doing its slow decent through the western sky, coloring everything in its path. In the quiet of the evening, removed from the street level rush, she drifted back through the months to summer. To that first toes-dip back into the pool. To Garrett.

If she'd had any idea what she was in for would she have done it anyway?

Yes.

Again and again and again.

Because while it lasted it had been incredible. Amazing. And having her heart break was better than never feeling it at all.

The scrape of feet moving over the rooftop sounded behind her and a tingle of awareness skirted across her skin.

Not Sam.

Garrett.

Her breath left her lungs in a rush and her fingers splayed wide over the rail as she tried to tell herself to be calm. To be strong. But all she could think was that he'd orchestrated this. He'd gone to the lengths of pulling Sam into whatever his plan was. After all this time, maybe he still wanted something.

Stepping beside her, Garrett set two mugs of cider on the rail and then wrapped a thick blanket around her shoulders from behind, so she wouldn't have to turn away from the blazing sky before them.

His hands shaped her upper arms, but he left a space between them.

"I never should have left the way I did. I shouldn't have behaved like I had some right or claim or justification for going nuts about you talking to another man. Not when you'd offered me something so much more and I'd turned it away."

Her shoulders slumped as that crazy bit of hope she'd been clinging to slipped through her fingers.

He was here to apologize. After all this time. Because Garrett…was *Garrett*. She'd become a responsibility somewhere along the way, and he was simply incapable of not facing up to it.

"I wasn't trying to play a game with you, Garrett. Not consciously anyway. I just… When Paul showed up—"

"You don't owe me an explanation. It doesn't change

what I did. I'm sorry and wish I'd had the clarity of thought to do something else."

Walk away? Maybe take that blonde who'd been flirting with him home?

She didn't want to think about that night. Right now she just wanted to remember all the things that had gone right. The fun. The ease. The promises fulfilled.

"Okay," she said, her following deep breath meant to be the break between one topic and the next. "So—been enjoying many sunsets lately?"

"I've been watching them—but, no. Not exactly enjoying them."

She turned then, drawn more by the man behind her than the star around which her very existence revolved. "Garrett, you've to got to stop holding yourself accountable for everything. If you've been worried about me—"

"I have."

This was why she was looking into accountancy firms across the country. Why she'd set up an interview for the next week.

She shook her head, but he just went on.

"Because if you feel even half as hollowed out and lost as I do, I don't know how you're surviving." Garrett looked past her to the sky beyond and then back to meet her eyes. "I watch the sunsets I've been waiting years to be able to enjoy and all I can think is how empty they are without you. I tell myself this connection is nothing I can't walk away from or get over. But there's *nothing*—nothing about it. We have a bond, and I'm finally starting to understand just how significant it is. It's about friendship and caring and attraction and the kind of sweet insanity of need I couldn't understand until I met you. It's about me wanting you to be a part of everything I do because everything I do is about a thousand times better when you do it with me. I was an idiot for taking it for granted, selling it short. Selling *us* short. Trying to let you go and doing such a poor job I don't think I'll ever be able to forgive myself."

Nichole's hands were on his chest then, the blanket slipping off one shoulder. Garrett caught it before it fell from the other. He tucked it around her and used it to pull her close.

"Garrett, what are you saying? That you want to give this a try for real? You think you might—?" Her voice cracked and she had to stop and blink back a tear. "You might want a future together?"

The muscles of Garrett's throat worked up and down as his jaw flexed. He gathered her hands in the warm hold of his own and held her gaze. "No. I'm saying I don't think I can live with a future where *we* aren't. Today I—I misheard something and got it in my head you were pregnant."

Nichole's chin snapped back. "Oh, God. I'm not—"

"No." He gave her a wry smile. "I know. But for the sixty seconds I thought you were…*damn,* Nichole, that might have been about the most terrifying, best moment of my life. Because suddenly I could see how incredible it was going to be…and how much there was to lose. A lifetime of everything I wanted condensed into a single minute. There was only one course of action and I wanted it. *Get Nichole back and marry her today.*"

Garrett drew a breath and closed his eyes. "But then it was over. Because it's Erin who's pregnant…not you."

He wanted her. Not some casual bit of fun. Not just the good time while it lasted. Pure elation pushed beneath her ribs as her stunned mind tripped and staggered over the words she'd never expected to hear. Processing each one until—

"What? Erin's pregnant?" She gasped, wondering if George still lived.

"Stop searching my clothes for blood. George is fine. They're getting married and I'm happy for them—mostly. But that doesn't matter right now."

She couldn't be hearing him right. Not about any of this. And especially not about his sister's pregnancy and impending marriage ranking as a lower priority than what was happening with *her*.

But that was what Garrett was saying. It was what was in his eyes. In the way he held so fast to her hands. Like he thought she might get away before he'd had the chance to make his case.

God, he was a fool.

"Garrett—"

"Nichole, all I could think when I figured out it wasn't you was *no!* Because that meant I didn't have anything to tie you to me. And I'd been such an ass I didn't know if I'd ever be able to get you to give me another chance. But I need another chance—because I swear to you, sweetheart, I can make you as happy as you deserve to be."

"Garrett—"

"And now I'm glad you aren't pregnant. But only because I want you to know this isn't just some sense of responsibility or obligation driving my actions. It's that I'm finally seeing what was in front of me the whole time—what I didn't have enough experience to recognize. I love you."

Words she'd never thought to hear. More beautiful than she could have imagined.

"Nichole, you have to—"

She was through trying to talk to him. Tugging her hands free, she reached up and grabbed his gorgeous, agonized face and pulled him into her kiss. For an instant there was only the blissful press of lips. Sweet contact and connection.

And then Garrett's arms slipped around her, pulling her into the solid strength of his body. He parted her lips with a desperate urgency that echoed her own. Murmuring her name against her mouth again and again before pulling back with a curse and looking into her eyes.

"Being without you has been the worst kind of torture. I thought I was afraid of losing my freedom, of ending up trapped in something beyond my control. But I didn't know what real fear was until I realized I'd lost the one person who makes me feel free. Alive. Complete."

"You haven't lost me. I'm right here." In the tight hold of his arms. With all that devastating blue shining down on her in a way that went straight to her soul and warmed her from the inside out. "I'm yours, Garrett."

"Then I'm never going to let you go. And I'm never going to give you a reason to want to leave, either, because I couldn't take it again. I couldn't take that feeling of being dead inside after knowing what it finally was to live."

Her palm cupped the solid line of his jaw as she peered up at him with a watery smile. Voice thick with emotion, she answered, "You won't have to."

"Promise?"

She nodded. With all her heart.

Garrett straightened, the muscles along his throat moving up and down as he swallowed.

"Good, because I love you, Nichole." Then, as if in slow motion, he went to one knee in front of her.

Her heart started to race and she shook her head as something other than joy began to push its way into her chest.

Within the cradle of his big strong hands sat a neat

black leather box opened to reveal a breathtaking diamond solitaire. "Marry me?"

"Garrett, no. I don't— I'm not—" She was terrified of that ring. Though by far the most beautiful, it was not the first she'd been offered. What if she put it on and he changed his mind again? What if they planned some elaborate wedding, invited everyone they knew, and then he woke up with the sense they'd rushed?

She couldn't take it. Not with him. Not after believing she'd lost him already.

"I won't let you down again, Nichole. If you can trust me with it, I'll take care of your heart for the rest of my life."

She looked down into those soulful eyes and realized this was no boy making a man's promise, nor some guy caught up in a moment. This was Garrett, who only made promises he could keep and who took his responsibilities more seriously than anyone she'd ever met. Garrett, who only knew how to love with his whole heart. Garrett, the man she wanted more than her next breath, who was worth any risk she had to take.

She did trust him. And he was offering her everything she'd ever dreamed of.

"Yes," she whispered, vowing never to forget the look of joy and relief spreading across his face. "I'll marry you."

He took a great breath and slid the ring onto her finger.

For a moment neither of them moved as they stared at the symbol of the commitment Garrett had just made.

"I like the look of my *forever* on your finger."

Nichole closed her eyes at his gruffly spoken words, letting that subtle distinction sink in to the very center of her heart.

Not just a ring. He was giving her a promise with no end. A lifetime together.

It was a perfect fit.

"I do too. It's beautiful, Garrett."

Pushing to his feet, he wrapped one hand around the small of her back, pulling her flush against the warm heat of him. When his mouth met hers it was in a kiss as soulful and lingering as his promise of forever.

When the kiss ended he pressed his forehead against hers. And then, cupping her jaw in his big hand, he said, "So, we've got a few hours… I didn't know if you were going to agree, or if I was going to have to try to whisper you into it, but we're booked on a flight for Vegas tonight."

At her shocked expression he let that half-smile of his crook its finger at her heart. "What? You didn't think I'd give you a chance to change your mind, did you? We might have missed the sunset tonight, but I want you wearing my name before sunrise tomorrow."

"I love you," she whispered.

That wicked smile fell from his lips, leaving nothing but the stark honesty of his answer. The promise she could believe in. The future they would share.

"I love you too."

* * * * *

ONE MORE SLEEPLESS NIGHT

BY
LUCY KING

Lucy King spent her formative years lost in the world of Mills & Boon romance when she really ought to have been paying attention to her teachers. Up against sparkling heroines, gorgeous heroes and the magic of falling in love, trigonometry and absolute ablatives didn't stand a chance.

But as she couldn't live in a dream world for ever she eventually acquired a degree in languages and an eclectic collection of jobs. A stroll to the River Thames one Saturday morning led her to her very own hero. The minute she laid eyes on the hunky rower getting out of a boat, clad only in Lycra and carrying a three-metre oar as if it was a toothpick, she knew she'd met the man she was going to marry. Luckily the rower thought the same.

She will always be grateful to whatever it was that made her stop dithering and actually sit down to type Chapter One, because dreaming up her own sparkling heroines and gorgeous heroes is pretty much her idea of the perfect job.

Originally a Londoner, Lucy now lives in Spain, where she spends much of the time reading, failing to finish cryptic crosswords, and trying to convince herself that lying on the beach really *is* the best way to work.

Visit her at www.lucykingbooks.com

For Emma.

CHAPTER ONE

THERE WAS SOMEONE in the house.

With the slam of the front door ringing in her ears, Nicky sat bolt upright in bed, her heart hammering like a pneumatic drill, alarm racing along her veins and her fingers gripping the edges of her book so tightly her knuckles were white.

A couple of seconds ago she'd been lying back against the pillows, happily lost in the romantic world of *Don Quijote.* She'd been trotting across the dry deserted plains of La Mancha in search of knight errantry and adventure, and vaguely contemplating the intoxicating notion that for the first time in weeks she might actually be beginning to relax.

Then the door had slammed and she'd hurtled back to reality. All thoughts of fighting off imaginary giants had shattered. Any hope of tilting at windmills had evaporated. The sense of relaxation had vanished, and now every instinct she had was alert and quivering and one hundred per cent focused on the fact that *there was someone in the house.*

And not someone she knew, she thought, her brain galloping through the facts as her blood chilled and a cold sweat broke out all over her skin.

Because as much as she'd like to believe otherwise, there was no way the heavy footsteps stamping over the rough flagstones of the hall and echoing off the walls could possibly belong to Ana, the pint-sized housekeeper. Or Maria,

the laid-back cook. Or any of the other staff employed on
the estate for that matter. Some of them might be big and
burly enough to possess a tread like the one now heading
up the stairs, but none of them would be in this part of the
house at this time of night.

No one was, apart from her.

And, of course, whoever it was who'd reached the landing, dropped something that hit the floor with a thud and was
now striding down the long wide corridor towards her room.

Nicky's heart hammered even more fiercely and her blood
roared in her ears as it struck her that the footsteps were getting louder. Closer. That any minute now they'd stop, he'd
be at her door, the handle would turn and—

Images of what might happen then slammed into her head,
vivid and terrifying, and as the alarm rushing around her
turned to full-blown panic she started to shake. Her vision
blurred, her breath stuck in her throat and she went dizzy,
and her heart was now beating so hard and fast it felt as if it
were about to burst from her chest.

She was a split second from passing out, she realised fog-
gily, and then the panic exploded inside her because if she
did pass out then she'd be toast.

And she really didn't want to be toast. She didn't want
not to be able to find out whether she might actually be able
to sort out the mess her life had become. She'd waited too
long. Suffered too much. Tried too hard…

So no, she told herself, struggling through the haze in her
head and battling back the panic. No way was she giving up
now and no way was she fainting.

Dredging up strength from who knew where and taking
a series of deep breaths, Nicky determinedly reined in her
spiralling-out-of-control imagination and willed her heart
rate to slow because she really had to calm down.

Now was *not* the time to lose it. Now was the time for cool assessment and a plan, because, regardless of what might lie in store for *her*, she was damned if she was going to let whoever it was get his grubby hands on her precious camera. Even if it had been sitting in a cupboard and gathering dust for the last few months.

Besides, she'd been in situations far more hazardous than this and had escaped at least *physically* unscathed so why should this be the one to get the better of her?

The most important question right now therefore was: what was she going to do? Simply lying here, frozen still and quivering with panic, wasn't going to get her anywhere, was it? Nor was dithering. No, it was time for action.

Allowing the instincts that had served her so well for so long to take over Nicky raced through the options. Options that weren't all that abundant, she had to admit, but never mind. She only needed one to work with and—aha!—now she had it. And in the nick of time, it seemed, because the footsteps had slowed right down and were a fraction of a second from stopping altogether.

Setting her jaw and clutching the book even tighter, she thanked God she'd picked an unabridged and illustrated copy of *Don Quijote* for her bedtime reading—which came in at a whopping thousand pages and weighed a ton—and silently slid from the bed.

What a week.

Striding down the corridor towards the sliver of light that shone from beneath the door at the end of it, Rafael rubbed a weary hand over his face and stifled a yawn.

He didn't think he'd ever had one like it, and frankly he'd be happy never to experience one like it again, because he couldn't remember a time when the muscles in his body hadn't ached or when his nerves hadn't been wound so tightly, let alone the last good night's sleep he'd had.

The crippling exhaustion could be attributed fairly and squarely to the merger he'd been working on recently and which had finally gone through this morning. It was a deal that had required delicate negotiation, tactful management, endless patience and long, long days at the office. All of which, of course, he'd been happy to handle. He was used to it, and sorting out other people's problems with their businesses was what he did best.

What he hadn't been so happy to have to deal with, however, and what was causing the unbearable tension in his nerves, were the myriad demands that the women in his life had chosen to unleash on him over the last few days.

Firstly, Elisa, the woman he'd been dating but had finished with a fortnight ago, had pitched up at his office the day before yesterday apparently unable to accept they were over. Despite the fact that he'd repeatedly pointed out he'd never promised her anything more than a casual fling, she'd been convinced she could change his mind, and the set of her jaw and the look in her eye had told him that no matter what he did or said she wasn't going to give up easily, as her subsequent battery of phone calls had proved.

Too busy and too knackered to deal with a full-on showdown right then and there, Rafael had sighed, muttered something about discussing it another time, and had eventually pacified her enough to bundle her out and send her on her way.

He'd barely got over *that* confrontation when his mother had been on the phone complaining about the fact that his father was once again holed up in his study and showed no signs of emerging. She'd demanded Rafael do something about it, although quite what she'd expected him to do he had no idea, because for one thing when his father retreated there was no shifting him, and for another he'd never paid his son any attention before so why would he start now?

When he'd eventually prised out the reason behind his father's withdrawal—the flap his mother was getting in over the organisation of a charity ball months away—he'd told her he could quite understand why his father had locked himself in his study, and that if it were *him* he wouldn't emerge until the night of the ball was long gone. At which point his mother had hung up on him in a fit of pique.

Then hot on the heels of *that* phone call, his eldest sister had invited him to a dinner party she was holding tomorrow night, which he suspected she'd engineered for the sole purpose of lining him up with one of her many single friends.

Rafael did *not* need help with his love-life, as Lola was well aware, but she'd inexplicably made it her life's mission to see him hitched again. Which was a thoroughly futile exercise because he had no intention of ever remarrying, especially not to any of his sister's friends, given the traumatic mess it had caused the last time he'd tried it. Once was quite enough, as he'd told her on countless occasions, but Lola had an infuriating habit of brushing him aside with a dismissive wave of her hand, and it was getting to the stage where if she didn't back off he might well lose it.

By the time his youngest sister, Gabriela, had begun her relentless onslaught of phone calls and emails, in the interests of self-preservation Rafael had made the snap decision to ignore her and everyone else, and flee the madness that was temporarily defining his life.

Whatever Gaby wanted it could wait, he'd assured himself, jumping into his car and telling his driver to make for the airport via a quick detour to his flat for a suitcase, then hopping on his plane and heading south.

He'd done the right thing by escaping, he told himself now. He'd known it the second he'd got out of his car a couple of minutes ago and for a moment had just stood there in the inky velvet of the night, listening to the blessed silence, breathing in the scent of earth and jasmine as the dry heat wrapped itself around him, and feeling some of the excruciating tension gripping his muscles ease.

Quite apart from probably collapsing with exhaustion, if he'd stayed in Madrid the usually strong bonds of filial and fraternal affection might well have snapped, so he refused to feel even a pinprick of guilt at disappearing without a word. His mother and sisters would survive perfectly well without him for a week or two. And as for his father, well, over the years he'd proved eminently capable of looking after himself by burying himself in his beloved books whenever there was a sudden surge of emotion about the place, as was being demonstrated by his current study sit-in.

So no. No guilt, he told himself, stopping at the door, wrapping his hand round the handle and turning it. He deserved a break. He needed one. All he wanted was a week or two of peace and quiet at the vineyard he'd had no option but to neglect for the last few months. He wanted long early morning walks among the vines and endless lazy afternoons drinking wine by the pool. He wanted rest and relaxation. Fresh air and sun and, above all, solitude. Was that *really* too much to ask?

Rafael opened the door a fraction to reach in and flip the switch he presumed had been left on by mistake, and his last coherent thought as the door slammed back, as something struck him hard in the temple, as pain detonated in his head and everything went dark inside as well as out, was that evidently it was.

Yes!

With a heady mix of adrenalin and triumph racing through her, Nicky heard the intruder groan, watched him stagger back in the shadowy darkness, and blew out the breath she'd been holding for what felt like hours.

Hah. That would teach whoever it was that she was not to be messed with. That she might be in a bit of a state at the moment, that she might be out here miles from anywhere and practically all alone, but that she was far from defenceless.

Her attack-being-the-best-form-of-defence plan had been an excellent one, and with the element of surprise on her side he hadn't stood a chance.

Still didn't by the looks of things, she thought with a surge of satisfaction as he swayed to one side, hit the door frame and, with a torrent of angry Spanish, ricocheted off it.

Oh, he didn't sound at all happy, but Nicky ignored the urge to wince and refused to feel guilty at the thought she might have done him some real damage because why should she when she was the potential victim here?

Not that she felt particularly victimish right now. In fact she'd never felt more victorious, which, after weeks of feeling nothing but listless, desperate and hopeless was very definitely something to be tucked away and analysed.

Although that analysis might have to wait until later, she thought, the satisfaction zapping through her slowly dissipating. Because with hindsight maybe her strategy hadn't been quite as brilliant as she'd thought.

He was filling the doorway and therefore blocking her only means of escape, and now, judging by the way he was giving his head a quick shake and straightening, he was making an alarmingly speedy recovery.

Her stomach churned with renewed panic as her mind raced all over again. Oh, heavens. If she wanted to leg it and make it to safety she was going to have to administer a second blow. One that would this time fell him like a tree and incapacitate him for the few minutes she'd need to clamber over him and run.

With barely a thought for the consequences and focused solely on survival, Nicky channelled every drop of adrenalin, every ounce of aggression she possessed, and raised the book again.

But before she could slam it down, he hit the switch, lunged forwards and grabbed her. Stunned by the sudden brightness of the light and by the sheer force of the bulk that crashed into her, Nicky let out a shriek and lost her balance.

As if in slow motion she felt herself go down. Felt her assailant follow her. Felt a large hand clamp onto the back of her head and a strong arm snap round her back. She heard the thud of the book as it landed on the carpet and wondered vaguely what she was going to do for a weapon now.

After what seemed like hours but could only have been a second, she hit the floor. Her breath shot from her lungs. Her vision blurred, her head swam and her entire body went numb. For a few endless moments the only thing she could hear was the thundering of her heart and a weird kind of roaring in her ears.

And then the dizziness ebbed and the shock faded and as feeling returned she became aware of the warm ragged breath on her cheek. Of the hammering of a heart against her chest. And of the very considerable weight half lying on top of her, crushing the breath from her lungs, pressing her into the floor and showing no signs of shifting.

Or of anything for that matter, she realised dazedly, which meant that she had the advantage and she had to use it. Now.

Preparing to knee him where it would *really* hurt and hoping that that might succeed where *Don Quijote* had failed, Nicky glanced up to get a good look at the man she'd need to describe to the police.

And froze, her leg bent slightly at the knee and her hands flat against the hard muscles of his shoulders.

She stared up into the face hovering inches above hers, up at the dark-as-night hair, the thickly lashed, startlingly green eyes, the deep tan and that mouth, all so exquisitely put together, the face she'd seen countless times in the photos on Gaby's mantelpiece—although admittedly never in its current furious state—and her breath shot from her lungs all over again. Only this time in one shuddery, horrified gasp.

The triumph vanished. The satisfaction disappeared. The thundering adrenalin and mind-scrambling panic evaporated in a puff of smoke. And in their wake came a flood of red-hot mortification.

Because, oh, dear God…

As unlikely as it seemed, and despite the fact that she'd been assured he was in Madrid and would never show up at the estate he'd lately abandoned, she'd just brained her host.

CHAPTER TWO

WHAT THE—?

WITH all the breath knocked from his lungs slowly returning, Rafael stared down at the figure sprawled beneath him barely able to believe his eyes.

This was the person responsible for the pain splintering his head apart and the juddering agony shooting up his arms from his wrists to his shoulders? This… This…*woman*?

Judging by the force of the blow he'd received he'd been expecting a six foot plus chunk of man, armed with a crowbar and sporting a balaclava at the very least, which was why he'd retaliated so vigorously and lunged.

He would never in a million years have guessed that his assailant would turn out to be a woman probably two-thirds his size. Or that she'd have the long dark wavy hair that was fanning out over his hand and the floor and the big blue-grey eyes that were widening with shock and alarm and horror. And he'd never have imagined that she'd be half naked.

Yet unless the thwack to his head was making him hallucinate, it appeared that, what with the long limbs entangled with his and the feel of her silky hair and soft skin beneath his hands, that was exactly the case.

Cross with himself for even noticing what she looked like and what she was—or wasn't—wearing when it couldn't have been less relevant, Rafael scowled, and since that made the pounding in his head worse he let out a rough curse. He felt as if someone were drilling a hole through his skull while repeatedly punching him in the stomach.

He hurt. Everywhere.

As must she, given that he was lying on top of her and probably crushing the life out of her, he thought, hearing her muffled groan.

She released his shoulders, let her knee drop and clapped one hand over her eyes, and he eased his arms away from underneath her, rolled off and lay back flat out on the floor. He closed his eyes and breathed in deeply in an effort to stifle the pain and try and make some kind of sense of the last couple of minutes, but it didn't work because none of this made any sense at all.

'Oh, my God,' said his assailant, her voice sounding hoarse with appal and breathlessness, and very English. 'I'm so *so* sorry. I had no idea... Are you OK?'

OK? Rafael wasn't sure he'd ever be OK again. If anything, the pain in his head was getting worse. What on earth had she lamped him with? Surely not just a fist. If that was all it had taken he was in a worse state than he'd imagined.

'Rafael?' This time her voice was lower, softer, more concerned. Sexier, he thought, and got a bit sidetracked by the image of the two of them lying not on a cold hard stone floor but a soft warm bed, wearing considerably less clothing, with that voice whispering hot filthy things in his ear.

And then she gave him a decidedly unsexy little slap on the cheek.

Rafael flinched as the erotic vision vanished, and refocused. God, she'd just attacked him and he was *fantasising* about her? What was his problem?

And what was *her* problem? Wasn't practically knocking him out enough? Had she really had to slap him too? What did she have lined up next? A methodical and thorough assault of his entire body?

Vaguely wondering what he'd ever done to womankind to deserve this torment on top of everything else he'd had to endure lately, he gingerly opened his eyes.

And saw stars all over again because she was on her knees, leaning over him, and he was getting an eyeful of creamy cleavage. So close he could make out a spatter of faint freckles on the skin of her upper chest. So close he could smell the delicate floral notes of her scent. So tantalisingly close all he'd have to do was lift his head a handful of centimetres and he'd be able to nuzzle her neck.

At the thought of *that*, his mouth watered, a wave of heat struck him square in the stomach and for the first time since she'd hit him he forgot about the pain throbbing away in his temple. The image of the two of them in that bed slammed back into his head, more vivid than before now that he had more detail to add, and he blinked at the intensity of it.

'Thank God,' she murmured, letting out a shaky breath, which made her chest jiggle and his pulse spike. 'Are you all right?'

How he managed it he had no idea but Rafael made himself drag his gaze up and look into her eyes. Eyes that were filled with worry, set in a face that was pale and, he thought, letting his gaze roam over it, perhaps a bit thinner than it ought to be.

There was nothing thin about her mouth, however, he decided, staring at it and going momentarily dizzy as a fresh burst of heat shot through him. Her mouth was wide and generous and very very appealing, especially what with the way she'd caught the edge of her lower lip between her teeth and was nibbling at it.

'Ow,' he muttered, forcing himself to remember the faint sting of the slap because the alternative was yanking her down and giving in to the temptation to nibble on that lip himself, which was so insanely inappropriate given the circumstances that he wondered if the blow to his head might not have done him a serious injury.

'I'm sorry—again—but I thought you'd passed out.'

'I'm fine,' he said, although actually nothing could be further from the truth, because now he was imagining that mouth moving over his, then pulling away and sliding over his skin, hot and wet and sizzling, and the throbbing in his head was breaking loose and rushing down his body with such speed and force that he had the horrible feeling that when it got to his groin he might do exactly as she'd feared and pass out.

He lifted his hand to his temple and touched it, as much to see if she'd drawn blood as to find out whether deliberately and brutally provoking pain might dampen the maddening heat.

'Do you think you might be concussed? Should I get help?'

'No, and no,' he said irritably because while on the upside she hadn't on the downside it didn't.

'Let me take a look.'

Before he could stop her she'd leaned down and reached across him and was now sifting her fingers through his hair. Her breasts brushed against his chest, then hovered perilously close to his mouth, and the heat churning through him exploded into an electrifying bolt of lust.

God, what the hell *was* this? he wondered, bewilderment ricocheting around his brain. Since when had he reacted so violently to a woman he'd barely met? And since when had he had to fight so hard to keep a grip on his supposedly rock-solid self-control?

'Leave it,' he snapped and wrapped his hand round her wrist to stop her going any further.

To his relief she went still, then frowned and, as he let her go, mercifully straightened and sat back. 'Well, if you're sure.'

Rafael hitched in a breath, briefly closed his eyes and ordered himself to get a grip before he embarrassed himself. 'I'm sure.'

With what felt like superhuman effort he levered himself upright and set about engaging the self-control he'd never had such trouble with before. He drew his feet up to hide the very visible evidence of the effect she'd had on him, rested his elbows on his knees, and began to rub the kinks out of his neck with both hands. He let out a deep sigh. So much for peace, tranquillity and nice quiet solitude.

'I really am sorry, you know,' she said, her voice sounding rather small.

'So you said.'

'I thought you were a burglar.'

'If I was, I wouldn't be a very good one,' he muttered, remembering the way he'd slammed the front door and thundered up the stairs in his haste to crash out and wipe the last week from his brain. 'I wasn't exactly subtle.'

'Well, no,' she admitted, 'but at the time a cool, logical analysis of the situation wasn't uppermost in my mind. I acted on instinct.'

And how he'd suffered for it. Her instincts were so dangerous they should come with a warning.

As should that body. Because she might have backed off but she was still far too close for his comfort. She was now kneeling beside him and sitting back on her heels and her smooth bare thighs were within stroking distance. At the thought of sliding his hands up her legs, his fingers itched and he dug them just that little bit harder into his neck.

'The next time I come across a closed door,' he said, setting his jaw and trying not to think about silky thighs and itching fingers, 'I'll knock.'

She nodded. 'Probably a good idea.'

'All I thought I was doing was simply switching off a light that had been left on by accident. Who knew helping the environment could be so lethal?' He glanced at the book lying innocently on the floor behind her and frowned. 'What the hell did you hit me with?'

'Don Quijote,' she said, wincing and going pink.

That would certainly account for the bruise he could feel swelling at his temple. 'I always thought that book was utterly deadly,' he said darkly, 'but I never thought I'd ever mean literally.'

'You were supposed to be in Madrid.'

At the faint accusatory tone of her voice his eyebrows shot up. 'Are you suggesting that this,' he said, breaking off from massaging his neck to indicate his head, 'is somehow *my* fault?'

She frowned. 'Well, no,' she said, sounding a bit more contrite and biting on that damn lip again. 'But if you'd been expected I imagine Ana would have warned me and then I'd have been listening out for you instead of attacking you.' And then she lifted her chin and pulled her shoulders up and back, which did nothing to help his resolution to keep his eyes off her chest. '*Were* you expected?'

No, his decision to come down here had been uncharacteristically on the spur of the moment, and with hindsight that might have been a mistake, but that wasn't the point. Rafael arched an eyebrow and threw her a look that had quelled many a thick-headed CEO. 'I wasn't aware I needed to be.'

'No, of course you don't,' she said, flushing a bit deeper. 'It's your house. Sorry.'

And that was the third time tonight she appeared to be one step ahead of him, he thought with a stab of annoyance.

In addition to taking him by surprise earlier, she apparently knew his name and that this was his house. Whereas he knew nothing about her apart from the fact that she was probably British, looked incredibly hot in her skimpy T-shirt and knickers and had skin and hair that felt like silk beneath his hands. The latter two of which, he reminded himself for the dozenth time, weren't in the slightest bit relevant.

Giving himself a mental slap, Rafael pulled himself together. He'd had quite enough of being on the back foot for one evening. Quite enough of having his nice ordered life being thrown into increasing disarray. It was high time he asserted some kind of control over this particular situation at the very least, and focused on what was important.

'You're right,' he said coolly as he fixed her with his most penetrating stare. 'So perhaps you wouldn't mind telling me who you are and what you're doing here.'

She blinked at him for a moment or two, then gave him a tentative smile. 'Well, I'm Nicky.'

She said it as if it should have been obvious, and Rafael frowned. 'Nicky?'

'Sinclair.'

He racked his brains for a spark of recognition but came up with nothing. 'Is that supposed to mean something?'

'I was rather hoping so.'

'It doesn't.' He was pretty sure he didn't know any Nickys, Sinclair or otherwise, and equally sure he didn't want to if they were anything like this one.

'Oh.'

Her smile faded and something tugged at his chest. Rafael ignored it and concentrated on his original line of questioning. 'And what are you doing in my house?'

'I'm here on holiday.'

His eyebrows shot up. Since when had the *cortijo* been open to visitors other than his family? 'On holiday?'

'That's right.'

'How long have you been here?'

'Two days.'

'And how long were you planning to stay?'

She shrugged then looked uneasy. 'Well, I don't know. I hadn't really thought.'

Hmm. He really ought to have made more of an effort to come down here over the last few months, tricky merger or no tricky merger. In the five years he'd had the place he'd generally managed to make it down once a month, but lately he'd been so tied up with work he'd had no option but to stay in Madrid. He'd received the usual weekly reports about the vineyard, of course, but heaven knew what had really been going on in his absence.

'Are there any more of you?'

She looked at him warily. 'No, just me.'

That was something to be grateful for, he supposed, shoving his hands through his hair before he remembered the bruise, and grimacing as a fresh arrow of pain scythed through him.

It shouldn't be too hard to get rid of her. His plane was sitting at the airport a mere half an hour away and could take her anywhere she wanted to go at a moment's notice. Within the hour he could be enjoying the solitude he'd been hankering after.

There was no question of her continuing her holiday, of course, because quite apart from the fact that the house wasn't open to visitors—of either the paying or non-paying variety—none of his fantasies about escaping everything for a few days had featured a hot house guest with a penchant for violence.

Besides, he'd finally reached the end of his usually fairly long tether, and he'd had enough. Of everything. So he'd send Nicky on her way, wipe the bizarrely traumatic events of this evening from his memory, and set about relaxing.

But not while they were both still on the floor, he decided, getting painfully to his feet then holding out his hand to help her up.

'You have absolutely no idea about any of this, do you?' she said a little wistfully as she put her hand in his and stood up.

'No,' he muttered, so disconcerted by the sizzle that shot through his blood at the contact that for a second he had no idea about anything.

'I knew it would turn out too good to be true.'

She sighed, slid her hand from his and Rafael ignored the odd dart of regret to focus instead on the way her shoulders were slumping. 'What would?' he asked, detecting an air of defeat about her and for some reason not liking it.

'Coming to stay. Gaby said it would be fine.'

That captured his attention. 'You know Gaby?'

She nodded and gave him another wobbly little smile. 'I do. And she said she'd clear it with you, but she didn't, did she?'

That would teach him to issue an open invitation to his sisters to use the place whenever they felt like it. Rafael thought of the barrage of phone calls and emails that his sister had bombarded him with and which he'd disregarded, and frowned at the niggling stab of guilt. 'No.'

'I thought not.' She sighed again and seemed to deflate just that little bit more.

He watched it happen and to his intense irritation his chest tightened. There was a vulnerability about Nicky that plucked at the highly inconvenient and usually extremely well-hidden protective streak he possessed. Which was nuts, of course, because presumably the kind of woman to wallop him over the head as she had wasn't in the least bit vulnerable. Or in need of protection.

Nevertheless, right now she looked crushed, as if she had the weight of the world on her shoulders, and Rafael found he couldn't get the words out to tell her to leave, however much he wanted to. Besides, if she was a friend of his sister's and he threw her out, he'd never hear the end of it.

He sighed and inwardly cursed. 'Look, it's late,' he said, deciding that he was way too tired for this kind of mental gymnastics and as it was pushing midnight he could hardly turf her out now anyway. 'Let's discuss this in the morning.'

'OK,' she said, with a weariness that made him want to do something insane like haul her into his arms and tell her everything was going to be all right. 'Thanks... And goodnight.'

'Goodnight,' he muttered, then turned on his heel and strode off down the corridor, thinking with each step that the night had been anything but good so far, and what with the traces of arousal and heat still whipping around inside him and the apparent disintegration of his brain it didn't look as if it were going to get any better.

Well, this was all just typical of the crappy way her life had been going lately, wasn't it? thought Nicky glumly, watching Rafael stop to pick up the suitcase he must have dumped at the top of the stairs earlier and then disappear round the corner.

Why would her stay at the *cortijo* be turning out as she'd hoped when nothing had done recently?

Feeling utterly drained by the events of the last half an hour on top of those of the past six months, she shut the door, retrieved *Don Quijote* from the floor and padded over to the bed. Setting the book on the bedside table, she slipped beneath the sheets and switched off the light.

How had things gone so badly wrong? she wondered for the billionth time as she stared into the darkness and felt the relentless heaviness descend.

Six months ago she'd been unstoppable. So full of energy and verve and enthusiasm, and fiercely determined not to let what had happened in the Middle East defeat her. She'd snapped up every assignment she'd been offered and had thrown herself into each one as if it were her last. She'd travelled and worked every minute she had, pausing only to hook up with the scorchingly hot journalist with whom she'd been having a sizzling fling.

Everything had been going marvellously, exactly as she'd planned, and she'd enjoyed every minute of it. She'd taken some of the finest photographs of her career and had some of the best sex of her life, and she'd congratulated herself on beating any potential demons she could so easily have had.

See, she'd told herself on an all-time high as she collected an award for one of her pictures and smiled down at the man she was sleeping with. All those colleagues who'd muttered things about PTSD had been wrong. Apart from the occasional nightmare and a slight problem with crowds, she hadn't had any other symptoms. And besides, she wasn't an idiot, so as a precaution she'd embarked on a course of counselling and therapy, which had encouraged her to make sense of what had happened, and get over it. As indeed she had, and the full-to-the-brim life she'd been leading, the work she'd been doing and the award she'd won, were all proof of it.

For months she'd told herself that she was absolutely fine, and for months she'd blithely believed it.

Until one day a few weeks ago when she turned out to be not so fine. That horrible morning she'd woken up feeling as if she were being crushed by some invisible weight. Despite the bright Parisian sunshine pouring in through the slats in the blind and the thousand and one things she had to do, she just hadn't been able to get herself out of bed.

She'd assured herself at the time that she was simply having a bad day, but since then things had got steadily worse. The bad days had begun to occur more frequently, gradually outnumbering the good until pretty much every day was a bad day. The energy and verve and the self-confidence she'd always taken for granted had drained away, leaving her feeling increasingly anxious, and to her distress she'd found herself refusing work she'd previously have jumped at.

Bewildered by that, she'd stopped picking up her phone and had started ignoring emails. And not just those from colleagues and employers. When staying in touch with friends and family had begun to require too much energy she'd stopped doing that too.

She'd given up eating properly and had started sleeping terribly. When she did eventually manage to drop off the nightmares had come back, but now with far greater frequency than before, leaving her wide awake in the middle of the night, weak and sweating and shaking.

Her previously very healthy libido had faltered, withered and then died out altogether, as, inevitably, had the fling.

Barely going out, hardly speaking to anyone, and with so much time on her hands to sit and dwell, Nicky had ended up questioning practically every decision she'd ever made over the years. She'd begun to doubt her abilities, her ideals and her motivation, and as a result cynicism and a bone-deep weariness had invaded her.

Down and down she'd spiralled until she'd been riddled with nerve-snapping tension, utter desolation, crippling frustration, and the dizzyingly frightening feeling that she might never be able to haul herself out of the slump she tumbled into.

Burnout, Gaby had diagnosed over a bottle of wine a

week ago when Nicky had finally hit rock bottom, although what made her such an expert she had no idea. Gaby, who was currently feng shui-ing the mansion of a businessman in Bahrain, was an on-and-off interior designer—more off than on—and wouldn't know burnout if it came up and slapped her in the face.

Nevertheless, as she'd sliced through Nicky's symptoms, and then relentlessly gone on about the importance of balance and rest and looking at things piece by tiny piece, Nicky had decided that perhaps Gaby might have had a point, which was why when her friend had come up with a plan she'd so readily and gratefully agreed.

Go to Spain, Gaby had said. *Get away from it all. Take some time out and restore your equilibrium. Rest. Sunbathe. Get a tan. You can recuperate at my brother's house. He's never there so you can stay as long as you need. Don't worry about a thing. I'll sort it all out.*

At the time Gaby had made it sound so easy, and, as she hadn't exactly had any ideas of her own, she'd booked a flight the following morning, buoyed up both by the thought of having something to focus on other than her own misery and at the heady feeling that *finally* she might be about to see the blurry flickering light at the end of a very long, very dark tunnel.

And OK, in the two days she'd been here she hadn't noticed much of a difference to her emotional state, but she knew she needed time at the very least.

Time it looked as if she wasn't going to get, she thought now, her heart sinking once again as she sighed and punched her pillow into a more comfortable shape, because it was blindingly obvious that Gaby hadn't managed to sort anything out, and it was equally blindingly obvious that, despite her friend's breezy assurances to the contrary, she wasn't welcome here.

Nicky closed her eyes and inwardly cringed as the image of Rafael's handsome scowling face drifted into her head. Quite apart from the initial burglar/assault misunderstanding, throughout the whole subsequent conversation they'd had he'd been tense and on edge, and had looked so mightily hacked off that she'd got the impression that he really resented her being there. Which meant there was no way she could stay.

If she did—and that was assuming he didn't chuck her out in the morning—*she'd* feel like the intruder, and she had quite enough on her plate already without adding guilt to her ever-increasing pile of problems.

So who knew whether the peace and tranquillity of the *cortijo* might have eventually worked their magic? Whether a couple of weeks of enforced rest and relaxation might not have been just what she needed? She wasn't going to get the chance to find out because one thing she'd learned from years of working in hostile environments was never to hang around where you weren't welcome.

Therefore no matter how depressing she found the idea, first thing in the morning she, her suitcase and her nifty little hire car would be off.

CHAPTER THREE

Despite his misgivings about any improvement to his night, he'd actually slept remarkably well, thought Rafael, smothering a yawn and setting the coffee pot on the stove.

When he'd eventually made it to his room after leaving Nicky, he'd downed a couple of painkillers and then taken an ice cold shower, which had respectively obliterated the pain throbbing in his head and the heat racing through his veins. He'd crashed into bed and had been asleep barely before his considerably less painful head had hit the pillow. Consequently he'd woken up in a much better mood.

Back in full possession of his self-control and all his faculties, he'd had ample opportunity to assess the events of the previous night and had come to the conclusion that he'd overreacted. Big time. He'd been tired and overwrought. In pain and on the defensive. All entirely unsurprising of course given the circumstances, but nevertheless he *had* overreacted.

For one thing, he told himself, lighting the gas ring beneath the pot and straightening, he doubted that Nicky, with her big blue eyes, tumbling dark curls and long slender semi-naked limbs, could be nearly as distracting as he'd imagined last night, and the cold light of day would soon prove it.

His reaction to her last night might have been startling, but it was nothing to get worked up about. Any red-blooded heterosexual man would have responded like that to a gorgeous near-naked woman practically draped over him. It would have been unusual if he hadn't.

Nor were the oddly erotic images that had peppered his dreams anything to worry about either, because that was just his subconscious processing what had been an unexpected and surprisingly traumatic half an hour.

For another thing, last night he'd somehow managed to see Nicky as some kind of threat to his peace of mind, which was a sign of just how tired and at the end of his tether with women he'd become because the very idea was ridiculous. Since his divorce he'd made sure that no woman—apart from family members, and he couldn't unfortunately do much about them—had ever had such an effect on him, and a woman he barely knew certainly posed no risk.

The second conclusion he'd come to was that there was no earthly reason Nicky couldn't stay. Why they both couldn't. The place was big enough, and however exhausted and fed up he was it wasn't Nicky's fault. Nor was it her fault that he'd ignored Gaby's phone calls and emails and was therefore unprepared for a guest. And yes, she'd lamped him so hard it would have made a saint curse the heavens, but perhaps that was understandable in the circumstances.

Besides, he couldn't get the image of her standing there enveloped by that air of defeat and desolation out of his head, and it had been niggling away at his brain all morning. For someone supposedly on holiday Nicky didn't look very happy. And who holidayed by themselves anyway? Not even he did, and he valued his solitude highly.

Rafael poured some milk into a jug and stuck it in the microwave, then leaned back against the rough wood worktop and rubbed a hand along his jaw as he contemplated the contradiction.

He supposed Gaby might have been able to shed some

light on the situation if he'd been able to get hold of her, but her phone had been off all three times he'd tried. And the emails and messages he'd eventually got round to checking had said nothing more than 'call me' with varying degrees of urgency.

But that didn't matter. He didn't need to speak to his sister to recognise that there was more to Nicky and her 'holiday' than met the eye. In fact, he'd repeatedly gone over the way she'd deflated right there in front of him and got the feeling that she was in some kind of trouble. And if that *was* the case, then despite the fact he had no interest in—and even less intention of finding out—what kind of trouble she might be in, he'd never forgive himself if he sent her on her way and something subsequently happened to her.

So she was going to have to stay.

Which was absolutely fine, he assured himself, hearing a strange rumbling making its way across the floor above and abandoning the coffee to go and investigate. He had plenty of things to be getting on with, and staying out of Nicky's way while she got on with whatever she was planning to do would be simple enough.

And if he *did* still feel a lingering attraction towards her, well, he'd easily be able to handle that too. After what he'd had to contend with lately, suppressing tiny pangs of inconvenient desire would be a walk in the park. Especially now that he was well rested, firing on all cylinders, and most importantly, firmly back in control.

Leaving might be the right thing to do, thought Nicky as she trudged along the corridor hauling her suitcase behind her, but it didn't make it any easier, because what was she going to do when she got back to Paris?

Moping around her flat didn't particularly appeal. Neither did booking another holiday and having to go through the whole packing/airport/people thing again. And she supposed she could track down her parents and see if they needed any help, but right now their relentless cheerfulness might be more than she could stand.

Oh, if only Rafael hadn't chosen this of all weekends to visit… If only Gaby had managed to get in touch with him… If only she hadn't bashed him over the head…

If only…

Her spirits sank even further. There'd been so many 'if only's in her life lately. She'd never used to believe in regrets, and she'd never used to wish for the impossible. However since her meltdown it seemed she'd done nothing but, and she was becoming thoroughly sick of it.

Nicky gritted her teeth and yanked her suitcase over the edge of the rug that the wheels were rucking up. She *had* to stop all this before she lost what was left of her sanity. She really did. Regrets and impossible wishes and 'if only's were pointless, especially now, because there was nothing to be gained from wishing she could stay, and even less from dwelling on what might have been. However hard she might find it, she *had* to drag herself out of the past and start thinking about the future.

'Good morning.'

At the sound of the deep voice rumbling through her gloomy ruminations, Nicky came to an abrupt halt and stared down. Rafael was standing in the doorway to the kitchen, barefoot and rumple-haired, wearing khaki shorts, a black polo shirt and the kind of lethal smile that had undoubtedly brought about many a swoon but left her depressingly unmoved.

'Good morning,' she replied, despite thinking there wasn't much that was good about this one.

'Did you sleep well?'

Not particularly, but at least she hadn't had that hideous

recurring nightmare. 'Like a log,' she said, mustering up what she hoped might pass for a smile and feeling faintly glad there were no small children around to scare. 'You?'

'Beautifully.'

'How's the head?'

'Much better.'

That was one less thing on her conscience at least. 'Thank goodness for that.'

'It had more to do with paracetamol than goodness, but it's fine.' His gaze shifted to her suitcase and he arched an eyebrow. 'Going somewhere?'

Nicky bit back a sarcastic comment about his spectacular powers of observation because her frame of mind this morning was hardly his fault, and settled for the more boring but less offensive truth. 'The airport.'

'Oh?' he said mildly. 'Why?'

For a moment she just stared at him. Why? *Why?* Had a good night's sleep somehow wiped the previous evening's events from his memory? 'Because I don't fancy the long drive home,' she said, this time unable to hold back the sarcasm.

Rafael merely shrugged and grinned. 'Then stay.'

Nicky went still and blinked down at him, confusion stabbing at her brain. Maybe she'd misheard him or something. Or maybe she was hallucinating, conjuring up the words simply because she wanted to hear them. Whether she'd misheard or was imagining things, she definitely had the sensation that she'd woken up in some kind of parallel universe, because the Rafael who was leaning nonchalantly against the door frame, folding his arms over his chest and smiling up at her, bore little resemblance to the extremely grouchy man she'd met yesterday. *That* one had looked as if he just wanted her gone, so who was *this* one who was now suggesting she stay?

'What?' she said weakly, as a tiny ray of hope that she might not have to leave after all flickered through her bewilderment.

'Stay.'

'Really?'

He nodded. 'Really.'

The hope surged for a second and then stopped, hovered, and, because such good fortune didn't happen to her these days, the cynicism that was never far away swooped down and crushed it.

Nicky frowned and narrowed her eyes. Such a volte-face? Just like that? She didn't think so. 'Why?'

Rafael lifted his eyebrows. 'What do you mean why?'

'Last night I rather got the impression I wasn't very welcome.'

'No, but then you'd just hit me over the head. I wasn't in a very hospitable mood.'

She tilted her head and shot him a sceptical look. 'But this morning you are?'

'Apparently so.'

'Have you spoken to Gaby?' If Gaby had told him why she was here, then maybe he'd changed his mind out of pity.

'No. I tried, but her phone was off.'

'I didn't have any luck either,' she said, mightily relieved that Rafael didn't know the truth because the last thing she wanted was pity. 'She seems to have gone AWOL.'

'Probably sensible given the conversations I imagine she can expect.'

'Probably.'

There was a pause, then he said, 'So would you like to stay or not?'

Nicky bit her lip and scoured his face, but found nothing there to suggest he was anything other than one hundred per cent serious. She saw nothing but warmth in the depths of his eyes and in his smile, and felt a reciprocal stab of warmth in the pit of her stomach. Totally unexpected and alien, but so welcome it gave her the strength to push the cynicism aside for once.

Oh, what was the point of dithering any longer? Of course she was going to stay. There was trying to do the right thing and then there was being a stubborn idiot. Besides, she could stand there and try and figure out Rafael's motivations for hours, but she doubted she'd ever succeed and frankly she didn't have the energy for it.

And anyway, did it really matter why he'd changed his mind? No. All that mattered was that he was offering her the lifeline she hadn't realised she so badly needed until it looked as if it had gone, and she'd be a fool not to grab it with both hands.

'Are you sure I won't be a bother?'

'Quite sure.'

'In that case,' she said, feeling the beginnings of what she thought might be the first genuine smile to curve her mouth in months, 'I'd be delighted.'

CHAPTER FOUR

IN HIS CONVICTION that sharing his house with Nicky would present no problem he'd been one hundred per cent right, thought Rafael as he lit the barbecue later that evening. Handling his house guest and, more importantly, his response to her, was simply a question of remaining in control, and so far he'd been doing splendidly.

He could easily have let himself be swayed by the glorious sight of her on the landing this morning, but had he? No, he had not. He'd been ice cool. Unflappable. And as strong and steady as the Rock of Gibraltar that reared out of the sea a hundred kilometres to the south.

The flash of heat that had shot through him when he'd clapped eyes on her striding along and dragging her suitcase behind her, looking strangely and grimly determined, was merely down to the sky-high temperatures of Andalucia in August. Never mind that the sun had only been up for half an hour; the heat started early down here.

Throughout their subsequent conversation his grip on his self-control had only got firmer.

He'd barely noticed that her strapless dress was the exact colour of her eyes, clung to her curves and showed off inches of flawless skin. He'd paid no attention whatsoever to the way the sun pouring in through the window behind her rendered the skirt of her dress practically transparent and revealed the legs that had featured so prominently in his dreams.

When she'd slid her gaze to his temple and asked him how it was the sensation that he could somehow feel her fingers sifting through his hair again had been nothing more than a figment of his imagination. When he'd watched her nibble on that lip of hers and had felt a sharp twist of his stomach, it had had more to do with a hunger for breakfast than that of any other kind.

And if, when she'd agreed to stay and flashed him that sudden dazzling smile, he'd thought he'd gone momentarily blind, it was undoubtedly down to more of the eye-wateringly bright sunshine spilling in through the window.

Even now, with her sitting at the wrought iron table on the terrace, wearing a halter-neck dress that gave her a cleavage like the Desfiladero de los Gaitanes gorge he'd abseiled down last summer and the scent that had so intoxicated him last night, he was utterly unfazed. The tiny nick he'd given his finger when she'd tasted the wine and let out a soft little sigh of appreciation and the knife he'd been using to slice off a couple of steaks had slipped didn't hurt in the slightest.

Yes, he'd done well indeed, he told himself again as he sprinkled salt onto each of the steaks and then added a grind of pepper. Spending much of his day out in the fields among the grape-laden vines—not in an effort to avoid her or anything, of course, but because he'd needed to catch up with his estate manager—had clearly done the trick. Whatever attraction he'd felt for Nicky last night, whatever mental wobble he'd suffered, he'd most definitely conquered it, and he was well and truly back on track.

Rafael Montero really was the best looking man she'd seen in a long time, thought Nicky, lifting her glass to her mouth and watching him as he deftly flipped the steaks and seasoned the other side.

Last night and this morning she'd been on too much of an emotional roller coaster to appreciate his rugged good looks, and anyway, after grabbing a coffee he'd pretty much vanished until now so she hadn't really thought about it. But after spending the day reading by the pool she felt more relaxed and more aware of her surroundings than she had in months, and now he was right there in front of her—and now she was looking—she could well see his appeal.

Taking a sip of wine and savouring the cool crisp flavours that rippled over her taste buds, she let her gaze drift over him with the detached appreciation of the photographer she was.

He had the kind of height and breadth that made her own five feet seven now rather gaunt frame feel unusually small, thick dark hair that was made for ruffling, and a pair of shoulders that looked strong enough to bear all manner of burdens. His back was broad and beneath the white T-shirt that stretched across it she could see his muscles flexing as he moved.

She leisurely lowered her gaze down over his waist, his very fine bottom and long tanned legs, and then let it wander back up again. There was an air of tightly controlled restraint about him, a latent strength and power, and she had a sudden memory of that body lying on top of hers, heavy and hard and strong...

Oh, what a crying shame her sex drive was all out of batteries, she thought dolefully as she watched him slowly turn round and give her a view of his front, because he really was magnificent.

If only she'd met him a year ago...

Nicky hadn't exactly bed-hopped before she'd hit the doldrums but she'd always liked men. She'd loved the thrill of new attraction and the whole host of possibilities it opened up, in particular that of hot delicious sex with men she respected and admired but could leave without a twang of the heartstrings.

So if she'd met Rafael a year ago she'd have flirted like mad and after gauging his amenability to the idea would probably have set about seducing him into her bed.

Not so now, though, because as she completed her perusal of his spectacular body and found herself looking into that gorgeous face once again did she feel even a glimmer of a spark? A tingle of lust? A flicker of heat? No, she did not, which was depressing in the extreme because if a man like this didn't do it for her, then who would?

Nicky stifled a sigh and lifted her glass to her lips again.

'Have you quite finished?'

The dry tone of Rafael's voice made her jump, and she coughed and spluttered as the wine went down the wrong way. And then she went bright red because, regardless of how she did or didn't feel about him, it was still mortifying to have been caught ogling him.

'Yes. Sorry,' she gasped, clasping a fist to her chest and giving it a good thump.

'Are you all right?'

'Wine,' she managed by way of explanation, and cleared her throat. 'I'm fine.'

He picked up a bowl from the table beside the barbecue, brought it over and set it down in front of her. 'Have a prawn.'

Nicky wasn't sure having a prawn was all that advisable when she'd evidently lost control of her oesophagus, but took one anyway. 'Thank you.'

She dipped it into the little pot of aioli, then sucked it into her mouth and opened her eyes wide in delight as the juicy taste of the sea and salt exploded on her tongue. 'Wow, these are amazing.'

'Local,' Rafael muttered, his gaze on her mouth and his jaw tightening. 'Expensive.'

She smiled. 'But worth every *céntimo*.'

He didn't say anything, just kind of growled and shrugged and continued to stare at her mouth.

A funny tense kind of silence stretched between them and Nicky was beginning to wonder whether she might have a blob of aioli on her lip or something, when Rafael suddenly frowned, gave himself a quick shake, then threw himself into the chair opposite her.

'So how has your day been?' he asked rather more curtly than she thought the question deserved.

'Idyllic,' she said, swiping a paper napkin from the box to wipe her fingers and dabbing her mouth just in case, and telling herself that she must have imagined the flash of tension and the curtness because as far as she could see there wasn't anything to get tense or curt about. 'Ghostly pale isn't really me so I've decided to work on my tan. Me and my bikini barely moved from the pool all day.'

A muscle started hammering in his jaw and she thought she heard him grit his teeth. 'Sounds great,' he muttered.

'It was,' she said, briefly wondering if his obvious displeasure was down to her hogging of his pool. 'Do you mind?'

'About what?'

'Me monopolising your pool.'

'Not at all,' he said, lifting his gaze back to hers and giving her a tight smile. 'Make yourself at home.'

'Thank you,' she said, and, unable to fathom what the inscrutability of his demeanour was about, decided to continue with the small talk he'd initiated before any more of that weird uncomfortable tension had the chance to return. 'And how has *your* day been?'

Rafael rubbed the back of his neck, let out what sounded like a deeply exasperated sigh and sat back. 'Fruitful.'

'In the literal or metaphorical sense?'

'Both.'

'How come?'

'I spent the whole day with my estate manager discussing plans for an early harvest.'

'I imagine you must have had a lot to catch up on.'

Rafael arched a quizzical eyebrow. 'Why would you imagine that?'

'Gaby said you haven't been here for months.'

'I haven't.'

'Why not?' It seemed a shame when the place was a little slice of heaven on earth.

'I've been busy with work.'

'And now you're less busy?'

'For the moment.'

'So you're on holiday too?'

The minute the words were out of her mouth Nicky wished she hadn't brought up the subject of holidays, because as Rafael fixed her with that startling green gaze of his and leaned forwards she had the feeling that she might be about to regret it.

'I suppose I am,' he said. 'And talking of holidays...' He paused and she automatically tensed because judging by the probingly intense way he was looking at her there was no 'might' about it. 'Tell me more about yours.'

'What about it?' she asked and inwardly winced at her faintly prickly tone.

'You're here by yourself.'

'Evidently.'

'And indefinitely.'

'Is that so surprising?' Her fingers tightened around the

stem of her wine glass as she wondered where he was planning to go with this.

He tilted his head and regarded her for a second. 'I suppose not, but don't you have work to get back to?'

She forced herself to relax before her defensive air piqued his evident interest in the reasons for her 'holiday' even more. 'Not right now,' she said, deliberately breezily. 'I'm freelance.'

'In what field?'

'I'm a photojournalist.'

'What do you specialise in?'

Not a lot at the moment, she thought darkly, and decided to focus on the Nicky of a year ago rather than the wreck she was at the moment. 'Human interest stuff mainly. Droughts. Conflict. Public protests. That kind of thing.'

'It sounds dangerous.'

Nicky shuddered as the incident that had sparked off the traumatic chain of events that had led her here flashed through her head. 'It can be. On occasion.'

'So why do you do it?'

Wasn't that the million dollar question? 'Because I love it,' she said, channelling her old self and dredging up the motivation and beliefs she'd started out with. 'I love the idea of capturing a split second in time for ever. The look on a face, the mood of a crowd...' She stifled another shudder. 'I know it's a cliché but I really do believe that a picture is worth a thousand words. I also believe in the justice of it, in showing people the truth and the story behind the headlines.'

Or at least she had done. Now, though, she wasn't sure what she loved about her work or what she believed in. 'Plus I'm good at it,' she added, because it was high time she started thinking positively.

'I'm sure you are,' he said, breaking eye contact to take

a prawn of his own and toss it into his mouth. 'How did you get into it?'

Released from that probing gaze, Nicky felt as if she'd been holding her breath and had just remembered to let it out. 'I entered a picture in a competition when I was ten and won,' she said, giving herself a quick shake to dispel the light-headedness.

'Impressive.'

'I was addicted. I entered a lot of photos to a lot of competitions.'

'And what did you win?'

'A then state-of-the-art SLR.'

'And it all went from there?'

She nodded. 'That camera became my most treasured possession.' A snapshot of her young self with the camera inevitably hanging round her neck flashed into her head and a wave of nostalgia rose up inside her. 'I took it everywhere with me. I'd spend hours just sitting and watching the light and even longer making pretty much everyone I came across pose for me. I must have irritated the hell out of them... Anyway,' she said, dragging herself out of the past and back to the present, 'eventually I went to journalism college, got a couple of assignments and things kind of took off after that.'

'That simple?'

She shook her head. 'No. Actually it took years and it was incredibly hard work.'

'It sounds fascinating.'

She sat back and lifted her eyebrows. 'Does it?' For her the fascination had worn off a while ago.

'To a mere businessman like me it does.'

Nicky's eyes widened and her jaw dropped at the understatement. 'A mere businessman? You?'

Rafael raised his eyebrows and lifted his glass of wine to his mouth. 'What's wrong with that?'

'Nothing. But from what I've heard there's nothing "mere" about you at all.'

He went still, his glass hovering an inch below his lips and his eyes fixed on her with a disconcerting intensity. 'Why? What have you heard?'

Heavens, what hadn't she heard? Beneath the full force of his unwavering gaze Nicky fought the urge to squirm—and where had *that* come from anyway?—and considered what she'd learned about him. Given that she and Gaby had been neighbours for two years, and close friends for the last one of those, she'd learned plenty.

She'd heard that Rafael was some kind of corporate troubleshooter and that he was brilliant at everything, whether it was business, languages or women. She'd learned that he was thirty-two, a control-freak workaholic who didn't know when to stop, and that he'd had a brief but disastrous marriage. She'd also discovered that, despite his apparently innate talent for identifying and fixing problems, much to Gaby's and her sisters' frustration, he channelled this talent into his business, and steered well clear of entangling himself in any trouble that might involve his siblings.

Not that she'd be spilling all that out, of course. If anyone revealed that they knew so much about *her* she'd have had them arrested on the grounds of an invasion of privacy. 'Oh, this and that,' she said vaguely, aware that he was waiting for an answer.

'So you and Gaby haven't been discussing me?'

He looked so unexpectedly and endearingly put out by the idea that Nicky found herself in the unusual position of grinning. 'Well, you may have come up once or twice in conversation.'

He grimaced. 'I don't know whether to be flattered or worried.'

'You should be flattered.'

The grimace eased. 'Why? What did she say?'

'That you're a corporate troubleshooter and you like solving problems,' she said, deciding that if she condensed the facts it wouldn't sound too stalkerish, and actually feeling relieved to be talking about him rather than herself. 'That you're very driven and that your successes are stellar, both with work and with women.' She paused and then added, 'Oh, and that you're divorced.'

Rafael winced and she instantly wondered exactly what had gone wrong with his marriage. 'So perhaps not quite so successful with women.'

Telling herself that she had no business wondering and even less asking when they barely knew each other, Nicky tilted her head and had to agree. 'No, perhaps not.'

'Gaby has been chatty,' he said dryly, twisting the stem of his wine glass between long brown fingers.

'She's fond of you. And proud.'

Her heart squeezed in the same way it had done every time Gaby had either sung her brother's praises or lamented his failings.

She really ought to be used to it by now because, while the envy she felt at Gaby and Rafael's evident closeness had taken her by surprise at first, she'd lived with it for as long as she'd known her neighbour. If anything, though, instead of lessening the envy had grown and, the more she'd listened to Gaby, offering words of either awe or sympathy depending on the circumstances, the more she'd come to realise that she didn't have anyone who knew her or whom she knew quite that well. And in the early hours of the mornings when she'd been unable to sleep she'd begun to wonder if she might not be in the state she was in if she too had had someone that close to turn to.

'It must be nice to have siblings,' she said a little wistfully as the image of a two-point-four family popped into her head.

'Don't you have any?'

'Nope,' she said, pulling herself together because there she went again, wishing for the impossible. 'It's just me and my parents.'

'Lucky you,' he muttered, then got up and headed to the barbecue.

As she watched him slap the steaks on the grill Nicky frowned. She'd always got the impression from Gaby that while there was frustration aplenty between the sisters and their brother there was also a lot of affection. 'Really?'

She heard him sigh. 'No, not really,' he said, leaving the steaks to sizzle and spit on the grill and returning to the table. 'They're fine. Except when they're hassling me.'

'Do they do that often?'

'More often than I'd like,' he said, sitting back down and taking a mouthful of wine.

'So what do you do about it?'

'Well, the last time it happened I came down here.'

The tone of his voice made her insides cringe. 'Which was when?'

He set his glass down and gave her a look. 'Yesterday.'

Oh, dear. 'Looking for a bit of peace and quiet?'

He nodded. 'Only to be attacked with *Don Quijote*.'

Nicky felt her cheeks flush with mortification. 'I really am sorry about that, you know.'

'Don't worry, it was infinitely less traumatic than the quadruple whammy of one mother, two sisters and an ex-girlfriend.'

As her blush receded Nicky resisted the urge to roll her eyes because if *that* was what he considered traumatic he should try what she'd been through in the last six months. She'd take a mother, two sisters and an ex over the ghastly effects of burnout any day. 'Which was highly traumatic, I imagine,' she said as sincerely as she could, which wasn't very.

He raised an eyebrow at her arch tone. 'It seemed so at the time. Especially on top of such a busy time at work.'

Nicky reined in her cynicism because everyone had their hangups and actually what made hers any worse than his? 'Do they often gang up on you?'

'My sisters?'

She nodded.

Rafael tensed a little and her curiosity rocketed. 'Not since I was about eight.'

'Why? What happened when you were eight?'

'I chose not to let it bother me.'

The words were spoken casually enough but she caught the almost imperceptible tightening of his jaw and for some bizarre reason her heart squeezed again, only this time she didn't think it was with envy. 'Did it work?'

'Beautifully,' he said dryly, and gave her an easy smile that thankfully made the squeeze release its grip on her heart. 'Trying to rile someone who won't be provoked isn't much fun. They very quickly lost interest and left me alone.'

'Ingenious.'

He shrugged. 'Not so much ingenuity as a need for self-preservation. Anyway it worked because we now get along pretty well.'

Fleetingly wondering if choosing not to let things bother him was a strategy he still employed to deal with difficult situations, but realising that there was no way she could ask such a personal question, Nicky decided it would be safer for her heart and its surrounding muscles to move on to more neutral ground. 'So what does corporate troubleshooting involve?' she asked, toying with her glass as the mouth-watering scent of sizzling steak drifted towards her.

'I sort out companies in difficulties.'

'What sort of difficulties?'

'Anything really. A board might have a problem with

staffing or be going through a tricky merger or there might be issues with the management. I go in wherever I'm needed and leave when I'm done.'

'So you fix things.'

'I do.'

'Have you ever failed?'

'Not so far.'

'Do you fix people too?' she asked as it suddenly occurred to her that he might be able to fix her. And then almost as quickly she dismissed the idea as ridiculous because, for one thing, why would he want to help her when he didn't even get involved with his sisters' problems? And for another she was pretty sure that no one could fix her but her.

He shuddered. 'Absolutely not.'

'Why not?'

'Because it would inevitably get…emotional…and therefore messy.'

'And you don't do emotion or mess,' she said with a nod because the way he'd hesitated, the way he'd just flinched, said it all.

'Not if I can help it.'

As Nicky wasn't particularly fond of either, emotional detachment when it came to personal relationships was something she could definitely identify with, but nevertheless…

'Not even for your sisters?'

'Especially not for them.' He frowned. 'I wouldn't even offer them advice.'

'Really?' she asked, becoming increasingly intrigued by these insights into family life because as an only child she knew nothing about the dynamics of siblings, and with parents who championed independence she'd become so self-reliant she couldn't remember a time she'd asked for advice about anything.

'Absolutely. If the advice I hypothetically gave them was

wrong I'd invariably end up being blamed and if it wasn't
taken then what would be the point of giving it in the first
place? It would be a no-win situation, not to mention an insanely frustrating one.'

There was a certain amount of logic to that, Nicky supposed, and frankly what did she know about how families
worked? 'Do they often ask you for advice?'

'They've learned not to,' he said darkly, and rose to head
over to the grill to flip the steaks.

'Well, I don't know about the others, of course,' she said,
remembering the long conversations during which Gaby
had bemoaned her brother's lack of emotional support, 'but
I think Gaby might appreciate being able to ask from time
to time.'

Rafael turned and shot her a humourless smile. 'Gaby's
the worst. She once asked me for advice years ago, which I
gave her. She didn't take it and when things didn't work out
she still blamed me.'

'Oh.' That Gaby had failed to mention. 'What happened?'

'You'll have to ask her. How long have you known her?'
he said, coming back to the table and reaching for the bottle
that sat in the middle of it.

'Two years.'

He poured her some more wine. 'Well, wait another thirty
and then you'll see.'

'I'll bear it in mind.'

'How did you meet anyway?'

'She lives next door to me.'

His eyebrows lifted as he topped up his own glass, then
sat down. 'In Paris?'

'That's right.'

'Yet you're British.'

And Gaby was Spanish. So what? 'It's a great place to be

based for the work I do,' she said, and told herself she really had to stop being so absurdly defensive. 'And yes, technically I'm British but I prefer to think of myself as a citizen of the world.'

He shot her a quizzical glance. 'Rootless?'

Hmm. Nicky tilted her head and pondered the question. She was certainly free and footloose. But rootless? She'd never really thought of it like that, but maybe Rafael was right because she'd been on the move for as long as she could remember.

Her parents had travelled extensively throughout her childhood—and still did—and she'd always gone with them wherever they'd been. As a result she'd never really had a base. She'd certainly never had a family home, or, come to think of it, a home of her own since. Even the flat she lived in now, with its minimalist décor and sparse furniture and general air of transience, was rented.

In fact the most permanent thing in her life was the suitcase she'd lived out of for the last ten years, a suitcase that was extremely well travelled and very battered but hanging in there. A bit like her, really.

'Perhaps,' she said, dragging her thoughts back on track and coming to the conclusion that Rafael was right about her lack of roots. 'And delighted to be so,' she added firmly, because that was about the only thing about her that hadn't changed in the last six months and it seemed important to remember it.

'Really?'

She nodded. 'Absolutely. I get itchy feet if I hang around in one place for too long. And the idea of staying in one place permanently...' She shuddered. 'Talk about stifling.'

'How come?'

'A by-product of my upbringing, I imagine.'

'Which was?'

'Internationally varied. My parents are anthropologists. They were—and actually still are—always heading off to investigate long lost tribes and things in far-flung places, and more often than not I accompanied them.' She paused and tilted her head. 'Remember that winning photo I took?'

Rafael nodded.

'It was of a Yanomami child. The Yanomami live in the Amazon rainforest,' she added in response to the quizzical look on his face. 'I was nine when I took it and it wasn't my first time in Brazil either. In fact, by the time I went to boarding school at the age of eleven, I'd got through three passports.'

'You've had an exciting life.'

She shrugged and felt her smile fade because lately it hadn't seemed quite so exciting. 'I've been lucky.'

There was a second or two of silence while he just looked at her and then he said, 'And yet with all that excitement you choose this place for a holiday?'

The words might have been spoken softly, but that didn't stop Nicky tensing. And it didn't stop a dart of wariness from flickering through her, because there it was again. The flash of perception—so similar to his sister's—in the dark green depths of his eyes, which told her that if she wasn't careful he'd be able to see far more of her than she wanted him—or anyone else—to.

'Well, why not?' she said, knowing she sounded on edge but feeling too unsettled to do a thing about it.

'It just seems a little sedate for someone so adventurous and globetrotting, that's all.'

Sedate was good, she thought, and determinedly pulled herself together. Sedate was exactly what she needed, so there was nothing wrong with sedate.

'Yes, well, adventure isn't always all it's cracked up to

be,' she said with as breezy a smile as she could manage, 'and sometimes even the most globetrotting of globetrotters needs a break, so thank you for inviting me to stay.'

CHAPTER FIVE

ALLOWING NICKY TO stay was the worst decision he'd made in years, thought Rafael grimly, staring out into the inky darkness of the night. What on earth had he been thinking? Had he *completely* lost his mind?

So much for all that peace and tranquillity he'd been after. And so much for all that rest and relaxation he'd hoped for. He'd never felt less peaceful, less tranquil, less rested or less relaxed. In fact, he was even more tense now than when he'd arrived and it was all entirely down to his unwanted house guest and the startlingly dramatic, insanely irritating effect she seemed to have on him.

How he'd ever managed to convince himself that he wasn't aware of Nicky he'd never know. Not aware of her? Hah. That was a joke. He must have been mad to even think it because over supper it had become pretty bloody obvious that he'd never been more aware of anyone, so since when did he do such complete and utter self-denial?

Rafael grimaced and knocked back another inch of his brandy. And to think that he'd blithely assumed he was doing so well. That his legendary self-control was fine. God, he was a stupidly arrogant idiot because he hadn't been doing well at all. He'd been doing dismally, and he hadn't even realised it.

He should never have suggested supper. If he'd known

what torturous agony *that* was going to be he'd have gone straight from the vineyards to his bedroom and stayed there until he was sure the coast was clear, but that was what hubris and the cook's weekend off could do to a man.

As a result, he'd had the most uncomfortable couple of hours he'd had in years, starting with the odd prickling he'd felt all over his skin when he'd been seeing to the steaks and had become conscious of the fact that Nicky was watching him.

He'd slowly turned, thinking that she might be mortified into jerking her gaze away, but was she? No. Those enigmatic blue-grey eyes of hers had continued to travel over him, languidly and totally unashamedly, and he'd been pinned to the spot, his body going into sensory overdrive and his head swimming.

But even then he'd just about held it together. Until he'd hit upon the idea of offering her a prawn in the foolhardy hope that moving on to food and small talk was the best way forward, and it had all gone downhill from there.

The prawns had been *such* a bad idea. There she'd sat calmly sucking them down and letting out those little soft moans while talking about her work, his siblings and her upbringing, and with every passing minute his head had got fuzzier and his body had wound tighter.

With his head filling with images of what Nicky might look like in nothing but a bikini as she lay by his pool, his stomach had twisted and his pulse had picked up until the desire he'd persuaded himself he'd conquered had slammed back with a force that had nearly floored him, and as hard as he'd tried he hadn't been able to stamp it out.

God only knew what they'd talked about after that because as night had descended he'd fallen more and more under her strangely hypnotic spell, until all he'd really been able to focus on was the way her mouth moved when she talked, the auburn streaks in her hair that the soft flickering candlelight picked out, and her funny little wistful smile.

Thank heavens she'd got up and announced she was off to bed when she had because he hadn't been sure how much longer he'd have been able to resist the growing pressure of desire.

It was completely baffling, he thought now, scowling down into his unexpectedly empty glass. He'd known her for less than twenty-four hours so how had things got so bad so quickly? When exactly had Nicky got into his head? And more importantly when exactly was she going to do the decent thing and get out? Because he really didn't want her in there.

For one thing, he absolutely did *not* need the hassle of a new affair so hot on the heels of the last disastrous one and, for another, what on earth was the point of wanting her when the attraction was so clearly one-sided?

Rafael set his glass on the table and let out a low growl of frustration. He'd had more than enough experience to rec-ognise the signs of mutual physical attraction, and Nicky hadn't displayed any of them at any point. Which he should have been fine with, seeing as he was no longer a hormone-ridden teenager but a mature rational man of thirty-two, so the fact that he *wasn't* apparently fine with it annoyed him even more.

What *was* going on? And what the devil was he going to do about it?

He leaned forward to pour himself another brandy with which to contemplate the dilemma, but he'd barely reached for the bottle when a yell tore through the warm still night.

The shock of it made his heart lurch and his arm freeze in mid-stretch, and the anguish in it made goosebumps break out all over his skin. All thoughts of unrequited lust fled from his head and instinct took over.

Shoving his chair back, Rafael leapt to his feet, his heart thundering and adrenalin pounding through his veins. He wanted to race indoors and charge up the stairs. He wanted to fling back the door to Nicky's bedroom and see if she was all right. He wanted to find out why she'd yelled, what was wrong with her, and why she was really here. He wanted all that with such sudden clamouring urgency that every inch of him was tense and tight, poised and ready to—

He froze in his tracks as reason suddenly swooped down and barged aside instinct, and his blood ran cold.

God, what the hell was he thinking?

No. Absolutely not.

He didn't *do* concern. He didn't *do* rushing to the aid of damsels whether in distress or not. And he definitely did *not* want to know what was wrong with Nicky or what had caused her to cry out.

He shoved his hands through his hair and swore beneath his breath. He hadn't been lying when he'd told her he didn't sort out other people's personal problems. He might have grown up constantly being told by his mother that as their only brother he had a duty to protect and look out for his sisters, but he'd never met a group of girls who needed looking out for less. And the women he'd met subsequently—bar one—only confirmed the conclusion he'd reached that the so-called fairer sex was emotionally far tougher than the men he'd come across, and more often than not didn't appreciate help with any issues they might have.

Steeling himself against the lingering urge to act on his instincts and go and check on her regardless, Rafael set his jaw and made himself sit down. Whatever was plaguing Nicky was none of his business, and whatever had made her yell like that was probably nothing but a bad dream. Besides, it wasn't his job to fix her, and judging by her defensiveness

when they'd been talking earlier he doubted she'd appreciate the interference.

So he was doing the right thing by leaving her alone, he
assured himself as he splashed some more brandy into his
glass. Nicky would be fine, and come the morning he'd have
forgotten all about it so there was absolutely no need to give
it any further thought.

Sitting back and downing half his drink, Rafael resolutely
put it out of his head and turned his attention to his vines.

Nicky woke up a second before she cracked her head on the
tarmac. As usual.

Once again she'd been trapped in the midst of a swirling
mass of humanity, the bright colours blurring her vision,
the thunderous noise deafening her and the increasing air
of menace intensifying the panic and fear rocketing through
her.

Once again she'd lost her balance and had desperately
tried to counteract the momentum of the crowd by grabbing
at air, at anything really, but with the crush of people pressing in and around her it was to no avail. And once again
she'd felt herself go down and had filled with the sickening
heartbreaking awareness that once she hit the ground she'd
never get back up...

At least she hadn't cried out, she thought, staring blankly
up into the jet black darkness of the night, her heart pounding, sweat pouring off her and her head swimming with the
horrible images that *still* haunted her sleep.

As mercies went it was a small one, but it was a mercy
nevertheless because she knew from past experience that she
was perfectly capable of letting out a yell that could wake the
dead. Or, at least, Gaby, who'd pounded on her door often
enough, demanding to know if she was all right.

If she'd yelled out this time Rafael would undoubtedly

have heard and very possibly would have rushed in to see what was wrong. So it was a relief she hadn't because she really wasn't up to explaining.

Willing her heart to steady and her breathing to slow, Nicky sighed and flung an arm over her eyes and reminded herself for what felt like the billionth time that the shakiness and the fear pounding through her would pass. As they always did.

But, God, she was sick of the whole sodding lot of it. She was sick of the lack of control she had over her subconscious, sick of the hold that something that happened months ago still had on her—and her inability to get over it—and sick of being so prickly and defensive all the time.

It had to stop. Today. Now.

But how?

As the turbulent images faded and her trembling stopped something Rafael had said earlier flickered through her head. Something about not letting things bother him. Or rather, about *choosing* to not let things bother him...

Well, that was what she'd do too, she thought with grim resolution, because she had a choice, didn't she? Maybe not about what went on while she was asleep, but while she was awake? That was a different matter entirely.

So today was going to be different. Today she was going to think positively and not dwell on the past. Today she'd choose not to care.

CHAPTER SIX

GUILT WASN'T A feeling Rafael was all that familiar with, but the guilt—and shame—he felt about not going to see if Nicky was all right last night was seriously beginning to grate.

So much for assuming he'd have forgotten all about it by this morning. He'd barely thought about anything else, because he might have gone to bed convinced he'd done the best thing by leaving her alone, and he might have congratulated himself on stoically resisting the urge to give in to his instincts, but over the course of the morning the doubts that had crept in overnight had intensified and nothing was making them go away. Not the knowledge that he had at least put his ear to her door on his way to bed, not the reassuring sounds of movement coming from her room at the crack of dawn, and not the jaunty whistling he'd heard coming from the landing moments before he'd shut the back door behind him.

Not even the hard physical work he'd engaged in in the vineyards had been enough to put it from his mind because, regardless of the consequences, he *should* have paid attention to his gut and checked up on her. Quite apart from it being the gentlemanly thing to do, Nicky was a guest in his home and therefore her welfare was technically his responsibility, however much he might not want it to be.

Which really left him with only one course of action, he

thought, narrowing his eyes and glowering at the blindingly white *cortijo* he was striding towards. Never mind that it directly contravened his policy of not getting involved. Never mind that it could potentially open up a whole messy can of worms. He had no option but to ask Nicky outright what was going on, and the sooner the better because the doubts and the guilt and the shame were driving him nuts and he didn't think he could stand any of it much longer.

Pushing open the back door he strode into the hall and briefly wondered where to start hunting for her. She shouldn't be too far away. If she wasn't in the house she'd probably be—

'Rafael?'

At the sound of her voice he automatically stopped and turned. And went still as all the blood rushed to his feet and his plan to clear his conscience shot clean out of his head.

Standing in the doorway of the kitchen, Nicky wasn't too far away at all. On the contrary she was uncomfortably close, and, in a bright red bikini top, a very short turquoise skirt that sat low on her waist and nothing else, her nose a little pink from the sun and her hair still semi-wet from the pool and hanging in thick waves to her shoulders, very very appealing.

Unable to stop himself, Rafael ran his gaze over her, over the swell of her breasts, pushed up and in by the bikini top, the dip of her waist, the flat abdomen and the flaring of her hips and then down to below the hem of the itsy-bitsy skirt and those long slim legs, which he'd envisaged wrapped around his waist so often in his dreams.

She looked like some kind of siren and as lust shot through him, so hot and fast it nearly brought him to his knees, he had the feeling that if he wasn't careful, if he didn't focus on what was important here, he could well find himself being lured to his doom.

Which wasn't nearly as ominous a notion as it ought to have been. In fact as he stood there staring at her, desire pounding through him and his head whirling, doom was looking increasingly tempting, and he had to ball his hands into fists to stop himself lunging for her because he was pretty sure that that kind of behaviour would get his face slapped.

With superhuman effort Rafael swallowed hard, ruthlessly deleted all images of sultry temptresses and entwined legs from his brain, and pulled himself together because wanting her was *not* why he'd decided to seek her out. 'What?' he muttered.

'I—' She stopped and looked at him with sudden concern. 'Are you all right?'

'Absolutely fine,' he said, frustration with himself making him sound brusquer than he'd have liked. 'What about you?'

'Me?' she asked, blinking up at him in surprise. 'Oh, I couldn't be better.'

Rafael frowned. 'Are you sure?'

'Of course,' she said, and flashed him an overly bright smile. 'Why on earth wouldn't I be?'

He thought he saw her smile falter for a second, but it was back in the blink of an eye and he couldn't be certain. 'Did you sleep well?'

'Fabulously.'

'Really?'

She nodded. 'Absolutely. It must be all this fresh air and sun.'

Hmm. He tilted his head and noticed the dark shadows beneath her eyes that belied her words. 'Right.'

'You sound sceptical.'

If it hadn't been for the guilt swilling around inside him, Rafael would have let it go, but if anything the guilt was growing so instead he braced himself and made himself say, 'I am.'

'Why?'

'Because in the middle of the night I heard a yell.'

Nicky's eyebrows shot up and she froze and for a moment there was such utter silence that he could hear the hum of a tractor he knew to be miles away. 'A yell?' she said at last, way too casually to be convincing.

'That's right.'

'And you thought it was me?'

'Who else would it have been?'

She shrugged and shifted her weight from one foot to the other while her gaze slid from his and focused on a point somewhere over his left shoulder. 'I've no idea. An owl perhaps?'

An *owl*? 'It was you. What happened?'

She bit her lip, dithered for a second and then clearly decided there was no point in denying it any longer. 'I had a bad dream,' she said with a dismissive wave of her hand. 'It was nothing.'

'It didn't sound like nothing.'

The smile she gave him this time was tight. 'Look, Rafael, I appreciate your concern, really I do, but I don't want to talk about it.'

'Don't you think it might help?'

'No,' she said firmly. 'It really was nothing, and I'd be grateful if you'd drop it.'

Rafael stared at her for a second, mulling over whether he should push her further for an explanation, but then mentally shrugged and did as she asked. He'd tried, but he could hardly force her to tell him, and anyway if it really *was* nothing then he didn't need to.

In fact he ought to be relieved she didn't want to discuss it. He'd done what he'd set out to do. By bringing the matter up he'd assuaged the guilt, and Nicky's request that he leave things alone reaffirmed his judgement that she wouldn't have appreciated the interference even if he *had* rushed to her aid, so he was completely off the hook. And he hadn't even had to mop up any messy emotional stuff.

So where was the relief? Where was the satisfaction? And why was he feeling faintly piqued by her reluctance to talk about what was troubling her instead of being pleased at such a successful outcome to his quandary?

'OK, fine,' he said, nodding and deciding to attribute the baffling—and faintly disconcerting—paradox to a long morning in the sun.

'Thanks,' she said, brightening considerably and shooting him a beaming smile that had desire once again rushing through him. 'You know, you're just in time.'

To do what? Succumb to her allure and his total mental collapse? Or pick her up, toss her over his shoulder and carry her up to bed? 'For what?' he said hoarsely, and cleared his throat.

'Lunch. Or what passes for lunch in my world.' Her mouth curved up into a funny little half-smile and his stomach felt as if someone had grabbed it and twisted. Hard. 'I'm not much of a cook, I'm afraid—not enough time spent in the kitchen probably—but I've cobbled a salad together from last night's leftovers and was wondering, would you like to join me?'

No was the answer he should have been looking for if he wanted to retain any kind of sanity, but clearly he didn't because all he could think right now was that he was hungry, her smile was as inviting as the idea of food and his brain was so addled with lust, confusion and frustration on top of the lingering pangs of guilt and shame he could barely remember his own name, let alone come up with some kind of suitable excuse.

'Sure,' he said and wondered what she'd think if he walked up to the wall and started banging his head against it. 'Why not?'

'It'll be five minutes.' She tilted her head and regarded him thoughtfully. 'In the meantime, why don't you take a dip? You look a bit hot and bothered.'

Watching her saunter back into the kitchen, Rafael resisted the urge to get up close and personal with that wall, and instead shoved his hands through his hair while calling himself all kinds of idiot for being so weak.

Maybe a long morning beneath the hot sun had resulted in more than just the paradox of being piqued instead of pleased that she didn't want to talk through her issues. Maybe it was also responsible for an evident meltdown of his brain cells, because one way or another Nicky was driving him demented, as was his total inability to know what to do about any of it.

Perhaps a swim wasn't such a bad idea, he thought darkly, heading upstairs to don his swimming shorts. The icy water of the pool would no doubt have the same effect as a cold shower, and it might even clear his head long enough for him to work out how to fix the exceedingly uncomfortable problem he was still facing.

Something had to be done, because he might have sorted out one dilemma but there still remained the issue of the unrequited lust he was suffering from, which if it continued any longer could well end up doing permanent damage to his body.

The question was, what to do?

Frowning as he began to assess the options, Rafael threw a towel over his shoulder and headed back downstairs. Taking care to avoid the kitchen and the dangers that lurked within, he stepped out onto the patio and strode along the path that led to the pool, frustratingly none the wiser.

He dropped the towel on a sun lounger, walked up to the edge of the pool and dived straight in.

Perhaps he should ask Nicky to leave after all, he thought, relishing the way the icy shock that hit his body obliterated the heat inside him, and beginning to scythe through the shimmering water as he made for the other end. Maybe *he* should leave, although frankly he didn't see why he had to when it was his house.

Or maybe, just maybe, he was going about this all wrong.

Rafael reached the end and surfaced. He rubbed the water out of his eyes and drew in a deep breath as a bubble of clarity burst in his head.

God, he was, wasn't he? He was going about this in *completely* the wrong way, and frankly if he conducted his business in such a manner he'd be bankrupt within weeks. Because how could he fix this—or any problem for that matter—when he wasn't in full possession of the facts?

As was very definitely the case here. He didn't have all the facts, did he? All he knew was the way *he* was feeling, the desire and need and longing *he* was burning up with. He had no idea how Nicky felt about anything. For all he knew she could be burning up in the same way he was.

OK, so she hadn't shown any sign of it so far, but then he was pretty sure he hadn't either, so she could well be just as crazed with lust as he was and equally adept at concealing it. After all she'd been eyeing him up yesterday evening at supper, hadn't she?

And if that *was* the case then maybe she was waiting for him to make the first move. Or maybe she was as baffled by all this as he was and was also struggling to work out what to do about it.

Hmm. Whatever Nicky was or wasn't doing, and frankly his head hurt just trying to work it out, he clearly needed a new, more obvious strategy.

* * *

So much for a new and more obvious strategy, Rafael thought darkly an hour later as he fought back the urge to grind his teeth.

Honestly, short of yanking Nicky into his arms and kissing the life out of her he didn't think he could have been more obvious.

Over lunch he'd hit her with his full arsenal of moves, which admittedly wasn't huge as he'd never had to work so hard to entice a woman into his arms, but nevertheless he thought he'd done his best.

He'd complimented her on the salad that hadn't been nearly as bad as she'd made out, and had then set out to be as attentive as he could. Although she'd been remarkably unforthcoming, he'd asked her dozens of questions about herself and her work, and had happily complied when she'd turned his questions back on him. He'd been genuinely interested and he thought she'd been the same.

Encouraged by that he'd shot her endless warm smiles, flashed her wide grins he'd been told were devastating, and been as charming as he knew how. He'd even left his T-shirt and shorts off after his swim to give her ample opportunity to ogle his near-naked body should she wish to do so.

But had any of it made even the faintest scrap of difference? No, it had not. There he'd been practically combusting with lust—not least because now he didn't have to imagine what she looked like in a bikini—and Nicky couldn't have been less bothered.

To his growing frustration she'd hadn't shown the slightest interest in his body and had been spectacularly undevastated by his smiles. In fact, at one point, after a wide, and, he'd thought, particularly blinding smile, she'd frowned and had had the cheek to ask him if he was feeling all right.

Now she'd settled herself on a sun lounger, was rubbing

suncream into the legs that had been haunting his dreams, and he was slowly going insane. Unable to drag his gaze away, he had a sudden vision of those hands roaming all over him, caressing every inch of him, and his body hardened.

With desire thrumming through him Rafael picked savagely at the label of the bottle of water they'd shared over lunch.

Dammit, why didn't Nicky find him as attractive as he found her? He'd been told he was reasonably good-looking and that his body wasn't too bad. He had all his hair, which was apparently something of a rarity in men over thirty, and, apart from the edginess he'd been feeling over the last couple of days, he was generally fairly even-tempered.

So what was wrong with her?

He glowered at the label for a second and then ruthlessly cut off that train of thought because it smacked of arrogance and petulance and those were two traits he hoped he didn't possess.

He didn't expect every woman to fall at his feet; it was just that quite a few had done in the years since his divorce, so it was frustrating—not to mention hugely unflattering—when he came across one he wanted who didn't.

With a growl of frustration Rafael abandoned the bottle and lifted his glass to his mouth instead. He let a cube of ice slide between his lips, crunched down on it and winced at the sudden hit of cold.

'Would you mind doing my back?'

Rafael jerked and choked on a chunk of ice. He coughed. Pounded his chest. Swallowed hard. And then as the implication of her words hit his brain his blood roared in his ears and his heart lurched so violently he nearly passed out.

God, she really was going to kill him. Because if the mere thought of his hands on her sent him into spasms of lust what would happen when he actually touched her for real? Which he was going to have to, of course, because what else could he do?

Slathering her in warm slippery cream might well unravel what was left of his self-control but he could hardly refuse. Not when lunch had been cleared away a while ago and he was doing nothing but trying not to watch her, picking at that damned label, crunching ice and slowly going out of his mind.

Rafael dragged in a deep steadying breath and told himself to calm down. All he had to do was think of Nicky as one of his sisters, whose backs he'd rubbed cream into loads of times in the past, and it would be fine.

'Not at all,' he muttered, getting to his feet and pulling his shorts on over his trunks in the hope it might disguise his body's reaction to her. As the cotton scraped over his sensitive skin he gritted his teeth and determinedly drummed up images of icicles and igloos.

With not a little discomfort he walked over, knelt down beside her and took the bottle from her outstretched hand, and tried not to jump when their fingers brushed.

'Thanks.' Nicky beamed up at him, then settled on her front and to his horror reached behind her and unclipped her bikini top.

It was fine, he told himself again, his jaw so tight he thought it might snap. It was just a back. A long smooth one, yes, but just a back. In the same way that that was just a bottom and those were just legs.

Except that they weren't because none of her was just anything. It was all slim. Toned. Perfect.

He drew in a breath and let it out agonisingly slowly in an effort to brace himself. He could forget trying to consider Nicky a sister because it wasn't working. And he could forget the icicles and igloos because they weren't working either. He was now thinking glaciers. Ice hotels. The Arctic.

All of which melted the instant he put his hands on the silky warm skin of her shoulders. At the feel of her beneath his palms as he slid them down her back, his senses shut out everything but her. The soft texture of her skin... The dizzying scent of the lotion as he smoothed it over her. The dazzling sight of all that bare hot flesh... The muffled sounds of her sighs...

He wondered what she'd taste like and his mouth watered with such longing that his knees nearly buckled beneath the onslaught of it all. His head swam and his body burned and he couldn't help letting out a deep ragged groan.

The sound of it, so rough, so desperate, snapped him out of the sensuous whirl and brought him crashing back to reality. He jerked his hands off her, snapped back and shoved them through his hair, not caring one bit that they were still covered in cream.

God. What was he doing? What was he thinking? Had he truly lost his mind? And could he even begin to hope she hadn't heard it?

Apparently not because she tensed a little and her breath hitched. 'Rafael, are you all right?' she murmured sleepily.

'Yes,' he muttered, totally thrown by the dizzying realisation that he'd been so wholly caught up in her. 'Why?'

'You sighed. Deeply.'

'I'm fine.'

She twisted her head round, squinted up at him and frowned. 'You don't look fine. You're glowering.'

'Just thinking,' he said, and told himself he really had to get a grip before all the need, confusion, tension and frustration that were swilling around inside him snapped and he did something truly insane like flip her over, get them both naked and then sink himself inside her.

Her eyebrows shot up. 'Heavens, about what?'

'Nothing,' he said sharply and lurched to his feet. 'You're done.'

'Thank you,' she said, wriggling slightly to refasten her top. Then she sat up and stared at him. 'It doesn't look like nothing. You look like you want to rip something apart with your teeth.'

Such as that bikini? The vision of Nicky writhing beneath him as he tore the red cotton from her body slammed into his head and practically robbed him of breath. Desire clamoured even harder at the flimsy barriers he'd erected and he had the terrifying feeling that he was losing the battle to contain it any longer.

'It's work, that's all,' he said, and took a quick unsteady step back because he had to get out of here now.

'Can I do anything to help?'

Yes. Quite a few things. 'No,' he said hoarsely.

'Oh, OK.' She frowned and bit that luscious lower lip and that was the last straw really. The lust he'd been struggling to keep at bay finally crashed through the barriers and his resistance evaporated beneath the force of it.

What the hell? He thought he'd been obvious, but clearly he hadn't been nearly obvious enough. And what did he have to lose? His self-control was already in tatters. His brain was already in shreds. What would a slap to the face do that she hadn't already done to him?

'Do you *really* want to know what the problem is?' he growled, way beyond the point of no return to question the wisdom of his actions.

Nicky nodded. 'I do.'

He reached down, wrapped his hands around her arms and hauled her to her feet. '*This* is what my problem is,' he muttered, barely registering her splutter of shock as he pulled her against him.

He buried one hand in her hair, clamped the other to the

small of her back, and as she gasped crushed his mouth
down on hers. He plunged his tongue between her parted
lips, the desire racing along his veins, burning through his
blood and setting fire to his guts. She tasted just as good as
he'd imagined. Like honey. Like heaven. And she felt soft
and lithe, fitting into his body as if made for him.

His head spinning with dizzying need, Rafael groaned
into her mouth and pulled her even tighter against him. He
angled her head and deepened the kiss, his relief at finally
having her where he wanted her making him so giddy that it
was some time before he realised that she wasn't responding.

But she wasn't, he realised dazedly, easing the pressure
of his mouth and softening the kiss. She was just sort of…
there. Hanging limply in his arms. Completely inert.

Her heart wasn't hammering like his, dammit, her body
wasn't plastering itself uncontrollably against his and her
breathing wasn't all ragged and shaky. She clearly wasn't
being rendered boneless by the experience as he was, which
meant that for the first time since confusing lust for something more and proposing to Marina he'd just made a grave
error of judgement.

Rafael jerked back, let her go and as he stared down at her
stunned expression it all became abundantly clear.

Nicky *didn't* feel the same way about him. She *hadn't*
been waiting for him to make the first move, and she hadn't
been baffled or struggling or any of the other things he'd
thought she might have been doing. It had all been in his
wildly overactive, desperately hopeful and seriously deluded
imagination.

In other words he'd been a complete and utter fool.

CHAPTER SEVEN

OH MY GOD, thought Nicky in astonishment, touching her mouth and staring wide-eyed at Rafael as he took a step back and raked his hands through his hair.

What on earth had *that* been all about?

One minute, faintly concerned by the strangled groan he'd let out while rubbing cream into her shoulders, she'd been politely enquiring after his health, the next she'd been dragged into his arms and had the life kissed out of her.

And why would he do that? she wondered dazedly before her head cleared of the shock and the dizziness, and the only feasible answer came to her. Surely he couldn't *fancy* her, could he?

No. It was impossible. He'd shown no indication that he did. In fact, what with the whole braining him business and the way he'd kept himself so busy over the last twenty-four hours and—with the exception of supper last night—very definitely out of her way, she'd got the impression that she was more of a nuisance than an attraction. Which she could well understand because she hadn't exactly been the ideal house guest so far.

Yet there was no denying the intensity and the passion behind that kiss. She could still feel the heat of his mouth moving over hers, the pressure of his hands on her body and the tension that had vibrated through him. She could still feel his tongue sliding between her lips and tangling with hers with the kind of skill and focus that her former self would have revelled in. And she could most certainly still feel the hard length of the erection that had been throbbing so insistently against her abdomen.

Good heavens, she thought, blinking in surprise as it became pretty obvious that he did, in fact, want her. Who'd have imagined…?

If she'd given it much thought, which she hadn't, it would never have occurred to her that someone fancying her at the moment was possible. Why would anyone—especially a man like Rafael who could presumably have whichever woman he chose—when she looked like a wreck and felt about as attractive as a sack of potatoes? But as bizarre as it seemed, all the evidence suggested that was indeed the case.

So was *that* what lunch had been all about? Was that why he'd switched on the charm and shot her so many warm blinding smiles she'd had to slip on her sunglasses? Had she been *flirting* with her?

God, maybe it was and maybe he had. And like the hopeless idiot she'd become she hadn't had a clue about any of it. She'd taken his attention at face value, and, feeling so deliciously relaxed and so inordinately grateful that he'd respected her request to leave the subject of her nightmare alone, had casually returned his smiles and fielded his questions as if talking to an old friend.

Not only that but she'd asked him to rub cream into her back. She'd even taken her bikini top off, for heaven's sake. No wonder he'd flipped.

Oh, what a mess, she thought as despair and mortification flooded through her. What a horrible awkward mess. Rafael wanted her. Unfortunately she didn't want him. Where on earth did they go from here?

But before she could even begin to work out whether she

ought to offer him some sort of explanation for her lack of response, Rafael broke the excruciating tension.

'I do apologise,' he said with an icy cool formality that knocked her off balance for a second and had her suddenly wondering if maybe she'd got it all wrong. If maybe she'd imagined the scorching heat and the passion that had been pouring off him only a minute ago because there was absolutely none of *that* left, was there? Nor was there any sign of the raw, out-of-control desperation she'd sensed in him when he'd been kissing her. In fact the man standing in front of her with the blank expression on his face, the shutters down over his eyes and the air of tight self-control surrounding him was almost unrecognisable, and to be honest she found the abrupt switch perplexing and not a little disconcerting.

'Whatever for?' she said, dragging herself back to what he'd said and thinking that if anyone had to apologise, surely it was her.

'Assaulting you,' he said flatly. 'It was unforgivable. I'm sorry.'

What? 'Assaulting me?' she echoed her eyebrows lifting as the feeling of having stepped into an alternate reality grew. 'You didn't assault me. You kissed me. There's a difference.'

'Is there?' The flatness of his voice suggested he didn't agree.

'Of course.'

He shoved his hands in the pockets of his shorts and his jaw tightened. 'You didn't respond.'

And that made him think he'd assaulted her? Hmm, however unpalatable an in-depth explanation for her lack of response might be, she couldn't let him think that. 'Well, no,' Nicky admitted, 'but that wasn't your fault.'

'Wasn't it?'

'No.' She shook her head vehemently and gave him a

faint smile. 'I mean, let's face it, you're gorgeous and most women would have swooned at that kiss.'

'But not you.'

Her smile faded. 'No. But really, it's not you. It's me.'

She didn't think it would be possible but Rafael went even stiller and his jaw tightened even more and she inwardly cringed because it might be true but it was still one of the most hackneyed lines on the planet. 'It really *is* me,' she added, but that didn't sound any better.

'Forget it,' he said with a dismissive shrug.

'I can't,' she said, 'because you have no idea how much I *want* to find you attractive.' He winced and she sighed in despair because instead of making things better she was only making them worse. 'If you'd just let me explain…'

'You don't have to explain anything.'

'I do.'

'There's really no need.'

'I think there is.'

And then his stonily blank mask slipped for a second, his eyes suddenly flashing as he glowered at her. 'Look, Nicky,' he snapped and she jumped. 'For the briefest of moments I found you attractive. Maybe it was the heat. The wine. Or the sun. Whatever. It was an error of judgement on my part, a mistake and an aberration. I apologise for it and you can be sure it won't happen again, but it really doesn't warrant discussion.'

'Yes, it does—' she began, but broke off when he whipped up his hand to put a halt to whatever she'd been about to say.

'No. This morning you asked me to leave the subject of your nightmare alone. Now I'm asking you to return the courtesy. So please. Just leave it.'

'But—'

'Now.'

At the hard, unyielding tone of his voice Nicky fell silent.

She looked at him for a long few seconds and then gave up. What was the point of trying to force an explanation and an apology onto him when he was in such an unreceptive frame of mind? There'd be plenty of time for that later anyway, once they'd both had a chance to cool down and reflect. Although frankly, if Rafael got any cooler he'd qualify for cryogenic preservation.

'OK. Fine,' she said grudgingly. 'I'll drop it.' *For now.*

'Good,' he said curtly and swiped up his T-shirt. 'Now please excuse me. There are things I need to see to.'

The distant sound of her mobile ringing in the kitchen filtered through the haze of her sleep-filled siesta, and Nicky yawned and stretched. She got up and padded down the stairs, her head beginning to spin yet again with the strange turn of events that the afternoon had taken.

So much for attempting to explain her behaviour, for trying to apologise. She'd done her level best, she really had, but for some reason Rafael had thwarted her every attempt.

In fact she probably shouldn't have bothered to try in the first place, she thought as she headed in the direction of the increasingly loud ringing, because hadn't he told her that he steered well clear of emotional mess? He had, so presumably the last thing he was hankering after was a spilling out of her soul, and in that they were in perfect agreement. Actually, apart from Gaby, it was about the only thing she and Rafael *did* have in common.

And as they were never going be anything more than the merest of acquaintances she really didn't need to waste any more time worrying about it. She had no need to ponder the odd way he'd gone from scorchingly hot to icily cold by the pool. No need to question the steely indifference he'd chosen to adopt, and no need to try to work out what was going on in his head any more than he needed to try and work out what was going on in hers.

No, she needed to pour all her energy to recovery. Recovery and staying well out of his way.

Spying her phone vibrating on the huge scrubbed pine table that sat in the centre of the kitchen, Nicky walked over, picked it up and hit the little green button. 'Hello?'

'Nicky!' came the relieved shriek down the phone, and at the sound of Gaby's voice she pushed all thoughts of perplexing men to one side and felt herself smile.

'Well, hello, stranger,' she said, pulling out a chair and sitting down.

'God, I'm sorry. I lost my phone and all the numbers and *everything* and it's taken an age to get a new one.'

'So that's why I couldn't get hold of you.'

'No one's been able to. It's been a *total* pain.' As Gaby's entire life was contained in her phone, Nicky could imagine her distress.

'How's Bahrain?'

'Hot. And depressingly dry, in all senses of the word. But more importantly, how are you?'

Hmm. Now wasn't that the question of the century? Quite honestly, what with everything that had been going on lately Nicky wasn't sure she knew any more. 'Fine,' she said in the absence of having any idea what else to say.

'Really?'

'Well, getting there,' she amended as it suddenly struck her that maybe she was. Maybe the *cortijo had* begun to work its magic, because, now she thought about it, of all the emotions that had been churning through her in the last couple of days—and there'd been plenty—despair and desolation had been conspicuous by their absence.

'Good. And how are your chakras?'

She thought about it a bit more and felt surprisingly light, as if the dark heavy weight she'd been carrying around for so long was beginning to lift a little. And then her smile deepened as the light at the end of that tunnel glowed a fraction brighter. 'Beginning to align, it would seem.'

'Hah,' said Gaby triumphantly. 'I knew it. God, I'm good.'

Nicky sat back in the chair, lifted her knees and planted her heels on the edge of the seat. 'Not that good,' she said dryly, wrapping her arm around her ankles and hugging her knees to her chest. 'I thought you swore your brother never came down here.'

'He doesn't. Or at least he hasn't for ages.'

'He does now.'

There was long, rather stunned silence. 'Rafa's there?'

'Yes.' At least she imagined he was. Probably seeing to those 'things' that had suddenly demanded such urgent attention.

'Good Lord. Why?'

Nicky paused and racked her brains because she could hardly tell Gaby her brother had been escaping his sisters. 'I think he was after a bit of rest and relaxation,' she said vaguely.

Gaby blew out a breath. 'Oh, I *am* sorry.'

'Why? It's not your fault.'

'No, I guess not. I mean, I did try and contact him, but he wouldn't answer any of my calls and he didn't reply to any of my emails…It never occurred to me he'd actually show up, though.'

'Well, he did,' Nicky muttered, catching sight of a slip of paper propped up against the vase of flowers sitting in the centre of the table. She leaned forwards to read the short note and then sat back and frowned, not at all sure what to make of it. 'But now it seems he's gone.'

There was a pause. 'Gone? Gone where?

'Back to Madrid.'

'Why?'

An excellent question. 'Work, according to the note I've just found.'

There was a moment's silence while Gaby processed the information. 'That doesn't make any sense at all.'

'Well, it is Sunday,' said Nicky, propping the piece of paper back where she'd found it. 'So I guess he had to get back for Monday.'

'But it's August,' said Gaby, sounding utterly baffled. 'No one works in August.'

Nicky bit her lip and tried to ignore the niggling suspicion that he'd planned to stay longer than just the weekend and had it not been for her he'd still be there. 'Apart from Rafael apparently,' she said, and then added as much to reassure herself as Gaby, 'You said yourself that he's a workaholic.'

Gaby sighed. 'That's true, I suppose. What else did his note say?'

'Not a lot. Just that I'm to enjoy the rest of my holiday.'

'I second that… So tell me everything. How did Rafael take you being there?'

Nicky grimaced as snapshots of the last couple of days flashed through her memory. 'I don't think he was entirely happy about it.' Which had to be the understatement of the century.

'No, well, he only has himself to blame,' said Gaby huffily. 'If he'd bothered to get in touch I could have explained everything.'

'It was fine,' said Nicky and hoped she wouldn't be struck down for the little white lie. 'Rafael spent most of the time talking to his vines and I've spent most of it reading by the pool. And that's—er—about it.'

Gaby hmmed sceptically. 'Now why do I get the feeling you're not telling me everything?'

Probably because Nicky sounded as guilty as hell, even

though she didn't really have anything to be guilty about. But heavens, now really wasn't a good time for Gaby to have one of her flashes of insight, because she was, after all, Rafael's sister, and, while Nicky didn't have any siblings so she didn't know for sure, she doubted Gaby would feel comfortable knowing exactly what had gone on by the pool any more than *she* would be discussing it.

'Nicky?'

She stifled a sigh and ran a hand through her hair. 'I can't imagine,' she said and cringed because it would have been hard to sound less convincing.

'Could it be because you're being uncharacteristically evasive?'

Nicky could virtually see her friend's antennae quivering, and pinched the bridge of her nose. 'I'm not being evasive,' she said. Evasively.

Gaby sucked in a breath and then said in a steely voice that Nicky had never heard before, 'What did he do?'

Nicky felt herself go bright red and thanked God Gaby wasn't around to see it. 'Nothing.'

'Rubbish. I know my brother. Did he make a pass at you or something?'

She wriggled in her chair and thought that however uncomfortable it made either of them, she'd have to come clean because one thing she'd discovered about her neighbour was that she might be all about balance and peace and chakras but she could be ruthlessly relentless in her pursuit of the truth when the mood took her.

'It was just a kiss,' she said lightly. 'That's all. Rafael kissed me, we had a—ah—little chat about it, and then at some point between then and now he must have gone.'

Long seconds of silence ticked by. So many of them, in fact, that Nicky wondered if they'd been cut off. 'Gaby? Are you still there?'

'I'm here.'

'Did you hear what I said?'

'I did.'

'And are you reassured?'

There was a pause and then it was as if Gaby sort of exploded. 'Reassured? *Reassured?* Are you joking? I'm not reassured in the least. In fact I'm going to kill him,' she spluttered. 'I'm going to bloody kill him.'

Rafael slammed closed the door to his flat, dumped his things in the hall and headed straight to the fridge for a cool refreshing beer. Flipping off the lid, he lifted the bottle to his mouth, leaned back against the counter and took a long swallow.

God, what an afternoon.

As the harrowing memory of it slammed back into his head for the thousandth time since he'd packed up and left he closed his eyes and let out a long deep breath.

How could he have got it all so badly wrong? How could he have so totally lost control like that? How could his rock-solid resistance to temptation have vaporised quite so comprehensively?

His behaviour had been unfamiliar, unexpected and completely unprecedented. And as for the primal urge to stake some sort of claim on Nicky, the one that had surged through him and had made him reach down and grab her, well, that had simply been as scary as hell.

At least in the aftermath of the kiss he'd managed to wrestle back *some* degree of control, he thought with a shudder. At least he hadn't high-tailed it to the safety of his vines as he'd been so tempted to do, but instead had stayed there, strong and resolute and in control. And at least he hadn't revealed any of the turmoil and confusion and still-scorching desire that had been churning through him. That really would have finished him off.

Yes, cool indifference and a refusal to let her speak had been the right way to handle it because he'd had no intention of engaging in a discussion about what had happened and he certainly hadn't wanted her to rake over the way he'd behaved or analyse his many deficiencies.

Leaving had been a good idea too because, for one thing, Nicky might have agreed to back off but the look in her eye had been fiercely determined and he'd got the impression she was planning to revisit the discussion at the first available opportunity.

For another, he might not have wanted to admit it, but her rejection of him had hurt and he didn't really need to be constantly reminded of it every time he laid eyes on her.

And lastly, with his self-control in such bits he couldn't guarantee that kissing her wouldn't happen again, and if that wasn't the most terrifying thought on the planet he didn't know what was.

So he'd walked away from her with what little pride he'd had left, utterly exhausted and defeated and struck by the realisation that finally, *finally* he'd reached breaking point.

Rafael sighed and rubbed a hand over his face. It had truly been the most shattering, frustrating, painful weekend he'd had in years and frankly he couldn't wait to see the back of it.

At least it was nearly over, he told himself, glancing up at the clock. He'd use what was left of it and the rest of the beer in the fridge to wipe it from his head, and put Nicky out of his mind once and for all. Then all the stuff churning around inside him would settle down, things would get better and he'd start to feel normal again.

With any luck.

The sound of his phone ringing jerked Rafael out of his thoughts. He dug it out of his pocket and as he glanced at the screen he inwardly groaned because apparently things weren't going to get better just yet.

Resisting the temptation to ignore the call because look at what had happened the last time he'd done that, he hit the answer button and lifted the phone to his ear.

'Gaby,' he said, and took another swig from the bottle. 'Good of you to get in touch. How's Bahrain?'

'Don't you give me any of that good-of-you-to-get-in-touch-how's-Bahrain crap,' said his sister, sounding so uncharacteristically fierce that he tensed, every one of his instincts instantly jumping to high alert. 'What I want to know is, what the hell did you do to my friend?'

Carefully setting down his beer, Rafael forced himself to relax and stay cool. 'I take it you've spoken to Nicky.'

'I've just got off the phone to her.'

'How is she?'

Gaby blew out a furious breath. 'Oh, she's fine. Just fine, considering… Me, though, I'm in a state of shock.'

He closed his eyes for a second and ignored the urge to hang up and blame it on a low battery. 'Why? What did she say?'

'That you'd kissed her.'

'I see.'

Gaby spluttered a bit more. 'Is that it?'

Rafael stifled a sigh. 'What else do you want me to say? You seem to know everything already.'

'Not everything,' she said furiously. 'One thing I'd really like to know is, how *could* you?'

Pretty easily, he thought, as the memory of Nicky in his arms and how she'd got there flashed in his head. Stamping down on the sudden surge of desire that rushed through him, he forced himself to focus on the conversation.

'What's your problem, Gaby? Why the outrage?'

In contrast to him Nicky hadn't seemed particularly upset

by the kiss earlier so what was his sister so het up about? Had Nicky had time to reflect and reached the same conclusion that he had? Had she decided that he had in fact taken one hell of a liberty, and said as much to Gaby? 'It was only a kiss,' he muttered as a sense of unease and a ribbon of self-disgust wound through him.

'That's precisely the problem,' his sister said vehemently. 'Nicky does *not* need kissing. She's in enough of a mess as it is without you adding to it.'

Rafael frowned. 'What kind of mess?'

'It's not for me to say.'

'Gaby...'

'No. She asked me not to. But it's serious.'

A chill ran through him. 'Is she ill?'

'No. At least not physically, I don't think. But what I *will* say is that she's been going through a really rough time lately and could do with a bit of head-space. She needs a break and time to get herself back together. Alone.'

And just like that, as if he didn't have enough to contend with, a bucketload of guilt landed on top of all the frustration and desire and self-recrimination, and his head began to pound with the force of it.

God, he should have realised something wasn't quite right with Nicky. In fact, he had, hadn't he? Within five minutes of meeting her he'd noticed the paleness of her face and the fact that she was a little too thin. He'd seen the way she'd tensed up when they'd talked about her work yesterday evening at supper, and he'd registered the way she'd been so reticent to talk about herself today at lunch. And then what about that nightmare she'd had, and he'd conveniently let drop?

Yes, all the signs that she wasn't entirely OK had been there. And what had he done? He'd paid it all the barest attention and then like a self-centred jerk switched his focus to himself, completely consumed by the heat and desire she'd

aroused in him and outraged by the fact that it wasn't reciprocated.

And then he'd jumped on her.

As yet more self-disgust unfurled in the pit of his stomach
and spread throughout his body Rafael wished he'd never
made the decision to head south. He wished he'd stayed
right here and suffered whatever torture that dinner party
might have held, whatever lengths Elisa might have gone
to to make him change his mind, because frankly none of
it would have been as unpalatable as having to live with the
knowledge that his behaviour over the last forty-eight hours
was nothing to be proud of.

'Well, I'm back at home,' he said flatly, 'and as I have no
intention of laying eyes on her ever again, Nicky can have
all the head-space she needs.'

CHAPTER EIGHT

MUCH TO HER surprise, Nicky was enjoying the rest of her so-called holiday immensely. Whether it was because the *cortijo* was so quiet and tranquil it was impossible not to relax, or whether it was because Rafael was no longer around to bamboozle her poor frazzled brain, she had no idea. All she knew was that in the fortnight since he'd left, she'd settled into something of a routine that largely revolved around eating, sleeping, reading and sunbathing, and she was feeling better than she had in ages.

The Monday following his stealthy departure Maria had returned after her weekend off and had resumed her mission to feed Nicky up. A seemingly never-ending stream of dishes had appeared, each so mouth-wateringly appetising that Nicky couldn't have resisted even if she'd wanted to. Slivers of melt-in-the-mouth *jamón*. Little earthenware pots of sizzling hot green peppers. Bowls of steaming paella. Strong crumbly manchego cheese. Spicy chorizo, sun-warmed tomatoes picked straight from the vines and freshly baked bread... She devoured it all and as a result had put on a few pounds, which she reckoned suited her.

Filled with good food, she'd been sleeping a lot better. Once she'd got used to the creaks and groans of the two-hundred-year-old house, she found the silence of the night comforting, and tended to crash out the minute her head hit the pillow. Not stirring until dawn, she enjoyed a sleep that was deep and restorative and nightmare-free.

Well, *almost* nightmare-free. She'd had it again once a week ago, triggered, she suspected, by a phone call from her therapist who was ringing to see how she was, but that was it. Most nights she seemed to dream of Rafael, which was bizarre given that he barely crossed her mind during the day.

Feeling physically so much stronger, Nicky had taken to exploring. The minute she opened the shutters to the coral pink streaks slashing across the sky, she was up, showered and dressed and heading outside into the relative cool of an Andalucian August morning.

As the sun inched higher she wandered up and down the rows of vines, letting the heady scent of ripening grapes and dry, dusty earth envelop her and feeling the warmth of the soil beneath her flip-flops stealing right into the depths of her bones and absorbing the cold that had been there for so long.

She'd got into the habit of having a nap after lunch, then spent the afternoons swimming and reading. In the evenings she sat on the terrace, looked out over the gently rolling landscape, nibbled on tapas and drank wine, the warm night air vibrating with the chirrup of cicadas and redolent with the scent of mosquito-busting citronella.

Not only had she been sleeping—and looking better—but she'd also tentatively been getting back in touch with friends and colleagues. Yesterday she'd even emailed her parents to find out where they were and how they were getting on.

Best of all, this morning she'd woken up, seen the fabulous light that she saw every morning, and without even thinking about it had picked up her camera. Her body buzzing with anticipation and her heart racing, she'd gone outside into the vines as usual, but, instead of idly ambling through them and thinking about nothing, this time she'd found herself automatically studying the way the light fell on the fat ripe grapes and bounced off the browning crumbling leaves, and focusing on contrast, angles and composition.

She'd rattled off a series of pictures and before she'd known it the sun was high in the sky and she was sweltering and dirty and aching all over. And she'd never felt so good, so giddy with delight, so *relieved*.

All she had to do now, she thought, pulling her eye mask down and settling against the pillows for her customary siesta, was wait for her libido to come back and she'd be well and truly on the road to recovery.

There was someone in the house.

Jolted out of the deep sleep she'd been enjoying, Nicky sat bolt upright in bed and tore off her eye mask, her pulse hammering, her blood roaring in her ears, and every one of her instincts quivering with awareness.

The slam of the front door echoed off the walls and the heavy thud of footsteps pounding up the stairs resounded through the house, shaking the *cortijo*'s foundations and rattling the windows.

Her ears pricked. Each step seemed to hit the floor in time to her heartbeat, getting closer, louder, faster as they thumped along the corridor, making straight for her room. Her stomach churned and she went dizzy.

It was just like before, she thought, her breath catching. Only this time it was the middle of the day. This time she wasn't white-knuckled and terrified. This time she wasn't frantically hunting around for a weapon and trembling with panic. And yes, her heart was pounding, but it wasn't with fear; it was with something else entirely because those footsteps sounded familiar. Very familiar. And even though they'd been gone a while now they were, apparently, back.

Before she could even begin to try and work out why, her

door flung back and there was Rafael, standing in the space where it had once been, looking haggard and drained, but dark and intense and utterly gorgeous nonetheless.

For one agonisingly long moment neither of them spoke. On Nicky's part, her head had gone so blank that all she could do was stare at him. And as for Rafael, she somehow got the impression that he didn't trust himself to speak. He looked to be barely clinging onto his control, as if it were taking every ounce of his strength to stay where he was. He looked like a man at the end of his tether. Like a man on the edge, and the rush of heat that swept through her made her entire body shudder and a thousand shivery little thrills scuttle up and down her spine.

Her eyes locked with his, held, and her heart skipped a beat at the fire that blazed in their depths.

'What are you doing back here?' she said, her mind spinning because no reason she could think of for his return seemed likely.

'I couldn't stay away,' he said hoarsely, his jaw tight as he stared back at her. 'I tried. But I couldn't.'

Nicky swallowed to work some moisture into her desert-dry mouth. 'Oh,' she breathed. 'Why not?'

'I can't get you out of my mind,' he said raggedly. 'You're driving me crazy.'

'What do you want me to do about it?' she said, her voice sounding oddly husky while her heart pounded so madly she thought it might break free.

And then the taut mask of his expression collapsed and the raw naked desire that was revealed nearly made her swoon. 'Put me out of my misery.'

The sizzle in the pit of her stomach flared into life and exploded, rushing through her veins like a tidal wave, drowning out all rational thought and dissolving her bones.

Somehow managing to get to her feet, Nicky slowly

walked over to him, and smiled as she took his hand and drew him towards her. She took a step back, he took one forwards and like that they tangoed towards the bed she'd just slid out of, their gazes bound by an invisible thread of want, barely touching, yet generating so much electricity that she could feel the air vibrate with it.

The backs of her knees hit the edge of the mattress, but he didn't stop and as he came up against her and took her in his arms she wound her arms around his neck and lifted her head. He lowered his and their mouths met. Opened. Fused.

She closed her eyes and sank into him and what had started as a slow, seductive meeting of mouths deepened, grew more passionate, more frenzied.

Electrifying desire shot through her and, unable to stop herself, she pressed herself closer and moaned into his mouth. Lost in a whirlpool of sensation, she felt him ease her back and down onto the bed and then clothing disintegrated and his hands were everywhere, sliding over her burning skin and touching and exploring every inch of her, her neck, her breasts, her stomach and then the molten, aching centre of her.

His mouth followed, creating devastation wherever it roamed, and within minutes she was moaning his name, writhing and panting and tilting her hips, her insides winding into an impossibly tight knot.

As wave after wave of sensation cascaded over her, Nicky groaned. Whimpered. Whispered in his ear and raked her nails across his back as she told him what she wanted.

And then he was above her and pushing inside her. Moving slowly at first but soon, with her pleas for more filling the room, driving in and out of her faster and harder, making her whole body tighten and tremble until she couldn't bear the pleasure any longer and—

Nicky woke with a start, her heart pounding, her breathing ragged, her skin coated in sweat and her insides adrift.

Oh, dear God. What was *that*?

She whipped her eye mask off, winced at the sudden flood of bright light that hit her eyes and then rapidly blinked. Which might have helped her eyes adjust, but did nothing to clear her head of the erotic images swimming around it, nor anything to dispel the tingles of residual pleasure that were rippling through her body and telling her that it could well have been what she thought it was.

Groggily levering herself up, she sat there stunned for a moment or two, then, taking a couple of deep breaths to try and clear her head and calm down, she braced herself and looked down at her T-shirt-and-knicker-clad body. Down to where the skin of her chest was flushed, her nipples were rock hard and her stomach and her legs were still twitching.

Heavens, she thought in astonishment, pressing her palms to her cheeks and feeling them burn even more fiercely at the dawning realisation that there was no longer any doubt that it had been *exactly* what she thought it was.

Well, well, well…

She flopped back and felt a wide smile spread across her face as she stretched and revelled in the unfamiliar lethargy of her body. Details of what she and Rafael had done in her sleep flitted through her head, in vivid Technicolor and spectacular clarity, and her smile deepened as heat flooded through her all over again.

Oh, thank *God*. It looked as though her much-missed sex drive was back. And about time too because she'd been beginning to fear it might *never* happen. Despite her secret efforts to encourage it…

The way her libido had reappeared might have been somewhat startling but that her dream had featured Rafael didn't surprise her in the slightest. When he'd initially gone she'd pretty much completely cast him from her mind, but at some point over the last fortnight he'd started to invade her thoughts with increasing frequency.

She'd found herself recalling the heavy weight of him lying on top of her flat out on the floor, that first night. Or remembering how well his T-shirt had stretched across the muscles of his back when he'd been lighting the barbecue and preparing the steaks.

In her mind's eye she'd kept seeing his long brown fingers twirling the stem of his wine glass and the heat in his eyes when he'd watched her eat all those prawns. And she'd kept thinking about all those smouldering sexy smiles he'd given her the next day at lunch and the feel of his hands massaging suntan lotion into her back.

And then, of course, there was that kiss by the pool.

She'd been dwelling on that a *lot*… The need in his eyes as they'd blazed down into hers. His warmth as it wrapped around her. The hard, lean planes of his body. His large hands holding her, pressing her against all that muscle and strength. That mouth, moving over hers with such skill and determination, and then the hard length of his erection pressing against her. Even the icy aloofness with which he'd dealt with the aftermath of it had been sexy in a perverse kind of way.

Not wanting to jinx things, she'd put the tingles that had run through her whenever she'd thought about him down to too much sun, but there was little point in denying it now.

She wanted him. She *wanted* him. Right now, at the mere *thought* of him, her body was weakening and softening. She just had to conjure up one of those devastating smiles and— ah, yes—her pulse was racing and her bones were melting and her temperature was rocketing in a way that had nothing to do with the midday heat.

And if she could feel all this just by thinking about him,

imagine what would happen when she and Rafael finally got together…

Nicky shivered. They'd be explosive. Dynamite. Fabulous.

If they got together, she amended, frowning suddenly and feeling the heat and desire ebb a little. Because it was all very well discovering that her libido was back and she wanted him quite desperately, but getting together would be pretty tricky when she was here and he was in Madrid, wouldn't it?

Not to mention the fact that it was entirely possible he wouldn't be interested in getting together anyway. Yes, he might have wanted her for that nanosecond he'd kissed her, but the way he'd gone so cool and indifferent minutes afterwards—although spine-tinglingly sexy—was hardly the sign of someone craving more, was it? Nor was the way he'd then vanished.

For a second her stomach plummeted, and then she jackknifed up, pulled her shoulders back and stiffened her spine.

No, she thought, determination swooping down to fill every corner of her body and obliterating the remnants of her orgasm. After everything she'd been through she was damned if she was going to let this opportunity slip by just because of five hundred miles and a trickle of doubt.

She had to at least *see* if Rafael might be up for turning her dream into a reality because frankly, what with the excellent progress she'd made so far, she'd never forgive herself if she didn't.

CHAPTER NINE

WHERE HE'D GONE wrong last time, thought Rafael, sitting at the desk in his study in his penthouse and twirling a pen between his fingers, was in believing that he could ignore someone whose presence was so tangible even when she physically wasn't.

That was why he hadn't been able to get Nicky out of his head the weekend he'd been at the *cortijo*, he realised now, despite spending such relatively little time in her company. That was why she'd occupied his thoughts while he'd been out there in the fields, why she'd invaded his dreams, and why he'd imagined he could smell her scent even though she'd been nowhere to be seen. It was never easy to ignore a guest, however out of sight, and he'd been nuts to assume that it would be.

Distance was what he'd needed in order to wipe Nicky and the temporary but devastating havoc she'd wreaked on his well-ordered life from his mind. Distance and time. Both of which he'd had plenty of lately.

The two weeks he'd been back in Madrid had been exactly what was required to restore calm to his life, harness his self-control and rebuild the defences she'd so swiftly and comprehensively destroyed. And just what he'd needed to finally relax.

With pretty much the whole of the country shutting down

in August and almost every Madrileño beetling off to the coast or the countryside, Rafael had figured the solitude would suit him perfectly, and had stayed put.

He could easily hang out here, he'd told himself. His flat was at the top of one of the most luxurious buildings in Madrid, and had all the trappings one would expect from a penthouse, so it hadn't exactly been a hardship.

He'd spent hours poring over his beloved first edition of John Gerard's *The Herball or Generall Historie of Plantes*, and pottering around his extensive and plant-stuffed roof terrace. He'd ploughed up and down the building's lavish outdoor pool and had frequented the gym. He'd been out a couple of times with the few friends who had stayed in the city, and in between all that he'd started to research his next job.

From Nicky he thankfully hadn't heard a word. Nor had he heard from any of the other women who'd been so hellbent on upsetting his existence. Apart from a text from Elisa informing him that she was on the Costa Brava should he feel like joining her—which he didn't—she too had been mercifully quiet. Even his family appeared to have better things to do than hassle him, and had left him alone.

Which all bode extremely well for the long sabbatical from women he'd decided to take in the wake of everything that had happened recently.

He glowered at his laptop and his mood darkened as he reminded himself exactly how dangerous Nicky, in particular, was. The others might be thorns in his side, but she was the one who turned him into someone he didn't recognise and didn't want to be. Someone who'd unravelled so quickly and comprehensively that he hadn't given even the most fleeting consideration to the values with which he conducted his relationships.

Because not only wasn't she too well—as his sister had

so brutally informed him—but Nicky was also a friend of Gaby's, and how that fact had managed to elude him at the time he had no idea.

Rafael's blood chilled as he thought about the far too close a shave he'd had. OK, so at some point during that weekend he'd evidently lost his mind, but how on earth could he have so *totally* forgotten his vow to not get involved with any friend of his sisters? It truly beggared belief.

Hadn't he learned the hard way that down that route lay disaster? Hadn't his brief, disastrous marriage proved it? And hadn't he sworn that he'd never let it happen again? He'd nearly lost one sister over the whole sorry episode and he had no intention of losing another. Ever.

Rafael had never imagined being *pleased* to have been rejected, but time and time again over the last fortnight he'd thanked God Nicky hadn't been interested in him, because if she had, and things had gone beyond one brief kiss, who knew what kind of chaos that might have caused?

But it was fine, he thought, letting out a long slow breath of relief. He'd escaped. Narrowly, but who cared? Narrowly was good enough.

Whatever had been going on in his head that weekend, and frankly it made him shudder to think about it, it was over. It had been a blip. A one-off moment of weakness, and ultimately entirely forgettable.

As was Nicky.

Now she was actually here Nicky wasn't at all sure that she'd done the right thing by coming. Yesterday afternoon, when, filled with delight and relief that she was more or less back to her old self, she'd made a plan that involved jumping on a train bound for Madrid this morning, it had felt like the most sensible, the most *right* decision she'd ever taken.

But now she was standing at Rafael's front door, her fin-

ger poised at the bell, and all the bubbling self-confidence
and heart-pounding adrenalin were draining away leaving
nothing but an unfamiliar bundle of nerves twisting her
stomach.

Because what if he wasn't in? What if, despite Gaby's
claim to the contrary, he was away at the coast as everyone
else seemed to be? What if her mad dash to Madrid hadn't
been the best decision she'd ever made but stupidly and uncharacteristically reckless and completely in vain?

Oh, this was ridiculous, she thought, frowning at a knot in
the wood of the front door and giving herself a mental slap.
She'd gone to great lengths to get here, starting with wan-
gling Rafael's address out of Gaby on the very flimsy pretext
of needing to forward some post, then facing the daunting
prospect of a crowded station, and she was not going to give
up this opportunity to find out whether her disturbingly long
period of sexual abstinence could be at an end.

She'd had enough of being a wimp at the mercy of her
hangups, and, besides, what was the worst that could happen? That he didn't answer? Or that he did, and slammed
the door in her face?

Telling herself that she'd cross those bridges if and when
she came to them Nicky took a deep breath, pressed the bell
and waited.

As the seconds ticked by with agonising slowness she ran
a hand through her hair and nibbled on her lip. Shifted her
weight from one foot to the other and fiddled unnecessar-
ily with the zip of her handbag until the jitteriness bouncing
inside her got so bad her knees started trembling.

Honestly, what *was* the matter with her? She never used
to get this nervous, so why now? Briefly closing her eyes
and telling herself to calm down, she took a series of deep
measured breaths until her pulse slowed and the pressure
inside her eased.

Just in time, she thought, hearing the sound of footsteps approaching on the other side of the door and feeling a flood of relief wash over her at the realisation that at least *someone* was home and her journey hadn't been entirely in vain.

Nicky opened her eyes as whoever it was—and she fervently hoped it was Rafael—stopped at the door, and, during the pause in which he presumably checked her out through the spyhole, she fixed her sunniest smile to her face and gave him a little wave.

Neither of which he appeared to appreciate, judging by the brief but heartfelt burst of Spanish that hit the door. She winced and dropped her hand to her side, and then jumped at the thud that sounded like either a fist or a head being thumped against the door.

Oh, dear. That didn't sound too promising, did it? In fact that sounded as if he wasn't pleased to see her at all. But that was fine. She had a plan, and she wasn't about to back out of it just because he might not be cooperative. In fact she couldn't wait to put it into action.

If only he'd open the damned door and let her in.

As the seconds continued to roll by and she found herself *still* face to face with a great flat lump of solid oak, Nicky was contemplating cupping her hands to the door and demanding he let her in when there came a muffled sigh, the latch clicked, the door swung open and there he was, towering over her, tall and broad, his face and his eyes utterly inscrutable.

But, at that particular moment, whether or not Rafael was pleased to see her didn't seem to matter, because as she looked up into his face and then straight into his eyes a great thump of desire thwacked her right in the stomach and nearly wiped out her knees.

The memory of him kissing her, his big, hard body wrapped around hers, flew into her head, making her pulse race and her breathing go haywire. As he thrust one hand into the pocket of his shorts she glanced at the other one resting on the door frame and had a sudden vision of his hands running over her sun-warmed skin. Heat wound through her and pooled in the pit of her stomach and she went dizzy.

God, if she'd needed any confirmation that her sex drive was back she had it. It was back with such a vengeance it was kind of mind-blowing to think that at one point she hadn't been interested in him at all.

Taking a deep breath before she started hyperventilating and melted into a puddle of lust, Nicky blinked to dispel the images and swallowed hard. 'Hi,' she said a lot more breathily than she'd have liked.

'Nicky,' he said flatly.

'Rafael,' she said, choosing to ignore the distinct lack of enthusiasm in his voice and giving him a beaming smile. 'How are you?'

'Fine.'

'Can I come in?'

He frowned. Hesitated for a moment, and she had the sudden disconcerting feeling he was going to slam the door in her face. But then the frown disappeared, that oddly sexy aloofness returned and as he held it back instead her stomach settled. 'Of course.'

'Thank you.'

She stepped inside, taking great care to fleetingly and subtly brush against him, and felt a dizzying little dart of satisfaction when he flinched. Excellent. Rafael might be trying to project an air of studied indifference and supreme self-control, but chemistry didn't seem to be going along with it any more than she was. Which was lucky because her plans for the afternoon relied heavily on chemistry.

'How did you know where to find me?' he said, closing the door behind her and sounding as if he wished she hadn't.

'Gaby gave me your address.'

'I didn't hear the buzzer.'

'I didn't ring it.'

'So who let you in?'

'A fellow resident.' She didn't see any need to mention that, not at all sure he'd want to see her, she'd abandoned the buzzer in favour of hovering outside, waiting for someone to go into the building and slipping in behind them. 'From downstairs, apparently. He was charming.'

'I'm sure he was.'

'He spoke flawless English.'

'How convenient.'

'Wasn't it?'

Rafael folded his arms over his chest, leaned back against the console table and fixed her with that unwavering stare that before had made her squirm with discomfort and now made her squirm with something else entirely. 'So how have you been?'

'Fabulous,' she said as longing spread through her veins as slow and thick and delicious as treacle.

Languidly and thoroughly he ran his gaze over her, from the hair on her head right down to her pink toenails, and as she endured his scrutiny every inch of her in between burned. By the time he'd finished making his way back up she was shaking inside with the effort of not hurling herself at him.

'You certainly look fab—' He broke off. Frowned. Swore probably, she thought, beneath his breath. 'Well,' he finished.

'Thank you,' she said and reminded herself that there'd be no hurling of anyone anywhere yet because she needed to concentrate. 'I feel well.'

'Would you like a drink?' he said, pushing himself off the console table and striding off in the direction of the kitchen.

'Anything soft and cold would be great,' she said and followed him despite the lack of invitation. 'It's hot, isn't it?'

He walked over to the fridge and took out a jug of orange juice and she took the opportunity to ogle his bottom. 'Very,' he muttered, and she got the delightful feeling he wasn't just referring to the temperature.

As Rafael plucked a couple of glasses from the cupboard next to the fridge and poured the juice Nicky watched the muscles of his back twist beneath the cotton of his T-shirt and her palms itched with the need to touch him.

He turned abruptly and handed her a glass.

'Thank you,' she said, taking it, lifting it to her mouth and taking a long swallow. Skin-pricklingly aware that his eyes were on her, she ran her hand down her throat as she did so. 'Yum, delicious.'

Rafael didn't move but she thought she caught the tell-tale hammering of a muscle in his jaw, and smiled.

'So this is a nice place,' she said, turning slightly to look around his apartment and deciding that actually nice was way too bland a word for the incredible vision that met her eyes.

It was open plan, the kitchen partly cut off by a wide breakfast bar giving way to a dining area, which then flowed into a vast and comfortable-looking sitting room containing a wide deep sofa, several well-worn armchairs and a coffee table piled high with magazines.

Bookshelves lined the far wall and sagged beneath the weight of the dozens of books that were stacked upon them. Light spilled in through the floor-to-ceiling windows filling the room with light and shadows. Plants sat on every horizontal surface and art hung on every vertical one.

It was the sort of flat a girl could get very cosy in, thought Nicky, if that was her intention, which in *her* case, of course, it wasn't.

'I like it,' he said abruptly.

'You like plants,' she observed.

'I do.'

'It's spacious,' she murmured and wondered where his bedroom was. 'Light. Airy.'

'And remarkably close to my office,' he said dryly.

'How handy.'

'Isn't it?'

And that seemed to be that for small talk, Nicky realised as she swung her gaze back to him and they lapsed into a tense little silence.

The seconds ticked by and Rafael just stood there looking at her with those penetrating green eyes and that unfathomable expression, barely moving a muscle, and she just stood there helplessly staring back, the tension inside her winding tighter and tighter as the heat flowing though her picked up speed and intensity.

As their gazes held the silence stretched, began to thicken and sizzle with electricity until it finally became unbearable and Nicky came to the conclusion that as he appeared to have no intention of doing anything to break it, she was going to have to.

'So,' she said, blinking to snap herself out of it and smiling brightly, 'I guess you must be wondering what I'm doing here.'

One dark eyebrow lifted. 'I can't imagine it was solely to discuss the weather, the architectural features of my flat and my interest in plants,' he said, sounding impressively bored.

'You'd be right,' Nicky answered, completely undeterred by his indifference because she was on a mission and nothing was going to sway her from it.

'So?'

'Well, firstly I just wanted to say that I thought you leaving without saying goodbye was rather on the rude side.'

He shrugged. 'Like I said in my note, I had work. But you're right. I apologise.'

'Accepted. Secondly, I wanted to see if you were all right.'

This time both eyebrows shot up. 'Why wouldn't I be?'

'When I last spoke to Gaby I rather got the feeling she'd like to do you some harm.'

Something flickered in the depths of his eyes but it was gone before she could identify it.

'As you can see I'm perfectly fine. And while I appreciate your concern,' he added, clearly not appreciating it at all, 'a phone call would have done.'

'True on both counts,' she agreed with a brief nod. 'But a phone call would certainly not have done for the main reason I'm here.'

'Which is?'

Deciding that neither a subtle approach nor skirting around the issue would break through such determined lack of emotion, but that getting straight to the point might at least provoke some sort of reaction, Nicky took a deep breath. 'Right,' she said, pulling her shoulders back, straightening her spine and looking him straight in the eye. 'Well. You see, the thing is, I'd like to give that kiss another try.'

When he'd looked through the spyhole and seen Nicky standing on his doorstep, smiling and waving, distorted but still lovely, Rafael had thought that someone somewhere really had it in for him. That he must have done something really terrible in a former life, because this was the second time she'd surprised him at a door and, while she might not have been armed with *Don Quijote* on this occasion, her impact had been no less devastating.

Which was why, feeling as if the whole sodding universe was conspiring against him, he'd been momentarily tempted to tiptoe back and hole up in his office in the hope that she'd give up and leave. However, given the not-particularly-subtle way he'd walked to the door, he'd realised that unfortunately that wasn't an option so he'd had to brace himself and let her in.

To a man whose defences weren't as indestructible as his now were, Nicky Sinclair, tanned, relaxed and smiling, wrapped in a dress that showed off her lovely curves and shod in high peep-toe wedges that added inches to her already willowy height, might have presented the ultimate temptation.

But not to him. Oh, no. Distance and time had given him ample opportunity to fortify his defences and they were now sky-high, unbreachable and as solid as rock, so he was immune.

If his detached approach felt like harder work than it should have done, it was merely that he'd been briefly thrown off balance by her unexpected appearance. And if he'd nearly dropped his glass when she'd mentioned trying the kiss again, well, that was simply surprise at her boldness, nothing more.

'What kiss?' he asked nonchalantly, aware she was waiting for some kind of response.

Nicky shot him a look that suggested she wasn't convinced by his nonchalance one little bit, and arched an eyebrow. 'The one you gave me that last Sunday. The one by the pool.'

'Oh, that kiss,' he said as if it hadn't been on his mind constantly over the last fortnight.

'That's the one. So what do you think?'

'About trying it again?'

She nodded.

'Well, it's an interesting proposal,' he said, and shot her the hint of a cool and with any luck condescending smile, 'and a very flattering one, of course, but I'm afraid it's out of the question.'

Nicky tilted her head and bit her lip as she stared at him. 'Out of the question?'

He nodded. 'Out of the question.'

'Why?'

Good point. Why was it out of the question? he wondered, his gaze dropping for a split second to that lip before he snapped back to his senses and dragged his eyes back up. 'I'm rather surprised you'd want to.'

'Are you?'

Now *she* was the one who sounded surprised, and frankly that was odd because surely she couldn't have forgotten her total lack of interest in that kiss. 'You didn't seem all that keen at the time,' Rafael said, and reminded himself that whatever it was that was stabbing at his chest it couldn't be hurt because he'd got over all that weeks ago.

'No, but things have changed.'

'How convenient.'

'Not entirely, but is my perceived lack of interest your only objection?'

'Not by a long shot.'

'Then what else is it?'

For a second he just stood there looking at her, his mind boggling. God, where to start? 'For one thing *I* don't particularly want to.' That was as good a place as any.

'Why not?'

'It wasn't exactly a success the last time we tried it,' he drawled, thinking that that was at least partly the truth. 'So why on earth would I want to go through it again?'

'It would be better this time. I guarantee it.'

'There isn't going to be a this time.' And he could guarantee *that*.

There was a brief pause while she glanced at his jaw,

his shoulders, and lifted her eyebrows. 'Are you absolutely certain about that?' she said eventually. 'Because you look remarkably tense for a man who isn't interested in experimenting with one harmless little kiss.'

Harmless? Kissing Nicky? Hah. Rafael forced his shoulders to loosen up and then shrugged. 'Well, I'm not,' he said as if he couldn't be more relaxed. 'I, for one, have moved on.'

She nodded and bit her lip. 'Ah.'

'As I told you at the time my attraction to you was mercifully short-lived, and I got over it days ago.'

'Oh, yes. I remember. It was an aberration. The sun or the wine or something.'

Now it was his turn to arch an eyebrow because she sounded so continually sceptical and somehow knowing that it was seriously beginning to wind him up. 'Is it really that hard for you to believe your charms aren't irresistible?'

'Of course it isn't.' She regarded him thoughtfully and as she did so an odd thread of trepidation began to wind through him. 'But if you're not interested, as you claim, if you're no longer attracted to me, and if that kiss was so unimportant, why for the last ten minutes have you been staring at my mouth as if desperate to feel it beneath yours again?'

The foundations of his defences wobbled, and Rafael set his jaw to hold back the sudden burst of desire that he'd managed to convince himself he'd obliterated but was now pounding away at them. 'I haven't.'

'You have.'

'Must be a trick of the light.'

'Right,' she said with a slow nod. 'And I suppose the way your eyes are darkening, the way you're clenching your fist and that muscle hammering in your jaw must be tricks of the light too?' Her gaze dropped to the zip of his shorts behind which he was helplessly swelling and hardening. 'Not to mention the way your—'

'OK, enough,' he said, and slammed his glass down on the counter, suddenly so sick of the way his body, his senses and everything about this conversation were so out of control that he couldn't hold back. 'Maybe I am attracted to you.'

'Aha, I knew it,' she said with a triumphant little smile.

'Maybe I would like to kiss you again,' he continued, now on an unstoppable roll. 'Maybe I would like to drag you to the floor, strip you naked and bury myself inside you, but it's not going to happen.' About that he was absolutely certain. 'Nor am I going to let you kiss me, however seductively you try and dress up your request.'

For a second Nicky just looked at him, that damnably distracting mouth dropping open in shock at his outburst. 'But why ever not?' she said, her breathing ragged and her cheeks pink.

'Because you're not well,' he said tightly.

Her eyebrows shot up. 'What?'

'You're not well.'

She frowned. 'Have you been speaking to Gaby?'

'Yes.'

'What did she say?'

'That you needed a rest.'

'Which I've now had,' she said, taking a step towards him. 'Yes, I'll admit that I haven't been all that great, and my lack of response to you initially was part of it, but I'm better now. Much better.'

As if that made any difference, he thought, wishing he could take a giant step back and get out of her mind-scrambling orbit. 'I'm delighted to hear it,' he muttered roughly.

'So much so that over the last couple of weeks I've found myself thinking about you. About that kiss.' She paused and tilted her head. 'And whenever I did there was this kind of spark. Right here.' She splayed her hand low on her abdomen.

Rafael focused on a huge arrangement of flowers sitting on the breakfast bar to her right. 'Good for you.'

'It was. It is. And it could be good for both of us because now there's more than just a spark.'

'You could spontaneously combust and it wouldn't bother me one little bit.' Were those dahlia pinnatas?

'I feel I'm about to.'

'That's your prerogative.' They were, and if he wasn't much mistaken there were some spathiphyllum wallisii in there too. He looked a little harder. Yep. Definitely spathiphyllum wallisii.

Nicky let out an exasperated sigh. 'Rafael, what *is* your problem?'

He reluctantly dragged his gaze back to her and pushed his hands through his hair. 'You're a friend of Gaby's,' he stated flatly.

A pause. 'And?'

'And I don't get involved with friends of any of my sisters.'

'Why on earth not?'

'I did it once and it didn't work out well.'

'What happened?'

God, what hadn't happened? 'I married her.'

'Oh.'

'Quite,' he bit out. 'It went wrong and in the ensuing mess I nearly lost my sister as well as my wife. Do you really think I'd want to risk that happening again?'

'Do you really think it would?'

'I've no idea, but it could and I have no intention of putting it to the test. So forget it. Just forget it.'

Nicky slowly tapped her mouth with her index finger as she presumably considered his position. 'Look, Rafael,' she said eventually, pulling her shoulders back and fixing him with a disconcertingly probing look. 'Aren't you rather over-analysing this? I'm not suggesting we get married or anything. Or even really get involved in a relationship. Heaven forbid, that's the last thing I want. All I'm suggesting is a kiss.'

Just a kiss? Was she nuts? He let out a sharp laugh. 'Really? Do you honestly think it would stop there?'

'Well, OK,' she said with a grin, 'if we're being honest, I'm hoping not. I'm hoping that if the kiss works out well then maybe we can take things further.'

'Further's the problem,' he all but snapped.

'Why? When is an afternoon of hot sex ever a problem?'

'When it gets complicated.'

'It won't,' she said firmly. 'It never does with me. Look, now I've got my health back I'm not interested in anything permanent, truly. So neither you nor your relationship with Gaby are under any threat whatsoever from me.'

She walked over to him, smiled up at him, desire blazing in the blue-grey depths of her eyes, and put her hand on his chest. 'Come on, Rafael,' she said softly and his vision blurred. 'Haven't you wondered what it would be like? A proper kiss. With *both* of us involved…'

Rafael felt as if he'd been thumped in the gut. Her proximity blew all rational thought from his head and left it empty of everything except harsh clamouring need. His skin beneath her hand burned and his head pounded. He *had* wondered what it would be like. Endlessly. And that was precisely the trouble.

'Honestly, it's just one little kiss,' she said, her hand sliding higher, curving round his neck and threading through his hair. 'How can one little kiss hurt?'

Beneath the onslaught of her scent, her warmth and her innate sensuality those cracked and weakened foundations crumbled, and down crashed his defences.

As they lay in smithereens at his feet once more Rafael

knew he didn't stand a chance. That since the moment he'd seen her through the spyhole he'd *never* stood a chance. He'd tried, but Nicky had battered down every one of his objections with logic and one smouldering smile after another, and now the pressure of wanting her was just too much.

There'd be time for explanations and regret and the chance to figure out what the hell was happening later. But right now he was drowning in need and he couldn't resist any longer.

With a strange sense that somehow this had been inevitable from the moment they'd met, Rafael gave up and gave in. 'Come here,' he muttered, and yanked her into his arms.

CHAPTER TEN

OH, THANK GOD for that, thought Nicky as Rafael crushed her against him and slammed his mouth down on hers.

She'd known it would be tough to convince him that kissing her again was a good idea, but she'd never imagined it was going to be *that* hard. Goodness, the man was stubborn.

For a moment back there she'd feared her seduction skills were so rusty he'd never crack because she'd hurled everything she had at him and he'd just stood there firing back all those reasons why he wasn't going to kiss her, tight-jawed and as implacable as rock.

Well, almost as implacable as rock, she amended, her head beginning to swim as desire swirled around inside her, because she'd finally broken through all that idiotic denial, the not particularly convincing aloofness and all those baffling objections and, boy, was she glad she had.

Gone was the rigidly stoical Rafael of seconds ago, all buttoned up and resistant, and here was the man by the pool. Six feet three inches of wild and uncontrollable passion.

Her lips parted and as he pushed his tongue between them she groaned and sank against him. One of his arms wrapped itself around her waist and he buried his other hand in her hair, in an exact imitation of how he'd kissed her before but with one crucial difference.

And that was her response. There was nothing cold and

numb about that this time. His tongue touched hers, and she jerked as if electrocuted. Sparks shot straight through her and her blood began to sizzle. Heat pooled in her pelvis and spread throughout her body like a fever.

As they kissed the heat intensified and her insides began to burn as if a thousand fires had sprung to flame in the pit of her stomach.

Unable to help herself, Nicky moaned. Oh, how she'd missed this. This heady feeling of wanting. Of being wanted. Of the delirious desperation that intense need caused. She'd missed the feeling of drowning in desire, the unstoppable thundering of her heart and the giddy aching of her body.

For the first time in weeks she felt truly alive. Vibrant and on fire, and she pressed herself closer, wrapped her arms tighter, and kissed him back even more fiercely.

After what felt like hours, they broke off and she stared up at Rafael and blinked, fairly reeling at the strength of her reaction to him. His eyes were glittering, dark with desire, his breathing was ragged and she could feel his heart thundering against her. As it seemed he couldn't move or speak either she thought that perhaps he was as stunned as she was, and the knowledge sent primitive satisfaction surging through her.

'Well?' she murmured huskily.

He blinked, frowned, and then gave his head a quick shake. 'Well, what?'

'Didn't I guarantee it would be better this time?'

He blew out a soft shaky breath. 'You did.'

'And?'

'It was better.'

There was nothing wrong with better, thought Nicky, but the imp inside her, the one who'd been slumbering away for weeks now, was waking up. It yawned and rubbed its eyes and made her say with a coquettishness that she didn't usually go in for, 'Just better?'

'Much better.' His mouth curved into a faint smile and he raised his eyebrows. 'Why? Think you can improve?'

'Oh, there's always room for improvement,' she murmured and lifted her head for another divine kiss.

And this time when their mouths met Nicky's brain well and truly went AWOL, because within seconds Rafael had taken control and was angling her head and deepening the kiss and sliding his hand up her side as he kissed her.

His hand curved round her breast and settled, and at the feel of it caressing her achingly sensitive flesh she sighed into his mouth. He brushed his thumb over her nipple, sending more of those tiny electric shocks skidding through her, and she melted against him.

Oh, this was heavenly, she thought dazedly. Absolutely heavenly. Instinctively she tightened her arms around his neck and tilted her pelvis against his erection and rubbed. He groaned and pulled her even closer, kissed her even harder and blew her mind.

By the time they broke for breath this time her bones had dissolved and she was glad he had some kind of hold on her because otherwise she'd have collapsed into a puddle of lust on the floor.

'God, I'd love to see how we can improve on that,' she said shakily, and thought that she doubted it was possible because how could you perfect perfection?

He brushed a lock of her hair back and tucked it behind her ear. 'Would you?'

The oddly tender gesture coupled with the hint of promise in his voice and the suddenly wicked glint that appeared in his eye shot her pulse so far through the roof and stole her voice so totally that all she could do was nod.

He let her go and nudged her gently back. 'Then take off your dress.'

A great boulder of desire rolled the length of her body, nearly wiping out her knees, and she swallowed hard. 'Now?' she breathed, and inwardly winced at the way he'd evidently turned her brain to mush because was he really talking about next week?

He gave her a slow smouldering smile that had her stomach flipping like a pancake. 'Now.'

How could she do anything but comply when she was so completely spellbound by him and the dizzying effect he had on her?

Everything but him and the way he was looking at her faded into a blur. As she slipped out of her shoes, her hands went to her side of their own accord and she slid the zip of her dress down and with Rafael watching her every move so closely Nicky was aware of her body in a way she never had been before.

The whisper of her zip sounded abrasively loud in the eerie silence of the afternoon. The soft cotton of her dress brushing against her skin sent tiny shivers scuttling down her spine, and her fingers trembled a little as she slipped the straps off her shoulders and let the dress fall to the floor in a pool of pale yellow. Her heart reverberated like a kettle drum and her blood roared in her ears as she watched Rafael swallow once, then slowly run his gaze over her nearly naked body.

Beneath his scrutiny, a shudder rippled through her and then she went so hot she wouldn't have been surprised to look down and find that the lace of her strapless bra and knickers had gone up in flames.

'What now?' she asked, perfectly happy to have him take charge when it made her feel like this.

'Sit down.' His voice was satisfyingly hoarse and she

smiled at the thought that despite his attempt to resist her, he was as much at the mercy of this as she was.

'Where?' she asked, because the only chairs she could make out in her very fuzzy peripheral vision were the kitchen bar stools and they didn't look nearly sturdy enough for what she hoped was about to happen.

He scanned the living space. 'The sofa, I think.'

With her pulse kicking with anticipation, she smiled, then turned and made her way over to the wide, deep chocolate-brown sofa, feeling her body moving languidly and her hips sashaying in a way that had nothing to do with any conscious thought on her part and everything to do with a primitively innate desire to attract.

She sat down before her knees could give way and looked up at him. 'How do you want me?'

'Sit back.'

With desire and heat making the blood racing through her veins sluggish and her limbs heavy, Nicky languorously sank back against the soft velvet and inched her knees open a fraction.

'Is that better?' she said huskily.

'Much.'

'So what are you doing still over there?'

'Contemplating exactly where to start.'

As her mouth went dry and heat pooled between her legs Nicky thought that he'd started already. 'Will you be long?'

'I might be.'

'Why?'

'I've just discovered a hitherto latent fascination with revenge.'

She shivered deliciously. 'Revenge?'

He nodded. 'And I think I could be getting a taste for it.'

'Are you planning to make me pay for that disaster of a first kiss?' she said a little raggedly.

'I might be,' he said and the look in his eye told her that there was no 'might' about it.

Wicked excitement spun through her. 'How?'

'By making you beg.'

Oh, heavens. 'I've never begged for anything in my life.'

'You will.'

Her heart thumped so hard her ribs ached. And then, just when she didn't think she could stand the tension much longer, he pushed himself off the counter and began to prowl towards her, not taking his eyes off her as he approached.

He came to a stop in front of her, loomed over her for a moment and then dropped to his knees. He pushed her legs apart and inched forwards and her excitement ratcheted up so dizzyingly it was all she could do not to grab him and pull him first up and then down on top of her. Achingly slowly he leaned into her and the spicy scent of him wound up her nose into her head and made a mess of her brain.

When his mouth finally brushed over hers, Nicky moaned and nearly passed out with relief because for a moment she'd thought she was going to have to start begging right there and then.

But he didn't linger. Instead he moved his mouth down over her chin, her neck and the skin of her upper chest, leaving tiny trails of fire wherever it touched, and at the same time he slid his hands up her thighs. The muscles beneath his fingers quivered and the skin beneath his mouth burned and then his teeth grazed her nipple beneath the lace of her bra and she gasped.

As he tugged her hips forwards and carried on kissing his way down her body Nicky closed her eyes and let her head drop back because it was all getting too much for her poor battered senses and, unlike some of her previous lovers, Rafael didn't seem to need instruction.

Quite the contrary, she thought briefly as he dotted a

trail of kisses over her stomach and then lower, and ran his tongue along the edge of her knickers. He knew exactly what he was doing.

And then she gave up thinking altogether in favour of biting her lip and arching her back and clenching her fists against the cushions to stop herself grabbing his head and pushing it where she so desperately wanted his mouth.

She whimpered and felt him smile against her skin and then he was lifting her hips, hooking his thumbs over the sides of her knickers and drawing back to slide them down her legs. He pulled them off and began stroking and kissing his way up over the inside of one of her knees, up along her inner thigh and then he was there. Right at the heart of her where she was burning and aching and so, so hot. He spread her legs even further apart, exposing her completely, and she let out an involuntary little moan. And then just when she thought she might be ready to beg after all, he licked along the length of her and a burst of pleasure exploded inside her.

Holding her in place, he licked and sucked and nibbled and stroked and within seconds Nicky's head was swimming and her body was on fire and all her senses zoomed in on his tongue and the chaos it was creating.

After such a long time of nothing she was a writhing mass of sensation. As he continued to lay siege to her body shudders racked her. Need clawed at her insides. Her muscles filled with tension.

He slipped a finger, then two, into her wet heat, found her g-spot with deadly accuracy, and what with the relentless onslaught of his tongue, the feel of his fingers inside her and the ecstasy spinning out of control deep within her, it was all just too much.

Far too soon everything tangled into one great jumble of feeling, soaring and swelling until it hit a peak and, with his name on her lips, she shattered, breaking wide apart and spinning off into delirious oblivion.

When the stars eventually stopped exploding behind her eyelids, when her heart finally slowed and when the strength eventually returned to her limbs, Nicky let out a long shuddery breath and opened her eyes.

'Been a while?'

She lifted her head and glanced down to find Rafael staring up at her, his eyes glittering with desire, satisfaction and a hint of surprise.

'You could say that,' she said huskily, then added because it seemed appropriate, 'Thanks.'

'It was my pleasure.'

'No, no, the pleasure was all mine. Literally.' And embarrassingly, she thought, feeling a blush steal into her cheeks at the memory of how abandoned, how vocal she'd been.

Rafael grinned. 'Yes, well, don't worry. There'll be plenty of time to even up the score.'

'You mean there's more?' she asked, widening her eyes with disingenuous innocence as a ribbon of fresh desire wound through her.

'Much more.'

Nicky smiled and stretched. 'I'm glad to hear it because you haven't even got naked yet.'

He looked down over her once again with that heated gaze and her stomach melted. 'Technically neither have you,' he said.

Arching an eyebrow and giving him a saucy little smile, Nicky reached behind her back, unclipped her bra and tossed it over the back of her sofa. 'Situation remedied,' she declared. 'And now, in the interest of fairness, it's your turn.'

Rafael's gaze dropped to her breasts and a muscle began to hammer in his jaw. 'Since you're so good at it,' he murmured, 'why don't you do it?'

'Bedroom?'

'Conventional. Who'd have thought?'

She shrugged. 'What can I say? I'm a fan of horizontal surfaces and space.' Although upright on the sofa wasn't such a bad alternative.

'In that case,' he said, holding out his hands, taking hers and pulling them both to their feet, 'the bedroom's this way.'

CHAPTER ELEVEN

OH, YES, THOUGHT Nicky, standing beside the bed, letting her gaze drift over Rafael and wondering where she was going to start. Coming to Madrid had been *such* a good idea and she was going to have so much fun with him because for this afternoon at least he was all hers, and she felt like a kid in a sweet shop, her fingers itching to delve and her mouth watering with the need to sample the wares.

'Are you just going to stand there and look?' said Rafael, and she looked up to see his face was dark and tight. 'Because I am this close—' he held up his thumb and forefinger a millimetre apart '—to tossing you onto the bed and ravishing you, and, believe me, finesse will not feature heavily.'

And there'd be nothing wrong with that, she thought, her heart jumping as desire shot through her all over again. But now that she'd got her mojo back—and how—she wanted to indulge every newly awakened sense.

So with her breath catching in her throat she put her hands on his stomach and slid them up, lifting his T-shirt as she did so and feeling his muscles twitch beneath her palms. He raised his arms to help her and she stood on tiptoe to pull the T-shirt over his head and up over his arms. She let it drop to the floor and then ran her hands back down his lowering arms and across his shoulders and then down over the broad tanned expanse of his chest.

Unable to resist, she leaned forwards and flicked her tongue over his nipple. Rafael inhaled sharply and she could feel his body tighten. With restraint. With desire.

'God, I'd forgotten how tantalising undressing a man could be,' she murmured.

'Done it often?'

'Once or twice.' Although never with someone quite like him. Relieving him of his clothes had to be one of life's greatest secret pleasures because he was physically quite magnificent.

Swallowing hard, she moved her hands down, undid his belt, the button of his shorts and then slid down the zip, relishing every glorious second.

And to think that that day he'd kissed her by the pool she'd had ample opportunity to admire the body on display. To ogle and want and touch. And she'd ignored it. What a waste.

Well, she wasn't ignoring it now. And she wasn't going to waste a second.

She slid her hands beneath the waistband of his boxers and moaned in anticipation as she eased them and his shorts over the thick, hard erection that she could feel beneath. He stepped out of them and she took a step back to simply admire. God, his body was incredible. It was all lean, hard muscle and taut restrained power and she couldn't wait to have the full force of it unleashed on her.

'Lie down,' he said in a voice that wasn't altogether steady.

Nicky's heart thumped madly as she did as he said and lay back on the bed, because, oh, there was definitely something to be said for a gorgeous man who knew how and when to use his power and liked to be in control.

And right now, with the way his eyes were burning over her, she was quite willing to submit herself to whatever delicious torment he had planned. There'd be plenty of time for payback later, she decided, and felt a wide wanton smile steal across her face.

'That smile looks dangerous,' he said, his eyes blazing down at her.

'Could be.'

'Sirens,' he muttered. 'I'm doomed.'

'What?'

'Sirens.'

'What about them?' she said, and stretched in what she hoped was an enticing manner because there was drawing things out and indulging her senses and then there was just plain being sadistic, and the way she was lying spreadeagled on the bed while he still remained upright and beside it definitely fell into the latter category.

'They had a tendency to lure sailors to their deaths with their song,' he said.

'Lucky you're not a sailor and I can't sing, then, isn't it?'

'You have plenty of other attractions.'

'So are you just going to stand there and look at them?' she asked, recalling his earlier words to her and deciding to hurry things up a bit. 'Or are you planning to do the decent thing and join me, because I am this close—' she held up her thumb and forefinger a millimetre apart '—to pulling you onto this bed and ravishing you.' She paused and smiled and batted her eyelashes up at him. 'And, believe me, finesse will not feature heavily.'

That seemed to do the trick. Rafael let out a strangled groan, jerked forwards and, planting his hands either side of her head, came down heavily on top of her. At the sudden urgency of his actions Nicky's breath shot from her lungs and lust spun through her.

'You know, I'm coming to the conclusion that finesse is vastly overrated,' he said roughly.

'You have no idea how glad I am to hear you think so,'

she said softly, loving the feel of his weight on top of her and wrapping a leg around his waist.

And then his mouth was on hers and she couldn't remember what she'd been glad about because his hands were in her hair, his tongue was in her mouth and both were rendering her to a mindless tangle of electricity, desire and delicious, delicious tension.

She ran her hands over the tight muscles of his shoulders and his back and dug her nails in, which took the kiss to another, more frenzied, more desperate dimension in which clashing teeth, melding moans and writhing limbs dominated.

Her head was so foggy, her brain so utterly destroyed, she was only dimly aware of Rafael pulling one hand from her hair and sliding it down her neck and then over the agonisingly sensitive skin of her upper chest.

But when it came to a rest on her breast all that electricity, desire and tension shot through the roof. Nicky groaned into his mouth and arched her back as his hand cupped her and he rubbed his thumb back and forth over her nipple and a burst of white-hot pleasure exploded deep inside her.

He dragged his mouth away and shifted a little, and she gulped in a shaky breath as it closed over her other nipple.

Biting her lip to stop herself from crying out at the stabs of ecstasy that were jabbing at her, she pressed her fingers into his head and tilted her hips to grind into his erection. She writhed. She whimpered. She simply couldn't help it.

'Ready to beg yet?' he said hoarsely against her breast.

God, probably, she thought dazedly, but in a bit because she wanted more and could take more. 'Not nearly,' she said, and then added in the hope it would make him double his already sensational efforts, 'You'll have to try far harder than that.'

So he did.

His mouth resumed its devastating assault on her breast and his hand slid lower and lower until it reached the juncture of her thighs and then his fingers were parting her and sliding into her and the feeling was so electrifying she would have jackknifed upright had he not been pressing her down.

He stroked her, relentlessly, expertly and her insides wound so tightly she felt they might snap at any moment. Heat coiled in the pit of her stomach. Tremors began to rack her body and shivers raced through her veins as the excitement swelled and spread into every cell of her body. She was hovering on the brink, a nanosecond away from splintering, clenching around his fingers and hurtling off into oblivion when suddenly he stilled and his head lifted.

Nicky groaned in protest as her orgasm instantly ebbed. 'Why are you stopping?' she said, her voice rough and raspy.

His green eyes gleamed down at her. 'Beg me,' he muttered.

What? Oh, his timing was good, she thought as a stab of such intense longing shot through her that she nearly did as he asked. Or very very bad, depending on your point of view. She didn't know which hers was.

'Sadist,' she murmured.

'Beg me,' he said again.

'No.'

'Masochist.'

'You'll pay for this,' she said, reaching down, taking him in her hand and stroking. She felt him tense and shudder so she rubbed her thumb across the tip and gently squeezed.

'I have a feeling we both will,' he said raggedly, stopping her hand, then abruptly rolling slightly and twisting away.

Nicky watched as he rummaged around in the drawer of the bedside table and pulled out a condom. He ripped open the packet, slipped it on and then he was back on top of her, his eyes blazing down at her and his erection nudging at her entrance. Hovering. Waiting. Wanting her completely and utterly at his mercy, which she was.

She opened her legs wider. Tilted her hips higher. And then he was driving into her with a rough groan and she thought that she was about to die and go to heaven.

'Oh…' she said, letting out a long shuddery breath as she felt him fill her.

'Incredible,' he muttered, going utterly still for a second before beginning to move. Deliberately slowly, ruthlessly measuredly and maddeningly in control.

And while there was certainly a time for languid and leisurely, right now she was in the mood for fast and frantic because the friction was becoming unbearable, the tension excruciating, and the pleasure relentless, and it wasn't enough. The climax that had remained so tantalisingly out of reach when he'd stopped and asked her to beg still hovered at the edges of her consciousness.

He was holding it off, holding them both back, and no matter how much she writhed and rubbed against him he didn't relent. She pulled his head down for a searing kiss and felt sparks shoot through her at the touch of his lips, his tongue, but none of it made the slightest difference. The only thing that all her efforts achieved was her own torment because with each tilt of her hips, with each twist and turn of her body and with each kiss she simply grew more and more frenzied until she was way beyond the point of any kind of control.

'Oh, God,' she mumbled, hearing the desperation in her voice and not caring one little bit. 'Please…'

And then a second later his control seemed to dissolve and a wildness took over his movements and Nicky found she cared even less, because gone was maddeningly slow and ruthlessly measured, and he was now thrusting into her over and over again, going deeper, harder, faster until she didn't think she could bear it any longer.

The delirium inside her escalated with each thrust, sweeping her up in it, higher and higher until the great ball of pressure inside her erupted and she hurtled over the edge, her body exploding into a thousand tiny fireworks of ecstasy.

She shook, convulsed and trembled in his arms, the tremors shuddering through her nearly breaking her apart and then she felt him bury himself deep inside her one last time, groan and pulsate into her, and unbelievably she came all over again.

For several long, long minutes neither of them moved. Nicky wouldn't have been able to even if Rafael hadn't collapsed on top of her because she felt utterly sated and utterly drained. As weak as a kitten, and quite extraordinarily good.

'Wow,' she managed once her breathing had eased, her heart rate had slowed and her surroundings had swum back into focus.

'Quite.' Even with his mouth muffled by her shoulder, Rafael sounded as stunned as she was.

'What was that?'

Gently easing out of her, he rolled to one side and propped himself up on an elbow. 'One harmless little kiss apparently.'

She looked up at him and slowly smiled. 'Ah, but it didn't hurt, did it?'

'The kisses didn't,' he said raggedly. 'However the damage to my back might be irreparable.'

'Sorry,' she said, too happy revelling in the aftermath of what had been the most glorious sex of her life to feel in the slightest bit apologetic. 'Is it that bad?'

'Not that bad. And I think I can live with it. Especially since you begged so nicely.'

She jerked her gaze to his and arched an eyebrow at the teasing glint in his eyes. 'I did not beg.'

'Yes, you did. I remember it clearly.'

'I pleaded. There's a difference.'

'You think?'

His grin was too smug to ignore. 'I'll show you.'

'How?'

Giving him a deliberately smouldering smile, Nicky pushed him onto his back, climbed on top of him and watched with satisfaction as a flicker of wariness leapt in his eyes.

'You'll see,' she said, and began to slide down his body.

'You know, you're absolutely right,' said Rafael quite a while later when he was able to think again. 'There is a difference.'

Nicky glanced up and grinned. 'Told you.'

'Feeling smug?'

'A little.'

And actually she had every right to, he thought, because frankly the afternoon had been astounding. When he'd initially pulled her into his arms he'd had the feeling that they'd be good together, but nothing could have prepared him for the explosive way they'd responded to each other. Over and over again she'd come apart in his arms and beneath his mouth, and he'd shattered in and beneath hers more times than he could count. It was truly staggering.

Now it was dusk and she was sitting cross-legged in his bed wearing one of his T-shirts and eating a tortilla he'd whipped up, tousled haired, sleepy-eyed and looking thoroughly ravished, and with any luck the night would be equally astonishing because unbelievably he wanted her again.

As the desire that had never really gone away surged through him for the dozenth time this afternoon Rafael felt himself harden and stabbed his fork into a piece of tortilla.

What was it about Nicky that made him lose such control and forget about everything but her? Where had all those 'thoughts of revenge come from? And as for wanting to make her beg, what the hell had that been all about?

The need to possess her, to make her succumb, had been all-consuming, and, for someone who'd always been so focused and in control when it came to sex, the realisation that all it took was a gorgeous woman, weeks of frustration and scorching chemistry to derail him so spectacularly like that was kind of harrowing.

'And tired,' said Nicky, yanking Rafael out of his thoughts in time for him to see her smothering a yawn and stretching languidly. 'You've worn me out. It's a good thing I stocked up on rest at the *cortijo*.'

And that was another thing, he thought as the comment she'd made earlier about not being well flashed into his head and a wave of guilt washed over him. Forget the mental gymnastics *he* was going through. What about the extremely physical ones he'd spent the afternoon subjecting her to?

He swore softly beneath his breath. Nicky had been ill and never mind that everything they'd done had been entirely mutual, he should have taken more care. Better still, he should have held his ground and resisted her in the first place, but there was little use in beating himself up about that again.

'Rafael?' she asked, the tinge of concern in her voice making him feel even worse. 'Are you all right?'

'Are you?'

She blinked and shot him a dazzling smile that slowly flipped his stomach. 'Of course I am. I feel fabulous. Why do you ask?'

'You said you hadn't been very well.'

She raised her eyebrows. 'True, but I also said I'd recovered. As I think we've just admirably demonstrated.' She frowned. 'I hope you don't think you hurt me or anything.'

Rafael stiffened with resolve because he'd let too much

slide and he wasn't about to let this go. 'If you've been ill, can you blame me?'

There was a pause, then she set her fork down and looked at him, pinning him to the mattress with those stormy grey-blue eyes of hers. 'OK,' she said, linking her fingers in her lap and leaning forwards earnestly. 'Here's the thing. Yes, I haven't been particularly well, but neither have I been exactly ill.'

As his once sharp but now apparently addled brain tried to work out what she meant and failed, Rafael frowned. He'd had a first class education initially at public school in England, then at Cambridge and finally at Harvard, and he'd always assumed he was pretty much bilingual, but perhaps he'd been deluding himself all these years. Perhaps somewhere along the way he'd missed the lesson on nuance, because right now he couldn't work out what she was saying. 'I'm afraid you've lost me.'

'I nearly lost myself.'

'How?' he asked, now even more perplexed.

'Burnout.'

'Burnout?'

'That's right. Gaby diagnosed it a few weeks ago and I think she was right.'

The image of the Nicky he'd first met flashed though Rafael's head. She'd been pale and gaunt. Exhausted and troubled. Tense, prickly and on edge. And enveloped by that disturbing air of desolate defeat.

All classic signs of burnout, he realised, and all of which he'd seen before. Hell, he'd even got work because of it but it had never occurred to him that that was what Nicky had been suffering from. But then he'd been so caught up in wanting her and wondering why she didn't want him that little else *had* occurred to him.

'What caused it?' he said, and forced himself to focus on

her instead of barrelling off down the road of self-recrimination yet again.

She tilted her head and regarded him for a moment, as if internally debating whether or not to tell him. Then she straightened as if bracing herself, and for some reason his chest tightened. 'Remember how I told you I was a photo-journalist?'

He nodded and took a deep breath to ease the pressure. 'I looked you up on the Internet. Your work is incredible.' Although actually incredible didn't begin to describe it. The pictures she took were powerful, provocative, beautiful and thought-provoking. He'd read that she'd won awards and as he'd scrolled through the gallery on her website he'd been able to see why.

She beamed. 'Thank you.' Then she sobered. 'Well, anyway, a year or so ago I was on assignment in the Middle East, covering a demonstration about rights for women. It was all going fine. Very peaceful and I got some excellent shots. But then some men turned up—family members of a few of the women, I found out later—and took exception. Especially to me and my camera.'

He thought he heard her voice shake a little and the pressure in his chest returned. 'What happened then?'

Nicky sighed. 'To be honest I don't remember all that much about it. One minute I was taking pictures, the next I was surrounded and being jostled and pushed to the ground. But I guess eventually my instinct for survival kicked in because somehow I managed to escape and make my way back to my hotel.'

Rafael felt his jaw clench. Why on earth had she put herself in such danger? Surely no photograph was worth risking one's life for?

'Of course I'd had training in how to deal with things like that,' she continued, 'but it was the first time it had happened to me and, in all the panic, I kind of forgot everything I'd been taught.'

'Were you badly hurt?'

'Depends what you mean by badly. I only had a couple of broken ribs so I guess I got off pretty lightly really. My camera, however, suffered infinitely more. It was smashed to bits. Luckily, though, I'd managed to take out the memory card before they got hold of it.'

'It must have been terrifying.'

Nicky shrugged. 'It's not an experience I'm particularly keen to repeat, I admit. And I'm not a huge fan of crowds.'

'I'm not surprised. So is that what your nightmares are about?'

This time she didn't bother pretending she didn't know what he was talking about. 'Pretty much.' She added, 'Sometimes the details vary but only slightly. Lately though they've been getting fuzzier and I have them far less often than I used to so that's good. Anyway it all happened ages ago, and I'm fine about it. Really.'

Hmm. Was she? 'So where does the burnout come in?'

Nicky blinked and gave him a rueful smile. 'Oh, well, I was so determined to prove that what had happened hadn't affected me that I went a bit overboard on the work front.'

'Overboard?'

'Put it this way. I didn't so much get back on the horse as saddle it up and take it round the Grand National a couple of times. I started working every waking hour I had and barely stopped for breath.'

Rafael frowned. 'Was that sustainable?'

'No. I was hurtling from time zone to time zone so much that I had no idea whether it was morning or night. It played havoc on my sleep and eventually I just wore out. Even taking my camera out of its case ended up becoming a major task and that scared me witless because if I can't take photos

I don't know what else there is.' She ran a hand through her hair. 'I think I just kind of gave up. It was so tiring treading water, I simply stopped. And once I'd done that then I really began to sink.'

'That doesn't sound good,' he muttered, knowing it was an understatement but too mystified by all the stuff beginning to churn around inside him to respond with anything more sensible.

'No, well, it wasn't,' she said dryly, 'but it's why I ended up at your house. It's why when we met I was in a bit of a state. And it's why when you kissed me I couldn't respond, even though I desperately wanted to. When I told you that my lack of response to you wasn't you but me, I meant it. Along with everything else I'd lost all interest in sex. It was like I was dead inside.'

'But not any more.'

She grinned. 'Not any more. And I've been taking pictures again. Of your vineyard. Do you mind?'

Did he mind? God, it was the least he could offer after all she'd been through. After all he'd put her through, and not just this afternoon. 'Of course not.'

Her smile deepened and his stomach twisted. 'Great. Well, anyway, it turns out your sister is quite the psychiatrist because she was the one who decided a rest and a time-out to regroup was the answer and she was right. That *cortijo* of yours was exactly what I needed.'

No, what Nicky needed was looking after, Rafael decided darkly, because God, he'd thought he'd had a tough time of it lately, but, compared with what she'd been through, a merger, a handful of demanding relatives and a persistent ex were nothing. And she might act as if she was over what had happened but was she? Really?

'So what plans do you have next?' he asked, ignoring the little voice inside his head demanding to know where he thought he was going with this, because she might not really be over it and she might need looking after but he definitely wasn't the sort of person who should be getting involved.

She lifted her eyebrows. 'You mean beyond some more of that lovely restorative sex?'

'Beyond that.'

She blinked and shrugged. 'I don't know. I'm not very good at living beyond the present.'

'Well, I'm at a loose end… You're at a loose end… What would you say to tying our loose ends together for a while?'

She grinned. 'I'd say does that line really work?'

Rafael frowned because oddly enough it hadn't been a line. 'I have no idea. You tell me.'

[faded text from previous page bleeding through]

CHAPTER TWELVE

APPARENTLY IT DID because a week later Nicky was back at the *cortijo* with Rafael, and she was loving every minute of it.

And why wouldn't she be when she was being so well attended to? she thought, feeling a sleepy satisfied smile spread across her face as she yawned and stretched gingerly so as not to wake Rafael, who was still asleep beside her.

Since they'd been back he'd been pretty much the perfect host. Not only had he made sure she was well fed and well rested, but he'd kept her entertained too. He'd taken her to the beach and taught her the basics of kite surfing. He'd driven her up into the coolness of the hills to a fabulous little restaurant overlooking a sparkling lake and fed her lobster. He'd spent an afternoon showing her round the vineyards and explaining how the *fino* she'd acquired quite a taste for was made. And then yesterday he'd asked her if she'd like to help with the harvest and they'd spent the day cutting away fat heavy bunches of grapes, until she couldn't bear her aching back any longer and had begged him for a massage.

As for the nights—and the siestas—well, those were something else. Nicky had always thought she'd had an active and relatively adventurous sex life but sleeping with Rafael took it to a whole new level. Over and over again she hit heights she'd never reached before, experiencing pleasure she hadn't known existed. The lavish attention he paid her body and the wild intensity with which he devoured her blew her mind every time.

She didn't regret telling him all about her recent history one little bit. Back then, sitting on his bed in Madrid in the wake of that extraordinary afternoon, it had felt like the ideal opportunity to test her emotional strength, and it had been everything she'd hoped for.

Opening up to him had been wonderfully liberating and that feeling of relief and freedom still lingered so she'd had no problem with answering the dozens of other questions he had about what had happened. She'd happily spilled out the details he'd asked for and at some point during the last week she'd felt something shift inside her. Something heavy dissipate. And she rather thought that at last—*finally*—she seemed to be getting over what had happened to her.

How she'd ever imagined that she and Rafael had nothing in common other than Gaby and a dislike of complicated relationships Nicky would never know. Apart from being astonishingly compatible in bed, they shared a love of the outdoors and travel. Of good food and hard work. Of books and art. Intrigued, she'd interrogated him about his fascination with plants and he'd been equally curious about her unconventional upbringing.

They seemed to be able to talk, laugh and argue about virtually everything under the sun. In fact pretty much the only thing that they *hadn't* talked about was his marriage, and it sat between them like the proverbial elephant in the room. Or at least *her* corner of the room because, while Rafael was no doubt perfectly happy to leave it alone, she was becoming quite obsessed with wanting to know all about it.

As she'd got to know him better, she'd found herself wondering what kind of husband he'd been, what his wife had been like, what kind of marriage they'd had and why it had failed. None of which she needed to know, of course, because she certainly wasn't interested in him—or anyone else for that matter—in a matrimonial kind of way, but that didn't stop her whiling away endless hours wondering.

And because she could never ask such intrusive questions her imagination had been working overtime. He'd be protective, she'd decided. Passionate. Loyal. And caring. Oh, he might like to make out that he was only interested in himself but that wasn't true at all, was it? Over the last few days she'd gathered plenty of evidence that contradicted *that* claim. She'd seen it in the way he'd provided food and water and shade for the temporary workers who'd been brought in to help with the harvest. In the way he'd frogmarched the housekeeper, Ana, to her room when she'd been stoically trying to carry on her duties through a streaming summer cold.

And in the way he'd kept a distant yet watchful eye on *her*.

Not that he'd needed to keep an eye on her because she was doing fine on her own, but that didn't stop warmth stealing through her whenever she glanced at him and caught him looking at her with what she thought might be concern and heat and something else that she was struggling to identify.

The warmth would have been worrying if she hadn't known perfectly well that she and Rafael wouldn't—couldn't—last. She hadn't been lying when she'd told him she wasn't interested in anything long-term; now she was back to her usual self, she fully intended to resume her old life and globetrot her way across the planet in the way she knew and loved.

Besides, they'd soon be going their separate ways. Once the summer was over Rafael would head back to Madrid and work, and she'd be back in Paris and lining up work of her own. And if that didn't sound quite as appealing as it should, well, that was just nervousness about having been out of the game for a while, nothing more.

Rafael stirred and Nicky frowned. Hmm. Maybe the fact

that this thing between them would inevitably come to an end—and sooner rather than later—was something she ought to keep in the forefront of her mind. She couldn't stay here for ever, and right now she might be having a great time but it wouldn't do to get lulled into a false sense of security, which would be all too easy to do seeing as this last week had been so idyllic.

She should probably stop spending quite so much time in his bed, she thought, carefully disentangling herself from the sheet and shifting away from him. In it she tended to lose all sense of perspective and reality and, while it was utterly lovely, getting used to it wouldn't do her any favours at all. Even if she wanted to, with the way she scooted around the world, living in hotel rooms and out of a suitcase, she simply couldn't afford to get used to anything.

Barely managing to resist the temptation to flop back and wake Rafael up in the most delicious way she could think of, Nicky was in the process of swinging her legs round when a hand snapped round her wrist and stopped her in her tracks.

'Where are you off to?' he said sleepily.

She twisted round and glanced down at him, drinking in the rumpled hair and sexy smile, and for a moment couldn't remember. 'I thought I might get up.'

He rubbed his eyes, gave his head a quick shake and shifted up onto his elbow. 'Why?'

'Because it's five in the afternoon.'

'So?' He stroked her wrist and her stomach all but disappeared.

Nicky swallowed and racked her brains for a reason to get up when there wasn't one. 'My feet are getting itchy,' she said even though they'd never felt less itchy.

'OK,' he said, sliding his hand up her arm and making goosebumps pop up all over her skin, 'so how about a trip into town?'

'That sounds great.'

'Then into town we'll go,' he murmured, and then pulled her down and back into his arms and gave her a kiss that frazzled her brain and made a mockery of her pathetic effort to resist him. 'Later.'

Quite a long time later, Rafael was sitting with Nicky at a table in a square in the centre of town, toying with the stem of his wine glass and wondering if he ought to be worried about what was going on here.

There were certainly things he *should* be worried about. Work or, rather, his lack of interest in it was one, for example. Nicky's friendship with his sister and its odd insignificance was another. Above all, he really ought to be concerned about the way that virtually anything that related to life beyond the physical and metaphorical boundaries of the vineyard simply didn't seem to matter.

Anything related to *real* life, in fact.

What was going on with Nicky wasn't real, he reminded himself, glancing over at her from behind his sunglasses and seeing a dreamy, wistful kind of smile curve her mouth. It couldn't last for ever, and nor did he want it to. Never mind that she was remarkably easy to be with. Never mind that she was fascinating. And never mind that night after night she blew his mind. She'd soon be going home, as would he, and he was absolutely fine with that.

So why did the thought of this being over and of her disappearing from his life for good leave such a bitter taste in his mouth? Why did it make his stomach twist and his chest squeeze? And when had the idea of going home started to sound quite so unappealing?

Rafael's fingers tightened around his glass and he shifted in his chair as it struck him that perhaps he wasn't quite as happy about the temporary nature of this thing with Nicky as he'd tried to convince himself.

Come to think of it, why did it have to be temporary anyway? Why couldn't they continue seeing each other even after they'd returned to their respective homes?

Nicky might have said she wasn't looking for a relationship but presumably she'd meant one that tied her to one place, that compromised her freedom. But over the last week he'd come to understand and respect her sense of wanderlust and he'd never ask that of her. Besides, why would he even want to when her independence, her self-sufficiency and her commitment to her work were among the things he most liked about her?

In that respect they were perfect for each other, so what would be wrong with a hot, steamy, long-distance affair? Nothing, as far as he could work out, so perhaps he ought to suggest it and see what she had to say...

'So what did your wife think of all this?'

Nicky's question yanked him out of his thoughts and he froze with shock at the unexpectedness of it. His wife? She wanted to talk about his *wife*? Now?

Forcing himself not to tense up, Rafael swivelled round to look at her. She was frowning and she'd gone a little pink and he got the impression that it was a question she hadn't intended to ask.

He wished she hadn't because the subject of his marriage wasn't one he cared to dwell on, but now she'd brought it up he could hardly pretend she hadn't, however much he might want to. He supposed he was lucky to have got away without having to discuss it for this long.

But never mind. It was fine. Just because she'd asked didn't mean he had to tell her anything other than the basic facts, did it?

'My wife?' he echoed.

'Well, your ex-wife,' she amended with a slight smile.

'She didn't think anything about this.'

Nicky frowned. 'What do you mean?'

'She never came down here.'

Her eyebrows shot up. 'What, never?'

'No,' he said coolly. 'I've only had the vineyard for five years and she was always more interested in city life anyway.'

'What was her name?'

'Marina.'

'And what was she like?'

'Blonde. Beautiful.'

'Naturally,' she said dryly.

'She was also temperamental and difficult.'

Looking slightly mollified by that, Nicky sat back. 'So what went wrong?'

Suddenly feeling as if he were sitting on knives, Rafael shifted uncomfortably in his chair. 'Hasn't Gaby told you?'

'No. She's loyal and I didn't like to ask.'

'Let's just say it didn't work out.'

'Yes, the divorce part of it kind of gives that away.'

He shrugged. 'There you go, then.'

Nicky fell silent and for a moment Rafael thought with blessed relief that was that. That she'd understood that he didn't want to talk about it, and that as far as he was concerned the topic was now closed.

But apparently it wasn't, at least not for her, because she was lifting her sunglasses off her nose and up into her hair and giving him a look that suggested that she didn't think him brushing over it quite so dismissively was on.

'Is that it?' she said, clearly not impressed. 'Is that all I'm getting?'

'Isn't that enough?'

'Not nearly.'

'Tough.' That was all he was prepared to divulge.

Nicky harrumphed and folded her arms over her chest. 'Well, that doesn't seem entirely fair, does it?' she said eventually.

Rafael lifted an eyebrow at her indignation. 'What doesn't?'

'I tell you all about the stuff that happened to me yet you get to avoid talking about what happened to you? I don't think so.'

The urge to tense up was back but he stamped it down and pasted a bland smile to his face. 'But the difference is that you *chose* to tell me. Willingly. And I don't particularly like talking about my marriage.'

'I'm sure you don't,' she said archly, 'but you might find it surprisingly therapeutic. I did, after all.'

'I don't need therapy. I got over it years ago.'

She fixed him with another far too perceptive look. 'Really?' she asked with a scepticism that made him want to grind his teeth.

'Absolutely.'

'In that case, why the reluctance to talk about it? And why do you still have such a thing about getting involved with your sisters' friends?'

This time Rafael couldn't stop his jaw from clenching because as he contemplated her irritatingly shrewd questions he realised she had a point. And he, therefore, didn't have much of a choice if he didn't want her thinking she was right. 'Fine,' he said as if it didn't bother him in the slightest. 'What do you want to know?'

Rafael's marriage might have been occupying her mind a lot lately, but Nicky had never had any intention of actually bringing it up.

However she'd been gazing in the direction of the

wedding-goers gathering in front of the church on the other side of the square and idly wondering whether he and the beautiful but temperamental Marina had been married here or in Madrid and what the dress had looked like, when the warmth and the wine and a sheer sense of contentment had obliterated her inhibitions and the question had simply spilled out of her mouth.

Once it had there'd been little point in hoping he hadn't heard her and even less in trying to back-pedal. And if she was being completely honest, she wouldn't have retracted it even if she could because the curiosity had been practically killing her.

She wanted to know everything, and now, thank *God*, it seemed she'd have to wonder and speculate and imagine no longer. 'Why don't you start at the beginning?' she said.

Rafael set his jaw and looked as if he were bracing himself. 'I met Marina through my younger sister.'

'Gaby?'

'The next one up. Elena. She and Marina were best friends. Elena had a party to celebrate her birthday and we were introduced. We dated and three months later we got married.'

Nicky nearly fell off her chair because that didn't sound like the action of the keen-on-control Rafael she'd come to know. 'Wow, that was quick.'

'Too quick with hindsight,' he said dryly.

'How long were you married for?'

'A couple of years.'

'What happened?'

He grimaced. 'Once the honeymoon was over—literally—it became pretty clear that we had nothing in common.'

Nothing? She couldn't believe that. Not when, as she'd discovered, he was intelligent and interesting and had well-formed opinions on an impressively wide range of subjects.

'You must have had *something* in common,' she said, 'otherwise why get married in the first place?'

He rubbed a hand along his jaw and nodded briefly. 'OK, there was one thing,' he conceded and as a pang of jealousy darted through her Nicky wished she hadn't pressed the point. 'But naturally it wasn't enough. We were too different. And too young.'

'How old were you?' she asked, dismissing the jealously as entirely normal and ignoring it.

'I was twenty-three and Marina was twenty.'

'Didn't anyone try and stop you?'

'Of course, but you know how I feel about advice. I'm as bad at taking it as I am at giving it.' He gave her a tight humourless smile. 'Besides, I'd just got back from Harvard and, having had the best education on offer, I thought I knew everything.'

'But you didn't.'

'Apparently not. I certainly knew nothing about how to handle the mess we'd got ourselves into. We argued. A lot. In fact,' he added with a frown, 'we argued about pretty much everything.'

'That sounds stressful.'

'It was.' He stopped and for a moment he seemed to be completely lost in the memory of it all before giving his head a quick shake and snapping out of it. 'Anyway, things went rapidly downhill until I ended up virtually living at the office and Marina ended up having an affair.'

Nicky winced. 'Ouch.'

Rafael sighed. 'I can't say I really blame her. We should never have got married in the first place. The whole thing was a disaster from start to finish and it's not something I'm in a hurry to do again.'

At the thought of him, normally so focused and so in control, so way out of his depth and floundering in the face of such unfathomably emotional upheaval, Nicky felt her heart squeeze. 'So how did your sister take it all?'

He went very still and a muscle ticced in his jaw. 'It wasn't the easiest of times,' he muttered eventually. 'We didn't see all that much of each other for a while. It was…awkward.'

'Just awkward?' she asked, thinking that for someone who clearly adored his sisters—even if they did occasionally drive him up the wall—'awkward' was more likely to mean 'gut-wrenching'.

'OK, yes, it was more than awkward,' he admitted, 'but you know all about the healing powers of time.'

She nodded. 'I do indeed.'

'We got through it eventually but that isn't something I'd care to repeat either.'

No, she could see why he wouldn't want to repeat any of it. And she could equally see why he went to such great lengths to avoid emotional mess now because she'd do the same in the circumstances. Who needed it?

Feeling faintly guilty at having made him relive what had clearly been a difficult time, Nicky decided the situation needed lightening.

'It's just as well I'm not blonde, beautiful, temperamental or difficult, then, isn't it?' she said, flashing him a teasing smile.

Rafael stared at her, bewilderment flickering across his face. 'What?'

'Well, when this is over we should be able to part as friends, don't you think? I certainly don't intend to lose Gaby's friendship over it.'

For a moment there was utter silence and Nicky wondered what she'd said. Then Rafael seemed to pull himself together and shot her a quick stomach-melting smile. 'This is quite different,' he said, and signalled for the bill.

* * *

It *was* different, thought Rafael, shoving his hands in the pockets of his jeans and leaning back against a low wall as he watched Nicky hunker down at the bottom of some steps and lift her camera to her eye.

And thank God for it because his relationship with Marina had been a disaster. A complete disaster, and not just because they'd been young and had had precious little in common. Yes, those had obviously been contributing factors to the breakdown of their marriage, but what had really been at the heart of it all was Marina's clinginess and neediness and his inability to handle any of it.

With hindsight he should have foreseen problems right from the start, or at least the minute he'd learned about her overprotective parents, the sheltered life she'd led and her desperate longing to escape.

If he'd been thinking straight he'd have paid attention to the great neon warnings his brain kept flashing at him and steered well clear, but in all honesty they'd met and he'd been so dazzled by her looks he'd stopped thinking at all.

It hadn't helped that meeting her had coincided with his return to Spain after years of hard academic work and little play. He'd been demob happy and hell-bent on making up for lost time and she'd been only too willing to help. So he hadn't stopped to think about what effect their whirlwind romance might have had on her and it had never occurred to him that she'd start to view him as some sort of saviour.

But she had, and before long the signs of her dependency on him had become apparent. She'd turned possessive, jealous and obsessive, calling him a dozen times a day just to check where he was and what he was doing. She'd stopped seeing the few friends she had and tried to stop him seeing the friends he had.

He'd unwittingly found himself responsible for her happiness and he hadn't known what to do. And then it had got even worse because by the time he realised how needy and stifling she'd become—and how unhappy he made her—he'd also realised that he'd confused lust with love and that by marrying her he'd made a massive mistake.

And the awful guilt-inducing truth of the matter was that he hadn't even thought about trying to sort things out, trying to make it work, because ultimately he hadn't cared. Not during their fiercest arguments, not when Marina had had the affair and not even when she'd filed for divorce.

In fact the bureaucratic nightmare of the divorce had given him a greater headache than his marriage had, and the distress it had caused his sister, who'd been torn between her brother and her best friend, had given him greater heartache.

Which was so wholly *wrong* he'd vowed never to let himself get into that kind of a situation again. Never again was he going to mistake lust for love, thought Rafael, narrowing his eyes and setting his jaw as he watched Nicky, who was totally absorbed in what she was doing. Nor did he intend to ever get himself into a relationship where he might find himself depended on. For anything. The responsibility of it all was simply too great and he'd only screw up. Again.

And that was why being with Nicky was so refreshing. He admired the way she kept her cards close to her chest, had the ability to sort things through in her own head and didn't ask anything of him. Above all he appreciated the way he could be himself, the way he didn't feel he had to be constantly on his guard in case she wanted more than he was able to give, because she never would.

The thought of pursuing a more long-term relationship with her popped up in his head once again and his muscles tensed and his heart beat a fraction faster as the need to get started on it right now surged up inside him.

What was the point in waiting? In deliberating? There

wasn't any, was there? Because it seemed to him that she was just as into this as he was, and he didn't think she'd say no. At least he fervently hoped she wouldn't.

Rafael was just about to push himself off the wall and head towards her when he saw her shoot to her feet, take a quick step back and crash straight into a group of tourists who'd gathered behind her and were listening to the guide gesticulating at the memorial she'd been photographing.

If he'd had time to think about it—and if it had been anyone else other than Nicky—he'd have expected her to brush herself off, give them a quick smile and a heartfelt apology and then stroll back to him.

But he didn't have time to think because it all happened so fast. So fast in fact that his brain slowed it right down.

He watched as Nicky froze and went white and then stumbled, and within what felt like aeons but could only have been a split second the little group was closing round her, hands reaching out to steady her.

As alarm began to flash through him he heard her cry of distress. Saw her lash out, and as he realised what was going on he didn't stop to think or consider his actions. He just reacted.

With his heart pounding as fiercely as he bet hers was and with adrenalin suddenly roaring through him, he raced over. Muttering a rough apology, he pushed his way through the crowd to where Nicky was standing, pale, sweating and shaking. He wrapped one arm around her waist, the other around her shoulders and drew her into a firm embrace.

'It's all right. You're OK,' he murmured against her hair, every cell of his body turning inside out with the need to absorb her panic and give her some of his strength. 'Lean on me. I've got you.'

CHAPTER THIRTEEN

I'VE GOT YOU.

As Rafael tightened his grip on Nicky's waist and led her away from the group of people and their curiosity at her extraordinary reaction to their mini collision, the words he was murmuring into her hair over and over spun round and round her head because now all the panic and confusion had evaporated it suddenly struck her that he *did* get her. He really did.

There she'd been a moment ago, surrounded and trapped and in the terrifying grip of a flashback, her heart hammering and panic drowning out the voice of common sense that was telling her the hands on her were only trying to steady her and that she wasn't in any danger. And then, just when her knees had been about to give way, just when she'd thought she'd been about to faint and almost falling apart at the awareness that she *still* wasn't as over everything as she'd thought, there *he'd* been, charging to her rescue like some kind of white knight, taking her into his arms and shielding her from the nightmare, warm and solid and so very reassuring.

She hadn't had to ask for his help. She hadn't had to spell it out. He'd somehow instinctively known what was wrong, and he'd put it right.

He'd got it.

He got *her*.

And not only a second ago, she thought dazedly as Rafael leaned back against the wall of the church and held her tight still murmuring soothing words into her hair. The truth of it was that over the last week he'd often appeared to be able to read her mind, apparently understanding exactly what she needed—whether it was space, silence or company—sometimes even before she did. And she'd been able to gauge his moods too.

It was as if they had some kind of connection and the weird thing was that, far from finding it unsettling as she should have done, she'd actually revelled in it. Which meant that not only did he get her, but that she *wanted* him to.

As *that* thought slammed into her head Nicky's slowing heart began to race all over again because hot on the heels of it came a whole load more, cascading into her head so fast that she went dizzy.

Oh, dear Lord. The attention and care he'd lavished on her in the last few days? She loved it. The feeling of being cherished, protected, looked after? She loved all that too. And as for the way he'd just rushed to her rescue, well, that melted just about every independent feminist thought she'd ever had.

She ought to have found it stifling, but she didn't. She ought to have been horrified that it went against everything she'd ever thought she'd valued, but she found she couldn't drum up much objection to that either.

And why not?

Because she was head over heels bonkers in love with him.

Nicky froze, her pulse going berserk and her knees threatening to buckle all over again.

She was in love with him. She had to be. What else could account for it all?

She'd never really thought about falling in love. Never

imagined she would. Never expected it. It wasn't that she didn't believe in it as a concept, and it wasn't as if she hadn't had a good example of it set by her parents. It was just that she'd never felt it herself before. She'd always been too busy to look for it. Too focused on staying on the move and remaining unattached.

But not any more because now she was thinking about it she was beginning to realise that she loved everything about him. And it had nothing whatsoever to do with the mind-blowing sex, because even when they weren't in bed she still had that wonderfully warm sense of contentment. Every time he smiled at her, every time he looked at her and every time he touched her. In fact every time he crossed her mind her heart turned over and she went soft and warm inside.

If that wasn't love, then what was it?

And just like that all those things that had been baffling her recently suddenly made sense. Her lack of enthusiasm about going back to Paris. The longing to learn everything there was to know about him. The brief jagged pain that scythed through her at the thought of them being over. The wrenching of her heart when she'd caught sight of the couple floating out of the church not five minutes ago, beaming and radiating happiness and wrapped round each other as they posed for photographs beneath a Mudéjar arch. And the couple of dark-haired green-eyed children she'd secretly imagined racing around the *cortijo*…

As her muscles gently collapsed beneath the deluge of emotion descending over her Nicky sank against him. God. Not a fan of emotional mess? Who had she been kidding? She'd never wanted it more. She wanted the roller coaster of the ride. The highs and the lows, the laughter and the arguments. She was bone-deep tired of being footloose and fancy free, of the endless travel and being alone. She wanted to settle down. She wanted someone to share her life with. She wanted Rafael.

Her heart thumped as her mind raced. But what about him? How did he feel about her? Could she even begin to hope he might love her back? Yes, she'd noticed his concern for her, the way he'd cared for her, the warmth with which he looked at her, but did any of that mean anything? Surely it had to mean *something*...

Listening to the steady beat of his heart beneath her cheek and taking strength from the arms around her and the warm hard body still supporting her, she sifted through all the evidence, analysing every look and every smile he'd given her, every little thing he'd said and done, and her heart thumped wildly as she came to the conclusion that he very well could.

And OK, from what she'd just learned about his marriage of course he'd be wary of loving again and wary of commitment, but maybe she could show him that with someone who understood him, with *her*, he needn't be.

Nicky closed her eyes and took a deep breath, inhaling the intoxicating scent of him as she struggled to absorb all these earth-shattering discoveries and would have swayed had she not been locked in his embrace.

'Would you like to go home?' he said softly.

And just when she thought her system couldn't cope with any more shocks, wham, there was another one, because didn't *home* sound like the most heavenly thing ever?

She'd never had a home before. Never wanted one. If she'd ever thought about it she'd have shuddered at the idea of anything so permanent. So cosy. So boringly domestic. But that long-held belief went the way of the others and exploded into smithereens because right now she couldn't think of anywhere she'd rather be than with Rafael. At home. For ever.

Feeling that the world had somehow tilted violently and

then settled back down all upside down, Nicky dazedly leaned back in his arms, smiled up into his eyes and said, 'Yes, please.'

The fact that Nicky didn't seem to have anything to say during the car journey back to the *cortijo* suited Rafael down to the ground because there was so much stuff churning around in his head he didn't think he'd be able to hold anything remotely resembling a conversation even if she'd wanted one.

At some point between taking her in his arms to lead her to safety and getting in the car something had changed. What precisely it was he couldn't work out. All he knew was that something was different, it was deeply unsettling and for some reason it threw his idea of a long-term relationship with Nicky right on its head.

He'd been leaning back against that wall and holding her close when he'd felt her stiffen, then soften. All of a sudden it had seemed to him that she was pressing just that little bit closer and not because she wanted to get horizontal and naked with him but because she wanted to simply be with him.

For some reason the idea of it had made him reel. It had made him prickle with foreboding and fill with trepidation. And then, before he'd had time to recover and to reassure himself that he was merely still shaken up by what he'd seen Nicky just go through and must have imagined it, she'd smiled up at him, her eyes shining and her face all soft and dreamy. She'd looked at him as if he were her knight in shining armour and his heart had given a sudden lurch because at that moment tough, resilient, independent Nicky had been replaced by someone he didn't recognise.

And frankly it spooked the hell out of him.

'Rafael, are you all right?'

His hands tightened on the steering wheel and he wished they were home already so he could put some distance between them. 'Fine,' he muttered. 'Why?'

'You're very quiet.'

'Just thinking, that's all.'

'About what happened back there?'

'Partly.'

'Me too.' There it was again, that dreamy wistfulness in her voice drifting through the dark, winding through him and twisting his gut into knots. 'Thank you for coming to my rescue.'

Rafael tensed and felt a bead of sweat trickle down his spine as his stomach instinctively clutched tighter. 'You're welcome.'

'I'll have to make sure you're around every time I find myself unexpectedly in the middle of a crowd.'

Her words hit his brain and Rafael went utterly cold, because despite the faint teasing note in her voice he didn't think she was joking. And if she wasn't joking, then he was in a whole lot of trouble. And if he was, then it was all entirely of his own making.

The knowledge struck him like a blow and he inhaled sharply. God, he'd been a fool. He'd told Nicky to lean on him and that was precisely what she'd done. And not, he could now see, in a solely literal sense. Nor only back in that square. She'd been leaning on him ever since he'd brought her back down here and like a blind idiot he hadn't seen it.

In fact he'd been *provoking* it.

He'd thought he'd simply been keeping an eye on her. Making sure she was OK. Spending time with her, getting to know her and encouraging her to talk about what had happened in the Middle East to help her get over it. But what he'd really been doing over the course of the last week was creating an environment in which she was *bound* to come to depend on him.

How he could have forgotten that she might not be as fully recovered as she claimed he had no idea. Hadn't she woken up in the early hours, sweating and trembling, only a couple of nights ago? She had, and without a thought for the consequences he'd gathered her in his arms and held her until she'd stopped shaking with fear and started quivering with something else entirely.

And then back there in the square he'd rushed to her side, and that must have fanned the flames because, God, the way she'd smiled up at him... As if he'd rescued her from more than just a flashback...

Rafael's blood chilled. He wasn't that man. He couldn't be. He couldn't be responsible for her well-being because he'd only fail and very probably set her back months.

So he could forget any idea of a long-distance, more permanent relationship, he thought with grim resolve. Things had already gone far too far and the minute they got back to the *cortijo* he'd be putting a stop to this affair, this budding relationship, this whatever it was, once and for all.

'Rafael?'

'What?' he growled, completely lost in thought.

'I think I love you.'

Perhaps Rafael's car in the dead of night wasn't the best place to blurt out she loved him, thought Nicky, clinging onto the door handle as the car swerved briefly before being hauled back under control, but really she hadn't had much of a choice. She'd never been one to tackle things anything other than head-on, so once she'd realised she loved him and wanted something more with him the need to spill it out had bubbled and built until it just sort of erupted from her.

But maybe she should have told him while they were in

bed or something because she didn't know what reaction she'd been expecting but she'd known what she'd been hoping for, and the short sharp curse, the fierce scowl, and the crackling tension that was suddenly filling the space between them wasn't it.

But it was way too late for regret. Her declaration was out there, the words were echoing between them in the thick darkness and there was no taking it back. All she could do now was brace herself for his response.

Releasing her death grip on the door handle, Nicky swivelled slightly to look at him and, with her heart in her throat, waited.

And waited.

And waited.

But to her growing bewilderment Rafael remained resolutely silent, his jaw tight and his focus fixed on the road ahead, and with every kilometre that the car gobbled up she went a little colder.

'Aren't you going to say anything?' she asked, when the deafening silence finally became unbearable.

'What do you want me to say?'

At the complete lack of emotion in his voice it dawned on her that this conversation was unlikely to go the way she'd have liked, and Nicky filled with apprehension. 'I don't know,' she said, suddenly feeling all shaky inside. 'How about thank you? I'm flattered. I love you too. *Something.*'

'I'm sorry,' he said flatly, 'but you don't love me.'

For a moment she thought she must have misheard, but no, he really had just told her that she didn't love him.

As it sank in Nicky felt her eyes widen and her jaw drop because of all the responses she could have imagined an outright denial of her feelings would never have occurred to her. 'What?' she breathed.

'You don't love me. You just think you do.' He shot her

a quick unfathomable look. 'I'm not some kind of white knight, Nicky.'

She blinked. 'I know you're not.'

'Do you?' His jaw tightened.

'Of course.' She might have had a moment of fancy back there in the square but that was all it had been because she knew perfectly well that, not only did Rafael have feet of clay like everyone else, but she didn't need a knight.

'I can't be responsible for your well-being.'

Confusion spun through her. Had she missed something? Had they had a conversation she'd forgotten about? They must have done because where was all this coming from? How on earth had they got from her telling him she loved him to this? And where had this God complex suddenly sprung from? 'What makes you think you are?'

'Your comment about needing me around whenever you find yourself in a crowd.'

'That was a *joke*.'

'It didn't sound like one.'

And maybe it hadn't been one *totally*, but that wasn't the point. 'I see,' she said, folding her arms over her chest and feeling her blood beginning to simmer in response to his baffling attitude. 'And you've deduced from that that I've somehow cast you in the role of knight in shining armour?'

'Haven't you?'

'Of course not.'

'It wouldn't be your fault if you had.' His face tightened. 'This last week has been a mistake,' he muttered, almost as if talking to himself. '*My* mistake.'

Did he really believe that? The hurt that suddenly cut through her momentarily robbed her of breath. 'Why?'

'Because I've let you become dependent on me and I shouldn't have.'

She let out a slow measured breath to stop the top of her

head blowing off. 'You know, your arrogance is truly staggering,' she said, staring at him in stupefaction as all the
lovely warmth and the dizzying sense of wonder that had
been bubbling away inside her for the last hour or so evaporated.

Rafael whipped his head round to give her a quick glance
and she saw astonishment written all over his face. 'What?'

'I'm perfectly capable of being responsible for my own
well-being,' she said, silently adding, *You jerk*. 'Like it or
not, I'm in love with you.' Although right now she really
wished she weren't. 'And it has nothing to do with my recovery or dependency or whatever you think you've been
doing over the last week.'

'You can't be,' he said flatly. 'We haven't known each
other long enough. You're confusing love and lust, that's all.'

Nicky fought not to gape at him as her head spun. What
the hell was going on here? Who was this? Where was the
Rafael she'd fallen in love with? The warm, thoughtful man
who'd made her laugh and who'd made such passionate love
to her. The one she'd got to know and admire. He had to
still be there somewhere but why had he switched himself
off like this?

And then suddenly a great wave of hurt and disappointment swept through her, boiling her blood and firing her indignation. If he didn't feel the same way about her as she did
about him that was fine. Painful, but fair enough. But this
casual and cold dismissal of her feelings? No, that wasn't
right and it wasn't fair.

'How dare you?' she breathed.

'What?' he said, casting her a quick cool glance as if he
genuinely didn't have a clue what she meant.

'How dare you just brush me off like that?'

He shrugged. 'Because I know what I'm talking about.'
The condescension in his voice made her want to slap him.

'It happened to me. In my marriage. I thought I married for love. It turned out to be nothing more than lust.'

'And you think that's what's going on here?'

'If it's not dependency, then very possibly. Have you ever been in love before?'

'Well, no, but—'

'Then how do you know that what you claim to feel for me isn't love, but simply lust?'

And once again he rendered her speechless. She just sat there, totally bamboozled by his logic and unable to breathe. She felt winded, as if he'd struck her square in the chest.

And then sensation came flooding back, and all that hurt and disappointment and frustration at his reaction now combined with dizzying and unfamiliar red hot anger, and the whole lot of it surged through her in one great unstoppable wave.

'I'll tell you how I know,' she said, feeling what little control she had when it came to him slipping away but too consumed by all the emotions tossing around inside her to do anything about it. 'I know because even if we never made love again I'd still want to be with you. I know because I admire you and respect you and because I think you're amazing. Yes, I love the way you make me feel, but it's so much more than that.' She glared at him. 'And you know how I *really* know it's love and not lust?'

'How?' he said, sounding as if he couldn't be less interested.

'By the way that your casual dismissal of what I feel is practically crucifying me.'

Rafael went still, but he didn't look at her. 'If I've hurt you, then I apologise, but perhaps it's for the best.'

'For the best?' she echoed.

'Better now than months down the line.'

God, she really had got it wrong, hadn't she? Terribly,

agonisingly wrong. 'Are you honestly saying that you feel nothing for me?'

Rafael frowned. 'I wouldn't say nothing. I like you a lot and I can't get enough of you in bed. But as I said, that's just lust.'

'And what about if sex wasn't part of the equation?'

'I would rapidly lose interest.'

His voice might be flat and cold but the muscle ticcing madly in his jaw suggested he wasn't as unaffected as he was trying to make out, and suddenly a tiny ray of hope burst through the tangle of hurt and confusion and anger within her. 'I don't believe you.'

He shrugged. 'That's up to you.'

As all the things he'd done for her, the way he'd held her, made love to her, talked to her flashed through her head she took a deep breath and a massive gamble. 'I think you love me too.'

'You couldn't be more wrong, because I don't.'

She let out that breath in a furious exasperated rush, suddenly utterly fed up with him. 'God, I've never met such a stubborn, thick-headed man in my life. Nor one who is such an emotional coward.'

That jerked him out of his indifference. He snapped his gaze to hers, his eyes blazing. *'What?'*

Nicky gripped her seat belt and refused to quail. 'You're an emotional coward, Rafael.'

He snapped his gaze back to the road. 'What the hell do you mean by that?'

'Every time the going gets tough, every time something crops up that you don't want to deal with, you retreat.'

'I do not.'

'No?' she said. 'OK, well, let's take a look at the evidence.'

'Don't be ridiculous. There is no evidence.'

'You think?' She held up her hand and ticked off her index

finger. 'Firstly there's your marriage. Things started getting difficult and you buried yourself in your work.'

'Don't even begin to presume you know what went on in my marriage,' he said icily calmly.

Nicky ignored his chilling fury. 'I wouldn't dream of it. But you even admitted that much, once you managed to get past your reluctance to talk about it in the first place. And then what about that time we met?' She wiggled her middle finger.

'What about it?'

'Weren't you escaping from the demands of two sisters, one mother and an ex-girlfriend?'

He gritted his teeth and his eyes flashed her a warning but she wasn't about to stop now. 'And then there was that kiss by the pool,' she fired at him, giving up with the fingers altogether. 'You might not have physically fled then, but emotionally you did, and you're doing it again now. Going straight into denial and retreating, just because I'm being honest and you can't deal with it. You look like you're itching to escape and the only reason you're not is because we're in your car flying along at seventy kilometres an hour and you can't.' She gave him a withering look. 'And you know something—while kind of understandable in a boy of eight, in a man of thirty-two it's pathetic.'

Her words hung in the air, suspended between them, the seconds ticking heavily by before he said, 'Yes, well, we can't all be wild, adventurous risk-takers like you.'

She stared at him. 'You see being honest and dealing with emotions as a risk?'

'Absolutely.'

'Then what about the rewards?'

'In my experience there aren't any.'

Ooh, she wanted to thump him. 'If you truly think that, then that's sad. Yes, I take risks—' and none more so than the one she'd taken just now '—but they're generally calculated ones. And even if one does go wrong—' as this one seemed to be doing '—at least I tried. But what do you do? You hide.'

'It's called self-preservation.'

'It's called immaturity.'

Rafael flinched as if she'd struck him, but Nicky hadn't finished. They might have arrived back at the *cortijo* and he might be yanking on the handbrake and reaching for the clip of his seat belt as if he couldn't get away fast enough, but she matched him for speed. 'You think you're so good at solving problems and sorting out things for other people,' she said, freeing herself and reaching for the door, 'but what about you? Who sorts you out?' She glared at him. 'Right now the biggest problem here is you and your absurd refusal to even entertain the thought about how you might feel about me, and you're not even bothering to try and fix it even though you could.'

'There's nothing to fix.'

'There could be.'

'There won't be.'

He got out of the car and slammed the door shut, and it finally hit her that she'd never be able to get through to him. That he'd been hiding his emotions away for too long and too well. Nothing she could say or do would ever have any effect on him and Nicky had suddenly had enough.

'Well, if that really is the case,' she said, her voice shaking with anger, 'then this time *I'm* the one walking away.'

Nicky was wrong, thought Rafael grimly as the slam of the front door reverberated throughout the *cortijo*, leaving nothing but an eerie silence and the echo of all those accusations.

Dead wrong. About everything.

As if he needed sorting out. As if he needed fixing. The

idea was laughable. He didn't need either. He was fine the way he was.

And if he did occasionally retreat, well, what was the problem with that? As he'd told her, it was simply a question of self-preservation, that was all. It worked for his father and it worked for him. He had it under control. It wasn't an issue. And it wasn't immaturity. And what would she know about it anyway? She didn't have a vast family that constantly badgered her, did she?

And OK, he might have been a bit thrown by that conversation about Marina and all the memories it had tossed up, and he might possibly have got it wrong about her being dependent on him, but as for them being in love with each other, well, that was completely absurd.

He wasn't in love with her and she wasn't in love with him. She couldn't be. They'd only known each other for a few weeks. It wasn't possible.

So it was a good thing she'd gone, wasn't it, because, God, all that emotion… It had been horrible…

Stifling a shudder, Rafael stalked into the drawing room and strode towards the drinks cabinet. He reached for the brandy and filled a glass and winced as all the things Nicky had said and the way she'd said them hit him all over again. He tossed his drink back in one and hoped the burning alcohol that hit his stomach would obliterate the memory of the last half an hour.

At least it was all over now, which was excellent because he didn't need this kind of hassle in his life. He didn't need this kind of upheaval. And he could certainly do without feeling like this.

Whatever it was that was coursing through him right now it couldn't possibly be something serious like hurt or disappointment or regret or anything. It was simply shock at the abruptness of her departure, that was all. And if he did feel a tiny pang of loss, well, that was only natural given the intensity and passion that their affair had had.

Like everything, recovering from it would simply be a question of patience and time, and with a bit of both he'd soon come to appreciate the lucky escape he'd had.

CHAPTER FOURTEEN

NICKY'S ANGER SUSTAINED her throughout the entire horrendous journey back to Paris. She bristled and fumed her way through the tiresome process of handing back her hire car, the booking of a last-minute, excruciatingly expensive flight, and, what with a three hour delay and a diversion to Orly, staying furious hadn't taken all that much effort.

The teeth-grinding frustration of international travel notwithstanding, all she had to do was remember how she'd laid her heart, her feelings, everything she had on the line and how Rafael had trampled all over them, and it rose up inside her all over again. She'd mentally called him every filthy name she could think of in both English and French, and told herself over and over again that she was well shot of him.

But the minute she closed her front door behind her the adrenalin and energy drained right away sweeping up all her anger and strength with it, and with a low anguished moan she crumpled into a heap on the floor.

As despair and misery filled the gaping hole left inside her, she finally gave in to the wretchedness and tears spilled down her cheeks because she might be well shot of him but she was still crazy about him. Her heart felt as if it were being wrenched from her chest. Her head pounded, her throat burned and she ached all over.

Oh, how could it all hurt so *much*? And why was she crying like this? She never cried. Now, though, it seemed she couldn't stop.

Burying her head in her hands as yet more tears welled up, Nicky reran the whole horrible conversation and with her anger at Rafael's reaction all burned out she now helplessly charged off down the road of self-recrimination.

Why, oh, why had she had to say anything? Why had she had to go and tell him she loved him? Why couldn't she just have kept it to herself?

She wrapped her arms around herself and rocked as regret spun through her. How could she have let rip at him like that? What gave her the right to fire all that stuff about his issues at him? And as for telling him he loved her, well, who the hell was she to assume that that was the case? He'd never given her that impression, had he? No, her common sense had been shot to pieces by everything that had happened in the previous half an hour and she'd jumped to that ridiculous conclusion all by herself.

She'd lost all control and because of it she'd never see him again. Her throat ached and her eyes stung all over again and she let out a quiet anguished moan as what little was left of her heart shattered.

God, if this was love then she was lucky to have escaped it for the past twenty-nine years because she'd never known agony like it. Never felt hopelessness like it, not even when she'd been at rock-bottom.

How long she sat there, crying and tormenting herself with what ifs and if onlys, she had no idea. All she knew was that by the time she was all wrung out and had no tears left, long silvery grey fingers of daylight were inching through the slats in her blinds.

With a deep sigh, Nicky wiped her eyes with the sleeve of her coat, sniffed unattractively and pulled herself together. This wasn't doing her any good, was it? She might be feeling battered and bruised but she couldn't stay here wallowing in self-pity for ever.

Groggily she got to her feet. She swayed a little and had to lean against the wall for support. Her limbs felt like jelly and she hurt everywhere but she gritted her teeth and made it into the kitchen because maybe things would look a bit brighter after coffee.

There was something remarkably restful about going through the motions of filling the pot with water, adding the coffee grounds to the filter and then screwing the top on. Something comfortably familiar, and as she put the pot on the hob, lit the gas and then leaned back against the counter to let it do its thing she determinedly rallied her spirits.

She might have screwed up whatever she and Rafael had had by recklessly telling him she loved him, but one good thing had come out of that whole mess of a conversation, and that was that she'd been right about wanting to settle down.

Despite the considerable progress she'd made she still—frustratingly—wasn't one hundred per cent back to her old self, so maybe she did need a bit of permanency to give herself the chance and time to focus on her.

And she might not have Rafael to settle down with but that didn't mean she couldn't do it anyway, did it?

Of course she could. She might love him, but she didn't *need* him. Even before she'd realised she loved him, she'd been toying with the idea of making changes to her life, and she was perfectly capable of making those changes on her own. In fact with no one else to consult, with no one to offer an opinion and advice, it would probably be easier.

She'd start now, she thought, pouring a cup of coffee and taking a hot fortifying sip. Thinking positively was the thing. Staying buoyant and remaining focused. And in the process she was bound to forget all about him.

* * *

This was getting ridiculous.

Rafael was sitting at his desk again, ignoring the files piled up in front of him again and staring blankly into space. Again.

With a growl of frustration he pushed his chair back, stalked over to the window and scowled down at the city spreading far below. What the hell *was* this? Why couldn't he focus? And where had this incessant restlessness and edginess come from?

He'd been back in Madrid for a week now, and every single minute of it had been diabolically awful.

He should have been fine. God knew he had plenty to occupy himself. The new job he'd taken on—sorting out a company whose management structure was so top heavy that it was in danger of toppling over—gave him enough work to keep him busy for months. But to his intense irritation he wasn't fine.

He couldn't concentrate on anything. He couldn't eat, couldn't sleep, and it was driving him nuts. He was cross, tired, hungry and frustrated, which, as he never usually got cross, tired, hungry or frustrated, only made it all ten times worse.

He should have been thinking about ways to flatten out his client's absurdly rigid management hierarchy. He should have been drawing up proposals and schedules and setting up meetings, but was he? No. All he could think about was that if ending things with Nicky had been for the best why wasn't he rejoicing at having had such a remarkably lucky escape? Why did her accusations keep ricocheting around his head as if on some bloody unstoppable loop? And why hadn't that stab of loss gone away?

He'd had plenty of time to forget her and he'd used up practically every drop of his patience trying to do just that, but neither had made a blind bit of difference because he simply couldn't get her out of his head. She was in there all the damn time, sometimes distracting him with her smiles, her voice and that maddening habit she had of biting on her lip whenever she was thinking, but more often sitting in the darkness of his car, spitting fury and flinging all those awful things at him.

For the life of him he couldn't work out why what she'd said was having such an effect on him. It wasn't as if he'd sat around deliberately dwelling on it. No. In fact he'd never been busier. Apart from the welcome distraction of work, he'd taken his mother out to a hip new restaurant. He'd caught up with Gaby. And yesterday he'd spotted a new bud on the baobab he'd grown from seed.

But the food in that restaurant had tasted like cardboard. All he'd wanted to ask Gaby was if she'd seen Nicky, and the new baobab bud left him oddly numb.

None of his usual fail-safe methods of self-preservation had worked and he'd now got to the stage he wished he could reach down, yank out everything that was churning around inside him and twisting him into knots and toss it in the bin because it was all driving him insane.

Especially the guilt that at some point over the last week had taken up what was turning out to be permanent residence in his conscience. The guilt that, along with the little voice that had been niggling away in his head, was beginning to suggest that firstly he'd behaved appallingly and that secondly Nicky might have had a point.

For days he'd tried to resist both. For days he'd been telling himself that his reaction to her declaration she was in love with him had been perfectly normal given his experience with Marina, and that of course Nicky hadn't had a point.

But right now he was just so *tired*. And not just physically. He was tired of resisting. Tired of constantly lying to himself—or at the very least denying the truth—and tired of trying to forget her.

Rafael rubbed a hand over his face as for what felt like the billionth time everything she'd said, everything she'd accused him of, ran through his head. And as something deep inside him finally gave way, fracturing and crumbling into dust, the truth smacked him right between the eyes.

Nicky had been deadly accurate in summing him up, hadn't she? He *did* back off and run when the going got tough. He'd started the moment he'd decided he'd had enough of his sisters hassling him when he'd been a boy and escaped to the end of the garden, and he'd never stopped. He'd done it with Marina, he'd done it with his sisters and his mother and his girlfriends and he'd done it with Nicky. Every time, every single time he faced anything that might require an emotional response he fought to escape. And if he couldn't he shut himself down.

Look at what had happened when Nicky had told him she loved him. He'd been cold. Dismissive. Cruel. He'd hurt her. Crucified her, she'd said. And why? Because he'd been unable to handle it. Unable to let himself believe it, because if he allowed himself to believe it then what else might he end up believing?

Rafael stumbled over to his chair just in time to sink into it and buried his head in his hands as the now unfettered truth rained down on him.

God, he *was* the problem, wasn't he? She'd accused him of being pathetic, stubborn and thick-headed, and he was, because was he *really* still hung up on what had happened with his marriage? It was nearly ten years ago, for heaven's sake. He wasn't twenty-three and Nicky wasn't Marina.

She wasn't needy and clingy and desperate for his attention, and of *course* she didn't depend on him for her recovery or her well-being or anything else. She'd been taking care of herself for years.

And he *did* know the difference between lust and love, didn't he?

Taking a deep breath, Rafael made himself face up to the facts he'd stupidly and lily-liveredly shied away from in an absurd effort to distance himself from Nicky and the way she made him feel, his pulse racing and his breathing shallowing.

It wasn't lust that had made him wish he'd been there to protect her when she'd been attacked on that assignment. It wasn't lust that had made him want to look after her that week at the *cortijo*. And it certainly wasn't lust that was making his heart ache like this.

It was love.

And how else did he know? He knew because when she smiled his world brightened. When she looked at him his stomach melted. During the last seven days it hadn't just been the sex he'd missed, but the very essence of her. He'd missed her laugh, her teasing and her vibrancy.

And he knew because for the first time in his life he wanted everything he thought he feared. He wanted to be someone she could depend on. Someone she could turn to for advice and support and comfort.

As wave after wave of emotion swept through him Rafael's hands shook with the force of it.

God, he loved everything about her. She was the bravest, most incredible woman he'd ever met and he'd been a blinkered, idiotic fool. Well, not any more, he thought, suddenly jerking upright and filling with grim determination. Enough was enough and he was through with hiding.

Making a snap decision, he leapt to his feet and scooped up his wallet and his car keys. She wanted honesty and emotion and risk-taking from him? She'd get it.

He could only hope he hadn't left it too late.

CHAPTER FIFTEEN

BUOYANCY, FOCUS AND positive thinking had been pretty hard to maintain when she'd been feeling so up and down but Nicky didn't think she'd done too badly over the last week or so.

For the first few days following her return home she'd swung like some sort of demented pendulum between utter misery at the thought of never seeing Rafael again and the grimly satisfying conviction that she was better off without him. But lately she'd come to terms with the fact that they were well and truly finished and that she was once again on her own, and, while she'd never claim to be happy about it, she had, at least, reached a place where she didn't feel winded whenever she thought about him or about what might have been. Well, not *every* time.

So by and large she reckoned she was making good progress, especially with the changes she'd decided to implement. She'd thrown out her suitcase. Made some calls. Fired off a couple of exploratory emails and bought a few bits and pieces for her flat. When she wasn't thinking about Rafael she felt calm, grounded, and, for the first time in her life, settled.

Any day now she might even be able to delete the photos she'd taken during the time she'd spent at the *cortijo* because while some of them were pretty good she knew perfectly well that that chapter of her life was over and that she needed to move on.

But telling herself to wipe the folder and actually doing it were poles apart, and every time she sat down to click on the 'delete' button she invariably found herself clicking on the 'play slide show' button instead.

Which was precisely what had happened a couple of minutes ago. She'd slid into her chair and opened up the folder, telling herself that she really would do it this time, yet here she was sitting at her desk, staring with longing at the monitor and trying for the billionth time not to think about what might have been if only she'd kept her big mouth shut.

The pictures slowly flipped across the screen and as they did Nicky felt her throat begin to ache all over again. Photo after photo of the grapes, of the vineyards and the people who worked in them, of the arid countryside, and more of Rafael than she'd ever imagined she'd taken flashed before her eyes.

She sighed and her heart squeezed as his gorgeous face filled the screen yet again. In this particular head-shot, he was looking straight at the camera, smiling at her, his eyes a lovely clear green in the bright sunlight, and as she surreptitiously hit 'pause' her mind instantly flew back to the moment she'd taken it. He'd been talking to one of the workers and as if he'd felt her eyes on him had suddenly looked up. Within moments he'd been striding over to her and taking her by the hand and dragging her into the house from where they hadn't emerged till dark.

A wave of melancholy washed over her and Nicky closed her eyes and pinched the bridge of her nose. Swallowing hard, she opened her eyes and set her jaw. She had to get a grip. She really did. She couldn't carry on wafting around like this. Foolishly indulging herself and romanticising everything that had gone on.

She had to do it now. Right now.

Naturally the pain would be sharp but it would be short and final and at *last* she'd be able to move on.

Taking a deep breath and bracing herself, she slid the mouse across her desk so that the cursor was hovering over the 'delete' button and her finger was hovering over the mouse. She dithered. She frowned. She bit her lip. Then she was lifting her chin, clenching her jaw just that little bit more and lowering her forefinger, about to press it and delete the lingering traces of Rafael from her life when the sound of her buzzer ricocheted through her flat and jolted her out of the bubble she'd been in.

No. She wasn't ready, she told herself, her heart thumping as she whipped the mouse up to close the folder instead of deleting it. She really wasn't. Maybe tomorrow…

Shaking her head in despair at her own pathetically weak resolve but reassuring herself that at some point this futile obsession with Rafael had to fade, she jumped up, headed to the kitchen and picked up the handset. 'Hello?'

'Hi,' came the voice from the other end of the intercom and she nearly dropped the handset because she knew of only one voice that deep, that sexy, and only one voice that spread through her like treacle and had the ability to make her shiver with nothing more than a simple 'hi'.

'Rafael?' she said, feeling her legs about to give way and sagging against the wall for support.

Maybe she'd been staring at those photos for too long. Maybe her poor battered imagination had finally succumbed to lunacy and had conjured him up out of nowhere, because what would he be doing at the other end of her intercom?

'May I come up?'

'No,' she said, her mind reeling and her voice breathy with shock.

'Please.'

'Gaby's still away,' she added as it dimly occurred to her that he might well be here to see his sister, not her, and it wouldn't do to get the wrong end of the stick again.

'I know. I haven't come to see her. I've come to see you.'

Oh.

Her heart stopped and then suddenly started galloping as it finally sank in that he was no figment of her imagination. That he really was here, standing on her doorstep and wanting to see her. 'Why?'

'Buzz me up and I'll tell you.'

Nicky closed her eyes and dropped her head back against the wall. Agh, what should she do?

Her head, which was remembering the way he'd been so cold, dismissive and cruel, was telling her to tell him to get lost, but her heart... Well, that was remembering the joy and happiness she'd felt when she'd realised she was in love with him and the pain and agony she'd felt at the knowledge she was never going to lay eyes on him again. And frankly there was no contest because deep down she'd been heartbroken and miserable and she was so very desperate to see him again.

But that didn't mean she was prepared to forgive him the minute he set foot inside her building, did it?

Nicky took a deep breath to calm her nerves and told herself to get a grip. 'Fine,' she said, managing to drum up a pleasing degree of diffidence. 'You can have five minutes.'

'Five minutes is all I need.'

She buzzed him in and then he was gone and she was hurrying to check her appearance in the hall mirror while constantly reminding herself to stay cool and detached. But it was so hard to stay cool and detached when her head was swirling with questions like: why had he come? What did he want? And what could possibly need only five minutes?

She opened the door and gripped the handle in a bid to

stop her hand shaking. She pulled her shoulders back and lifted her chin and slowly inhaled and exhaled to try and stay calm but it didn't work terribly well because Rafael hove into view, looking dishevelled, pale and not a little wild-eyed, and as her heart turned over at the sight of him and she nearly collapsed with longing she realised that everything she'd convinced herself over the last week, all that stuff about doing fine on her own and not wanting him, was rubbish because she wasn't doing fine and she did want him and she hadn't got over him nearly as much as she'd thought.

Throughout the flight to Paris, Rafael had gone over and over what he wanted to say to Nicky and how he planned on saying it. But now he was here, looking down into her beautiful blue-grey eyes, his heart thundering, his mouth dry and his whole world reduced to this square metre of Parisian real estate and the woman standing in it, every single word of his well-prepared speech shot straight from his head.

'Nicky,' he said, and cleared his throat.

'Rafael,' she said, sounding disconcertingly far more calm and in control than he was. 'Come in.'

'Thank you.' As she stood to one side he moved past her. She was tantalisingly within touching distance and he went dizzy with the effort of not stopping and reaching for her right then and there because, considering the way they'd parted, he didn't think that would be the best move he could ever make.

She closed the door and showed him into her sitting room and then whipped past him and leaned against the edge of her desk, her arms folded over her chest and her expression still utterly inscrutable.

What with the overall chilliness of her demeanour Rafael got the impression that she wasn't entirely happy to see him, but that was fine. That was what he'd expected and he was ready for it. Besides, he was fired up and on an unstoppable mission, in love with her and totally prepared to fight for her.

'So how have you been?' he said, shoving his hands in his pockets because they'd suddenly started shaking a little.

'Absolutely fine,' she said with a cool smile. 'You?'

'Grumpy as hell.'

'Oh?' she said, arching an eyebrow. 'What happened?' Before he could answer she held up a hand and flashed him a tight smile. 'No, no, don't tell me. Let me guess. One of your precious plants died.' Ruthlessly ignoring her sardonic tone, Rafael slowly shook his head. 'No? OK, then, your latest batch of wine is undrinkable? Or hang on, I know, someone actually dared to ask you for advice.'

Her sarcasm was nothing less than he deserved, and he told himself that if she really hadn't wanted to see him she'd never have let him in, and if she really no longer cared she wouldn't be trying so hard to pretend she didn't. At least he hoped to God that was the case. 'Something infinitely more troubling than any of that,' he said.

'Excellent.'

'How's work?' he asked, wondering if a sudden change in direction might crack her unpromising and actually faintly disconcerting façade.

But Nicky didn't bat an eyelid. 'Fantastic,' she said smoothly. 'I've been looking at diversifying.'

'Into what?'

'All sorts of things. Corporate stuff. Social events. The odd wedding and christening.'

Rafael tilted his head. 'That's quite a change.'

'A necessary one. What with all that travel my carbon footprint was getting way too big and my previous subject matter had begun to pall.'

'I remember.'

She arched that eyebrow once again. 'I'm surprised.'

'I remember it all.'

She went pink and her gaze slid over his shoulder. 'That's unforgivable,' she muttered and bit on her lip.

Rafael glanced around to see what was suddenly of such interest and as he did so he clocked the pictures on the walls, the cushions strewn over the sofa and armchairs, and what he could only describe as clutter littering the place.

Hadn't she told him once that her flat was only a rental? That she'd never bothered filling it as she didn't know how long she'd be staying? None of what he could see right now looked particularly temporary.

'Nice place,' he murmured, feeling a bit derailed by the knowledge.

'Yes, well, I decided if I'm going to settle down here then I might as well put some effort into it.'

He frowned. 'Settle down here?'

'That's right. I'm buying the flat off my landlord.'

She sounded so matter-of-fact, so sorted, it suddenly struck him that he might have left it too late after all and he went cold. 'Right,' he said as the room spun for a second. 'I see. Right. Congratulations.'

'Thanks. Is there a problem?'

'No problem.' He shoved a hand through his hair and told himself to stay focused. 'It's just something of a surprise to discover that someone who's always claimed to be rootless wants to put down after roots after all.' And without him.

'Well, why not?' she said indignantly. 'I'm twenty-nine. I can't drift around for ever.'

'This is true.'

'I need to start thinking about the future. You know, pensions and stuff.'

'Sensible.'

'It's normal.'

'It is.'

'So why the surprise?' Her expression cleared and she let out a little laugh. 'Oh, I get it. You expected to find me huddled in a pathetic heap, weeping buckets over you, didn't you?'

'No,' he said, because he hadn't. Although to be honest he hadn't expected to find her quite so together either.

'Why are you here, Rafael?' she said with a sudden weariness that for some reason scared the living daylights out of him. 'Surely it can't be to admire my interior-decorating skills.'

'It isn't.'

'And it can't be out of any concern for my welfare.'

'Can't it?'

'You of all people know it can't. So?'

She set her hands on her hips and glared at him and Rafael pulled himself together. However she felt about him now—and he *really* didn't want to contemplate the notion he'd managed to kill off her love for good back there in his car—the least she deserved was an explanation for his abominable behaviour the last time they'd seen each other. Taking a deep breath, he stuck his hands in the back pockets of his jeans and said, 'I came to tell you about my plants.'

Nicky really wished Rafael hadn't done that thing with his hands because up until that point she'd been doing so well.

Deeply concerned by the realisation that she still loved him as much as she ever had, she'd decided that channelling her inner ice queen was the way to handle his sudden heart-stopping appearance on her doorstep, and in her mind's eye she'd been standing there wearing a white dress encrusted with icicles, a vast pointy ruff made of glass round her neck and a white bouffant wig studded with a thousand tiny glittering crystals. She'd even mentally added a touch of white powder to her face and white lipstick to her mouth, and to her delight she'd had the feeling that he'd found her frostiness a bit uncomfortable. A little unsettling. And rather unexpected.

But then he'd stuck his hands in his pockets and it instantly dragged her attention away from all things ice and made it settle firstly on the stretched shirt behind which lay his chest, and then lower on the stretched jeans, behind which lay—

As heat blasted through her and incinerated the ice Nicky snapped her gaze back up and swallowed hard as she determinedly put all thoughts of his lovely warm body out of her head and concentrated on not giving in to her pathetically weak resistance and flinging herself into his arms.

'Your plants?' she echoed, hoping her disdain masked her sudden light-headedness. 'You came all the way to Paris to tell me about your plants? Why on earth would I want to know about your plants? What do they have to do with anything?'

'Very possibly, nothing.' He glanced up at the clock solemnly ticking away on the wall and gave her a faint smile that was most definitely *not* making the ice chips surrounding her heart melt. 'But I still have three minutes left.'

She frowned, momentarily distracted by his mouth. 'What?'

'You gave me five minutes. There are three left.'

So she had. 'Of course,' she said with an airy wave of her hand. 'Well, if you want to use them to talk about your plants, be my guest.'

Rafael tilted his head and stared at her for a few long seconds during which it seemed to Nicky that all she could hear was the apparently thunderous beat of her heart and the rasp of her breathing.

'You were absolutely right, you know,' he said eventually.

'About what?'

'Everything.'

Nicky blinked and went still because he'd suddenly gone all dark and serious and it was doing crazy things to her pulse. 'Everything?'

He nodded. 'Everything. I *do* back off whenever the going gets tough.'

'Oh.'

'Yes.' He rubbed a hand along his jaw but all that did was make her think about the times *she'd* run her hand along his jaw and how much she longed to do it again. 'I've been thinking about it and I reckon I probably picked it up from my father.'

'Your father?'

Rafael nodded. 'It's the way he deals with things. He's an academic. Linguistics. Anyway, whenever things get too overwhelming he buries himself in his study with his books.'

'I see,' she said, although frankly she was struggling to see anything other than him.

'And I have my roof terrace and my plants, my vineyard and my vines.' He shoved his hands through his hair, shifted his weight from one foot to the other and cleared his throat. 'Remember how I told you about the time when I stopped letting my sisters bother me?'

'Vaguely,' she said, because she wasn't about to confess that she'd been over every conversation they'd ever had so often that at times she'd wanted to tear her hair out.

'Well, before that, whenever things got too much I used to run to the end of the garden and take refuge there. It was my sanctuary. I used to—ah—talk to the trees and make up imaginary worlds where girls didn't exist…' He winced and she couldn't help melting just that little bit more at the way he was going through with all this even though it was clearly mortifying him. Then he took a deep breath. 'I guess growing up as the only boy among four sisters taught me that emotion is a weakness and one that can all too easily be exploited.' He gave her a faint smile and her stupidly fragile heart squeezed. 'Certainly boarding school didn't change that perception and in the end I became adept at not giving a damn. I told myself that life's a lot easier if you simply don't care about things. About people.'

Nicky swallowed hard in an effort to suppress all the emotions that were about to spring free from their confines, but she had the feeling that she was losing the battle. 'Sometimes you don't have a choice.'

He stared at her intently, his eyes burning into hers. 'No.' And then he shrugged. 'So there you have it,' he said with a small self-deprecating smile. 'I *am* an emotional coward. When you told me you loved me it spooked the hell out of me. I'd just realised that you made me feel things I'd never felt before and hadn't ever wanted to. We'd just had that conversation about Marina and all I could think about was how dependent on me she'd become, how manipulative she'd been and how horribly it all ended. I reacted horrifically and for that there's no excuse.'

And he sounded so flat, so bleak and resigned that suddenly everything she'd been trying to hold down spilled over. 'No,' she said fiercely, her heart racing and her throat aching. 'I was wrong.'

'You weren't.' He rubbed a hand over his face and then his entire body shuddered. 'But, God, Nicky, I'm sorry for letting you leave like that.'

And when his hand dropped and she saw the tormented expression on his face, the anguish in his eyes and heard the raw honesty in his voice, Nicky felt what was left of her pseudo-steeliness crumble. 'No, *I'm* sorry,' she said, her voice croaky and shaky with the rush of emotion. 'I should never have said any of it.'

'Yes, you should.' He raked his hands through his hair. 'I needed to hear it.'

'I was out of line.'

'You had every reason to be.'

'No, I didn't.'

'You did.' He stared at her, his eyes suddenly clear and focused absolutely on her. 'You don't back down from anything, do you?' he said with what sounded like awed wonder. 'You face everything head-on.'

Nicky swallowed down the lump that had suddenly lodged in her throat. 'I've never seen the point of not doing that.'

'You know, you're the bravest woman I've ever met.' His expression softened and the look in his eyes made her heart lurch madly.

'No, I'm not. I'm a mess. I can't even bump into someone without going loopy.' She unfolded her arms and gripped the edges of the desk just in case her knees actually did give way.

He began to walk towards her and with every step he took she became a little more breathless. 'You're beautiful.'

'You're insane,' she murmured as he stopped just in front of her, overwhelming her senses and scattering her wits.

'I'm certainly crazy about you.'

'What?' she breathed, her heart galloping and the awful tension inside her making her go a bit dizzy.

'Nicky, I love you.'

And then the world shuddered to a halt and time stopped altogether because she'd wanted it so badly, had wanted *so* much for this to be why he'd come, and she'd tried so hard not to let herself hope, and now she didn't have to.

'Really?' she said giddily.

'Really.'

'But I thought you only did lust.'

'So did I.' He put his hands on her upper arms and she felt herself tremble with longing. 'But that was another thing you were right about. I've been stupidly deluded this past week because how could I not be in love with you? You're incredible. Mind-blowingly gorgeous. Supremely talented and utterly fearless.' He looked down at her, his eyes blazing so fiercely that she could barely breathe. 'You completely dazzle me, Nicky. You make me want to experience every emotion under the sun. I'm sorry I've been such a thick-headed idiot for not realising it before, and I know how badly I hurt you, but maybe if you'd let me stick around for a while I could try and make it up to you.'

'How long are we talking?'

'Seventy years, give or take a few.'

'That sounds like a long time.'

He frowned. 'Too long for you?'

And then finally she let loose everything that had been caught up inside her and was suddenly grinning like a fool as love and heat and happiness poured through her. 'Not nearly long enough because I love you too.'

He dragged her into his arms as if he never wanted to let her go and buried his face in her hair. 'Thank God for that,' he muttered. 'Thank *God*.'

And then he drew back and cupped her face and kissed her until she couldn't think straight. By the time he pulled back, his breathing was as ragged as hers and his heart was banging frantically against hers.

'I know you're perfectly capable of looking after yourself,' he said, keeping her wrapped in his arms as he looked down at her, the love shining in his eyes almost stealing her breath, 'but do you think you might be able to lean on me from time to time?'

She tilted her head and grinned up at him as she pretended to consider. 'I should think that could probably be arranged.'

'And if you ever need advice or help or anything, in fact, might you think of asking me?'

'Only if you promise to do the same.'

'I do.'

She gave him a cheeky smile. 'Good, because frankly you could do with the help.'

'I know.'

Her smile wobbled for a second. 'And actually I could do with some too.'

He held her tighter and she could feel his strength surrounding her. 'Whatever you need.'

'I just need you.'

'You have me.'

Her heart swelled with everything she felt and her eyes stung. 'You should probably know,' she said shakily, 'I'm hopeless at relationships.'

'So am I.'

'I haven't even had a proper one.'

'Well, I've only really tried it once and it didn't exactly work out well.'

She shook her head in bemusement. 'So what on earth do we think we're letting ourselves in for?'

Rafael grinned and lifted her onto the desk. 'I have absolutely no idea. All I do know is that I can't think of anywhere else I'd rather be than with you and I can't think of anything else I'd rather be doing.'

He looked down at her, his eyes shining with love and the promise of a lifetime of happiness, and somehow she knew they'd be fine. Smiling up at him, she wound her arms round his neck and pulled him down and murmured against his mouth, 'Neither can I.'

* * * * *

THE ONE SHE WAS
WARNED ABOUT

BY
SHOMA NARAYANAN

Shoma Narayanan started reading Mills & Boon romances at the age of eleven, borrowing them from neighbours and hiding them inside textbooks so that her parents didn't find out. At that time the thought of writing one herself never entered her head—she was convinced she wanted to be a teacher when she grew up. When she was a little older she decided to become an engineer instead, and took a degree in electronics and telecommunications. Then she thought a career in management was probably a better bet, and went off to do an MBA. That was a decision she never regretted, because she met the man of her dreams in the first year of business school—fifteen years later they're married with two adorable kids, whom they're raising with the same careful attention to detail that they gave their second-year project on organizational behaviour.

A couple of years ago Shoma took up writing as a hobby—after successively trying her hand at baking, sewing, knitting, crochet and patchwork—and was amazed at how much she enjoyed it. Now she works grimly at her banking job through the week, and tries to balance writing with household chores during weekends. Her family has been unfailingly supportive of her latest hobby, and are also secretly very, very relieved that they don't have to eat, wear or display the results!

This and other titles by Shoma Narayanan are available in eBook format—check out www.millsandboon.co.uk

To Anna and Megan, my two wonderful editors, for
their patience and unfailing support.

CHAPTER ONE

'THAT,' PRIYA SAID, pointing dramatically, 'is the hottest man I have ever seen in my life.'

It was the first evening of their annual office convention and Shweta was already exhausted. The flight from Mumbai to Kerala was short, but it had been very early in the morning and she'd not slept much. Then the day had been crammed with intensely boring presentations that she'd had to sit through with a look of rapt attention on her face.

'At least look at him!' Priya was saying, and Shweta looked in the direction of her pointing finger.

A jolt of recognition made her keep staring for a few seconds, but there was no answering gleam in the man's eyes—clearly he didn't remember her at all. Not surprising, really. She'd changed quite a bit since they'd last met.

She shrugged, turning away. 'Not my type.'

Priya gave her a disbelieving stare. 'Delusional,' she said, shaking her head sadly. 'You're so out of touch with reality you can't tell a hot man from an Excel spreadsheet. Talking of spreadsheets—that's one guy I'd like to see spread on my sheets…'

Shweta groaned. 'Your sense of humour is pathetic,' she said. 'Every time I think you've reached rock-bottom you find a spade and begin to dig.'

Priya took a swig from her glass of almost-neat vodka. 'Yours isn't much better,' she pointed out. 'And, pathetic sense of humour or not, I at least have a boy-friend with a pulse. Unlike that complete no-hoper Siddhant…'

'Siddhant is not…' Shweta began to say, but Priya wasn't listening to her.

'Ooh, he's looking at you,' she said. 'I bet you can't get him to come and talk to you.'

'Probably not. I'm really not interested.' The man had given her a quick glance, his brows furrowed as he obviously tried to place her.

'You're a wuss.'

'This is childish.' She'd changed a lot since he'd last seen her—if he'd recognised her he'd have definitely come across.

'Bet you a thousand rupees.'

Shweta shrugged. 'Sorry, not enough. That pair of shoes I saw last week cost…'

'OK, five thousand!'

'Right, you're on,' Shweta said decisively.

The man across the room was looking at her again. Shweta took a comb and a pair of spectacles out of her purse. By touch she made a middle parting in her hair and, with little regard for the artfully careless style she'd spent hours achieving, braided it rapidly into two plaits.

Then she scrubbed the lipstick off her lips with a tissue and put on the spectacles. She still had her contact lenses in and the double vision correction made everything look blurry.

Even so, Priya's look of horror was unmistakable.

'What's wrong with you?' she hissed. 'You look like the Loch Ness monster. Where did you get those spectacles from? They're hideous!'

Shweta cut her off, nodding at the man, who was now purposefully headed in their direction. 'Mission accomplished,' she said, and Priya's jaw dropped.

She was still gaping at him as he came up to them. Close up, he was even more breathtaking—over six feet tall, and exuding an aura of pure masculinity that was overwhelming. He was looking right at Shweta, and the quirky, lopsided smile on his perfectly sculpted mouth made him practically irresistible.

'Shweta Mathur!' he said. 'My God, it's been years!'

He'd thought she looked familiar, but until she'd put on the spectacles he'd had no clue who she was. It was fifteen years since he'd seen her last—they'd been in middle school then, and if Shweta had been the stereotypical hard-working student, he'd been the stereotypical bad boy. He hadn't changed much, but Shweta had blossomed. She'd always had lovely eyes, and with the spectacles gone they were breathtaking, drawing you in till you felt you were drowning in them.... Nikhil shook himself a little, telling himself he was getting over-sentimental as he neared his thirtieth birthday. But the eyes were pretty amazing, even if you looked at them with a completely cynical eye. Her features were neat and regular, her skin was a lovely golden-brown, and even in her prim black trousers and top her figure looked pretty good. Somewhere along the line she'd even learnt how to use make-up—right now, in her bid to make him recognise her, she'd scrubbed off all her lipstick, and the vigorous treatment had made her un-expectedly lush lips turn a natural red.

'Hi, Nikhil,' Shweta said, holding her hand out primly.

Nikhil disregarded it, pulling her into his arms for a hug instead.

Shweta gave a little yelp of alarm. She'd recognised Nikhil the second she'd seen him—the slanting eye-brows and the hint of danger about him were pretty much the way they had been when they were both four-teen. But back then his shoulders hadn't been so broad, nor had his eyes sparkled with quite so much devilry. There was something incredibly erotic about the feel of his arms around her and the clean, masculine scent of his body. Shweta emerged from the hug consider-ably more flustered than before.

'You cheated!' Priya wailed. 'You crazy cow, you didn't tell me you *knew* him!'

Nikhil raised his eyebrows. 'Does it matter?'

Priya turned to him, eager to vent her ire on some-one. 'Of course it bloody does. You looked at her a cou-ple of times and I bet her five thousand she wouldn't be able to get you to come across and introduce your-self. She should have *said* she knew you.' She glared at Shweta. 'You're not getting that five grand.'

'Fine. And the next time your mother calls me to ask where you are I'll tell her the truth, shall I?'

Shweta and Priya shared a flat, and Shweta had spent the last six years making up increasingly inventive excuses to explain Priya's nights away from the flat every time her mother called to check on her.

Priya's eyes narrowed. 'Wait till I catch you alone,' she said, and flounced off in deep dudgeon.

Nikhil grinned and tweaked Shweta's hair as she shook it out of the braids. 'Still not learnt how to play nicely, have you?'

Oh, God, that took her back to her schooldays in an instant. And the feel of his hands in her hair… Shweta shook herself crossly. What was *wrong* with her? She had known Nikhil Nair since kindergarten, when both of them had been remarkably composed four-year-olds in a room full of bawling children. They'd grown up together, not always friends—in fact they'd fought almost constantly. A dim memory stirred of other girls sighing over him as they reached their teens, but she didn't remember thinking he was good-looking. Maybe she'd been a particularly unawakened fourteen-year-old. Looking at him now, she couldn't imagine how she had ever been impervious to him.

He was still laughing at her, and she tossed her head. 'And *you* are quite as annoying as you ever were,' she said, realising that she was willing him to comment on her hugely improved looks since the last time he'd seen her. He was looking at her intently, and as his gaze lingered around her mouth she wished she hadn't rubbed off the lipstick. She put up her hand self-consciously.

Given her general clumsiness, she'd probably smudged the stuff all over her face and now looked like Raju the circus clown.

He smiled slightly. 'It's all gone,' he said, and then, almost to himself, 'Little Shweta—who'd have thought it…? You're all grown-up now.'

'You haven't shrunk either,' she blurted out, and then blushed a fiery red.

Thankfully he didn't come back with a smart retort. 'I lost track of you after I left school,' he said instead, his eyes almost tender as they rested on her face.

Ha! Left school! He'd been expelled when the head-master had found him smoking behind the school chapel.

'What have you been doing with yourself?'

'Nothing exciting,' she said 'College, then a chartered accountancy course. Shifted from Pune to Mumbai. And I've been working here ever since.' The 'here' was accompanied by a gesture towards the stage, where her firm's logo was prominently and tastelessly displayed. 'How about you? How come you're here?'

She didn't know everyone who worked in the firm—actually, she didn't know more than two or three of the people from the Delhi office—but she would have bet her last rupee that Nikhil hadn't buckled to convention and become an accountant. School gossip had pegged him as the boy most likely to become a millionaire—it had also estimated that he was the one most likely to go to jail. Not because he was a cheat or a thief, but he had always had a regrettable tendency to get into fist fights.

'I'm helping organise the convention for your firm,' he said.

Shweta looked surprised. 'You work with the event management company, then?' she asked. 'Leela Events?'

Nikhil nodded. 'Sort of,' he said.

Leela Events was big, and organised everything from Bollywood movie launches to corporate bashes. This was the first time her firm had engaged them, but she remembered the HR director saying that it had been quite a coup getting them in for a relatively small event.

The doors of the banquet hall opened and Nikhil touched her briefly on the arm. 'I'll catch up with you in a bit,' he said. 'I need to go and start earning my living.'

Shweta watched him go, her senses in turmoil. She had never been affected so strongly by a man, and even all the alarm bells clanging in her head weren't enough to stop her wanting to pull him back to her side.

'He *owns* Leela Events,' Priya said, reappearing by her side. 'Hot *and* loaded. If you're thinking of making a play for him, now's the time.'

Shweta turned away, coming abruptly back to earth. She should have guessed that Nikhil wouldn't be working for someone else. Owning a company at twenty-nine. Wow! So, definitely on the millionaire path, then—if he wasn't one already.

'I'm with Siddhant,' she said, her tone turning defensive as Priya raised an eyebrow. 'Well, kind of….'

Siddhant Desai was the youngest partner in the accounting firm Shweta worked for. They had been dating for a while, and things were on the verge of getting serious, though Siddhant hadn't actually popped the question yet.

'Don't marry him,' Priya said impulsively. 'He's beady-eyed and boring and he…' She wound to a stop as Shweta glared at her. 'He's just not right for you,' she said lamely.

'I don't want to discuss it,' Shweta snapped, but she had a niggling feeling that Priya was right. She'd never pretended even to herself that she was in love with Siddhant, but he was nice, her father would approve of him, and she'd thought that she could make it work. Of late, though, he'd begun to get on her nerves with his constant carping and complaining if things didn't go exactly as he'd planned.

'Talk of the devil…' Priya said, and made herself scarce as Siddhant came up to join Shweta.

He was good-looking in a conservative kind of way, and right now he was in an excellent mood. Shweta gave him a critical look. He was *safe*, she decided. That was what had drawn her to him. But safe could be boring sometimes….

'Sweetheart, you shouldn't be drinking that muck,' he said, smiling at Shweta and trying to take her glass away from her. 'Let me get you a proper drink.'

'Apple juice *is* a proper drink,' Shweta said, stubbornly holding on to her glass. She never drank at office parties—alcohol had the effect of disastrously loosening her tongue. There was a very real risk of her mortally offending a senior partner and finding herself without a job. 'Look, they're about to begin,' she said, pointing at the stage to distract Siddhant.

It was set up on one side of the banquet hall, and designed to look like a giant flatscreen TV. A rather over-enthusiastic ponytailed male MC was bouncing around exhorting people to come and take their places.

'I'm back,' Nikhil announced, materialising at her side so suddenly that Shweta jumped.

'I thought you'd gone off to earn your living,' she said.

'Just needed to do a quick check and see that everything's on track,' he replied. 'I have a relatively new team working on this event—good guys, but I thought I should be around in case something goes wrong.'

The team was still very raw, and normally he wouldn't have left their side for a moment—only he hadn't been able to keep himself away from Shweta. He tried to figure out why. While she'd metamorphosed into quite a stunner, he met equally good-looking girls every day in his chosen profession. It was the tantalising glimpses he could see of the gawky, independent-minded girl he'd known in school that drew him to her. He'd always liked her, in spite of the unmerciful teasing he'd subjected her to. At fourteen, though, he'd never consciously thought of her as a girl. Now it was impossible not to think of her as a woman, and the change was singularly appealing.

'You're not the nagging kind of boss, then?' Shweta asked.

It sounded as if she approved.

'You don't hover over your people telling them what to do and how to do it, when they should have it done...?'

Nikhil laughed. 'It's a little difficult to be like that in my business,' he said. 'There's a lot of planning involved, but people need the freedom to take spot decisions.'

Siddhant cleared his throat and Shweta realised guiltily that she'd completely forgotten he was standing next to her. Nikhil noticed him as well, giving him a friendly smile as he held out his hand.

'Nikhil Nair,' he said.

Siddhant took his hand, sounding almost effusive. 'Yes, of course. Manish mentioned you'd be here. I'm Siddhant.'

Priya had been right, then—Nikhil had to be loaded. Siddhant was this friendly only with the very successful or the very rich.

'You're one of the partners in the firm, aren't you?' Nikhil asked with a quick smile. 'I understand you guys are putting on a performance for the team?'

Oh, God. The firm's senior partner, Manish, had come up with the brilliant idea of all the partners dancing to a Bollywood number. On stage. Manish himself could dance well, though he was grossly overweight, most of the rest were terrible—and that was putting it mildly. Siddhant wasn't as bad as some, only he was very stiff and self-conscious. Shweta cringed at the thought of watching him make a fool of himself in public.

'It's just something Manish thought would make us seem a little more approachable to the team,' Siddhant was saying. 'That becomes a problem sometimes in an industry like ours. By the way—marvellous arrangements this morning. Your team did a fabulous job. The elephants and the Kathakali dancers welcoming everyone…and that flash mob thing at lunchtime was also a fantastic idea.'

The flash mob *had* been brilliant. Shweta conceded that much. But Siddhant was sounding a little sycophantic. Maybe Manish had asked him to make a pitch to Nikhil. She had only a vague idea of how event management companies operated, and it was unlikely Manish knew more than her—he usually operated on the principle that any company that made money needed accountants.

'Thank you,' Nikhil said, clearly amused. 'Can I borrow Shweta for a minute?'

Siddhant looked a bit taken aback, and Shweta hastened to explain. 'We were together in school—met again after years today.' *Borrow* her, indeed. He made her sound like a library book—and a not very interesting one at that.

'Oh, that's good,' Siddhant said. His eyes darted between the two of them as if he was registering for the first time that Nikhil could pose some kind of threat to his slow-paced courtship. 'But aren't you staying for the performances? I thought there were some Bollywood stars coming down…'

'Seen them many times before,' Nikhil said, a quick smile flashing across his face. 'I'll try and be back before you guys go on stage. Wouldn't want to miss that.'

He slung a casual arm around Shweta's shoulders as he drew her away and she felt her senses instantly go on high alert. He must have touched her in school, she thought, confused, but she didn't remember feeling anything like this—what was wrong with her? He'd changed, of course, but how had he turned from the wild tearaway schoolboy she remembered to someone who drove her crazy with longing without even trying—it was totally unfair.

'Is Siddhant your boss?' Nikhil asked once they were some distance away. When Shweta shook her head he said, 'Hmm…something going on between you guys, then? He looked quite possessive for a bit back there.'

'He's just a friend,' Shweta said, but the colour flaring up to her cheeks betrayed her yet again.

Nikhil grinned wickedly. 'Just a friend, eh? He's still looking at us. OK if I do this?' He bent his head and brushed his lips against her cheek. It was a fleeting caress, but Shweta felt her heart-rate triple.

Nikhil stepped back a little and gave her a considering look. 'Will he come charging up and challenge me to a duel?' he asked.

She shook her head mutely.

'OK—what if I do this?'

Shweta swatted his hands away as he brought them up to cup her face. Feeling all hot and bothered, she said, 'Stop playing the fool, Nikhil!'

He stepped back, raising his hands in laughing surrender. 'I've stopped…I've stopped. You're dangerous when you lose your temper—I don't want you giving me another scar.'

'Rubbish!' she said.

'Not at all.' Nikhil pushed his shaggy hair off his forehead with one hand and she saw it—a thin white scar across one temple that stood out against his tanned skin. 'The last time I annoyed you I ended up with this.'

Shweta remembered it quite vividly. She'd grabbed a wooden blackboard duster off the teacher's table and thrown it at him. But it still hadn't wiped the mocking grin off his face. A thin ribbon of blood had trickled down one side of his face and he'd mopped it off with a grimy handkerchief. He'd been laughing all the while. Right, so that was one time she remembered touching him—evidently he hadn't had the same effect on her then as he did now.

'I'm sorry,' she said awkwardly. In retrospect she was—a few centimetres the other way and she could have blinded him.

'It wasn't your fault,' he said. 'From what I remember I was quite an obnoxious little beast—you helped knock some sense into me. And every time I look in the mirror now I think of you....'

He lowered his voice to a sexy rasp for the last part of the sentence, and Shweta felt a visceral reaction kick in. It wasn't *fair*—he was just playing around without realising what he was doing to her. And with Siddhant watching...

Belatedly, she remembered Siddhant's existence, and turned around to look for him.

'Too late,' Nikhil said. 'He gave you a minute and then he went in, looking like a thundercloud. You'll have to grovel to get him to forgive you.'

'Fat chance,' Shweta said shortly.

Nikhil's accurate reading of Siddhant was unnerving, though. Right from when they'd first started dating

Siddhant had given the impression that he was assessing her against a set of strict criteria. Rather like the way he screened job applicants, actually. At all times she was conscious of his approval or disapproval. He rarely lost his temper, retiring instead into a stately silence that she had to coax him out of. Completely out of the blue she wondered what a relationship with Nikhil would be like. Unpredictable, definitely, but lively— she could imagine impassioned arguments followed by equally passionate reconciliations.

'Dreaming of something?' Nikhil asked teasingly.

Her eyes whipped back to him. She shook her head, trying to stop thinking of what a passionate reconciliation with him would be like.

'Look, are you really keen on watching the show? It'd be nice to catch up, but I'm leaving tomorrow morning. Want to sneak off with me somewhere?'

Oh, yes, she *did* want to sneak off with him. Put like that, it sounded deliciously wanton—also, no one had ever suggested sneaking off with her before.

Shweta tried not to look over-eager. 'I can slip away. I'm not terribly keen on the Bollywood dancers anyway.'

'Maybe you should tell Siddhant you're leaving,' Nikhil suggested.

But Shweta had decided to spend at least one evening free of his petty tyranny. 'He's not even my boss,' she said. 'I'll message Priya so that she doesn't get worried.'

It was only once they were in the black SUV that Nikhil had hired for the day that it occurred to Shweta to ask where they were going.

'It's a place where the locals hang out,' he said. 'Good music, and the food's to die for. Not too swanky. But we can go to one of the five-star hotels around here if you'd prefer that?'

'Yes—like I'd choose the five-star hotel after *that* introduction,' Shweta said. 'And you should know I'm not the swanky restaurant type.'

'You might have changed,' Nikhil said. 'You don't look the same—for all I know you might have turned into a wine-sipping socialite, scorning us lesser mortals...'

Shweta punched him in the arm and he laughed. 'Still violent, I see,' he said, but his tone was more tender than mocking. She felt her heart do an obedient little flip-flop in response. At least now her reactions to him weren't coming as a surprise. All she had to do was work harder at concealing them.

They were on the outskirts of the city now, and driving down a narrow lane flanked by fields and coconut trees.

'OK if I roll down the window?' Nikhil asked.

When she nodded, he switched off the air-conditioning and got the windows down.

'We're lucky it's not raining,' he said. 'Kerala gets most of its rains in winter...'

'I know. I used to pay attention in Geography,' Shweta said pertly. 'Unlike you.'

Nikhil gave her a mocking smile. 'You were such a *gooooood* little girl,' he said, dragging his words out. 'Of *course* you paid attention.'

Shweta carefully controlled an urge to hit him on

the head with a high-heeled shoe. 'And you were such a *baaad* boy.' She copied his tone as closely as she could. 'Of *course* you paid attention to no one and were good for nothing.'

'Bad boys are good at some things,' he murmured suggestively.

Shweta flushed as all the things he was probably very, very good at sprang to mind. God, was he doing it on purpose? Probably he thought it was fun, getting her all hot and bothered. There was no way he could be actually flirting with her—or was he?

'Do you know where you're going?' she asked in her best auditor voice—the one that Priya swore made entire finance departments quake in their shoes.

Nikhil nodded. 'Almost there.'

The road had developed some rather alarming twists and turns, and he was concentrating on his driving. In Shweta's opinion he was going too fast, but she'd boil her favourite shoes in oil before she said anything— there was no point giving him an opportunity to make remarks about fraidy-cat accountants. She fixed her eyes on Nikhil instead, hoping the man would take her mind off his driving. It worked. The moonlight illuminated his rather stern profile perfectly, throwing the planes and angles of his face into relief.

He was really quite remarkably good-looking, Shweta thought. It was a wonder she hadn't noticed it in school, but she had an explanation. In those days she'd been completely obsessed by a rather chocolate-faced movie star, and had unconsciously compared everyone she saw with him. Nikhil was the complete opposite of chocolate-faced—even at fourteen his features had been uncompromisingly male. Her eyes drifted towards his shoulders and upper body, and then to his hands on the steering wheel. He had rather nice hands, she thought, strong with square-tipped fingers. Unbidden, she started to wonder how those hands would feel on her body, and she blushed for probably the twelfth time that evening.

The car negotiated a final hairpin bend, after which the road seemed to shake itself out and lose steam. It went on for a couple of hundred metres through a rather dense copse of coconut trees and ended abruptly on a beach.

'Are you lost?' she enquired. He shook his head. 'Come on,' he said, opening his door and leaping down lightly.

He was at her door and handing her down before she could protest. Locking the car with a click of the remote, he put an arm around her shoulders and started walking her to the beach.

Their destination was a small, brightly lit shack thatched with palm fronds. There were small tables laid out in front, some of which were occupied by locals. Nikhil chose a table with a view of the beach. The moon had risen now, and the sea had a picture-postcard quality to it. A motherly-looking woman in her fifties bustled out, beaming in delight when she saw Nikhil. She greeted him in a flood of Malayalam which Shweta didn't even bother trying to follow. She wasn't particularly good at languages, and Malayalam was nothing like Hindi or any other language she knew.

'Meet Mariamma,' Nikhil said. 'She's known me since I was a kid.'

Shweta smiled and Mariamma switched to heavily accented English. 'Am always happy to meet Nikhil's friends,' she said, dispelling any notion that this was the first time Nikhil had brought someone here with him. 'Miss Shweta, do sit down. I'll get you a menu.'

'I thought you didn't have one?' Nikhil murmured.

Mariamma said chidingly, 'You haven't been in touch for a long while. We got a menu printed—Jossy designed it on his laptop.'

'I'd love to see it, but I know what I want to order,' Nikhil said. 'Shweta, any preferences?'

'If you could order for me…' Shweta said, and Nikhil promptly switched back into Malayalam and reeled off a list of stuff that sounded as if it would be enough to feed the entire state for a week.

Mariamma beamed at both of them and headed back to the kitchen, her cotton sari rustling as she left.

'You come here often?'

'I used to—when I was a child. My grandparents lived quite near here, and Mariamma was one of my aunt's closest friends.'

'Your grandparents…?'

'Died when I was in college.'

Nikhil was frowning, and Shweta wished she hadn't asked.

'Are you in touch with anyone from our class in school?' she asked hastily.

He began to laugh. 'You need to be more subtle when you're changing the topic,' he said. 'No. I e-mail some of my old crowd on and off, but I haven't met up with anyone for a long while. Ajay and Wilson are in the States now, and Vineet's building a hotel in Dehra Dun. How about you?'

'I'm not building a hotel in Dehra Dun,' Shweta said, and made a face. 'I'm in touch with Vineet too. He's difficult to avoid. And a couple of other people as well.'

'Have they got used to your new avatar?' He was still finding it difficult to reconcile Shweta who looked like a million bucks but sounded like the old tomboyish Shweta he'd known for most of his adolescent years.

Shweta frowned at him. 'What avatar?'

'I remember you as a serious, pigtailed little thing, very grim and earnest all the time—except when you were climbing trees and challenging me to cycling races.'

'And now?'

'And now…' He smiled and leaned back in his chair. 'Well, you've chosen a grim and serious profession, all right, but in spite of that…something's changed. You've been rebelling, haven't you? You look different, of course, but that's just the contact lenses and the new hairstyle.'

A little piqued at his dismissal of the change in her looks, she said firmly, 'Well, I haven't been rebelling.'

'Sure?' he asked teasingly. 'You came away with me instead of staying back with that extremely eligible, extremely boring young man.'

'I haven't seen you for fifteen years,' she pointed out. 'I see Siddhant every day.'

'And your shoes…'

She looked down at them defensively. They *were* rather lovely shoes—high-heeled green pumps that struck a bright note against her sombre black trousers and top. She was wearing a silver hand-crafted necklace studded with peridots—the stones perfectly matched the shoes. In spite of having read a dozen articles that condemned matching accessories as the height of un-cool, she found it difficult to stop herself, especially when it came to shoes. Speaking of which...

'What's wrong with my shoes?'

'Nothing,' he said, looking amused. 'They're...very striking, that's all. But otherwise you're very conserva-tively dressed.' Before she could protest, he said, 'Sorry, I've been reading too many articles on pop psychol-ogy. But I stick by what I say—it's a slow rebellion, but you're rebelling all the same. I always thought your father was way too strict with you.'

'I've been living away from home for over seven years,' Shweta said indignantly. 'All my rebelling is long over and done with. And he's changed. He's not the way he used to be.' Her father had been a bit of a ter-ror when she was younger, and most of her classmates had given him a wide berth. It had taken Shweta her-self years to muster up the courage to stand up to him.

'If you say so.' Somehow seeing Shweta again had brought out the old desire in Nikhil to wind her up, watch her struggle to control her temper—except she was now all grown up, and instead of wanting to tug her pigtails and trip her over during PE class he wanted to reach out and touch her, to run his hands over her smooth skin and tangle them in her silken hair...

Realising that his thoughts were wandering a bit too far, he picked up the menu and started leafing through it. A thought struck him. 'You haven't turned vegetarian, have you?'

He looked relieved when Shweta shook her head. 'Thank heavens. I've ordered mutton stew and appams and prawn curry—I just assumed you'd be OK with all of it.'

'Of course I am. I've always loved prawn curry. Your mom used to cook it really well, I remember.'

'Which mom?' he asked, his mouth twisting into a wry smile.

Shweta felt like kicking herself. Nikhil was illegitimate, and had always been touchy about his family. His father had taken a mistress after ten years of a childless marriage, scandalising everyone who knew him, and Nikhil was his mistress's son. Perhaps it would have been less scandalous if he'd tried to keep the affair secret, but when he'd found out that Ranjini was pregnant he'd brought her to live in the same house as his wife. Until he was four Nikhil had thought having two mothers was a perfectly normal arrangement—it was only when he joined school that he realised he lived in a very peculiar household.

'Veena Aunty,' Shweta said.

Veena was Nikhil's father's wife. If they'd been Muslims Nikhil's father could have taken a second wife, but as a Hindu he would have been committing bigamy if he'd married Ranjini. Veena had taken the whole thing surprisingly well. People had expected her to resent Ranjini terribly, even if she couldn't do anything about having to share a house with her, but Veena appeared to be on quite good terms with her. And she adored Nikhil, which perhaps wasn't so surprising given that she didn't have children of her own. In his teen years at least Nikhil had been equally attached to her—all his sullenness and resentment had been directed towards his parents.

'How're they doing?' Shweta asked. 'Your parents, I mean.' She'd met them only a few times—her father had made sure that she didn't have much to do with Nikhil.

Nikhil shrugged. 'OK, I guess. I haven't seen them for over four years.'

Shweta's eyebrows shot up. 'Aren't they still in Pune, then?'

'Dad has some property in Trivandrum. They moved there when Dad retired. They're still there—though now Amma is pretending to be a cousin and Mom tells everyone that she's married to Dad.'

The words came out easily enough, but Shweta could see his jaw tense up and was very tempted to lean across the table and take his hand, smooth away the frown lines. He'd always called his own mother Mom, while his father's wife went by the more affectionate Amma.

'I guess it's easier that way,' Shweta said. 'Rather than having to explain everything to a whole new set of people.'

'Pity they didn't think of it when it really mattered.' His voice was tight, almost brittle. 'I don't know why Amma is letting them do this.'

'I'm sure she has her reasons. Maybe you could visit

them now that you're already in Kerala?' Shweta believed strongly in women standing up for themselves—in her view Veena was quite as responsible for the situation as Nikhil's parents.

'Not enough time—I've got to be back in Mumbai for another gig. Plus I'm not on the best of terms right now with my father.' He was still frowning, but after a few seconds he made a visible effort to smile. 'While we're on the subject of parents, how're your dad and aunt?'

'He's retired, so now he bosses the gardener and the cleaners around instead of his patients,' Shweta said, and Nikhil laughed.

Shweta's father had been a doctor in a fairly well-known hospital in Pune, and he'd inspired a healthy respect in everyone who knew him. Shweta's mother had died quite suddenly of a heart attack when Shweta was three, and her father's unmarried older sister had moved in to help bring up Shweta.

'And your aunt?'

'She's still keeping house for him. Though she grumbles about him to whoever's willing to listen—wonders how my mother put up with him for so many years.'

A lot of people had wondered that, but Nikhil didn't say so. He'd met Shweta's father several times—he'd been on their school board, and had chaired the disciplinary hearing that had led to his final expulsion from the school. Nikhil didn't hold that against him. He'd been on a short wicket in any case, given that the smoking incident had followed hard upon his having 'borrowed' their Hindi teacher's motorbike and taken his best buddies out for a spin on it. But he had resented Dr Mathur telling Shweta not to have anything to do with him.

The food arrived and Mariamma came across to ladle generous portions onto their plates. 'Eat well, now,' she admonished Shweta. 'You're so thin—you girls nowadays are always on some diet or the other.'

'I can't diet to save my life,' Shweta said. 'I'm thin because I swim a lot.'

Mariamma sniffed disapprovingly, but Nikhil found it refreshing, being with a woman who wasn't obsessed with her figure. His job brought him into contact with models and actresses, all of whom seemed to be afraid to breathe in case the air contained calories. In his view Shweta had a better figure than all of them—she was slim, but not stick-thin, and her body curved nicely in all the right places.

'Like the food?' he asked, watching her as she dipped an *appam* into the curry and ate it with evident enjoyment. For a few seconds he couldn't take his eyes off her lush mouth as she ran her tongue over her bottom lip—the gesture was so innocently sexy.

'It's good,' she pronounced.

He dragged his eyes away from her face to concentrate on his own untouched plate before she could catch him staring.

'Everything's cooked in coconut oil, isn't it? It adds an interesting flavour to the food.'

Nikhil thought back to the last time he'd taken a girl on a date to a restaurant in Mumbai that served authentic Kerala cuisine. She'd hardly eaten anything, insisting that the food smelt like hair oil. She'd been annoying in many other ways as well, he remembered. Rude to waiters and refusing to walk even a few metres to the car because the pavement looked 'mucky'. Not for the first time he wondered why he chose to waste his time with empty-headed women like her rather than someone like Shweta. He didn't want to delve too deeply into the reasons, though—self-analysis wasn't one of his passions.

'Can I ask you something?' Shweta said as she polished off her last appam. 'Why were you out to get me in school? We used to be good friends when we were really little—till you began hanging out only with the boys and ignored me completely. And when we were twelve or something you started being really horrible. You used to be rude about my clothes and my hair-style—pretty much everything.'

'Was I that bad?' Nikhil looked genuinely puzzled. 'I remember teasing you a little, but it was light-hearted stuff. I didn't mean to upset you. Maybe it was because you were such a *good* little girl—listening to what the teacher said, doing your homework on time, never playing truant… It was *stressful*, studying with you. You set such high standards…'

He ducked as Shweta swatted at him with a ladle. 'Careful,' he said, his voice brimming over with laughter as drops of curry sprayed around. 'I don't want to go back looking like I've been in a food fight.'

'Oh, God—and your clothes probably cost a bomb, didn't they.' Conscience-stricken, Shweta put the ladle down. 'Did I get any on you?'

Nikhil shook his head. 'I don't think so. If I find any stains I'll send you the dry-cleaning bill.'

She looked up swiftly, wondering whether he was being serious, but the lurking smile in his eyes betrayed him. 'Oh, you wretch,' she scolded. 'I've a good mind to throw the entire dish at you.'

'Mariamma will be really offended,' he said gravely. 'And if you throw things at me I won't buy you dessert.'

'Oh, well that settles it, then. I'll be nice to you.' He hadn't really answered her question, but she didn't want to destroy the light-hearted atmosphere by pressing too hard. 'But only till we're done with dessert.'

CHAPTER TWO

'ARENT YOU GOING to wear something under that? A *churidaar* or leggings?'

'It's a dress, Siddhant,' Shweta explained patiently. 'It's supposed to be worn like this.' Dresses had come back into fashion a couple of years ago, but evidently no one had informed Siddhant.

'I like you better in *salwar kameez*,' he said. 'Or even jeans. You look—I don't know—sort of weird in this. And the shoes…'

Shweta surveyed herself in the huge mirror in the hotel foyer. The simple pale yellow cotton dress set off her golden-brown skin and lovely black eyes to perfection. And the shoes were her favourite ones—flat open-toed white sandals with huge yellow cloth flowers on the straps. The flowers were even of the same genus/sub-species as the white printed ones on her dress, and until she'd come downstairs she'd been pretty happy with the overall effect.

During her childhood she'd been forced to wear truly horrible clothes—her aunt had had absolutely no sense of colour or style, and had usually bought Shweta's clothes at discount stores or got them made up by the local tailor. It didn't help that the tailor was the same one who'd made Dr Mathur's shirts. All her clothes had ended up with boxy cuts and mannish collars. She'd tried complaining to her father, but he'd told her she shouldn't be bothering about something as frivolous as clothes, and she'd been too much in awe of him to protest. It had only been when she was in college that she'd started choosing her own clothes and, while she knew her taste wasn't perfect, she hated anyone criticising what she wore.

'They're very nice shoes,' she told Siddhant firmly. 'Actually, all in all, I think I look pretty good.'

'I agree,' a voice said behind her.

She spun around to meet Nikhil's smiling eyes. Brilliant—now he probably thought she was needy and totally hungry for reassurance.

'I wasn't intending to criticise your clothes,' Siddhant said, after nodding stiffly to Nikhil. 'I just thought that jeans might be more practical, given that we're going sightseeing.'

He himself was dressed in khaki trousers and a crisp white short-sleeved shirt. Somehow, though, he managed to look a little stiff-necked and conservative next to Nikhil's rugged good looks.

Nikhil gave him an easy smile. 'We're driving to the backwaters and we'll spend the next few hours on a boat. It's hardly a Himalayan trek. Shweta—I came to ask you… You said you wanted to pick up some spices for your aunt, right? I've decided to stay back for another day, and I'll be taking the SUV out again—

you can ride with me. We'll stop at a spice garden I know—you'll get much better stuff there than you do in the stores.'

Shweta nodded happily. The alternative was to ride in a bus with the rest of the office crowd. Siddhant would be with the other partners in a specially rented van. Not that they were trying to be elitist, as he'd hastily clarified, but they had some urgent business to discuss, which was confidential, and it would be a pity to waste the travel time when all of them were together anyway.

He didn't look at all happy about Shweta going off with Nikhil, but there was little he could do about it. 'I'll see you at the boats, then,' he said.

'Yes, we should be there in a couple of hours,' Nikhil said. 'Come on, Shweta, we should leave now. See you in a bit, Siddhant. I was taking a look at the video of yesterday's dance, by the way—not bad at all. I wish I could have made it back in time for the actual performance.'

'Don't make fun of him,' Shweta said in an undertone as they waited for the car. 'He was pretty uncomfortable with this whole dance thing, but it was his boss's idea and he couldn't wriggle out of it.'

There was genuine surprise on Nikhil's face as he replied. 'I wasn't. OK, he isn't India's answer to Michael Jackson, but he did a good job. Must have practised a lot.'

'He's a bit of a perfectionist,' Shweta muttered.

She still hadn't figured Nikhil out. Maybe he'd been telling the truth the night before—he'd only been teasing her back then in school and she'd overreacted. An incipient persecution complex—that was what her father would call it.

'So is it serious, then?' Nikhil asked after a pause.

'With Siddhant? I don't know—we've not talked about it. We've been dating for a while, so I guess there's a good chance of us ending up together.'

'Are you in love with him?'

Startled, she felt her gaze fly up to his face. 'With Siddhant?' she asked again, stupidly.

He smiled. 'No, with that traffic policeman over there. Of course with Siddhant, you dimwit.'

'No,' she said, and then bit her lip. Impulsive frankness was all very well, but sometimes she wished she had more control over her tongue. 'I mean, I'm very fond of him, but it's a little too early. We've not actually…' Her voice trailed off as he began to smile. She must be sounding like an utter idiot to him. He'd already made it pretty clear that he didn't have a very high opinion of Siddhant, and her dithering was probably amusing him no end. Rapidly she moved the battle into enemy territory. 'What about you?' she asked. 'Are you in love with…well, whoever people might *think* you're in love with?'

'No, I'm not,' he said, his lips twitching.

A valet brought his black SUV around and Nikhil helped her in before heading around to the driver's side. The powerful engine purred to life as he turned the key in the ignition, but to her surprise he didn't start driving right away. Instead he was looking at her, his expression unfathomable.

'How keen are you on this spice-buying thing?'

'It's one of the must-dos if you're in Kerala, isn't it? Why? Is there a problem?'

'Well, the proper spice gardens are up in the hills,' he said. 'It's just that we had a good time yesterday—or at least I did—and I thought it would be good to hang out for a while without the rest of your group.'

Shweta took a few seconds to digest this. On the one hand there was something incredibly flattering about Nikhil wanting to spend more time with her. On the other the thought of slipping away for a clandestine rendezvous was a little unsettling. She hadn't got over her crush on Nikhil. If anything it was worse today— her stomach was going quivery just from her looking at him. Telling her stomach firmly to behave itself, she frowned at Nikhil.

'So there isn't a spice garden here at all?'

'There is.' Nikhil's smile was self-deprecatory. 'We can go there if you really want. Or we can go directly to the backwaters.'

'But we'll get there a lot earlier than the others,' Shweta pointed out. 'They haven't even started getting into the buses, and you drive like a maniac—you'll take half the time they will.'

'We'll take one of the small houseboats out,' he said. 'Just the two of us. It'll be more peaceful than joining a hundred accountants.'

'You really don't like accountants, do you?'

'I like some.'

His smile deepened as he looked right into her eyes,

and Shweta said hurriedly, 'OK, we'll take the boat,' before she could start blushing again.

Only later did she realise that he hadn't asked her if she wanted to come with him—he'd just assumed she would.

Once they reached the pier Shweta was glad Nikhil had made the choice for her. The small boat he was pointing out was a hundred times more charming than the double-decker monstrosities that were lined up for the rest of the group. And the backwaters were lovely—a network of canals opening into a huge, still expanse of water flanked by rows and rows of coconut trees. Little houseboats were moored by the banks, and there were water birds all around, gracefully swooping through the air to land on the water.

'Time slows down here,' Shweta said wonderingly as their boat was cast off and negotiated through one of the narrow channels into a wider stretch. 'It seems so far away from Mumbai.'

'It *is* pretty far from Mumbai.' There was a smile twitching at Nikhil's lips. 'Almost two thousand kilometres. But I know what you mean.'

'And people actually live in these boats?'

'These ones are mainly for the use of tourists,' he said. 'Take a look at the inside, if you want.'

The inside wasn't really all that impressive—it was just a small room with cane furniture, and in spite of the slow speed they had to be careful not to rock the boat by moving around it too much. And the bed in the centre was all too suggestive.

Suddenly very conscious that she was alone with Nikhil, Shweta said, 'It was nicer outside, wasn't it?'

'This isn't bad either,' Nikhil said. He was sprawled lazily on a cane chair, with a beer in one hand. 'Stop hopping around like a jittery kitten and sit down. I don't bite.'

'I should have brought my work phone,' Shweta said. 'There's an e-mail that's supposed to come in this morning from a client and I totally forgot.' She looked fretfully at her little yellow clutch purse. 'It wouldn't fit properly into this.' But the purse had perfectly matched her outfit, and she'd decided to leave her phone behind.

'You work very hard, don't you?'

It didn't sound as if he meant it as a compliment, and Shweta immediately went on the defensive. 'I don't work any harder than my colleagues do.'

'Nothing wrong with working hard,' he said. 'It's just that you don't seem to take any time out to have *fun*.'

He stretched out the word a little, and it was quite evident what kind of fun he had in mind. Despite herself, Shweta felt her cheeks growing warm.

'Don't make assumptions,' she snapped. 'I have enough fun, thank you very much. I needed to reply to this e-mail as soon as it comes in—that's why I'm worried.'

Nikhil got up and came to stand behind her. 'Do you want to go back?' he asked. 'We can if it's really urgent.'

For a second Shweta almost said yes. Not because the e-mail was all that urgent, but because Nikhil's proximity was throwing her nicely ordered world into turmoil. Then the ridiculousness of it all struck her and she shook her head.

'I'll phone him,' she said. 'It's just that this particular client is a bit picky—he calls up my boss for the smallest thing.'

As it turned out, though, the client was on a camping trip in Alibagh and had completely forgotten to send the e-mail before he left. He even had the grace to apologise for the delay.

'So that's OK, then,' she said after she rang off. 'I hate having work stuff hanging over me like that.'

'Stop thinking about work now,' Nikhil said, putting his hands on her shoulders.

Shweta went completely still as he started massaging her neck and shoulders gently. She could feel the tension seep out, but it was replaced by a set of entirely different sensations. She was acutely conscious of the strength in his lean hands. The temptation to turn into his arms was intense, and she felt positively bereft when he removed his hands after a few minutes.

'Why were you asking me about Siddhant?'

There was a little pause, then Nikhil said, 'I have a theory about the two of you. Look, I'm sorry—it's none of my business really.'

Of course as soon as he said that she *had* to know more.

'A theory about us?' she asked, trying to sound casual and unconcerned. Somehow, she had a feeling she wasn't fooling Nikhil one bit.

'You don't give a damn for him,' Nikhil said bluntly.

'But for some reason you've led him on to think that you're interested.'

Shweta flushed. Nikhil was only saying something Priya had been telling her for months, and there was no earthly reason she should feel the need to justify herself. She still found herself explaining, though.

'We've been dating for a while,' she said. 'I was planning to say yes if he asked me to marry him. It's only for the last month or so that I've not been so sure.'

'Why not?' he asked, his voice quiet.

Shweta felt that a lot depended on her answer. 'He's a little…' She'd been about to say *judgemental*, but it felt disloyal to be talking about Siddhant with Nikhil. 'I don't know what it is, really, but I don't think we'd suit.'

'You wouldn't.'

Her eyes widened at the bald statement. 'You hardly know either of us!' she said, and continued hastily when he raised his eyebrows, 'You knew me a long while ago. I was just a kid then. I've changed!'

'I'm sure you have,' Nikhil said. 'But you used to be a very straightforward person, and people don't change fundamentally. So what I find difficult to understand is why you'd even contemplate marrying a man you don't care two hoots about.'

Shweta glared at him. 'You just said it isn't any of your business, and I wholeheartedly agree,' she said. 'Why are you so bothered about me and Siddhant, anyway?'

'Because I don't want to feel guilty when I do this,' Nikhil said, bringing his head down to hers and kissing her mouth very, very gently.

Shweta stood stock-still, frozen in shock. A kiss was the last thing she'd been expecting, but the sensation was incredible, his lips warm and teasing against hers. Her hands came up involuntarily to clasp him around the neck. Oh, but it felt so good—familiar, and wildly exciting at the same time. She clung to him as the kiss deepened, giving a little gasp of protest when he finally stepped back.

'I've wanted to kiss you ever since I saw you yesterday,' he said, the edges of his voice rough with desire. 'It was all I could do to keep my hands off you.'

Shweta looked up at him, too shaken to speak. The kiss had awakened a swarm of emotions in her and she wasn't sure how to react.

Nikhil gazed back at her, his dark eyes smouldering. It was taking all his self-control not to pull her back into his arms. Her inexperience showed, though, and until he was sure of his own feelings he didn't want to go too far.

'Maybe we should go back outside,' he said, his voice softening as he put up a hand to touch her cheek. 'I don't trust myself alone with you for too long.'

Shweta felt like crying out in frustration. She *wanted* to be alone with him, to take the kiss further—but she could hardly say so. Mutely she followed him out on to the deck of the boat.

'The others should be on the boats by now,' he said. 'Do you want to wait till they catch up with us or go on to the village?'

'Go on to the village,' she muttered.

The last thing she wanted was a bunch of her colleagues gawking at her—Priya at least would be sure to smell a rat. And Siddhant… She needed to make it clear to him that it was off between them. Only it would be a slightly difficult thing to put across, given that he hadn't formally proposed in the first place.

Nikhil came to stand next to her, his sleeve brushing her bare arm as he leaned against the handrail. 'The boatman says we'll reach it in fifteen minutes,' he said. 'We'll get some time to look around the village then.'

Except that they didn't, because his new team head who was supposed to be managing the project had a sudden attack of nerves and Nikhil had to step in to avoid a crisis.

Left to her own devices, Shweta wandered around the little resort village, admiring the local handicrafts and watching a troupe of dancers rehearse their steps.

'Nikhil Sir is calling you,' one of the trainees said behind her, and Shweta turned to see Nikhil beckoning to her from the pier.

'The boats are about to come in,' he said as she joined him. 'We have a little surprise planned.'

He slung an arm casually around her shoulders and she had to fight the impulse to lean closer into his embrace. 'What kind of surprise?'

'Look,' he said.

The four large boats carrying the office gang were now lined up on either side of the narrow stretch of water.

'Aren't they docking?' she asked, puzzled. The boats seemed to be waiting for something. Before Nikhil could answer her, she realised what they were waiting

for. 'The snake boats!' she said. 'But how's that possible...? This isn't the time of year for the races, is it?'

But the snake boats were there—immensely long ca-
noes, with almost a hundred rowers per boat wearing
T-shirts in their team colours over *veshtis*.

Shweta clutched at Nikhil's arm in excitement. 'I've
always wanted to see the races!' she said. 'I used to
watch them on TV when I was a kid, but this is the first
time I've been to Kerala... Ooh, they're off!'

Nikhil smiled down at her, amused by her evident
excitement. The snake boats *were* a pretty amazing
sight. The teams of rowers, working in perfect synchro-
nization, propelled them down the channel faster than
the average motorboat. He was about to point out the
finer points of the race when something caught his eye.

'Damn,' he muttered. Releasing Shweta's arm, he
sprinted to the makeshift dais at the end of the pier
which his team was using to make announcements
from. The girl he'd put in charge was holding the mi-
crophone idly, her entire attention focussed on the snake
boats.

Nikhil grabbed the mike from her. 'Viewing boat
Number Two—yes, you guys on my left—please don't
crowd near the guardrail. Your boat is tilting. We don't
want you to land up in the water. Especially since I see
that many of you have taken off your life jackets.'

There were some squeals of alarm from the occu-
pants of the boat and they stepped back from the rail.
The boat was still tilting a little, though not at quite
such an alarming angle. Nikhil cast a quick eye around
the other boats.

'Keep an eye on them,' he instructed, handing the mike back to his hugely embarrassed event manager. 'Don't panic them, but make sure the boat doesn't go over. And once everyone's on land call for a quick team meeting—this shouldn't have happened.'

'It wasn't her fault,' Shweta protested as Nikhil rejoined her. 'How was she to know that everyone would go thronging to one side?'

'It's her job to know,' he said, frowning. He'd been so distracted by Shweta that he'd lost sight of why he was really here. He should be with his team, making sure that nothing went wrong, but he hadn't been able to tear himself away from her side.

She was leaning forward a little now, her lips slightly parted as she watched the rowers put in a last furious effort to get the snake boats across the finish line.

'I knew the purple team would win,' she said, her eyes glowing with satisfaction.

Nikhil wished he could pull her into his arms and kiss her. Instead, he put a casual arm around her shoulders, pretending not to notice the slight quiver that ran through her. 'There's still one more race to go,' he said. 'I bet the yellow T-shirts win this time.'

'Purple,' she said, aware that she sounded a little breathless. Nikhil's proximity was doing strange things to her pulse-rate.

'Dinner with me in Mumbai if yellow wins?' he said.

Shweta looked up at him. 'And if they lose?'

'If they lose I'll take you out for dinner before we leave Kerala.'

'A little illogical, that.'

'Not really,' he said, and his voice was like a caress.

Shweta acted as if she hadn't heard him. Flirting was not something she was good at, and she suspected that Nikhil was only flirting with her out of habit. She knew she hadn't changed all that much from her schooldays— her glasses were gone, and she had a better hairstyle, but inside she was still the studious, slightly tomboy-ish and totally uncool girl she'd been fourteen years ago. The kiss she couldn't explain away. It had felt as if the attraction was as red-hot on his side as hers, but he'd pulled away and hadn't tried to get her alone af-terwards. Of course they'd been under the gaze of his entire events crew—not to mention four boatloads of her colleagues.

'Watch,' he said as the snake boats lined up for the race.

Shweta dutifully turned her eyes in the direction he was pointing. His arm was still around her, and she found it difficult to concentrate on the race. Except for the frazzled girl with the mike no one else seemed to share her problem—even the waiters and perform-ers were crowding onto the landing stage to watch the race. As for her colleagues on the boats—they were going crazy, whooping and blowing paper trumpets, though this time they were careful to stay away from the guardrail.

The yellow team won by a few metres and Shweta exhaled noisily.

'Dinner in Mumbai,' Nikhil said, looking down at her. 'I'll let you go back to your colleagues for today, then.'

Was that a dismissal? It didn't feel like one, and the thought that he'd be in touch when they returned to Mumbai made her pulse race a little faster.

'Pretty impressive, Mr Nair,' a voice said near them.

Anjalika Arora was one of the Bollywood entertainers who'd performed for the team the day before. In her late thirties, she was still strikingly beautiful. She'd never really made it to the top in films—the few in which she'd played the female lead had flopped dismally at the box office, and over the last few years she'd appeared in glitzy productions with all-star casts where she'd been only one of four or five glamorous leading ladies with very little to do. The gossip magazines said that she made a fortune in stage shows, dancing to the songs from those movies.

Shweta looked at her curiously. This was the first time she'd met even a minor celebrity face-to-face. Anjalika looked like anyone else, only a lot prettier—dressed as she was today, in denim cut-offs and a T-shirt, and with her hair tied up, she could have been a soccer mom, dropping her kid off for a game. Shweta tried to remember if she had children or not. Unfortunately the financial newspapers she took didn't say much about the private lives of movie stars. She did remember picking up a magazine at the beauty parlour which had covered a high-profile reconciliation between Anjalika and her movie producer husband.

'How was your morning?' Nikhil asked, releasing Shweta as Anjalika gave him a socialite-type kiss on the cheek.

'Oh, brilliant—I spent most of it in the spa,' Anjalika said, giving Shweta a girl-to-girl smile. 'It's pretty good—have you been there?' Before Shweta could respond she'd turned back to Nikhil. 'Nikhil, I hate to bother you while you're working, but I'm sure your amazing team can handle things. I have this teeny query which I need your help on...'

'Yes, of course.' Nikhil smiled at Shweta. 'I'll be back in half an hour, OK?'

Shweta nodded, and Anjalika gave her another brilliant smile before hooking an arm through Nikhil's and drawing him away.

'Wants a pay-hike, does she?' one of Nikhil's crew members muttered to another.

The man he was speaking to shrugged. 'It's standard practice for her. She waits till the event's underway and then starts haggling for more money. I don't think Nikhil will buckle, though—he'll sympathise, and say he'll do what he can, but she'll be lucky if he gives her even a rupee more than was actually agreed.'

'Or maybe he'll pay her in kind,' the first man said in an undertone. 'Take her back to the hotel and sweeten her up a bit. She must be gasping for it—her husband's got a floozy on the side, and she isn't as young as she used to be.'

'Yeah, and *he's* hot stuff with the women. That's how he gets some of these star types to come in for the smaller events—gives them a good time in bed and they're ready to do anything for him. Then, once the event's done with, he's off.'

'OK—minds out of the gutter, please, and back to work.'

Nikhil's second-in-command, a hearty-looking lady called Payal, strode up to them—much to Shweta's relief.

'Let's see if we can get this bunch off the boats and into the village without anyone falling into the water.' She gave Shweta a friendly nod. 'Where's that idiot Mona? I believe she was busy gawking at the race while one of the guest boats was about to tip over.'

'It wasn't so bad,' a scarlet-face Mona muttered. 'I did let my attention wander a bit, but Nikhil stepped in.'

'Well, you're lucky he was in a good mood or you'd be hunting for a job right now,' Payal said. 'Come on— start announcing the docking order and get those snake boats out of the way now. I've had enough of them.'

Wishing she hadn't overheard the conversation, Shweta headed into the resort village. People always gossiped, and event management was on the fringes of show business, where stories were that much more outrageous—probably nothing of what the two men had said was true.

She'd just ordered a carved name-plate from one of the handicraft stores and the man had promised to have it ready in fifteen minutes. She was paying for it when Siddhant came up to her.

'That's beautiful,' he said, smiling as he saw the hand-carved letters that the man had mounted onto a wooden base. 'For your flat?'

Shweta nodded. 'My old one fell off and broke.' She watched Siddhant as he picked up the name-plate and ran his fingers over the letters. Try as she might, she couldn't summon up a smidgen of feeling for Siddhant. He was intelligent, and successful, and he'd probably make someone an excellent husband some day, but meeting Nikhil had driven the last doubts out of her head. Not that she was in any way serious about Nikhil, she hastened to tell herself. The conversation she'd overheard his team having had only underlined that she didn't stand a chance with him.

'I've hardly seen you since we got to Kerala,' Siddhant was saying. 'Let's walk around the village a bit, shall we? Unless you've seen it already? You must have reached it some time before we did.'

'Not seen much of it yet,' Shweta said.

She'd have to let him know somehow that it wasn't going to work out between them—the distinctly proprietorial air he adopted when she was around him was beginning to bother her.

CHAPTER THREE

THEY WERE SITTING down to lunch when Nikhil reappeared. Anjalika was nowhere to be seen—either she'd left, or was having lunch separately. Payal had mentioned to Shweta that her contract only included a stage performance, not mingling with the guests. Nikhil didn't come across to her, however. He spent a few minutes talking to the resort manager, and then the firm's HR head nabbed him.

Shweta found herself gazing at him hungrily. His clothes were simple—an olive-green T-shirt over faded jeans—but they fitted perfectly, emphasising the breadth of his shoulders and the lean, muscled strength of his body. At that point he turned and caught her eye—for a few seconds he held her gaze, then Shweta looked away, embarrassed to have been caught staring.

'This traditional meal business is all very well, but I wish they'd served the food on plates rather than on banana leaves,' Siddhant was saying as he tried to prevent the runny lentils from spilling over on to his lap.

'It wouldn't be very traditional then, would it?' one of the senior partners said dryly.

Remembering that the man was South Indian, Siddhant rushed into damage-control mode. 'Yes, of course. It's just that I'm not used to it. The food's delicious—we should seriously evaluate the option of getting South Indian food made in the office cafeteria at least once a week.'

One of the other partners said something in response and the conversation became general. Shweta felt pretty firmly excluded from it, however. She was sitting between Siddhant and another colleague who was all too busy trying to impress his boss. Priya and the rest of her friends were sitting across the room, and they appeared to be having a whale of a time. Siddhant himself was making absolutely no effort to bring her into the conversation with the rest of the partners—evidently he felt he had done enough by inviting her to sit with them at the hallowed top table.

Her phone pinged, and Shweta dug it out of her bag to see a message from Priya. *You look bored out of your wits*, it said, and Shweta looked across to see Priya miming falling asleep and keeling over into her banana leaf.

Shweta took a rapid decision. She wasn't very hungry, she'd finished all the food on her leaf—and the server was still two tables away. 'Siddhant, I need to go and check on something,' she said in an undertone during the next break in conversation.

Siddhant looked a little surprised. 'Right now?' he asked, and his tone implied that she was passing up on a golden chance to hang out with the who's who of the firm.

'Right now,' Shweta said firmly, and escaped to the corner where Priya was busy demolishing a heap of sweetmeats.

'What happened to your diet?' Shweta asked in mock-horror. Only the week before, Priya had embarked on an oil-free, sugar-free, practically food-free diet.

Priya shrugged happily. 'The diet's on vacation,' she said. 'This stuff is way too good to resist. Where's that hunk of a childhood friend of yours? I thought you'd finally seen the light when I saw you go off with him, but here you are back with Siddy-boy.'

'Don't call him Siddy-boy,' Shweta said, feeling annoyed with Priya. 'And I just spent the morning with Nikhil—we had a lot of stuff to catch up on. I didn't "go off" with him.'

'"Catching up"? How boring,' Priya said, making a face. 'If you aren't interested the least you could do is introduce me to him properly—he's *sooooo* hot…'

'And you're *so* not available,' Shweta said, getting even more annoyed. 'You have a steady boyfriend, remember?'

'Someone's getting jea-lous,' Priya carolled, and Shweta longed to hit her.

'Lunch over?' a familiarly sexy voice asked.

She turned to almost cannon into Nikhil. 'Yes,' she said ungraciously, wondering how much he had heard. Priya had a rather strident voice, and she hadn't bothered to keep it low.

'Sorry I had to rush off like that,' he said. 'Anjalika has this habit of creating problems halfway through an event.'

'No worries,' she said, sounding fake even to her own ears. It was a phrase she'd picked up from Siddhant, and she found herself using it whenever she didn't know how to react to something. Then natural curiosity got the better of her and she asked, 'Did she want more money?'

Nikhil looked nonplussed for a few seconds, and then he started laughing. 'I can see the team's been talking. Yes, she did. But she isn't going to get it.'

The team had been saying a lot, she thought. But, looking at Nikhil, she couldn't believe that he'd trade sexual favours for a reduction in Anjalika's fee. That was as bad as being a gigolo—worse, probably, because he didn't *need* to seduce older women for money.

'Don't look so horrified,' Nikhil said, tweaking a stray strand of hair that had escaped from the barrette she'd used to tie it back. 'This business is like that. There's a lot of last-minute haggling, and you can lose all your profits if you're not careful to tie people down with water-tight contracts before you begin.'

Forgetting the fact that pulling her hair was anything but a lover-like gesture, Shweta's relief at the business-like way he spoke was overwhelming. She'd been right all along then—his team had just been gossiping.

'Nikhil, the resort manager would like to speak to you,' Payal called out.

Nikhil made an exasperated gesture. 'I'll see you in the evening, then,' he said to Shweta.

Priya made a disappointed face once he'd left. 'Very brisk and practical, that was,' she said. 'D'you think there's something wrong with you? I was hoping you were on the verge of a mad fling with him, but you talk to him like he's your cousin or something. No chemistry at all.'

'Perhaps I'm more of a physics and geography kind of girl,' Shweta retorted. 'Grow up, Priya. Not every woman goes on heat when she sees a good-looking man.'

Siddhant had come up in time to hear the latter part of her sentence and he looked completely scandalised. Good job, too, Shweta thought spitefully as she refused his offer of a lift back to the hotel.

'I'll go in the bus with Priya,' she said. 'I'm sick of sitting around while you talk shop with the other partners.'

No chemistry. Perhaps Priya was right and she was imagining things, Shweta thought as she leaned her forehead against the cool glass of the bus window. There was that kiss, though, and the way he'd looked at her when they were watching the boat race…

'Siddy-boy didn't know what had hit him,' Priya said gleefully as she took the seat next to her. Evidently she'd forgiven Shweta for the bitchy comment about not all women being like her. 'He was so sure you'd be thrilled at being offered a seat in that stuffy old van with him and the other partners. There's hope for you yet.'

Shweta shrugged. 'I was irritated, and I said it without thinking. I'll end up apologising when I see him again.'

Priya looked disappointed. 'Don't—that'll spoil everything,' she said. 'Stay away from him a bit so that he gets the message. You're definitely off him, aren't you?'

Shweta nodded. Priya was as sharp as a needle, and there was no point trying to hide it from her. Far better that she used her rusty dissembling skills to conceal the fact that she was helplessly attracted to Nikhil.

'I don't know what you saw in him in the first place,' Priya said. 'You're smart and you're good-looking—you can do a lot better for yourself.'

'Like who?' Shweta asked dryly. 'Men aren't exactly queuing up asking for my hand in marriage. If I decided to hold a *swayamvara*, I'd probably have to pay people to come.'

Priya shrugged. In her view marriage was vastly overrated—but then, she'd spent the last six years fending off offers of marriage from several men, including her long-term boyfriend. She gave Shweta a considering look. 'You know what your problem is?' she asked.

'I don't, but I'm sure you're about to tell me,' Shweta replied.

'You treat all men like they're your buddies. So then they treat you like "one of the boys" and everything goes downhill from there. You need to build an aura— some mystique.' Priya gesticulated madly. 'Or, if all else fails, some good old-fashioned sex appeal would do the trick.'

Shweta shrugged. She'd long ago come to terms with the fact that, unlike Helen of Troy, whose beauty had launched a thousand ships, hers would only be able to float a paper boat or two. She was good-looking enough—lots of people had told her that—but men regularly bypassed her to fall for less good-looking but sexier girls. Not that it had ever bothered her much. Until meeting Nikhil again she hadn't felt the pull of strong sexual attraction. She'd just assumed it was something that people had made up to sell romantic novels and movies.

'I've booked us into the spa for a massage and a steam bath,' Priya said after a while. 'I forgot to tell you.'

Shweta shook her head. 'Take one of the other girls instead,' she said. 'I'm going for a swim.'

It was almost six when they got back to the hotel, and the pool was thankfully deserted. Everyone who'd managed to get a spa booking was headed there, and the rest were in the bar at the other end of the property. Shweta ran up to her room to change into her swimsuit, and was back at the pool in a few minutes.

The water was perfect, warm and welcoming, and she automatically felt herself relax as she got in. She did the first few laps at a brisk pace, working off the day's confusion and angst as she cleaved through the water. After a while, however, she flipped over, floating aimlessly on her back as she looked up at the sky. The sun was about to set, and the sky was a mass of lovely red-gold and purple clouds. Looking at it, she felt her troubles seep away.

A muted splash told her that someone else had joined her in the water, but she didn't turn to see who it was. Only when the sun set fully and the sky faded to a dull steel-grey did she swim to the side of the pool.

'You'll shrivel up like a prune if you stay in the water any longer,' Nikhil remarked.

A sixth sense had already told her who her silent companion was, and she didn't turn her head to look at him. 'Stalker,' she said in amiable tones. She felt in her element while she was in the pool, and more than equal to dealing with her old classmate.

He was by her side in a few swift strokes. 'What did you say?' he asked, playfully threatening her with a ducking.

'You don't even like swimming,' she said. 'You told me yesterday.'

'Depends who I'm swimming with.' The lights around the pool had come on, and his eyes skimmed over her appreciatively. 'Looking pretty good, Ms Mathur.'

She was wearing a much-used one-piece black swimsuit—but in spite of its age it clung faithfully to her slim curves. He could hardly take his eyes off her. Her wet hair hung down her back, and little drops of water were rolling down her neck and into her cleavage as she leaned against the side of the pool. Involuntarily, he raised a hand and trailed it down the side of the arm nearest him.

Shweta shivered in response, slipping back into the water before he could do more. She'd got a good look at him, and he looked pretty irresistible himself. His body lived up to if not exceeded the expectations it had aroused when he was fully clothed—all washboard abs, lean muscle and sinewy arms. He looked more like a professional athlete than a businessman. His damp hair flopped just so over his forehead, dripping into his deep-set eyes and he had just the right hint of devilry in his expression—all in all, Shweta thought, she could be forgiven for thinking him pretty irresistible.

'Well?' he asked, treading water next to her. 'Are you done practising for the Olympics? Can we get out before I catch my death of cold?'

'It's not cold at all,' Shweta said, but she swam to the side of the pool. It was difficult to hold a conversation with her ears full of water, and she didn't mean to try.

Outside the pool, Nikhil looked even more impressive, towering over her as she got out of the water. He took her hand to help her out and a jolt of electricity seemed to pass from his body to hers. Realising that she was staring up at him dumbly, Shweta made as if to step away—Nikhil, however, took her by the shoulders and pulled her against his body. Slowly, he lowered his head to hers, but just when she thought he was about to kiss her he pulled away.

'Someone's coming,' he said. 'You'd better go and change. I'll see you back here in fifteen minutes, OK?'

It took her ten minutes to shower, change into shorts and a sleeveless tee and get back to the poolside. He was waiting there for her, standing with his back to the pool. He'd changed as well, into khaki shorts and a white T-shirt. His hair was still damp, and as she came up he tossed the towel he'd been holding on to a deckchair.

'I'm leaving tonight,' he said abruptly. 'I'll see you in Mumbai soon—we have that dinner date, remember?'

Shweta felt quite absurdly disappointed. 'Are you leaving right away?'

He nodded. 'Almost. It's a long way to the airport.

I wanted to say goodbye, and I realised we haven't ex-changed numbers.'

'I don't have a piece of paper,' she said. 'And my mobile's back in my room.'

'Tell me your number. I'll memorise it, and I'll call you when I'm on my way to the airport,' he said. 'I'm not carrying my mobile either.'

Shweta told him her number and he listened care-fully, repeating it back to her to make sure he'd got it right.

'So…I'll call you, then,' he said, turning to climb the stairs that led to the hotel.

Shweta gazed after him in disbelief, and then ran up the stairs to overtake him. 'Just a minute,' she said. 'When you say you'll call me and we'll go out for din-ner, is that like a date, or something? Because I'm a little confused—you kissed me on the boat, and you were about to kiss me just now, if someone hadn't come along. But the rest of the time you act like I'm your old buddy from school—not that I was your buddy. We used to fight all the time, except in kindergarten. Actually, that's the last time I was able to figure out what you're up to—when we were in kindergarten. You've grown more and more complicated…'

Nikhil's brow creased with concentration as he tried to keep up and failed. 'I don't know what you're talk-ing about,' he said finally.

Shweta shook her head in exasperation. 'Forget it,' she said. 'I'm making a muddle of things as usual.'

'No—rewind a bit and let me understand this.'

His eyes were amused and caressing as he looked at her, and she felt her knees go just a little bit wobbly.

'You think I'm asking you out because I want to be your *buddy*?'

'Something like that,' she muttered—and gave an undignified little squawk as she was efficiently swept into his arms.

'A buddy?' Nikhil said. 'Hmm, that's an idea. Purely platonic, right?'

Shweta could feel her heart hammering, and pressed so close against his chest she was sure he could feel it too. When he bent his head to kiss her lips she tensed, going rigid in his arms. He kissed her very lightly, as if just tasting her lips, but when she unconsciously leaned towards him the kiss grew harder, more demanding. The sensation was exquisite, and Shweta felt positively bereft when he drew away.

She took a couple of quick breaths. 'Not purely platonic, then?' she asked, fighting to keep her voice steady.

'Not platonic,' he said, and his slow, incredibly sexy smile set her heart pounding away like a trip-hammer on steroids. 'That OK with you?'

It was more than OK, but Shweta couldn't say so without sounding impossibly over-keen. Trying to play it cool, she gave him a flippant smile. 'I can live with it,' she said—and gasped as he pulled her close for another scorching-hot kiss.

'I'll see you in Mumbai, then,' he said.

And before she could gather her senses enough to reply he was off.

Shweta watched him stride into the hotel. So much for there being no chemistry between them, she thought as a feeling of pure euphoria swept over her. Somewhere at the back of her head she knew that she shouldn't rush into a relationship blindly, but just now she wanted to enjoy the moment without bothering about the future.

CHAPTER FOUR

IT WAS MORE than two weeks after she'd returned to Mumbai that Shweta managed to meet Nikhil for dinner. He'd been out of town for a few days, and then she'd had a project to finish within some pretty crazy deadlines. After that, she'd gone down to Pune to meet her dad and her aunt. Now that she was finally back Nikhil had reserved a table at a rather swanky new restaurant at the Mahalakshmi race course for Saturday evening.

'Where are you off to?' Priya asked, lounging on her bed as Shweta made yet another attempt to get her eyeliner on straight.

'Nowhere special.' She wasn't sure why she was keeping her dinner date with Nikhil a secret, but she hadn't told Priya earlier and it would be more than a little embarrassing to tell her now. 'I'm meeting a couple of old college friends for drinks, and we might go out for dinner afterwards.'

'Can I come with you?' Priya asked. 'Rahul's out of town, and I'm so bored... Maybe one of your college friends could help cheer me up?'

'Sorry,' Shweta said, shooting Priya an amused

glance over her shoulder. 'They're not your type, and we have a lot of catching up to do. I'll tell you what— I'll lend you some of my DVDs. You can watch a nice movie.'

'You have rubbish taste in movies,' Priya said moodily, going over to the drawer where Shweta kept her DVD collection. 'It's all such grim, arty stuff—no chick flicks, and you don't even have a good action movie in this lot.' She watched Shweta as she outlined her mouth with lipliner and proceeded to colour it in with lipstick.

'You're meeting a *guy*,' she said. Shweta glared at her as she broke into a wide smile.

'Of *course*—that's why you don't want me to come along! I haven't seen you make so much effort over your face in months, and you changed in and out of three dresses before you chose this one. Who is it?'

'No one you know,' Shweta said, slamming her make-up drawer shut and squirting a last bit of perfume over herself.

'Nonsense. I know everything about you.' Priya thought for a bit. 'I know! It's that hottie from the Kerala trip. What was his name again? Naveen? Nirav? No—Nikhil. That's it—you're meeting Nikhil, aren't you?'

Despite herself, Shweta felt a warm tide of colour stain her cheeks.

Priya crowed with delight. 'I knew it! I knew something was happening. Come here and let me look at you—a special date needs some special advice.'

Shweta submitted to being examined from every

angle. Priya had a good sense of style, and it wouldn't hurt to take her opinion.

'Pretty good,' she pronounced finally. 'Except you could do with a little more colour in your cheeks. And I can't believe you didn't buy a new dress. This one's nice, but you've worn it lots of times before.'

'Nikhil's not seen it,' Shweta pointed out as she warded off Priya's attempts to put some more blusher on her cheeks. 'I don't want to look like I'm trying too hard.'

She gave herself a last look in the mirror. The midnight-blue dress was deceptively simple in cut and it showed off her curves to perfection. She wore a simple diamond pendant on a white-gold chain with matching earrings, and her shoes—as usual—were the exact shade of the dress.

'Are the shoes a bit much?' she asked anxiously.

Priya hesitated. 'A little too matching-matching, but that's OK—guys never notice such stuff.'

But Shweta was already kicking the shoes off, exchanging them for strappy silver sandals.

The intercom rang, and Priya ran to pick it up. 'Your cab's here,' she said.

Shweta had called for a taxi rather than hailing a black-and-yellow cab on the street as she usually did. It was normally a half-hour drive from where she lived to the race course, but a mixer truck had broken down in the middle of the road and the traffic was terrible. In spite of that, she got there a few minutes early. Nikhil wasn't there yet, and they had arranged to meet for a drink at the bar before they went down for dinner.

Feeling a little awkward and out of place, Shweta ordered a drink and sipped at it gingerly, surveying the room. The whole building had been redecorated recently—the bar had a high wooden ceiling with fake beams and lots of *faux*-antique wooden furniture and panelling. Shweta wrinkled her nose a little. She couldn't see why places that weren't really old tried to look that way.

'You don't look pleased,' Nikhil observed as he walked up to her.

Shweta jumped, spilling a bit of her drink. 'It's the way this place is done up,' she confided. 'They've tried to make it look like an old English pub, but it's not old and it's not English—and anyway the roof's all wrong. Pubs have low ceilings normally.'

'I'll tell the architect if I ever meet him,' Nikhil said, sounding amused. 'I'd apologise for being late—but I'm not, am I?'

'No. I have a pathological fear of being late myself,' Shweta said, 'so I end up being early for everything. I've even gone to weddings where I've reached the venue before either the bride or the groom. You're looking nice, by the way.'

That last bit had just slipped out—but he *was* looking exceptionally good. *Nice* didn't even begin to cover it. He'd had his hair cut since she'd seen him last, and the new, shorter hairstyle suited him. He was wearing a striped button-down shirt open at the collar, and black formal-looking jeans. The shirt was rolled up at the sleeves, and she could see his strong forearms, with a smattering of hair covering them. The temptation to reach out and touch was overwhelming.

'So are you,' Nikhil said, sounding more amused than ever. 'That's a lovely dress.'

'But most of the other women are wearing black,' she said. 'I'm feeling terribly out of place.'

Nikhil shrugged. 'Black is like a uniform,' he said. 'Pretty boring, if you ask me. Come on—let me get you another drink.'

Shweta hadn't even noticed that her first drink had gone. Something was not quite right. Nikhil seemed a lot more formal than he had when he'd met her last— and, while he was smiling a lot, the smile didn't reach his eyes.

'Is everything OK?' she asked.

Nikhil sighed and rubbed at his face. 'It's been a crazy week,' he said. 'Sometimes I'm tempted to throw this whole thing over and go and do something else. Maybe work in an office—it's got to be simpler.'

'More stars throwing tantrums?'

He shook his head. 'I wish. That's the easiest thing to handle. No, some of my clients are delaying payments. Big corporates. Apparently they hadn't got all the internal approvals in place before they hired me, and the bills aren't getting cleared. I've had to threaten legal action in two cases to get them to pay up. It isn't hurting me right now, because business is doing well, but unless I play hardball with these guys I'll have other clients trying to take me for a ride.'

Shweta was looking mildly shocked.

He laughed. 'Let's change the topic before your eyes

glaze over and you fall asleep on the table. How was your Pune trip?'

'Pretty good,' she said cautiously. Nikhil still looked on edge, and she would bet anything that it wasn't about a few missed payments.

'Your dad happy to see you?'

'I guess so.' Her father rarely displayed any emotion, but he'd cancelled his weekly bridge game to spend time with her, and that was saying a lot. 'He's growing old,' she said. 'He was forty when I was born, so he's pushing seventy now… I get a little worried sometimes.'

Shweta had grown up without a mother, and losing her father was one of her biggest fears. She rarely spoke about it, not acknowledging it even to herself, but the expression in Nikhil's eyes showed that he understood.

She hurried on before he could say anything. 'How's Veena Aunty doing?' she asked. She knew how fond Nikhil was of his stepmother—he was probably closer to her than to his own mother.

Nikhil's face clouded over. 'I haven't seen her for a while,' he said tightly. 'I had a bit of a bust-up with my parents. She lives with them, and I'm not keen on going there if I can help it. Amma's taken their side on the whole thing.'

'Maybe she has her reasons,' Shweta couldn't help saying. She'd always thought that Nikhil was a bit too hung up on the whole being illegitimate business. She could see why it had bothered him during his growing up years, but surely it was time to let go now?

Nikhil didn't seem to have heard her. 'I asked her to move here and stay with me,' he said. 'I have a decent flat, and I could hire someone to look after her during the day. It would be so much more dignified than letting those two take care of her. I told you, didn't I, that she's pretending to be Mom's cousin now?'

'Go to Kerala and try speaking to her,' Shweta said. 'You don't need to talk to your parents unless absolutely necessary.'

'My father's told me not to come near until I've apologised to him for what I said during our last argument,' he said. He stared broodingly into space for a few minutes.

Having run out of useful suggestions, Shweta stayed silent.

After a while Nikhil shook himself and seemed to come back to earth. He took a largish swig out of his glass and turned to Shweta. 'I'm not the best of company today, am I?' he asked, forcing a smile. 'It's just that you know the whole story—it's so much easier talking to you than to anyone else...'

Of course it was. For a few seconds Shweta felt such an acute sense of disappointment that she could hardly speak. That explained why Nikhil was seeking her out, she thought. He must have kept all this stuff about his parents bottled up for years, and it would be a relief being able to pour it out to someone who knew all about it—save him the embarrassment of having to tell whoever his current friends were that he was illegitimate.

But after the first wave of anger ebbed she was able to think about it more rationally. It was natural, his wanting to talk to her. And the kisses and dinner dates—perhaps he sensed how attracted she was to him and those were his means of keeping her hooked. Unbidden, her thoughts went back to that conversation she'd overheard between members of his team.

'I'll have another drink, I think,' she said.

Her mind was working overtime, she knew—maybe she was imagining things. Nikhil got up and went to the bar to fetch a refill, and she watched him silently.

'I resented you for a long time, you know,' he said quietly after handing her the glass. 'That's why I used to give you a hard time. You were the first person who made me realise that there was something wrong with my family.'

'Me?' Shweta's voice was incredulous. 'What did I do?'

'You asked me who my real mother was,' he said. 'I told you that both of them were my moms, but you said, "Whose tummy did you live in before you were born?" Until then I think I'd believed implicitly in the "babies are a gift from God" story. So it was a revelation in more ways than one.'

'I don't even remember,' Shweta said remorsefully. 'But I can quite imagine myself saying that. I went around once telling the whole class that Santa Claus didn't exist—some of the kids actually started crying.'

'Now, *that* I don't remember,' he said, and the smile was back in his voice. 'Maybe I got off lightly, then.'

'I thought it was very unfair,' she said after a brief pause.

Nikhil raised his eyebrows. 'What was? No Santa Claus?'

'You having two moms when I didn't have even one,' she said.

There was an awkward pause, and then Nikhil said, 'I never thought of it that way.'

The realisation that he was illegitimate had tainted most of his childhood. He'd grown up in a stolidly middle-class neighbourhood and the very fact that most of the rigidly conventional people around him had felt sorry for him had been a constant thorn in his flesh. It had never occurred to him that Shweta had envied him.

'It must have been tough for you, losing your mom when you were so young.' As soon as the words were out, he wished them unsaid. Shweta's face had closed up in an instant.

'I hardly remember her,' she said. 'And my aunt was there. She took good care of me.'

She'd always been like that when her mother was mentioned, Nikhil remembered. Something made him look down at her hands and he noticed a familiar mannerism—just like she'd used to in school she was tracing out words on her left palm with the fingers of her right hand. It was something she did when she was tense. Unconsciously he leaned a little closer, to try and make out the words, but her hands clenched into little fists, and when he looked up she was scowling at him.

'I'm sorry,' he said, his voice gentle.

'You're so *annoying*!' she burst out. 'You used to do that when we were kids—try and read what I was scribbling into my hand. I hate it! No one else—'

She broke off, realising that she sounded impossibly petulant and childish. No one else had ever noticed the habit, though she did it all the time. Not her father, or her aunt, or her boss, or Siddhant. Somehow that made her feel even more annoyed with Nikhil.

'Aren't we getting late for dinner?' she asked, sounding stiff and ungracious even to herself. 'I thought you had a reservation for nine o'clock?'

Nikhil nodded and got to his feet. 'Let's go,' he said.

She didn't even feel hungry, Shweta realised as she went down the stairs.

The ground floor of the restaurant was full now—and several people seemed to recognise Nikhil, turning to wave as he escorted her to the outdoor seating area. The women gave her curious looks, and she felt acutely conscious of her off-the-rack dress and casually done hair. Everyone else was dressed far more expensively than she was, and that somehow made her feel worse than ever. The evening was turning out to be a total disaster—the quicker she left the better it would be for both of them.

'I'm not really very hungry,' she muttered, glancing down at the menu.

Supposedly the food was Indian, but she hadn't even heard of half the dishes before. Probably they were designed to appeal to the large number of foreigners who were thronging the place. Shweta cast a quick look around. Most of the tables were occupied by glitzy types, except for one where a bunch of older people were celebrating someone's fortieth birthday. They were expensively but casually dressed, and seemed very comfortable in their own skins. The woman whose birthday it was caught Shweta's eye and gave her a wink. Instantly she started feeling better.

'I like the look of that group,' she told Nikhil. 'Especially the husband of the birthday girl. He's cute.'

'He's twice your age,' Nikhil said, following her gaze.

'But so what? He looks nice. I bet he was quite a heartbreaker when he was younger. And look at him now—he's so wrapped up in his wife, and she must be about the same age as him…'

Nikhil reached across and firmly took her glass out of her hand. 'I agree. They're very cute. But you need to stop staring,' he said. 'And they're forty—not eighty. It's perfectly normal to be wrapped up in each other even at that age. I didn't know you were such a romantic.'

'I'm not romantic at all!' Shweta gave him an indignant look. 'And I'm not drunk either. So you can give me back my glass, thank you very much.'

'I didn't say you were drunk,' Nikhil said, and gave her the glass back. 'Shall I order for you? You're holding your menu upside down.'

'It makes the same amount of sense both ways,' she said, and he laughed out loud.

After he'd finished ordering and the waiter had gone away, he reached out and took her hand across the table. 'I'm sorry,' he said. 'The evening's not gone the way it was supposed to, has it?'

'I'm not sure *how* it was supposed to go,' she said, meeting his gaze squarely across the table. 'But if it was supposed to be a date it's not been very date-like so far.'

Nikhil toyed with her hand for a few seconds without looking up. Then he lifted it and gently kissed her fingers one by one, his lips lingering against her skin. Completely taken by surprise, she watched him as if turned to stone. There was something incredibly erotic about the gesture—quite suddenly the date was living up to expectations after all.

'Why did you do that?' she asked when he finally looked up, and her voice was trembling slightly.

He took his time answering, bending to press one more kiss on her palm before he spoke. 'You looked like you could do with a kiss,' he said. 'And you're too far away for me to kiss you properly. We'll have to wait until we're out of here for that.'

She tried to be annoyed at being told that she looked as if she needed kissing, but she was so strung up at the thought of getting to kiss him properly later that she couldn't bother to be upset. The rest of her appetite seemed to have disappeared as well, but she obediently picked at her food when it arrived. After the first few mouthfuls she discovered that the taste was out of the world—and that she was hungry after all.

'I like watching you eat,' Nikhil said. 'You look like you're enjoying the meal, not counting calories.'

'I'll probably be as fat as a tub by the time I'm forty,' Shweta said.

She said no to dessert, however, and Nikhil asked for the bill. Shweta was almost jigging around in impatience while he waited for his credit card to be swiped and then signed the charge slip.

'Let's go,' he said finally, and she slipped her arm in his to walk out of the restaurant.

'I'll drop you home,' he said. 'But first…'

The path to the car park was deserted, and Nikhil pulled her into his arms and kissed her very, very thoroughly. 'I've been dreaming about this,' he said huskily. 'It drove me crazy, waiting two weeks till I could see you again.'

Shweta nodded in agreement before fisting her hands in his hair and pulling his head down for another kiss. This was one situation where his new haircut wasn't an improvement—it had been so much easier to get a grip when his hair was longer. Still, she did the best she could, and he reciprocated admirably. Both of them were a little breathless when they broke apart a few minutes later.

'I wish I could take you home with me,' he said. 'But it's too soon—I don't want to rush you.'

One part of Shweta's brain was quite sure that she didn't mind being rushed—the other part, however, grudgingly admitted that he was right.

'I'll call the car,' he said.

Shweta gave him a curious look. 'You mean you'll whistle to it and it'll come to you? Like in a Bond movie?'

Nikhil laughed. 'No, I brought my driver along because I knew I'd be drinking,' he said. 'Come here—we have time for one last kiss.'

And what a kiss it was. Shweta thought of protesting that she was in no hurry, that they could spend the rest of the night in the car park as far as she was concerned, but she had to bite the words back. Also, the kisses were getting a little too much for her self-control—another few and she'd be clawing the clothes off him. It was probably best that she go home before she completely disgraced herself. Either he wasn't quite as attracted to her as he said he was, or he had super-human self-control, she thought resentfully as they waited for the driver to bring the car around.

Once they were in the car Nikhil kept his hands off her completely. After he'd foiled her first two attempts to get closer to him Shweta sat grumpily in one corner, resisting his attempts to make polite conversation.

'Are you free next weekend?' he asked as she got out of the car.

She nodded. Definitely not as attracted as she was, she thought. Next weekend seemed like aeons away, with the week yawning like a bottomless abyss in between.

'Only I don't think I can wait that long to see you again,' he said, with a laugh in his voice as if he'd gauged exactly how frustrated she was feeling. 'OK if I pick you up after work on Tuesday?'

'Tuesday sounds good,' she said politely. 'Dinner again?'

He thought it over. 'Well, I guess we would need to eat,' he said. 'Though it wasn't exactly dinner that I had in mind…'

In her high heels she was almost as tall as he was. She stood on tiptoe and put a hand to the side of his face. Slowly she brought her lips close to his mouth and pressed them there. For a few seconds he stood frozen.

Worried that he'd move away, she moved her hands up to clasp his head and deepened the kiss, leaning into him, her body pressed provocatively against his. This time his response was far more satisfactory and he returned the kiss, his lips hot and hungry against hers, while his arms held her in a possessive embrace.

A piercing whistle from an upstairs window make them break apart and look up. Priya was leaning out of the window, waving madly.

'Stupid cow,' Shweta said crossly, once she'd got over her initial embarrassment. She made a face at Priya and gestured to her to go back inside. Priya gave her a huge grin, and mimed kissing. It took a particularly hard glare to get her to shut the window and go inside.

'I'll see you on Tuesday,' she said to Nikhil, but he gave her a quizzical look. 'Why do you and Priya share a flat? You don't seem to like each other much.'

Shweta stared at him. 'She's my best friend,' she said sharply. 'I thought you'd be able to figure that out without me having to tell you.'

She was unlocking her front door when she heard his powerful car start up and she gave a little groan. She'd been stupid, she realised, snapping at him like that. But Priya was the closest thing she had to a sister, and she'd reacted without thinking.

'You're a pestilence and a disease,' she told Priya crossly as Priya came out of her room with a big grin plastered on her face. 'A foul blot on humanity. A Nosey Parker. The worst excuse for a flatmate in all creation. The only—'

'Dry up,' Priya said firmly. 'I've saved you from a

terrible fate. Just think—what if Mrs Ahuja had looked out of the window and seen you standing on the pavement, making out in public? She'd throw both of us out of the flat before you could say *hot hunk*. Which he is, by the way. But that would have only annoyed her more.'

Sidetracked for a second by the thought of their terrifying landlady having spotted her kissing Nikhil, Shweta protested, 'She should be happy! She's always nagging me to find a "good boy" and marry him and have twenty children.'

'Reached that stage, has it?' Priya teased. 'Daydreaming about marrying Nikhil and having his children…? And without doing a single online compatibility test? What have you done with the real Shweta?'

Shweta flushed. Priya had caught her checking her compatibility with Siddhant on a matrimonial website's compatibility scorer, and she hadn't let Shweta forget it. But her words brought her back to reality with a rather sickening thump. She'd been so carried away the last few weeks, she hadn't really thought things through at all. Living in the moment was all very well, but she was in real danger of falling in love with Nikhil now.

Seeing the changing expressions on her face, Priya groaned. 'I shouldn't have opened my big mouth,' she said. 'Spit it out, now. What's bothering you?'

'I'm in this way too deep!' Shweta wailed. 'I don't know what's wrong with me. I've never made a fool of myself over a man like this before.'

'Then it's about time you did,' Priya said briskly. 'It's natural, Shweta. You're young—you need to loosen up, live life a little. I fully approve of this Nikhil person, by the way. He's super-hot, and he'll be amazing in bed. Even if he doesn't turn out to be the love of your life he'll give you a rocking time.'

'I don't want a rocking time,' Shweta muttered. 'I'm not the kind of person who rocks. I'm more into stones and pebbles.'

Priya ignored her feeble stab at humour and eyed her with misgiving. 'Don't tell me you're thinking of going back to Siddhant?' she asked. 'I hope you've told him it's off?'

'I told him the day after we got back from Kerala,' Shweta said.

It had been a difficult conversation. She'd expected Siddhant to be offended, but he'd been genuinely upset and hurt, and she'd felt dreadfully guilty. Not so guilty that she'd wanted to go back to him, obviously, but enough to stay awake a couple of nights beating herself up about it.

'He thought I hated you!' Shweta burst out suddenly. 'Nikhil, I mean. Not Siddhant. He doesn't know the first thing about me.'

'We bicker all the time,' Priya pointed out reasonably. 'You can't blame him if he thought we don't get along.'

'I did an internet search on him last week,' Shweta said. 'He hangs out at celebrity parties, and there are pictures of him with all these glamorous women… There's no reason for him to choose me over them. The novelty will wear off in no time, and then where will I be?'

'Right where you are now,' Priya said. 'But at least you'll have taken a shot at making things work with him so you don't have to wonder about it for the rest of your life.'

It was sound advice, and Shweta knew it, but when she was in her room, trying to go to sleep, the doubts all crept back. She'd never had a very high opinion of her own attractions, and the more she thought about it the more convinced she was that Nikhil would lose interest pretty soon.

She dozed off finally, but her dreams were troubled with images of Nikhil striding away from her as she ran faster and faster, trying to keep up with him.

CHAPTER FIVE

'So, WHAT DO you think, Shweta?'

Shweta looked up from her notepad in alarm. Busy daydreaming about Nikhil, she hadn't heard a word of what her boss had said to her. Across the table, Priya was nodding at her vigorously, so Shweta said, 'Um, I agree, of course.'

Deepa gave her a strange look. 'Were you listening, Shweta?' she asked. 'I asked if you had any major projects lined up for this week.'

'No, I don't,' Shweta said, wondering why Priya was still making faces at her.

'Good. Then you can fly down to Delhi and take over the audit Faisal was doing. The silly man's had an accident and broken his wrist—he won't be back to work for a week at least.'

Oh, great. 'When do I need to leave?' Shweta asked, hoping Deepa would say next week, or even Wednesday.

'Well, this afternoon would be good,' Deepa said briskly. 'Then you can meet Faisal before he goes for surgery. He's in no state to give you a proper hand-over, but at least he can tell you what to watch out for.'

'Serves you right for wool-gathering during a meeting,' Priya said when they met for lunch a couple of hours later. 'Have you told Nikhil?'

Shweta nodded glumly. 'I won't be able to see him for a few weeks now,' she said. 'He's leaving for Europe this Saturday, and he isn't back till the end of the month. *Damn* Faisal and his stupid wrist—he should have more sense than to go around breaking bones at his age.'

'It was hardly his fault,' Priya said. 'From what Deepa said, someone had spilt a drink on a dance floor and he slipped.'

'Whatever,' Shweta said, in no mood to be sympathetic. 'Pretty mess he's made of my plans.'

When she actually saw Faisal, though, she felt quite sorry for him. He was in a lot of pain, having broken his wrist in three places, and obviously terrified about going through surgery.

'Deepa must be furious,' he said, smiling up at Shweta wanly. 'This is a complicated audit, and now you've had to come down to take care of things. There'll be an additional cost which we can't bill to the client...'

'Stop stressing about it,' Shweta advised. 'Deepa knows you didn't fall down on purpose, and she'll figure out a way of recovering the costs. She's pretty smart about that sort of stuff.'

In the evening, while she was headed back from her client's office to the company's guest house, she couldn't help thinking that she could have been with

Nikhil instead. He hadn't even called—maybe he was going out with someone else instead. The thought almost made her stop in her tracks.

'There's a parcel for you,' the guest house clerk said as she came in. 'And you didn't leave your room keys with me this morning, so your room's not been cleaned. Should I send someone in now?'

'Yes, sure,' Shweta said, eyeing the parcel in puzzlement. It was a square box, done up in white paper, and it had her name on it in big bold letters. No courier slip or post office stamps. 'Who brought this?'

The clerk shrugged. 'A delivery boy. I thought it was someone from your office.'

Shweta picked up the surprisingly heavy parcel and carried it to her room. Her firm had a small office in Delhi—perhaps Deepa had asked for some files to be sent over.

But the parcel wasn't from Deepa. Opening it, Shweta was more puzzled than ever. There was a book of Urdu poetry on top—one that she'd wanted to read for a while but which wasn't available in Mumbai—and next to it was a box of expensive chocolates and a silk pashmina shawl. Under the shawl was a leather jewellery box that opened to reveal a pair of really beautiful earrings in antique silver. Right at the bottom of the box she found one of Nikhil's business cards. There was no note.

Shweta slowly put everything back in the box except for the book, which she put on her bedside table. The gifts were lovely, but Nikhil hadn't called or messaged her since she'd left Mumbai. Picking up her phone, she sat lost in thought for a few minutes. She could call *him,* of course—thanking him for the gifts would be the perfect excuse. On the other hand she might come across as being a little over-eager, perhaps even desperate. She wasn't sure of her feelings for Nikhil yet, and she'd already gone much further with him after two dates than she would have with anyone else.

In exasperation at her own indecisiveness she picked up her phone and dialled Nikhil's number before she could change her mind. It rang for a long while, and she was about to give up and put the phone down when he answered.

'Hey, Shweta,' he said. His voice was like liquid silk, making her go a little weak at the knees. Just as well she was already sitting down if two words could make her feel like this.

'Hi,' she said softly. 'Just called to thank you for the gifts—they're lovely.'

'Glad you like them,' he said. 'I told a girl in my Delhi office what to get. She's got pretty good taste.'

Shweta winced. It had crossed her mind that the gifts had been bought by someone else—there hadn't been time for him to buy the stuff himself *and* have it shipped over. She wondered what the girl had thought—the one Nikhil said had 'good taste'. Had she done this before? Bought gifts for Nikhil's girlfriends? Or had he given her some other explanation? Maybe that Shweta was a client, or an old friend? The last had the added advantage of being actually true. She couldn't help wondering how Nikhil would react if she told him that she didn't *like* the thought of one of his employees having to buy gifts for her.

'How did she find the book?' she asked instead. 'I checked with practically every bookstore in Mumbai, and I tried ordering it online as well.'

'She spoke to the publisher,' Nikhil said. 'The book's out of print, but he had some copies.'

'Well, thank her from me,' Shweta said, feeling awkward. 'The earrings are lovely too, and so is the shawl—'

'I'm missing you,' Nikhil said, cutting her off before she could mention the chocolates.

He'd had the gifts sent to her on impulse, and he was wondering whether it had been such a good idea after all. Maybe flowers would have been a better bet. But with a major product launch event starting in just under fifteen minutes he didn't have much time to speak to her.

'Nikhil, darling, I need some help.'

Nikhil turned around, cursing under his breath. The voice belonged to a singer who'd recently won an all-India reality show—she was hugely popular, and Nikhil had engaged her for several events. She was rather high-maintenance, and presumably something about the current arrangements was not to her liking.

'Give me a moment,' he said into the phone. 'What's wrong, Ayesha?'

She pouted prettily, making Nikhil grit his teeth.

'Your tech guys aren't letting my accompanists set up—they're saying that there's some dance number billed just before mine. Come on, Nikhil, I need you!'

'Right,' he said, and then, into the phone, 'Shweta...'

'You need to go.'

It was like Anjalika dragging him away in Kerala—except that this Ayesha woman sounded even more irritating.

'I don't think I'll be free till after twelve. Speak to you tomorrow, OK?'

'OK,' Shweta said. 'And thanks for...' But he'd already rung off.

When Nikhil called her the next afternoon Shweta was in a meeting and couldn't take the call. She tried calling him back once she got home. He was on his way to the airport. There were other people with him, and he sounded so distracted that Shweta finally told him she'd speak to him once he got back from Europe.

The rest of the week was intensely depressing. One of her client meetings turned acrimonious, and she had to drag Deepa and the client company's finance director into a conference call to sort things out. To say that neither of them was pleased was a serious understatement. The worst thing was that she knew no one in Delhi. She didn't feel very safe going around alone after it was dark, so she ended up staying in the guest house and watching TV every evening.

'I'll start sticking straws in my hair and talking to the walls soon,' she complained to Priya when she called. 'Even Faisal's gone back to Mumbai.'

'What news of the boyfriend?' Priya asked. 'No e-mails or phone calls?'

'None,' Shweta said glumly. 'He's in Greece. He's

probably forgotten all about me. And don't call him that. He's just an old friend.'

Priya snorted disbelievingly. 'Yeah, right—that's why the two of you had your mouths glued together the other week. Don't give up so easily.'

After Priya rang off Shweta looked at her phone thoughtfully for a while. There was nothing stopping *her* from calling or messaging Nikhil. Well, maybe not calling. She only had Nikhil's India mobile number. International roaming rates were terribly high—however rich he was now, Nikhil might not appreciate shelling out a small fortune just to hear her voice! Messaging, then.

She spent a few minutes composing a suitably witty, non-desperate message in her head. Finally she gave up, and went with, *How are things?*

Her phone rang after a few seconds and she picked it up, annoyed to find her hand shaking a little.

Nikhil's warm voice said, 'You wanted to know how things are?'

Feeling quite idiotically happy to hear his voice, she said, 'I didn't mean to disturb you. Just hadn't heard from you for a long while… Isn't it crazily expensive, calling from your India phone?'

'Ah, well, if I'd called from a local number you wouldn't have known it was me,' he said. 'And then you wouldn't have picked up the phone, and I wouldn't have got to speak to you.'

'You can call me back if you want,' she suggested.

Nikhil laughed. 'No, it's cool. Are you still in Delhi or have they let you come back home?'

'Still in Delhi. I'll be here for at least another week.'

Her voice must have sounded particularly mournful, because his softened immediately. 'Bear up—you'll hardly notice the time go by. Don't you have friends there?'

'No,' she said, and then, worried that she was turning maudlin, went on, 'But that's OK. I'm having a lot of fun exploring the city. How's Greece? Been partying a lot?'

'I've been working my backside off,' Nikhil said. 'This has to be one of the most difficult trips I've ever had to co-ordinate. And it doesn't help that I've been missing you like mad.'

Her heart suddenly thumping a lot louder than normal, Shweta said, 'I've missed you too.'

There was a longish pause.

'I'll be back in Mumbai around the same time as you,' he said softly. 'I'm looking forward to seeing you again.'

She was looking forward to it too, more than anything ever before, but she was worried her voice would betray too much emotion if she said so.

'Why's this trip turning out to be so difficult?' she asked instead, and she could hear the amusement in his voice when he answered.

'It's a huge sales convention for an insurance company. Very traditional Indian guys, half of them are vegetarian, and they want Indian food everywhere they go. I've had to fly out a platoon of cooks and enough rice and *dal* to feed the entire population of Bangladesh for the next three years. They want to dance to

Bollywood music every night till four in the morning, and the DJ's threatening to quit because he was hired for only two nights. And of course there's all the minor stuff, like equipment breaking down, or the hotel booking two men and a woman into the same room... Anyway, it's all sorted now, which is the main thing. And they've already confirmed that they'll hire us for their next convention.'

He sounded remarkably cheerful for someone who had such a lot to deal with, Shweta thought. She was getting the shudders even listening to him—she was the kind of person who couldn't bear the smallest thing not going according to plan.

'Poor you,' she said sympathetically. 'Any more star tantrums?'

'Anjalika's here,' Nikhil said. 'No tantrums yet, but we had to hike her fees up from what we paid her last time.'

An unfamiliar little dart of jealousy shot through Shweta. Anjalika and he had been featured in yet another glossy magazine article, in which Nikhil had been referred to as one of Mumbai's most sought-after bachelors and Anjalika as his 'constant companion'. Heroically suppressing the urge to say something bitchy, she said, 'I guess she's good at what she does, so it's OK.'

Nikhil wasn't fooled. 'She's just someone I work with,' he said. 'Don't let the gossip get to you.'

'I haven't heard...I mean, I have...but...' She floundered to a halt, feeling very grateful that Nikhil couldn't see her. It was bad enough reading every article about him with the eagerness of a celebrity stalker—his knowing she was doing it was a thousand times worse. 'Sorry,' she said. 'I couldn't help overhearing some of the people in your team when we were in Kerala.'

'Let me guess—they said that Anjalika works with me because I sleep with her?' She didn't answer and he said exasperatedly, 'She was the first celebrity who agreed to appear in one of my shows. She was short of cash and I paid her thrice her normal rate, but it's not something I've discussed with the team.'

'I guess it's a tough business,' Shweta said, feeling even more embarrassed by the explanation.

'Hmm…I could have always taken up a nice, normal nine-to-five job,' he said. 'Like my parents wanted me to. As my father says, I've no one to blame for where I am other than myself.'

Nikhil probably earned more than the rest of their high school class put together, but his father had still been disappointed that he hadn't taken up engineering or medicine. That was part of the reason why Nikhil hadn't spoken to his father for so long.

'I think you're doing pretty well,' she said. 'Even if your dad doesn't admit it, he must be very proud of you.'

'Oh, I doubt it,' Nikhil said lightly. 'Look, I need to go now. I have a whole bunch of insurance salesmen bouncing in and out of the Parthenon, and I need to make sure they don't do any damage.'

Shweta said goodbye to him, but she was sure he'd rung off because of what she'd said about his father. She'd met Mr Nair a few times in her schooldays, and he'd struck her as a rather nice man. Nothing like the cold-hearted villain Nikhil was making him out to be. And Nikhil's mom had been nice as well, though a little quiet and shy.

Nikhil had been right. The following week did pass by in a blur. On Thursday, though, Shweta began to get a nasty tickling feeling in her throat, and by the time she left the office on Friday she had a full-blown attack of sinusitis.

'Go home and drink lots of hot soup,' the finance director advised her during the closing meeting. 'It's the Delhi winter—you Mumbaikars aren't used to the cold.'

It wasn't all that cold, Shweta thought as she trudged to the Metro station. Winter hadn't set in yet, and the weather was still very pleasant. She'd visited the company doctor and got a prescription during lunchtime, but the medicines weren't helping. By the time she got to the guest house she was feeling really ill.

'You have a fever,' the guest house cleaning lady said, after putting a work-roughened but surprisingly gentle palm on her forehead. 'Are you sure you'll be able to take the flight tomorrow?'

'I'll decide in the morning,' Shweta said.

In the morning, though, she felt even worse, and knew there was no way she could get on a flight. She'd tried a short-distance flight once when she'd had only a mild cold, and the pain in her ears and sinuses when the flight took off had been excruciating.

'Ma'am, today is OK, but we have another booking from Sunday evening onwards,' the clerk said when she told him that she'd have to extend her stay at the guest house. 'I'm sorry, but you will have to ask the company to book you a hotel.'

Deepa was most unsympathetic when Shweta called her to explain. 'For God's sake—it's just a cold, isn't it? Can't you come back to Mumbai?' She exhaled in annoyance when Shweta told her she couldn't. 'Right, I'll ask my secretary to get you a hotel booking, then. This audit project's jinxed—first Faisal, then you. You guys are toppling over like ninepins.'

The hotel was a lot more luxurious than the guest house had been, but it was centrally air-conditioned, and even after fiddling around with the controls in her room for half an hour Shweta wasn't able to get the room any warmer. Finally she gave up and crawled into bed. She almost didn't get up to pick up her phone when it rang, but habit made her walk across the room and fetch it from her bag.

'Hi, Nikhil,' she said, but her bad throat made her voice so raspy that she knew he'd hardly be able to make out what she was saying.

'What's wrong?'

'Cold,' she said. 'Sounds worse than it is.'

'OK,' Nikhil said, sounding relieved. 'You'll be back in Mumbai tomorrow, won't you?'

'I've cancelled my flight,' Shweta said, 'and checked into a hotel because my room at the guest house isn't available. I'll come back some time next week, when I'm feeling more human.'

'Don't you know anyone there at all?' Nikhil asked.

The concern in his voice made her feel a lot better immediately.

'Should I send someone across from my Delhi office to help?'

'No,' Shweta said promptly. He'd probably send the girl who'd bought the presents for her, and Shweta didn't want strangers around. 'I'll manage—I can call the hotel guys for help if it gets too bad. Anyway, in Mumbai when I fall ill I have to look after myself. I'm used to doing it.' In actual fact she'd hardly ever fallen ill since she'd started working in Mumbai, and on the few occasions she had Priya had taken care of her.

'I don't like the thought of you being there all alone,' Nikhil said.

'Come down to Delhi and be with me, then,' Shweta said flippantly.

Nikhil disregarded that. 'Are you sure there's no one you can call? What about your father and aunt?'

'I haven't told them I'm ill!' Shweta said in alarm. 'Anita Bua's a world-champion worrier, and my dad's not much better. Don't you dare let them know.'

'I won't,' Nikhil said in mollifying tones. 'I just thought it might be nice for you to have family around.'

'It's very nice when I'm well,' Shweta said. 'It's a disaster when I'm not. I'll need to put the phone down now, Nikhil. I'm a bit groggy from the medicines, and my throat hurts if I talk too much. I'll message you the hotel number—we can talk tomorrow.'

Nikhil frowned after she'd rung off. Shweta hadn't sounded well at all, and he hated the thought of her being all alone in an unfamiliar city.

Shweta was still asleep when the phone rang shrilly in her room the next morning. She tried to ignore it for a while, but whoever was calling had the persistence of a Rottweiler, and with a final groan of protest she caved in and picked up the receiver.

'Yes?' she said, in a tell-me-one-good-reason-why-I-shouldn't-throttle-you kind of voice.

'Ms Mathur?' the girl on the phone said in a disgustingly cheerful voice. 'I have Mr Nair here, waiting for you—will you be able to come downstairs?' She broke off for a few seconds to have a muffled conversation with someone, then got back on the line. 'Oh, he says that you're ill and it would be better if he could come up to your room—is that OK?'

Half asleep, for a few seconds Shweta was thrown by the unfamiliar 'Mr Nair'. The only person she could think of with that name was her neighbour in Mumbai—he was a curmudgeonly lawyer in his mid-sixties, and she couldn't for the life of her imagine why he'd landed up at her hotel, asking for her. Then she woke up fully and realised that the girl meant Nikhil.

'I'll come downstairs,' she said, and then remembered that she looked an absolute fright. 'Actually, no— maybe you should send him up. Or—wait…not right now. Ask him to come up after ten minutes or something. I've only just got up…' She trailed off, aware that she was making a fool of herself.

The girl seemed to understand, however. 'Sure thing,' she said, and this time her cheerfulness didn't grate on Shweta's nerves.

With the prospect of meeting Nikhil in a few minutes the day seemed a lot brighter—even her throat didn't seem to hurt quite as much. She pushed the bedcovers back and went into the bathroom, washing and brushing her teeth in record time. She grimaced at her reflection. She very rarely fell ill, but when she did she made a thorough job of it. Her hair looked stringy and unwashed, and her eyes were puffed up, as if she'd been on a week-long drinking binge. Along with her hollow cheeks and chapped lips, they made her look like something the cat had dragged in.

The doorbell rang before she'd had a chance to do anything more than comb her hair and pull it back into a neat but rather limp and lifeless ponytail. Making a face at her wan reflection in the mirror, she went to open the door.

'Don't scream in fright. I've only just woken up,' she announced to Nikhil. Then she caught sight of the chocolates and flowers in his hands. 'Ooh, for me?'

'I was thinking of popping around to the Prime Minister's house with the flowers,' Nikhil said, strolling in and shutting the door behind him, 'but if you like them you can have them instead.' His face softened as he took a good look at her. 'Poor thing,' he said. 'You've lost weight since I saw you last, and your voice sounds awful.'

Shweta grimaced. 'Thanks—you're so tactful. How did you land up in Delhi?' Nikhil was still looking right at her, and there was a quality in his gaze that made her blush in confusion. 'I mean…I thought you were supposed to be in Mumbai. That's what you said when we discussed it last.'

'I was,' Nikhil said, reaching out and taking the flowers from her to put them on a table. 'But I thought

I'd come and check on you first. I've always had a thing for damsels in distress. Especially when they have deep, mannish voices and are wearing purple pyjamas.'

'Deep, *husky* voices, you mean,' Shweta said. She was having trouble keeping her voice steady. The thought of him having changed his plans to come and check on her was so moving that she took refuge in flippancy. 'And these pyjamas are the latest in chic nightwear. All the best people are wearing them—even in the day.'

Nikhil nodded seriously. 'I especially like the effect of the matching *chappals*,' he said, indicating her fluffy purple flip-flops. 'The green scrunchie is spoiling things a bit, though.' He got up and moved closer to her. 'Feeling any better?' he asked, reaching out to stroke her hair.

Quelling a mad impulse to press her lips into his palm, she nodded. 'Yes,' she said—and, before she could help herself, 'Oh, Nikhil, it's so good to see you!'

She wasn't sure who made the first move, but the next second she was in his arms, with her face pressed against his chest. He held her close, pressing his lips into her hair, moving his hands first soothingly and then rather excitingly over her back. She clung to him, inhaling the fresh clean scent of his body, nuzzling closer as he moved her into a more comfortable position. The material of his T-shirt was soft against her face, and she could feel the taut muscles of his chest through it.

'You'll catch a cold too,' she said, her much-maligned voice muffled against his chest. 'And stop kissing my hair. I haven't washed it for three days. I have just brushed my teeth though.'

Nikhil laughed at that, and gently tipped her face upwards. All thoughts of flippancy flew from her mind as she looked up at him, and she gave a little gasp when he brought his head down and kissed her very, very thoroughly. When he broke the kiss, moving his head back a little, she knotted her hands firmly in his hair and pulled his head down again. He succumbed without a protest.

'I wasn't intending to do this,' Nikhil said when they finally broke away from each other. 'You're not well. I just meant to make sure you have everything you need...'

'I have everything I need now,' she said, her eyes dancing as she reached out for him again.

He shook his head and took a firm step back. 'Be sensible,' he said.

'I'm not going to launch myself at you and rip off your clothes,' she said, a little annoyed at the way he'd stepped back. It was a pretty tempting idea, ripping his clothes off—though maybe not just now. Without his arms to support her she was feeling a bit dizzy. The virus evidently wasn't done with her yet. Unobtrusively, she started backing towards a chair to sit down. It wouldn't do to faint immediately after kissing him. It would give him entirely the wrong idea.

'Are you OK?' he asked.

So not as unobtrusive as she'd hoped after all. 'Just a little light-headed.'

'Have you eaten?'

She hadn't, and the guilty look on her face gave it away.

Nikhil gave a disgusted shake of his head. 'And here I am, grabbing at you like some sex-starved maniac. Let's get you something to eat first, and then we'll take you to a doctor.'

'It's OK—' she began to say, but her voice wasn't up to so much exercise and trailed off in an unlovely croak. Nikhil had ignored her anyway, and picked up the phone to order soup and toast from room service.

'Don't talk for a bit,' he advised once he got off the phone. 'I'll put your things together, and once you've had your soup we can get you checked out of the hotel.'

Shweta gave him an alarmed look. 'I have a small flat in Gurgaon,' Nikhil said. 'It's a bit of a drive, but I'll be able to look after you properly there.'

It sounded lovely, being looked after properly by Nikhil. He waited till she nodded, then said, 'I'll head back to Reception, then. Tell them to get the bill ready.'

Shweta watched him as he left the room. He was pretty amazing, she decided. The perfect combination of looks and charm and devil-may-care attitude.

The soup arrived, and after she had swallowed the last spoonful Shweta decided to test her voice again. 'The quick brown fox…' she started to say to the empty room, but her voice refused to rise above a whisper. Sighing, she got up to collect her scattered belongings and push them all higgledy-piggledy into her suitcase.

Nikhil came back when she was almost done with her packing. 'I thought I told you I'd do the packing for you,' he said. 'Go and get changed. I've arranged for a car.'

Shweta held out a hotel notepad to him on which she'd written, 'Have lost my voice.'

'A woman who can't answer back—perfect,' he said. She punched him in the arm.

To her annoyance, he didn't even react, merely saying, 'D'you need help getting ready?'

She shook her head. If she'd had the use of her voice she would have asked him exactly what kind of help he was offering, but writing the question down wouldn't have nearly the same impact. Instead, she picked up jeans and a T-shirt and went into the bathroom to change.

It was a long drive from Connaught Place to Gurgaon, and Shweta dozed on Nikhil's shoulder for most of the way. It was a relief to have everything taken care of for her. Nikhil had even paid her hotel bill, refusing to look at her scribbled notes asking him how much she needed to pay him back.

'We've reached my flat,' Nikhil said gently as the cab pulled up in front of his apartment building.

Shweta woke up and groggily got out of the car. She was trying to help the driver get her suitcases out when Nikhil firmly steered her towards the lobby of the building. A teenage boy was waiting for them with Nikhil's keys.

'I've cleaned the flat and stocked the fridge with food,' the boy said. 'Take a look, and if you need anything else give me a call.'

'Thanks, Krishna,' Nikhil said. 'Shweta, take the

keys and go upstairs—the flat's on the sixth floor, to the left of the lift. I'll pay the driver and be up in a minute with your suitcases.'

It was only when she was in the lift without Nikhil's supporting arm under her elbow that Shweta realised quite how ill she was feeling. Her head felt as if it was stuffed with cotton-wool, and her knees had a distinct wobble in them. She only just about managed to get into the flat and collapse onto the sofa. When Nikhil came in a few minutes later, she was already fast asleep.

Nikhil stood looking at her for a few minutes. She looked very young and defenceless as she slept, with her long lashes fluttering slightly with every breath and her hair spread around her in absolute disarray. He wondered what he was doing, bringing her into his home. He'd had more than his fair share of female company in the years since he'd left home and struck out on his own. Except for one short, relatively serious relationship, all his women had made it clear that they wanted a good time and not much else. He'd told himself he liked it better that way—love was for wimps. Now, however, the feeling that was overcoming him was a perilous mixture of attraction, affection, and good old-fashioned lust—it was difficult to sort the three out in his head.

Shweta shifted in her sleep, almost rolling off the sofa, and Nikhil was by her side in an instant. Deciding that she'd be a lot more comfortable in bed, he picked her up, being very careful not to wake her, and took her into the bedroom. She nestled closer to him as he tried to put her down on the bed, her hands curling into the material of his shirt. Finally he lay down next to her, gently removing her hands only once she'd settled down into a deeper sleep. Then he tenderly kissed her on the forehead and left the room.

CHAPTER SIX

'I FEEL PERFECTLY healthy now,' Shweta announced. 'And you're pampering me silly. I won't know what to do the next time I fall ill.'

'Call me,' he said, and his lips curved into an absolutely heart-stopping smile. 'No reason for you to look after yourself if I'm around.'

They were sitting across from each other at the breakfast table in his Delhi flat. It was five days since he'd come back from Greece and rescued her from the hotel, and he'd pulled out all the stops to make sure she'd got everything she needed to recuperate. She felt disloyal even thinking it, but Nikhil had been a lot more caring than her father or her aunt had ever been when she fell ill growing up. That was one of the disadvantages of being a doctor's daughter—illnesses were treated in the most matter-of-fact and unsympathetic way possible, even if her father was eaten up with worry inside.

Shweta gave him a saucy wink. 'If you promise to come over and look after me I don't mind falling ill every weekend.' Then, more seriously, she added, 'I haven't thanked you properly, have I? Other than Priya, I can't imagine any of my other friends doing so much for me.'

'They haven't known you since you were four,' Nikhil said. 'And they haven't spent their entire childhood being beaten up by you either.'

'Spent their entire childhood…' Shweta spluttered at him for a few seconds. '*You* were the one who used to drive me up the wall with your teasing and your stupid jokes. And I don't believe you've changed either.'

He laughed. 'Oh, I have,' he assured her. 'In more ways than one. By the way, I meant to tell you—you're looking pretty good this morning. Are you warm enough?'

His gaze swept over her, and Shweta felt a familiar little jolt of electricity go through her. They'd been living in the same flat for several days, but until now he'd made no move even to touch her—she could have been sixty years old for all the notice he'd taken of her. In a fit of pique she'd pulled out the shortest pair of shorts she'd brought with her and worn them today—they were a cheerful shade of pink, and she'd put on a T-shirt and a black knitted top over them. The Delhi winter was setting in, and her legs *were* beginning to feel a bit chilly, but she'd freeze to death before she admitted it.

'I'm warm enough. Thanks for asking,' she muttered. Really, he was overdoing his concern over her health—he sounded as if he was her uncle or something. It was as if the earlier Nikhil had vanished, along with the passionate kisses and the scorching looks. Now that she was feeling human again, Shweta was pretty sure she wanted the old Nikhil back.

'You don't need to thank me,' he said dryly. 'Just make sure you don't forget what the doctor said.'

The doctor had been pretty scathing about modern lifestyles and young women who let their immunity levels fall because of over-work and irregular meals.

Shweta winced. 'I'm not likely to forget,' she said. 'I was expecting him to ask for my dad's number so that he could call and tell my father what a dreadfully careless person I am.'

'He still might do that,' Nikhil said, getting up from the dining table. 'Now, are you sure you aren't cold?'

'I'm sure,' she snapped.

'What a pity,' he said. He was standing behind her now, only a few inches away, and she had to twist her body around to look up at him. 'I'd thought of some interesting ways of keeping you warm—especially since you're all recovered from your flu. But if you're sure…'

His voice had changed—became husky, caressing, and very, very sexy—but he was moving away from her. Never good at reading between the lines, Shweta found the conflicting signals frustratingly confusing.

'I *am* feeling a little chilly,' she blurted out.

He laughed, his eyes sparkling with devilry. 'So should I put the heaters on?'

For a few seconds Shweta felt positively murderous. This was like a grown-up version of the teenage Nikhil—making suggestive remarks, and then pretending he'd said nothing out of the ordinary. It was like flirting in reverse. Deciding that stamping her foot or

throwing a plate at him would be childish and imma-
ture, she sulked instead, turning her back to Nikhil
and pretending to be very busy clearing up the breakfast things.

Nikhil gave her an amused look. He knew pretty
much exactly what was going through her mind. When
he'd brought her home from the hotel she'd been so
ill that getting her back on her feet had taken priority over everything else. It had been tough having her
in the house and not even touching her, but he'd been
very careful not to take advantage of her weakened
state. Now, of course, she was fully recovered, and he
couldn't resist teasing her a little.

He came to stand right behind her as she plonked
dishes into the sink. She was muttering under her
breath, and he leaned closer and said, 'Sorry, I didn't
catch that.'

Shweta jumped a few inches into the air—Nikhil
could move very silently when he wanted, and she
hadn't heard him come up behind her. 'I wasn't talking to you,' she said.

'But I want you to talk to me.' His voice was pur-
posely mournful as he put his hands on her soapy forearms.

'I'm doing the dishes.'

'We'll ask Krishna to come and do the dishes later,'
he said, lowering his head and kissing the nape of her
neck very, very gently.

She could feel his breath ruffling her hair, and she
firmly repressed an urge to drop the dishes and turn
into his arms. 'You exploit Krishna.'

'Hmm…actually, on second thoughts, maybe I don't want him hanging around after all.'

His hands had moved from her arms to her waist. She just needed to lean back a little to be pressed up against his long, hard body…

'Maybe I'll help you do the dishes,' he was saying now. 'Then we can…umm…do other things.'

'Play Scrabble?' Shweta asked sweetly, and turned the kitchen tap on.

Oops—bad move. In her agitation she'd turned it too far, and a Niagara of water came gushing out. It splashed over the dishes, almost completely soaking the front of her black top. Nikhil leaned over her and turned the tap to a more reasonable setting. Taking her hands, he started rinsing the soap off. He did it very carefully and slowly, holding each hand under the water and running his own hands over it in a slow and sensuous movement that had her squirming against him in no time. Then, without releasing her, he reached out for a towel, and started drying her arms—still very, very, slowly. When that was done he turned her around to face him.

'You're completely…wet,' he said.

There was absolutely nothing suggestive about his tone, but Shweta shivered as he took the hem of her top and gently drew it upwards. She was wearing a T-shirt under it, and was still perfectly well covered when he got the top off and tossed it into a corner of the kitchen—she felt bare, though, when his warm gaze roamed over her body.

'Come to bed with me?' he asked softly.

For a few seconds Shweta's traditional upbringing reared its head, and she almost panicked and said no—but this was Nikhil. She'd known him all her life. She trusted him. Looking into his warm brown eyes, for the first time she began to think that she was probably in love with him, and with that realisation her last doubts fell away.

'Yes,' she said, and she sounded confident and very sure of what she wanted.

In the next second she was in Nikhil's arms. He held her very close for a few seconds, and then he swung her up into his arms and carried her to the nearest bedroom.

'I'm hungry,' Shweta announced, propping herself onto one arm and lazily trailing a finger down Nikhil's hair-roughened chest.

It was the middle of the afternoon, and the last few hours had been the best hours of her life. Far more experienced than her, Nikhil had been very gentle at first, careful not to alarm her. But, finding her eager and willing, he'd finally abandoned all restraint. Shweta's lips curved into a smile as she remembered quite how good it had been.

'Hungry, are you?' Nikhil frowned at her. 'Are you likely to turn cannibal? Should I be worried?'

Shweta laughed, and leaned down to nip at his lower lip lovingly. 'Mmm, that's a thought,' she said. 'You taste pretty good, actually…'

'I'll get up and cook lunch for you,' Nikhil said, sitting up in mock-haste and taking her with him. 'Just think—you might want to do this again some day, and if you eat me up you'll have to find a new man. He might not be quite as nice as me.'

Shweta pretended to think.

'I cook quite well,' Nikhil said as added inducement. 'And I'm house-trained—you won't regret it.'

'Can you do rice and noodles? With mushrooms?'

'Yes, ma'am, of course I can.' Nikhil paused to drop a row of little kisses on her shoulder, but raised his head as she spoke. 'And you can have chilli chicken with it, if you like. And ice cream. But I didn't make that—it's already in the freezer.'

'The ice cream is the clincher,' Shweta said. 'I'll allow you to live.'

Nikhil gave a mock sigh of relief and tried to get out of bed—Shweta pulled him back for a kiss.

'I thought you were hungry,' he protested as he found himself back in bed, with Shweta draped seductively over him.

'I can wait for a little bit,' she said. 'Right now you've got me interested in *you* all over again.'

It was late afternoon by the time they finally made it to the kitchen, and by then both of them were too hungry to bother about cooking an elaborate meal.

'Scrambled eggs. Or omelettes and bread,' Shweta decided after doing a quick scan of the fridge. She gave him a doubtful look. 'Did you mean it when you said you can cook? Because I'm not all that good. Priya does most of the cooking at home.'

'I meant it,' Nikhil said. 'I'm not *cordon bleu* level, exactly, but I can manage.'

He could do more than manage, Shweta decided as

she bit into a delicately flavoured omelette. There was a lot more to Nikhil than met the eye. 'Any other talents I should know about?' she enquired. 'Singing, maybe? Ballroom dancing?'

'Someone did try to teach me to jive once,' Nikhil said. 'Mrs Fernandes—remember?'

She did. Shweta had been his partner in a dance their class had been rehearsing for the school annual day. Mrs Fernandes had paired them up because, in her words, 'that boy' behaved a little better with Shweta than he did with the other girls. Shweta had been deeply annoyed, but Mrs Fernandes had known her father and she hadn't dared to protest. And because Mrs Fernandes had been well over fifty at the time, jiving had been the only 'Western' dance style she knew well enough to teach the class.

'I got expelled before that annual day, didn't I?' Nikhil asked. 'Who did you end up dancing with? Vineet?'

'I didn't participate,' Shweta said. 'Dancing wasn't really my thing.' She had been pretty upset when Nikhil was expelled—especially when she'd found out that her father had been on the disciplinary committee. She hadn't ever said anything to her father, but that was the first time that she'd seen him as a regular human being, capable of making mistakes.

'They weren't fair to you, expelling you like that,' she said.

Nikhil gave her a lazy smile. 'Oh, I think they were. I'd pushed their patience to the brink.'

'Vineet and Wilson were with you when you stole that bike,' she said.

She waved him aside impatiently when he murmured, 'Borrowed…'

'And Wilson used to smoke as well—all the time.'

'They were a lot smarter than I was,' Nikhil said, getting to his feet. 'And they didn't go looking for trouble.' He surveyed her mutinous expression. 'I don't hold it against your dad, if that's what you're worried about,' he said.

Shweta gave an impatient shrug. 'He's so…so…*set* in his ways,' she said. 'It doesn't even occur to him that he could be wrong about anything.'

Nikhil leaned across to take her plate. 'Finished?' he asked, and when she nodded her head, he said, 'Still like that, is he?'

Shweta nodded. 'It's my fault as well. I shouldn't bother so much about what he thinks. I don't even live at home now, and to be fair to him he's stopped trying to tell me what to do. But he has an opinion on everything, from my job to my clothes. He even had something to say when I chucked away those dreadful glasses and started wearing contacts.'

'How about your boyfriends?'

Shweta gave him an enquiring look.

'Does he have opinions about your boyfriends as well?'

'I'm sure he would, if I introduced any of them to him,' Shweta said.

Nikhil noticed that she was doing the scribbling

thing again—tracing words out on the palm of one hand with the fingers of the other.

'So far I've never bothered—I've not had much luck with men. I think he'd have liked Siddhant, only *that* particular story didn't go anywhere, did it?'

Nikhil nodded. If he'd been in a psychoanalysing mood there would have been a lot he could read into what Shweta was saying, but right now he had a more pressing concern.

'I assume he would be horrified if he got to know about me?' he said lightly.

Shweta shrugged. 'Not planning to tell him,' she said.

She looked a little tense, but her tone was so matter-of-fact that it took Nikhil a few seconds to absorb what she was saying. When he did get it, he felt a quick stab of anger go through him.

'Not planning to tell him now, or not planning to tell him ever?' he asked, keeping his voice carefully even.

Shweta bit her lip. She wasn't sure why Nikhil was cross-examining her—maybe he was trying to figure out how seriously she'd taken their sleeping together. And maybe he'd run for his life if he figured that she was planning to tell her family about him.

'I don't know,' she said. 'I mean, there isn't much to tell, is there? We're friends and…'

'Friends?'

'Well… Lovers, I guess. Only I'm not likely to talk to my dad about my sex-life, am I?' She might have told her mother if she'd been alive, but she didn't say that out loud.

Nikhil laughed, but there was very little genuine mirth in the sound. 'So that's all I am, is it? Part of your sex-life?'

Shweta looked at him uncertainly. She didn't recognise him in this mood, and she wasn't sure what was bothering him—he couldn't actually *want* her to tell her father that she was sleeping with him. That made about as much sense as sticking one's head into a beehive full of angry bees. Her father might have become a little less control-freaky as he grew older, but he was still rigidly conventional—he'd probably come after Nikhil with a hypodermic full of strychnine if he thought his precious daughter was being messed around with.

The thought that Nikhil might be feeling insecure crossed her mind, but she dismissed it. There was no reason for him to be insecure. She'd dropped into his arms like a plum ripe for picking. If anything, she should be the one getting clingy and emotional.

'I haven't *had* a sex-life before now,' she pointed out. 'So, if we're getting all technical about it, I'm just part of yours, aren't I?'

He didn't say anything, but his expression lightened a little. She sprang to her feet. 'Don't let's fight,' she coaxed, going over to him and putting a hand on his crossed forearms. 'I'm sorry if I said something I shouldn't have.'

Nikhil looked into her upturned face and his expression relaxed as he bent down to drop a kiss on her parted lips. 'It wasn't anything you said,' he assured her. 'Put it down to me being a little cranky.'

Shweta frowned. 'Must be the food,' she said. 'It

can't be the sex making you cranky. Or does it usually take you that way?'

Nikhil laughed and swept her into his arms. 'It most definitely doesn't.' His voice softened as he gazed into her eyes. 'You're pretty special, Shweta Mathur, do you know that?'

CHAPTER SEVEN

'WHY DON'T YOU move in with me?' Nikhil asked.

They were back in Mumbai and had been spending practically every free minute together for the last three weeks. Nikhil had never been happier. There was something about Shweta that centred him—it was as if she brought peace to his restless soul. He had been toying with the idea of asking her to marry him ever since they'd first kissed, and he'd made up his mind a few days back. An engagement first—perhaps a long one, to allow both of them enough time to get used to the idea of spending the rest of their lives together. Asking her to move in with him was the first step.

'Live with you?' Shweta wrinkled up her nose. 'Isn't that a little unconventional? We're in Mumbai, not Manhattan.'

In the last few weeks she'd figured that Nikhil was a lot more serious about her than his sometimes casual attitude suggested. On the other hand, there was his rather colourful past, and her own pathological aversion to taking risks—taking things slowly seemed to be the only sensible thing to do.

'I know we're in Mumbai.' Nikhil pretended to be offended. 'I might not have topped the class in geography, but the little fact that I live in Mumbai hadn't escaped me... Ouch—don't. You've grown into a terribly violent little thing, Shweta.'

Shweta gave him a last punch in the arm for good measure. 'Some men deserve to be treated violently,' she said, though she reached up and dropped a light kiss on his forehead, right where her unerring aim with the blackboard duster had left a scar many years ago. 'You'd get terribly out of hand if I didn't keep a strict watch on you.'

'Yeah right,' Nikhil said. 'So, how about it? It's not all that uncommon in Mumbai nowadays—lots of people live together.'

'I must say that's the most romantic proposal I've ever received,' Shweta said. 'Actually, "So, how about it?" is probably the most romantic proposal *anyone's* ever received. It should go down in the *Guinness Book of World Records* as an example for generations to come....'

Nikhil grinned at her. 'You'd have run a mile if I'd gone down on one knee,' he said. 'But I've got you a ring.'

In the short time they'd been together he'd figured that, while she was a romantic at heart, Shweta was deeply uncomfortable with romantic gestures—somehow she didn't seem to think she was worth them. And proposing to her was important. He wanted to make sure he did in a way that made it impossible for her to refuse just because she was embarrassed.

'Let's see the ring,' Shweta demanded, but inside her heart was pounding away at triple speed. A ring meant an engagement, and she'd never allowed herself to hope that Nikhil would go that far. He'd had dozens of girl-friends, after all—some of them well-known models and actresses. There was no reason to imagine that he was serious about her.

Nikhil took the ring out of his pocket and showed it to her. It was a square-cut champagne diamond, flanked with smaller stones in a pale-gold setting. She'd told him once that she didn't like traditional solitaires, and he'd gone out of his way to find something that was unusual yet classic in design.

Shweta looked at it for a few seconds. Misunder-standing her silence, he said, 'If you don't like it I can exchange it for something else.'

'No, it's lovely,' she said, and then she looked up at him and asked. 'Are you sure about this, Nikhil?'

'I'm sure,' he said. Then, more gently, he added, 'But I understand if you need some time to think things over. There's no hurry.'

He didn't seem too fussed about the whole thing, and Shweta felt her hackles rise. There was a little pause. 'Why do you want to get engaged?' Shweta asked fi-nally.

Nikhil looked surprised. 'Why do I…? Because I care about you! Why else?'

Why else indeed. It struck Shweta that Nikhil was taking a lot for granted. She couldn't blame him—she wore her heart on her sleeve, and it was probably very evident that she was in love with him. On the other hand, she didn't know how *he* really felt.

She bit her lip. 'I care too,' she said. 'It's just that I'm not comfortable with the thought of moving in with you. I know it's hypocritical, when we're sleeping together, but I'm a little conservative that way.'

Nikhil nodded. 'Are you OK with an engagement, though?' he asked, and his lips thinned as the pause lengthened.

'Maybe not just yet,' she said. She wasn't sure herself what was holding her back—a few minutes ago she'd been thrilled at the thought of being engaged to Nikhil. But dimly she felt that if she said yes now both of them would be entering into an engagement for the wrong reasons. One part of her said that she was making a stupid mistake, while the other part desperately wanted to get away and think.

'Right…' Nikhil said.

His voice was controlled, rather lifeless, and Shweta had a sudden twinge of doubt. Maybe he wasn't as blasé about the whole thing as he seemed. She watched him as he closed the ring box and put it on the table, but his face was impassive.

'I'm sorry, Nikhil,' she said helplessly.

'Is there something in particular that's bothering you, or…?'

Shweta shook her head. 'I just feel that we should take some time and think this through properly. I'm crazy about you, but it's been only three weeks, and you know what I'm like.'

Her face was appealing as she looked up at him, and

some of the rigidity left his face. 'Little Miss Take-No-Risks,' he said, with only the faintest trace of mockery as he took her hand and kissed it gently. 'I understand. But don't keep me waiting too long, OK?'

With a little sob, Shweta threw herself into his arms. She did love him—more than she could say—and it took all her will-power not to cave in and agree to an immediate engagement.

Nikhil hesitated for a second, and then he put his arms around her and held her close. Shweta's rejection had hurt, and it was a measure of the depth of feeling he had for her that he wasn't resentful. Maybe he'd gone about it the wrong way, he thought. A romantic gesture might have worked better. But he hadn't wanted to dazzle Shweta into agreeing to marry him only to regret it later.

'I can't understand you,' Priya said in despair when Shweta told her. 'Any fool can see you're completely besotted by him. Why would you say no?'

'It's too soon,' Shweta muttered.

'And you're scared?'

Her eyes flew up to meet Priya's. 'Not scared, exactly,' she said, and then, 'Or maybe, yes—I *am* a little scared. I'm not sure what Nikhil sees in me, and I need to know it'll last. He's dated all kinds of women, and he's never stuck with any of them for more than a few months.'

'I bet he's not asked any of them to marry him either,' Priya said. 'He's a very attractive man. You can't blame him if he's played the field a little. You need to trust him.'

'What are you? His PR agent?' Shweta asked crossly. 'I just need some time to think, OK?'

Priya shrugged. 'Nothing wrong with taking time, but don't keep him hanging around for too long. He doesn't look the patient type.' Her voice gentled as she saw Shweta's stricken expression. 'I don't mean he'll dump you if you don't agree to getting engaged,' she said. 'But he won't know why you're holding back, and he might get impatient and angry. Why don't you just speak to him a little more openly? Tell him what's bothering you.'

'But I don't know properly myself!'

'Would you get annoyed with me if I told you?'

'Probably,' Shweta muttered. 'I hate it when you go into your psychoanalyst mode.'

Priya laughed. 'I'm not trying to psychoanalyse you,' she promised. 'But it's pretty obvious—your dad closed himself off from everyone when your mom died, and somehow he's made you think it's safer to have a blood-less marriage of convenience rather than expose your-self to that kind of hurt.'

Shweta felt a lump come into her throat. 'They were very happy together,' she said. 'My mom and dad. I don't remember her much, but you can tell from the photos and when he talks about her... But that's got nothing to do with me and Nikhil.'

Priya sighed and left it at that. Perhaps it was best for Shweta to figure things out for herself. At least she'd progressed enough to realise that she belonged with

Nikhil and not with someone like Siddhant—hopefully, in time, she'd learn to trust him with her heart.

Things were a little awkward between Shweta and Nikhil for the next couple of days, but soon they swung back into an easy rhythm of spending weekends together, as well as a few evenings in the week when he wasn't working.

'Amma's decided to pay me a visit,' Nikhil said one evening over dinner.

His tone was neutral, but Shweta looked up sharply. 'Just her? Or your parents too?'

'Just her,' he said. 'Though I'm sure my parents have something to do with it. This is the first time she's travelled alone—and she's just recovered from a long bout of illness. But she's insisting I don't need to go and fetch her.'

Shweta didn't think that Veena's deciding to travel alone indicated anything, but she wisely refrained from arguing the point. Nikhil tended to get completely irrational when it came to his parents.

'So, do I get to see her?'

'Yes, of course. She'll be ecstatic about seeing you again. You're probably the only person she knows in Mumbai apart from me.'

'Ecstatic' was probably an exaggeration, but Veena was definitely very pleased to meet Shweta when she arrived in Mumbai. 'It's so nice to see you!' she said, beaming all over her thin, rather careworn face. 'It's been years since I saw you last—you were just a little girl! I remember when you came home after school one day; you were so polite and respectful. Ranjini and I couldn't stop talking about you!'

Shweta smiled back at her. 'It's good to see you too, Aunty,' she said. 'Will you be in Mumbai for a while?'

Veena's face clouded. 'I'm not sure,' she said. 'Nikhil's father's not very well, and Ranjini might find it difficult to manage on her own.'

It was the second time Veena had mentioned her husband's mistress, and Shweta found that her childhood memory was perfectly accurate in this instance—there was no trace of resentment in Veena's voice when she spoke about Ranjini. Not for the first time Shweta found herself thinking that there was a lot more to the elder Mr Nair's domestic arrangements than met the eye.

'Is it serious? Nikhil's dad's illness?'

Veena shook her head. 'Oh, no. His blood pressure's a bit high, and he's due for a cataract operation in his left eye.'

'They can manage a cataract operation perfectly well on their own,' Nikhil said as he came into the room carrying three cups of coffee on a tray. 'Now that you're here I'm not letting you go in a hurry.'

Veena's eyes were frankly adoring as she looked up at Nikhil. 'Oh, thank you,' she said, taking a cup from the tray. 'You shouldn't have. I was about to get up and make the coffee.'

'I'm buttering you up,' Nikhil said, giving her a lopsided smile. 'So that you stay here for as long as possible.'

'I can stay for a couple of weeks,' Veena said. 'After

that I'm pretty sure the two of you will be tired of having me around.'

'Of course we won't,' Shweta said impulsively. 'Nikhil's been looking forward to seeing you, and so have I. It'll be fun showing you around.'

Veena smiled, but said nothing, and Shweta couldn't help feeling that she'd leave once the two weeks were over.

Nikhil was looking a little tense again, and she hurried to change the topic. 'Do you still watch Bollywood films?' she asked Veena. It had been a bit of a joke around school—Mr Nair solemnly escorting his wife *and* his mistress to the movies every Saturday.

'Ooh, yes,' Veena said, sounding more like a sixteen-year-old than a grey-haired lady in her sixties. 'Some of these new actors are quite good. But I don't like the actresses much—all they seem to do is wear tiny clothes and dance around in front of the men.'

Shweta cast an involuntary look at her own rather short skirt. She'd come over directly after office, and it hadn't occurred to her to change.

'Oh, much tinier than that,' Veena assured her earnestly, catching the look. 'You look very nice, dear. I didn't mean to make you uncomfortable.'

Nikhil caught Shweta's eye and burst out laughing. 'Oh, God, Amma, you're priceless,' he said finally. 'Poor Shweta—now she'll lie awake all night wondering if you think her clothes are tiny.'

Veena gave him a reproving look. 'No, she won't,' she said. 'Do you watch movies now, dear? I remember your father didn't let you when you were a child.'

'He lets me watch them now,' Shweta said, beginning to feel a little cross. Childhood reminiscences were OK up to a point, but she didn't like to be reminded of how hemmed-in her life had been.

'Yes, of course,' Veena said. 'I didn't mean it that way. I suppose he thought Bollywood movies weren't suitable for a young girl, and he was quite right. But when your mother was alive they used to go to the movies every weekend—just like Nikhil's father and me.'

She hadn't known that, Shweta thought, feeling a pang go through her. All her life she'd thought her father hated movies, but maybe he'd just avoided them because they reminded him of his wife.

'Your mother was so lovely,' Veena was saying. 'Smita Patil was one of my favourite actresses, and I thought your mom looked a lot like her.'

'Shweta looks a bit like her too,' Nikhil said. 'Especially the eyes.' He'd seen that Shweta was looking a little overwrought, and he wanted to steer the conversation into safer channels.

Veena gave Shweta an affectionate look. 'Yes, she's as beautiful as her mother.'

'Thanks,' Shweta said, trying to smile.

There were very few people who still talked about her mom—her father had changed houses soon after her mother died, and he'd fallen out of touch with their old neighbours and friends. He spoke about her only rarely, and his sister hadn't known her very well. Veena hadn't known her well either, but to Shweta the few sentences she'd spoken had made memories of her mother come to life. So far she'd always thought of her mother in the abstract—not as a living, breathing woman who'd gone to the movies and looked like a famous actress. Smita Patil had died young as well, and that made the comparison even more poignant.

'You OK?' Nikhil asked when Veena left the room for a few minutes to fetch something.

She nodded. 'I didn't realise Veena Aunty knew my mother,' she said softly. 'But it felt good, hearing about her.'

Shweta refused to stay to dinner, pleading an early start the next morning as an excuse.

'But I'll drop in again soon,' she promised a visibly disappointed Veena as she left. 'I still remember the prawn curry you gave me when I came over to your house in Pune.'

Nikhil came to the door to see her off, and when he pulled her close she sought his lips hungrily with her own.

'Is Priya in town?' Nikhil asked in an undertone when he released her after a few minutes. Veena's visit meant that Shweta couldn't stay the night in Nikhil's flat, and the thought of the enforced separation was sheer torture.

'Very much so,' Shweta said. 'But you can come over anyway. I have my own room, and Priya has a boyfriend of her own. She isn't around much herself.'

Nikhil hesitated. 'I thought you weren't very keen on people knowing about us,' he said.

Shweta's eyes opened wide. 'Why would you think that?' she asked. 'Anyway, Priya knows—how d'you think I explain being away for so many nights? Prayer meetings?'

He smiled briefly, but still looked unconvinced. 'We'll figure something out,' he said. 'Maybe a hotel. I don't want to put you in an awkward situation.'

'It would be far more awkward sneaking into a hotel for a dirty weekend,' Shweta said, standing on tiptoe and firmly pressing her lips to his. 'Love you, Nikhil. Bye!'

'Bye,' he said, but he stayed at the door long after Shweta had disappeared into the lift—so long that Veena came out to look for him.

'What are you doing out here all alone?' she asked. 'Is everything OK?'

Nikhil nodded, forcing a smile to his lips. 'Everything is fine,' he said. 'I'm sorry—I started thinking of something.'

Veena gave him a worried look but refrained from asking any questions. She'd looked after Nikhil since he was a tiny baby—Ranjini had been young and nervous when he was born, and more than happy to relinquish him into an older woman's care. In some ways she felt more like his real mother than Ranjini, but she was always careful not to let it show.

'What do you want for dinner?' she asked. 'I can do rice and *avial*—or *dosas*. I have everything ready.'

'Come and sit down with me for bit, Amma,' Nikhil said. 'We haven't had a chance to talk properly since you arrived—I was rushing around trying to finish work, and then Shweta came over.'

'She's a lovely girl,' Veena said warmly. 'Are the two

of you…?' She left the question hanging delicately—she was of a generation and upbringing that didn't ask direct questions about people's love lives.

'I want to marry her,' Nikhil said heavily. 'She hasn't said yes yet.'

'You've asked her?' Veena had no illusions about her husband's son, and she was a little surprised at his saying he wanted to marry Shweta. So far he had flitted from one relationship to another, and Veena had got the impression that he was shying away from commitment—she had been all prepared with a little lecture on how he couldn't treat Shweta the way he did all his other girlfriends.

'Of course I've asked! Amma, we've been—' He broke off, not wanting to shock his stepmother, and continued in bitter tones. 'I know what you've been thinking—I could see it on your face when you were talking to her. You were feeling all protective, and you assumed I was playing the fool with her.'

'No, I didn't. I know you wouldn't deliberately hurt someone, but I *was* a little worried. She seems to be…' Veena hesitated a little '…very fond of you, and I wasn't sure if you felt the same way.'

'I've known Shweta since she was four years old,' Nikhil said. 'If I wasn't serious about her I wouldn't have come within touching distance of her, let alone—' He broke off again, because Veena was looking uncomfortable. 'Anyway, it doesn't matter. She's the one who needs more time to make up her mind.'

'If you're already…' Veena tried to phrase it as delicately as she could, and then, failing, hurried on.

'She's a girl. I would have thought she'd be in a hurry to marry.'

'It doesn't work that way nowadays,' Nikhil said with a short laugh. 'And I can quite see her point—her family's not terribly well-off, but they're very proud. Dr Mathur's only daughter marrying the illegitimate son of a building contractor would be a big come-down. Oh, and I got expelled as well—from a school where he was on the board of directors. Yes, I can see it going down a treat…his daughter wanting to marry me.'

Veena had turned very white. 'Is that what she told you?'

Nikhil shook his head. 'She doesn't need to say it. I know her father, and though she won't admit it I know she's completely under his thumb. She cares for me, but she's not sure if she cares enough to cut herself off from her family.' He noticed Veena's still expression and reached out impulsively, taking her hand.

'I'm sorry I started talking about it,' he said. 'It's not your fault, and I'm sure I'll win Shweta around in time.'

'Perhaps if I talk to her—' Veena started to say.

Nikhil cut her off. 'No, don't. It'll only make things worse. Now, come on, let's figure out dinner—I'll help you put something together.'

Veena allowed Nikhil to coax her into the kitchen, but she was deeply troubled. The rift between Nikhil and his parents was bad enough. The thought that Nikhil was suffering even today because of his illegitimacy was unbearable. She'd been happy when he'd set up his event management company, especially because she'd thought his background wouldn't matter in the rather bohemian crowd he mingled with. She didn't really approve of his girlfriends, with their artificially straightened hair and short dresses, but she'd hoped he would settle down with one of them. His marrying Shweta would be a dream come true. She was quite sure Shweta would come round in the end—it had been difficult to miss the depth of feeling in the girl's eyes when she looked at Nikhil. But Nikhil was the kind of man who brooded and let old resentments fester. Shweta's reluctance boded ill for a happy life together. He'd allow distrust to eat away at him—always assume she was ashamed of being seen with him.

'Stop looking so worried,' Nikhil teased, putting his arms around his stepmother and giving her a quick hug. 'What's eating you?'

'I'm trying to decide between *dosas* and rice,' Veena said. 'It's a difficult call to make—needs a lot of thought.'

'*Dosas,*' Nikhil decided. 'I've missed the way you make them.'

Shweta sighed as she put the phone down after a particularly difficult call with a client. The week had been dispiriting, to say the least. Nikhil had been busy with work, and when he hadn't, he'd had Veena to take care of. She'd tagged along a couple of times, but Veena's idea of suitable entertainment was to visit every major temple in the city, and Shweta had finally given up and gone home in sheer exhaustion. It didn't help that Veena kept giving her anxious looks. She seemed on the verge of asking her something, and Shweta was sure it had to do with her not being engaged to Nikhil yet.

That was another thing she was puzzling over. Nikhil wasn't pressuring her at all, and he'd been the perfect boyfriend so far. Yet still she held back from saying yes to him. Mainly it was because she was convinced he wasn't really in love with her. The physical attraction between the two of them was too strong to be denied, and at times it blinded both of them to anything else. Outside of it, Nikhil's eagerness to marry her could be explained by his feeling comfortable with her, just because she'd known him for so long and understood the complicated situation with his family. She suspected that he never talked about his parents with anyone else he knew in Mumbai. In spite of the wide circle of friends and acquaintances he partied with, he was essentially reserved and very lonely.

'Bad day?'

Siddhant had stopped by her desk and was smiling at her. Shweta nodded ruefully. 'The company I audited is disputing every comment on the report,' she said. 'Deepa's going to kill me when she finds out.'

Siddhant shook his head. 'Deepa's a tough boss, but she's a very fair person,' he said. 'She'll take your side.'

'I hope so.' Shweta still felt rather guilty about the way she'd treated Siddhant, especially since he'd been so nice about it. Perhaps the fact that she and Nikhil had been childhood friends helped—Siddhant hadn't reproached her even once, though he'd been shattered by the news. In the last couple of weeks they'd progressed to a polite friendship, and Shweta found herself liking him a lot more than she had when she'd been gearing herself up to marry him.

'How's Nikhil doing?'

Shweta sighed. 'Busy. Most of his big events are on Fridays or over weekends, and he needs to be around to make sure everything's running smoothly.'

'So you're not meeting up with him after work today?'

Shweta shook her head.

'Then let me take you out for dinner,' Siddhant said. 'We haven't caught up for a while, and there's no reason why we shouldn't stay friends even though…well…'

'Yes, sure,' Shweta said hastily before he could elaborate further. She had nothing else to do, and having dinner with Siddhant would help lessen the guilt she felt every time she saw him.

'Ask Priya if she'd like to join us,' Siddhant said.

He'd probably said that just to make it clear that he wasn't trying to woo her back—in any case, Priya was horrified at the thought of dinner with her and Siddhant.

'No way,' she said. 'It'll be the most awkward meal of the century, what with you having just jilted Siddy-boy. Have you told Nikhil you're going out with him?'

'No, I haven't,' Shweta said, justifiably annoyed. 'I didn't jilt Siddhant, by the way. He never even told me he was interested. And Nikhil's not the possessive kind—he won't care.'

As it turned out, though, he *did* care—he cared a lot more than Shweta had ever imagined. She'd put her phone on silent during dinner, because she didn't want

Siddhant to think she was being rude answering calls while she was with him, and the dinner had been pleasant, with both of them carefully sticking to neutral topics of discussion. Shweta couldn't help comparing him with Nikhil—Nikhil was terribly opinionated, often unpredictable, and she'd never been out for dinner with him without losing her temper at least once. But he made her feel alive and desired and cherished all at the same time. In stark contrast, her conversation with Siddhant was a mass of clichés and views picked up from the latest business magazines. Nice as he was, Shweta couldn't help thinking that she'd had a lucky escape.

It was only after Siddhant had dropped her home that Shweta checked her phone and found three missed calls from Nikhil.

'Where have you been?' he demanded when she called him back. 'I tried a dozen times. I was beginning to get worried!'

'You called me exactly three times,' Shweta said calmly. 'My phone was on silent—I'd gone out for dinner with Siddhant.'

There was a long pause. For a second Shweta thought that the call had got disconnected.

'With Siddhant?' Nikhil repeated slowly, a dangerous note coming into his voice. 'You went out for dinner with him? Alone?'

'Quite alone.' Shweta was annoyed now, and she let it show. 'Now, if you've finished cross-examining me, I'd like to go to bed. It's quite late.'

'I was planning to ditch one of my biggest launches of the year because I wanted to come and spend some time with you,' he said. 'Obviously I shouldn't have bothered. You were too busy to even take my calls, going out for dinner with your very eligible little toy-boy…'

He was almost spitting the words out—Shweta could feel the anger coming off him in waves. She could feel a reciprocal fury stirring in herself.

'I suppose I should have been sitting at home next to the phone on the off-chance you'd call?' she said. 'Grow up, Nikhil. This isn't the nineteenth century.' Irrelevantly, she wondered if they'd had phones in the nineteenth century. Perhaps not, but Nikhil was too worked up to pick holes in her logic.

'I don't expect you to hang around waiting for my calls,' he said through his teeth. 'I do, however, expect you to refrain from two-timing me with the man you were all set to marry two months ago.'

'Right—that's enough,' Shweta said, her voice absolutely cold with rage. 'I'm ringing off now, and don't you dare try to call me back. I don't think I want to talk to you ever again.'

She cut the call. Immediately the phone began to ring again, and she switched it off, her hands trembling with anger as she punched the buttons. The landline began to ring next, and she took it off the hook as soon as it stopped. Then she locked her bedroom door, so that Priya couldn't come in for a midnight chat, and plonked herself on her bed, staring into space. She was usually the kind of person who lost her temper and calmed down within a few minutes—now she was so furious she could hardly think straight.

Around fifteen minutes later she heard Priya come into the flat. The doorbell rang almost immediately afterwards and she assumed it was Priya's boyfriend, probably coming up to give her something she'd left behind in the car. She could hear Priya having a muffled conversation with someone on the landing—then footsteps came up to her door and someone tried the handle.

'Shweta?' Priya called out, knocking on the door.

'I've gone to bed!' Shweta yelled back. She knew she looked a fright—something like an avenging goddess on a bad hair day—and she didn't want Priya coming in and figuring out something was wrong.

'Nikhil's here,' Priya said.

Oh, great. That was all she needed—a scene in her flat in the middle of the night. She'd be lucky if the building's residents' society didn't turf them out—the society secretary had already started rumbling about male visitors not being allowed after eight p.m.

'I don't want to see him,' she said. 'Tell him to go away.'

Priya turned around and gave Nikhil a helpless look. She'd always had a soft spot for her flatmate's gorgeous boyfriend, and she thought Shweta was being completely unreasonable.

'Tell her I'm sorry,' he mouthed, and Priya relayed the message faithfully.

'He can go boil his head!' was the short and rather inelegant response.

Priya almost groaned aloud in despair. Of all the things to say! No wonder Shweta ended up with all the boring Siddhant types if this was the way she treated her men.

Nikhil's mouth was twitching with amusement, though—telling him to go boil his head sounded more like the fiery Shweta he knew than the ice maiden who'd put the phone down on him.

He'd realised he'd overstepped the mark the instant he'd made that remark about two-timing, and he was heartily sorry. He'd felt insanely jealous, though. He didn't believe for a moment that she had any feelings left for Siddhant, but the thought that she'd seriously considered marrying him when she wasn't even attracted to the man was a perpetual thorn in his side. It all boiled down to the same thing—Siddhant was eligible and he wasn't. Even if he did convince Shweta to marry him she'd always feel she'd settled for second-best. If he had any pride he'd give up on her, but the thought of spending the rest of his life without her was unbearable.

'Ask her if I can speak to her,' he said to Priya.

'No, he bloody well can't!' Shweta yelled from inside the room. 'Tell him to go away or I'll call the cops.'

There was silence outside the room for a few minutes, and then Shweta heard the front door shut. There was a tentative knock on her door, and Priya said, 'He's gone.'

'Good,' Shweta said grumpily. Shouting at Nikhil had lessened her anger somewhat—and in hindsight she could understand his being upset. Though she still couldn't see her way towards forgiving him for the accusation he'd made.

'Can I come in?'

'Are you sure he's gone? Because if he isn't I'll call your mom right now and tell her all about your boyfriend.'

'He's gone,' Priya said. 'Stop threatening me.'

Shweta got up and opened the door. Priya studied her carefully. 'You look like a homicidal maniac,' she said. 'Go and comb your hair, for heaven's sake. What was the hullabaloo about?'

'I had a fight with Nikhil,' Shweta said as she hunted for a comb.

Priya rolled her eyes in disgust. 'Really?' she said. 'Fancy that—I'd never have guessed.'

'He said I was two-timing him with Siddhant.'

'I did tell you that dinner was a bad idea,' Priya said. 'Though keeping loverboy on his toes isn't a bad strategy either. By the way, I don't think he's gone—I didn't hear his car start. He's got one of those expensive jobs, hasn't he? The engine sounds quite different. I noticed that when he pulled up in front of the building.'

Shweta went to the window. Sure enough, Nikhil's car was still there. She pulled the curtains together decisively.

'He can wait there all night if he wants,' she said. 'I'm not going to let him off so easily.'

Priya looked impressed. 'Remind me to take lessons from you on putting boyfriends in their place,' she said. 'That is if you still have a boyfriend at the end of this.'

Shweta was also privately beginning to wonder if Nikhil would still be around after the way she'd behaved. Perhaps she should let him in after all. Then his words came back to her and she stiffened her resolve. She hadn't asked him to wait outside—he should have listened to her and gone away for a while.

She drifted into an uneasy slumber after Priya left the room. Weird dreams plagued her, in which she ended up marrying Siddhant. Only at the last moment Siddhant slipped away, to be replaced by a giant alarm clock. After the fifth such dream she woke with a start. The luminous hands of her watch told her that it was three in the morning. Unable to stop herself, she got up and went to the window. Nikhil's car was still there.

'I give up!' she said in annoyance, and switched her phone on. Dialling Nikhil's number, she watched him as he sat up and took the call.

'Hey, Shweta,' he said.

His familiar voice sent little tendrils of longing through her. 'Why are you still here?'

'I'm not going until I get to see you and apologise,' he said. 'I was way out of line—I got jealous and lost my head.'

Shweta felt her resolve melt further at his admission. 'There was no reason for you to be jealous,' she said. 'If anything, I should be the one throwing jealous tantrums about you spending all your time with models and actresses.'

'I know. But what can I say? I'm not always rational.'

'Will you go home now?'

She couldn't see him clearly, but she could sense he was shaking his head. 'Not till I see you.'

'You'd better come up, then,' she said in resigned tones. 'You can't spend the whole night in your car.'

She went out and opened the front door. He was there in a few seconds. 'Your watchman was fast asleep,' he said as he came in. 'I don't think this place is very safe.'

'Well, I wouldn't have opened the door if you were a burglar,' Shweta said. 'Go into my room. I'll lock up and join you in a minute.'

He was sitting on her bed looking suitably contrite when she came in. 'I'm really sorry,' he said.

Shweta plumped down next to him. It was several days since they'd last been alone together, and her hands ached to touch him. It didn't help that he was looking particularly appealing—his hair had grown out a little and was flopping over his forehead in just the way she liked, and he was wearing a shirt in her favourite shade of midnight-blue. There was a slight stubble covering his face, and that added to his rather dangerous attractiveness.

'I can't handle anyone being controlling or possessive with me,' she said. 'My dad isn't possessive, but he's always been controlling—it took me years to break away from his influence, even after I'd grown up and left home. I'm not about to let myself be bossed around again, with you telling me whom I should meet and whom I shouldn't.'

'I understand,' he said, and it was clear he did. 'It won't happen again.'

It was getting more and more difficult to stay angry with him, and Shweta clenched her hands together in frustration.

'I don't even understand *why* you behaved the way you did!' she burst out. He raised his head, an arrested look on his face. 'I mean, I could have married Siddhant if I wanted to. *Why* would I dump him and start going around with you if it was him I wanted all along?'

Put that way, it was a difficult thing for him to explain—and in any case Nikhil wasn't sure he wanted to tell her everything.

'You were always thinking of *him* in terms of marriage,' he said, struggling to put at least part of his thoughts across without offending her. 'But marriage is the last thing on your mind as far as *I'm* concerned. I know you have your reasons. It's just a little...difficult to deal with at times.'

'You're a prize idiot,' Shweta said despairingly. 'Of *course* I was thinking marriage when I thought of Siddhant! I'm pushing thirty. I want to get married and have a family. I haven't ever had a serious relationship—all the men I know are good friends and not much else, and the few I've dated because I'm attracted to them turned out to be complete losers.'

'Didn't you consider an arranged marriage?' Nikhil was genuinely curious now—he'd never thought about the whole Siddhant thing from this angle before.

'There needs to be someone to do the arranging,' she said dryly. 'My father doesn't believe in arranged marriages, so a marriage of convenience seemed the best bet till you came along. *That's* why I was thinking of marrying Siddhant—he was pleasant enough, and he obviously wanted to marry me. And that's a rare combination, let me tell you.'

'Aren't *I* pleasant, then?' he asked, half-laughing, half-serious. Shweta looked into his eyes for a few seconds before getting onto her knees and leaning across to kiss him, slowly and lingeringly. It was the first time she'd had the opportunity to control a kiss in exactly the way she wanted—usually his reactions were so fast that she didn't get to explore fully, at her own pace. Now, however, he let her do as she liked, leaning back to give her better access as she unbuttoned his shirt and slid her hands across his chest, but not initiating anything himself. She gave a long sigh when she finally dragged her lips away from his.

'No, you're not pleasant,' she said. 'You're maddeningly attractive, and you make me want to throttle you and make love to you at the same time. Sometimes I think I won't be able to survive another minute if I don't have you. And you're there when I need you, and you're so thoughtful most of the time that I can't deal with it when you stop thinking and acting like an irrational idiot. So, no, you're not pleasant. But I love you all the same.'

'That's good enough for me,' he said, and there was a slight catch in his voice. 'Only I warn you—I'm not going to give up on convincing you to marry me.'

She put her arms around him, and this time he did respond, with a speed and suddenness that left her gasping for breath. Much later she thought that if he'd asked her to marry him at that instant she'd have agreed like a shot.

CHAPTER EIGHT

'WHY AREN'T YOU agreeing to get engaged?' Veena peered worriedly across the table at Shweta.

Nikhil was out of town for the day, and Shweta had offered to come over and spend time with Veena after work. Now, after ten minutes of being cross-examined by Veena on every possible aspect of her relationship with Nikhil, she was wishing she'd stayed back in the office.

'I'm not sure if he's really in love with me,' she said.

When they'd woken up the morning after they'd made up he'd turned to her and said, 'You know, you're the only person I know who's been really, really angry with me multiple times and hasn't ended up calling me an illegitimate bastard.'

Evidently he thought that was the ultimate proof of her goodness as a human being, and that had further confirmed her opinion on why he wanted to marry her. He might not be conscious of it himself, but he felt that he was safe with her—she knew everything about him, and she accepted him the way he was. In Delhi he'd told her that the only girl he'd been in a long-term relation-

ship with had broken off with him when she found out
he was illegitimate. He'd made a joke of the incident,
but Shweta couldn't help feeling that it had affected him
badly. And the facts spoke for themselves—since then
he'd had one meaningless fling after another.

'I don't know why you think that,' Veena was saying. 'He's crazy about you. He can't stop singing your
praises.'

Shweta sighed. This was why she hadn't wanted to
come. She didn't like discussing Nikhil with anyone—
and especially not his stepmother. She wasn't even sure
why she was holding out, not agreeing to marry Nikhil,
when every cell in her brain was crying out to her to
say yes. For the last few days she had been wondering
if she'd made a mistake—Nikhil had displayed every
sign of being deeply in love with her.

'It's complicated,' she said finally.

Veena stayed silent for a while, then she asked dif-
fidently, 'Does Nikhil talk about his parents?'

'Not much,' Shweta said, feeling more and more
uncomfortable. 'I get the impression he's not on good
terms with them.'

'No, he quarrelled very badly with his father when
he visited us last. But I know his father would forgive
him if he just made the first move—called him up, or
visited us in Kerala.'

'From what I understand, Nikhil thinks it's his father
who needs forgiving,' Shweta said sharply.

Veena looked even more distressed. 'He doesn't understand… It's my fault. I should speak to him, but it's
so difficult…'

'I don't think it's your fault at all,' Shweta told her. 'Let's talk of something else, Veena Aunty. I don't think Nikhil would be very happy if he knew we were discussing his parents.'

Veena changed the topic, but after dinner she came back to it again. 'Shweta, I know you think you shouldn't get involved, but it would help so much if you could speak to Nikhil once. He'll listen to you—he cuts me off every time I bring up the topic.'

Privately Shweta thought that Nikhil would cut her off as well—and a lot more rudely. Persuading Veena of this was way beyond her powers, though, and Shweta found herself agreeing to try and speak to him.

At least one person seemed happy, she thought gloomily as she left the flat—Veena was beaming. Clearly she thought Shweta would have everything sorted in no time.

Nikhil got back to Mumbai the next day, and he called her almost as soon as he landed.

'Can you get out of the office a little early today?' he asked. 'I thought we could meet up for a drink after work and you could come over for dinner with us afterwards—I was planning to order in so Amma gets a break from cooking.'

For once Shweta wasn't looking forward to meeting him, and she almost chickened out before better sense prevailed. Given that she'd been stupid enough to promise Veena that she'd speak to Nikhil, she might as well get it done with.

'I can leave by six,' she said. Deepa was out for a meeting, and it was best to leave before she got back.

'Great. I'll pick you up from outside your office.' He paused, then said softly, 'I've missed you.'

'Umm…me too,' Shweta said self-consciously.

There were multiple disadvantages to working in an open office—not least of which was everyone around her being able to hear what she was saying. She rang off as soon as she could, and went back to work—she'd dawdled a bit in the first half of the day, and would have to work like a beaver to be done by six.

Nikhil took her to a rooftop lounge bar in a swanky new hotel—thirty-four floors up, it had an amazing view of the Mumbai skyline on one side and the sea on the other.

The wind whipped at Shweta's hair, and she grimaced a little as she sat down next to him on an elegant black sofa.

'Don't you like it?' Nikhil asked.

'Oh, I do,' she said. 'It's just that if I'd known we were coming here I'd have dressed up a little.'

She was wearing a lime-green cotton *salwar kameez*, with matching leather slippers. Everyone else was in Western clothes, and there were a fair number of foreigners around. Nikhil himself was wearing an expensive-looking jacket over jeans and a white linen shirt, and his shoes looked as if they were designer-made.

His gaze softened as he looked at her. Her cheeks had turned pink and her hair was tousled by the breeze. She'd never looked prettier.

'You look perfect,' he said. 'I like you better in regular clothes than when you're dressed up with make-up on.'

Given that she'd spent a frantic ten minutes in the office loo, trying to do her face, that didn't say much for her make-up skills, but Shweta laughed.

'That's because you're used to hobnobbing with actresses and models all the time,' she said. 'It's a relief being with a frump.'

'You're not a frump.' Nikhil leaned across and touched her face lightly. 'I always thought you were beautiful—even when you were in school and wore those hideous glasses with black plastic frames.'

Shweta put her head to one side. 'That's a bit difficult to believe,' she said. 'Sure you aren't brainwashing yourself? Telling yourself you've always loved me and that it was fate, meeting me again…?'

'I'm sure,' he said, and tipped her face up to drop a kiss on her lips.

Shweta squirmed away—she was conservative enough to feel uncomfortable about kissing in public. 'Don't,' she said. 'There are other people around.'

He moved away a little and gave her an indulgent smile. 'You're cute when you're embarrassed,' he said.

'I'm even cuter when I wallop people with my handbag,' she retorted. 'And that's what going to happen to you if you try kissing me again.'

'I have a violent girlfriend,' Nikhil informed the server who'd just come up with their drinks. 'If you see blood pouring out of my head you'll know I've just been savagely attacked by her.'

'Yes, sir,' the man said gravely.

Shweta went scarlet. 'He's joking,' she said.

'Yes, ma'am.'

'And there aren't any oranges in my sangria. Only enough apples to make a pie with.'

He peered into her glass. 'I'm sorry, ma'am. I'll let the bartender know. I think the recipe we use doesn't have oranges in it. Can I offer you something else instead?'

'No, it doesn't matter.'

She looked so disappointed that Nikhil laughed.

'Why are you so stuck on the oranges?' he asked when the server had gone away. 'I think you injured that poor man's pride, finding fault with his recipe.'

Shweta glared at him. 'You'll be the one injured if you make any more stupid remarks. And a lot more than just your pride.'

Nikhil laughed and threw up his hands in surrender. 'I'm sorry...I'm sorry. Couldn't resist it.'

Slightly mollified, Shweta sat back and sipped at her drink. She'd had sangria for the first time in Spain, and loved the way they made it there. It just didn't taste as good without the oranges, but it would sound silly and pretentious to say so.

She was wondering how to broach the topic of his parents with Nikhil when she saw him take a jewellery box out of his pocket.

'I got you something,' he said.

He clicked the box open and there, nestled in black velvet, was a pair of exquisite diamond earrings. They matched the ring he'd given her earlier, and in the evening light the diamonds sparkled with all the colours of the setting sun.

'They're lovely,' she said. 'Thank you, Nikhil!' Taking them out of the box, she slid them into her ears.

Nikhil watched her and said, 'I wish you'd done the same with the ring.'

She was about to give a flippant reply, but there was something in his voice that stopped her. 'Nikhil—I've only asked for some more time,' she said helplessly.

He met her gaze squarely. 'You can have all the time you need. I'm not trying to pressure you into saying yes. It's just that sometimes—well, sometimes I wish I didn't have to wait.'

There was a short pause and Shweta kept on looking at him, scanning his eyes keenly. She'd come very close to agreeing to the engagement twice before, but doubts had held her back. Now she was almost a hundred percent sure that Nikhil was in love with her—the doubts were probably stemming from her own lack of self-confidence. There were risks, of course. Nikhil would never make a safe or comfortable husband, and with his lifestyle he would always be surrounded by women a dozen times more attractive than her. But which was better? Taking the risk of having her heart broken some years down the line, or making sure she got it broken right away by breaking up with him?

Nikhil looked away first. 'I'm sorry,' he said. 'This is way too heavy for evening conversation.' He picked up the jewellery box and put her old earrings into it, held the box out to her. 'Here—maybe you should put these away before you lose them.'

As she took the box from him she noticed that his hands were shaking a little—and his lips were compressed, as if he was suppressing a strong emotion with some difficulty.

'Have you got the ring with you?' she asked.

Nikhil's eyes flew to her face. He shook his head, but his eyes were ablaze with hope. 'I'm a little superstitious about carrying it,' he said. 'Does this mean…?'

'It means, yes—I'd love to marry you,' Shweta said. Nikhil promptly pulled her into his arms and did his best to kiss her senseless. Shweta emerged from his arms a few minutes later with her hair tumbled and cheeks aflame.

'I told you not to kiss me in front of other people,' she muttered, but she wasn't really angry this time.

Nikhil looked completely unrepentant. 'Special circumstances,' he said. His eyes were sparkling with devilry and he looked magnificent, with sunlight glinting off the angles of his perfectly sculpted face and his lean, strong body draped across the sofa.

'You know, this is a pretty nice hotel,' he said. 'What do you say to checking into one of the rooms and celebrating our engagement properly?'

It sounded too tempting for words, but Shweta frowned in mock annoyance. 'Absolutely not,' she said. 'We're not officially engaged until you give me the ring anyway. And I want to finish my drink.'

Nikhil watched her sip at the drink. Under his scrutiny she grew more and more conscious, finally spilling a bit onto her clothes.

'Stop it,' she said, swatting at his hand as he leaned

forward and mopped at the stain with a spotless hand-kerchief. 'You're doing it on purpose—looking at me like that.'

'Like what?' he asked innocently, leaning back in his chair. 'Can't I even look at my fiancée?'

His eyes were dancing with unholy glee and Shweta frowned at him. 'You know exactly what I mean,' she chided. 'Let's talk about something else.'

'There *was* something I wanted to ask you, actu-ally,' Nikhil said, and his abrupt switch to a serious tone made her look up in surprise. 'Would you object if Amma came and lived here in Mumbai?'

'I thought she didn't want to move?'

'I'm going to convince her,' Nikhil said, and there was a confident smile on his lips. 'I was originally going to ask her to move into my flat, but now I think it would work better for all of us if I get her another apartment in the same building.'

It was the perfect opening, and in spite of her mis-givings Shweta took it.

'Veena Aunty's not going to move here until you sort things out with your dad,' she said. 'She's spoken to me a couple of times about it.'

Nikhil frowned. 'I thought I told you—my father and I aren't on speaking terms any more.'

'That's exactly what's upsetting Veena Aunty. Look, I don't want to interfere, but for my sake just give her a fair hearing, OK? I won't bring the topic up again afterwards.'

'I'll speak to her,' Nikhil said. 'But right now I'm calling for the bill, and then we're heading to my office so that I can retrieve the ring. I knew it was a good sign, finding those matching earrings.'

'Yes, of course—*that's* why I agreed to marry you,' Shweta said. 'So that I could get a ring to match my earrings.'

He laughed. 'I'm too worried that might be true to ask questions,' he said. 'I know how important it is for you to have matching accessories.' He looked pointedly at her lime-green slippers and bag, and Shweta made a face. 'But let's come back here after we get the ring—I do want to celebrate properly.'

As it turned out they didn't end up going back—Nikhil remembered that the ring was in his flat, and that Veena was there, waiting for them for dinner.

'OK if I tell her?' Nikhil asked in an undertone when they reached his apartment. 'I'm sorry about this. I completely forgot that she was here, that I'd even told her we'd come back for dinner.'

'You told me,' Shweta said, suppressing a smile. It was rather endearing, his having forgotten all the plans he'd made for the evening just because she'd agreed to marry him. 'Let's tell her—and let's celebrate by ordering in the most expensive meal possible.'

To say that Veena was over the moon was an understatement. She hovered over Shweta and made gushing remarks and generally got in the way, but it was impossible to be annoyed with her because she was so genuinely happy. The only sour note was introduced when she asked Nikhil when he would tell his parents.

'I'm not planning to speak to them,' he said shortly. 'You can tell them if you want.'

Veena shot Shweta an appealing look, but Shweta didn't want to interfere in something that Nikhil evidently felt strongly about. She changed the topic and Veena followed her lead, though a worried frown still puckered her forehead.

Nikhil was just dropping Shweta back home, and she looked at him in surprise when he pulled the car over halfway between their apartments. 'Something wrong with the car?' she asked.

He shook his head. 'No, there's something wrong with me,' he said, leaning over her to release her seat belt and pull her into his arms. 'I'm likely to die of frustration,' he muttered against her lips as he began to kiss her. 'We should have checked into that hotel, and to hell with everybody else.'

The kiss was explosive, and when they finally broke apart Shweta found herself trembling.

'We're likely to get pulled in by the cops for indecent behaviour in public,' she said shakily. 'Let's go.'

Priya had some friends over, and Nikhil refused to come upstairs. He knew Shweta well enough to know that she'd feel awkward and embarrassed taking him into her room if other people were around.

'I'll see you soon,' he said, caressing her face.

Even the gentlest touch had the capacity to send her up in flames, and for a second she was tempted to forget her scruples and drag Nikhil up to her flat. Then she remembered Veena, and how scandalised she would be if Nikhil stayed the night with Shweta. Sighing, she stepped back and waved as Nikhil got into his dangerous-looking car and drove away.

Shweta spent the next day in a happy daze. So far she'd only told Priya about the engagement. Her father and aunt would need to be told soon, but Shweta wanted to tell them face to face. She was slightly apprehensive about her father's reaction. In spite of having finally broken away from her father's overpowering influence, she found herself regressing a bit now, when it came to her marriage—she wanted him to approve.

It was around seven in the morning on Saturday when her phone rang, and for a few seconds Shweta didn't recognise the agitated female voice. When she finally realised who it was, she said, 'Veena Aunty, you need to calm down—I can't understand a word of what you're saying.'

'I need to come and see you. Can you message me your address? I'll take a taxi and come.'

'What's happened? Is Nikhil OK?'

'Yes, yes, Nikhil is fine. But he's very upset with me, and I really need to see you before I leave.'

'Leave for where?' Shweta asked in bewilderment. Only the day before Nikhil had told her that Veena might be staying on for another week, to meet some distant relatives from the US who were passing through Mumbai.

'I'm leaving for Kerala today. Nikhil's father has booked the tickets. I just need to go to the airport and pick them up, he said. But I have an hour or two, and I need to speak to you.'

Shweta could get nothing more concrete out of Veena on the phone, and finally gave her detailed directions to her apartment. When she arrived Veena seemed a lot

more composed than she'd sounded over the phone—
only the way she was twisting her *sari pallu* betrayed
how upset she was.

'Why is Nikhil angry?' Shweta asked gently.

'I asked him to tell his parents about the engagement and he refused. Maybe I should have let it go, but
I thought it was important for him to call them—and
they will need to be involved in the preparations for
the wedding… Your father would think it very strange
if they didn't participate. Then Nikhil said he wasn't
even planning to invite them.'

Clearly that statement had led Veena to remonstrate
with him, and their argument had got completely out of
hand, with Nikhil storming out of the house at the end
of it. While Shweta sympathised with Veena, she could
see the whole thing from Nikhil's point of view as well.

'He hasn't really forgiven them for all he went
through when he was growing up,' she said gently. 'It
couldn't have been easy, dealing with all the gossip
around his being illegitimate.'

'If he wasn't illegitimate he wouldn't exist,' Veena
said. 'Better being illegitimate than not being born.'

As a statement, it was a difficult one to argue against,
but Shweta was finding it incredible that Veena, who
had far greater cause for complaint than Nikhil, was
staunchly defending her husband.

'I think he feels that his dad was very unfair to you.'

'He doesn't know anything about it,' Veena said. 'It's
I who wasn't fair to Nikhil's father. He's always been a
perfect gentleman.'

OK, this was really strange. Shweta gave up on trying to understand. Her face must have reflected her confusion, because after a pause Veena said with great difficulty, 'I could never be a proper wife to Nikhil's father.'

'Because you couldn't have children?'

'No, that's not what I mean. We never—never lived together like man and wife.'

Never living together *like man and wife* was presumably a euphemism for *we never had sex*, and Shweta finally began to understand. Not sure how to respond, she asked tentatively, 'So, was that because of a medical issue?'

Veena shook her head. 'Not a medical problem. It's not a very...*nice* story. I'm going to tell you, though—that's the only way to make you understand.' She waited till Shweta nodded in assent, and then continued. 'I grew up in a family in Kerala. My parents were very simple folk—they had a farm, and my father was out on the farm most of the day. My mother would be busy with the cooking and the housework and the younger children. I was the oldest and I had three younger brothers.'

She paused a little, and Shweta wondered where the story was going.

Veena continued, 'There was a distant cousin of my father's who used to come home often. He was a college graduate, but he was unemployed. He told my mother he would help me with my studies...'

And then Shweta knew. It was the kind of story she'd read in magazines and books and been horrified by—hearing Veena talk about it in her flat monotone was sickening in a more gruesomely immediate way, even couched in euphemisms.

'He misbehaved with me—I was only nine…' It was a heart-rending story.

'I'm so sorry,' Shweta said, and the words sounded pathetically inadequate. 'I can't imagine how you would have felt… Didn't you tell anyone?'

'I was scared,' Veena said, and smiled briefly. 'It was too shameful to talk about. And my mother was always so busy. It went on for three years, until I turned twelve and became a woman.'

Became a woman was a common way of describing reaching puberty, and Shweta didn't ask for an explanation.

'And then you married Nikhil's father?'

'It was an arranged marriage—my father chose the groom for me. Nikhil's father was well-educated, and he lived in Pune. I wanted to get away from the village.'

Shweta noted that, like most ultra-conservative women, Veena didn't call her husband by name— 'Nikhil's father' was the term she always used. Irrelevantly Shweta wondered what Veena had called him through the ten years before Nikhil was born.

'How old were you when you married?'

'Nineteen. At first Nikhil's father thought I was just shy and scared, because I was so young. Then he realised that something was wrong.'

'And you told him?'

Veena shook her head. 'He guessed. He asked who the man was. I couldn't talk about it. I never have. This is the first time I've—' She broke off and her face contorted with grief. 'Nikhil's father was so good to me. He was like a brother to me after that. I felt terrible— he was a young man and I was ruining his life. I could never have his children...'

'And then he met Ranjini Aunty?'

'We'd been married for ten years. He never reproached me. If I tried to apologise all he would say was that it wasn't my fault. But I knew he wanted a proper family—not a wife in name only who cooked and cleaned... And then he met Ranjini. He didn't want to hurt me, but they fell in love. They never wanted to tell me. It was only when they found out that there was going to be a baby that Nikhil's father came and told me. Even then he said that Ranjini would move to a different city and he would send money to look after the child...'

'You asked him to bring her home instead?'

'Yes.' Veena tried to smile. 'Nowadays it would be a lot simpler—I would have a job, and I could divorce him so that he could marry Ranjini instead. But I had no job, only a high school education, and I couldn't stand the thought of going back to my village. My parents would have died of shame. And I wanted to see a baby in the house—I wanted Nikhil's father to watch his son grow up.'

A thought struck Shweta. 'Was the man still there? In your village?'

Veena shook her head. 'He died in a motorcycle accident soon after I got married. So at least I didn't have to see him when I went home on visits. And I don't think he misbehaved with any other girls—he had begun to drink, and people stopped allowing him into their homes.'

There was a short pause while Shweta digested what she'd just been told.

Then Veena said, 'Nikhil isn't really illegitimate.'

'But I thought you said a divorce wasn't possible?'

'Not then. But around the time Nikhil got expelled from school we were shifting cities anyway, so his father and I filed for divorce by mutual consent. Ranjini and his father married soon after the divorce was finalised.'

Shweta stared at her. 'But why haven't you told Nikhil this?' she asked. 'It would make things so much easier for him!'

'He knows,' Veena said sadly. 'He was the first person we told. It made him settle down for a while, but then he started brooding about it and he turned very bitter. You see, he was always very attached to me. Both his parents were working, and I'd looked after him for most of his growing up years—I'd always loved children, and maybe I even spoilt him a bit. I was so worried about people misunderstanding, thinking I was ill-treating him because he was my husband's illegitimate child… At some point he started blaming his parents. He thought they had coerced me into agreeing to the divorce. Nothing I could say would convince him.'

'He's never told me about this,' Shweta said in a daze. 'And we've discussed it a lot. He even told me he was upset because his dad and mom are "pretending" to be married.'

'That's what he said to them as well. The last time he

was home he had a terrible fight with his father. And he got so angry yesterday, when I tried to convince him to make up with them… I can't stay with him any more. I feel like I've stolen Ranjini's son away from her.'

Shweta sat silently for a while, trying to absorb what she'd heard. She felt sorriest for Nikhil's father—to be vilified by his own son for a sin he hadn't really committed seemed grossly unfair.

'Do you want me to tell him—tell Nikhil, I mean?'

Veena shook her head in panic. 'No! I can't bear the thought of him knowing—he's more than a son to me. It would kill me, having him know what happened to me.'

Shweta stared at her in frustration. 'He'd understand, Veena Aunty, and he wouldn't mention it to you ever! It's the only solution—can't you see?'

Veena shook her head again. 'It would kill me,' she repeated. 'Promise me you won't tell him.'

When Shweta hesitated, she said, 'You have to promise me. Otherwise I'll need to cut off all ties between me and Nikhil.'

Which would only make matters worse. And in any case, whatever she might feel about it, the secret was not hers to share. Reluctantly, Shweta promised not to breathe a word to Nikhil.

'But what do you want me to do, then? What was the point of telling me this if you don't want me to tell Nikhil?'

'Convince him to come and meet his father,' Veena said. 'To reconcile with him. If his father wants to tell him part of the story I won't say anything. But Nikhil needs to make the first move.'

'So far my trying to convince him has been pretty disastrous,' Shweta said. 'But I'll try once again if you want.'

It was getting late, and Shweta called a cab to drop Veena to the airport. She even offered to come with her and help her get her ticket from the airlines, but Veena refused.

'I've troubled you enough today,' she said, giving Shweta a grateful kiss on the forehead. 'God bless you, child. I'm sure Nikhil will listen to you.'

Marvelling at Veena's completely misplaced confidence in her, Shweta waved her goodbye. Then she looked down at the ring on her finger, twisting it around a couple of times with a wry smile on her lips. She'd have to speak to Nikhil, but given a choice between bringing up the topic with him and getting a root canal treatment, she'd choose the root canal any day. Perhaps even without anaesthetic.

CHAPTER NINE

'THE LEAST YOU could do is hear me out!'

Nikhil said steadily, 'I've heard enough. Shweta, I hate to say this, but you have no idea of what you're talking about.'

'But you're not even illegitimate! Your parents got married, didn't they?'

'Yes, they did—but that's not the point. They coerced Amma into agreeing to the divorce.'

Shweta gave him an exasperated look. 'She was an adult woman! You can't force someone into a divorce like that. Does it never occur to you that she might have had her own reasons for agreeing?'

As soon as she said it Shweta realised that she was skating a little too close to the truth.

Nikhil was shaking his head, and though he sounded quite calm when he spoke a vein was throbbing in his temple. 'Yes, she *did* have her reasons. She had no job, and she was from a poor and terribly conservative family—they wouldn't have taken her back if my dad had thrown her out. She'd have probably starved on the streets!'

'Nikhil, I've met your dad. And I've heard Veena Aunty talk about him so much. There's no way you can make me believe that he forced her into a divorce.'

'Perhaps it wasn't that, then. Perhaps it was me.'

'Perhaps it was you, what? *You* threatened to throw her out?'

Nikhil shook his head. 'No. Maybe you're right, my dad would have supported her financially, but she'd never have seen me again—she had no rights over me. I wasn't related to her. Maybe that's what she couldn't deal with. She was barren herself, but she loved children. She'd looked after me all my life and she had no other real family. Even her parents were dead by then, and she wasn't very close to her brothers.'

If Shweta hadn't known it to be untrue, it would have seemed a very plausible story. For a second she wondered if she should just let the topic rest. She couldn't help remembering Veena's tortured expression, though, and in spite of her better judgement she ploughed on. 'Nikhil, it's stuff that's between *them*. You'll never know what really happened. Why don't you take them at face value? Veena Aunty's obviously happy with them, or she would have agreed to come and live with you.'

Nikhil asked abruptly, 'Why are you so interested in me making up with my parents all of a sudden?'

'I told you! Veena Aunty came to me and she was upset—I'm trying to help. But the more I speak to you, the more convinced I am that it's utterly useless trying to talk sense into your thick head.'

'And from what I can figure, Amma's worried that

your father will say no to the wedding if my parents aren't involved at every stage. I can't think where she would have got the idea other than from you,' he said.

The thought that she was ashamed of his background had been eating at him from the day they'd started dating. Shweta still hadn't told her father that they were engaged. He'd told himself that he would give her time, but in the face of her insistence that he reconcile with his parents it was difficult not to flare up at her.

'I've *never* spoken to her about what my father might say!' Shweta exclaimed. 'Really, Nikhil, you're pushing it a bit too far. Even if my father said no, that wouldn't stop me from marrying you.'

Nikhil shrugged, his eyes remote. 'Your father will hate the thought of us marrying, won't he?'

Shweta hesitated. She wasn't really sure how her father would react—she suspected he wouldn't be very pleased, but explaining to Nikhil in his current mood that her father had rigid views on most things and rarely approved of her decisions would be difficult.

'I'm not sure,' she said finally. 'It doesn't really matter, does it?'

He didn't answer.

Shweta said, '*Does* it, Nikhil?'

'It doesn't matter to me,' Nikhil said slowly. 'I know you keep saying you're out of your dad's shadow, but you're always trying to live up to his expectations.'

'What?'

'Now that you've found out that my parents are married after all you want me to reconcile with them, so that you can present a nice textbook family to your father. Reformed son, reasonably successful, legally married parents…'

Shweta stared at him for a few seconds, and then anger began to kick in. 'If I cared about any of that I wouldn't have got involved with you to begin with!' she said. 'I could have gone ahead and married Siddhant, or someone like that. Why would I bother getting engaged to *you*?'

There was another short pause, and then Nikhil said, 'I guess it helps that you actually enjoy sleeping with me.'

His voice wasn't even cold, it was matter-of-fact, and somehow that made it worse.

'You don't have a very high opinion of me, do you?' Shweta asked, fighting to keep her voice steady.

'I could say the same of you,' Nikhil said.

Quite suddenly, Shweta knew she'd had enough. Nikhil didn't trust her, and there was nothing she could say that would make a difference. It was ironic, really—given the number of relationships he'd had in the past, *she* was the one with a logical reason not to trust *him*.

'Maybe we should take a break from each other,' she said, and she was surprised at how calm she sounded. Jumbled thoughts were warring for attention in her mind—one part of her was grappling with a deep sense of hurt, while another was wondering whether she was going completely mad.

Nikhil had gone very still. 'Just because I won't listen to you and go running to my parents?'

She bit her lip. It wasn't that. It was because he didn't trust her, and because she still wasn't sure if he really loved her. At that point if Nikhil had made the slightest move towards her she would have probably collapsed gratefully into his arms. He didn't, though—he just kept looking at her, his expression grim.

'Not just that,' she said finally. 'I'm not sure you're really committed to us being together. It's just convenient because you've known me for so long, and…and because I know about your family and everything.'

There—she'd said it.

His face was like granite, but she floundered on. 'We don't really have much in common. I don't move in the same circles as you do, I wouldn't fit in with all your celebrity friends, and you'd get bored with me after a while.'

'Spare me,' he said. 'I've used the "it's-not-you-it's-me" line too often to be fooled by it. We'll take a break, then, if that's what you want.' When she didn't answer, he said, 'Let me know when you're ready to give it a go again.'

Shweta nodded silently and Nikhil turned towards the door. Halfway there, he turned back, and Shweta felt a ridiculous surge of hope go through her. His eyes were still grim, though, and the hope died as quickly as it had been born.

'If we do get back together it has to be on the understanding that you don't try interfering in parts of my life that don't concern you,' he said, and his voice was hard and uncompromising.

'I'll try to remember that—if I'm ever tempted to get back with you,' Shweta said hotly.

He shrugged. 'Always better to make things clear.'

Shweta suddenly saw red. Despite what he'd said, he seemed so *sure* that she'd come crawling back to him. Rather as if she was a child throwing an unnecessary tantrum. He wasn't even acknowledging that they had a genuine problem, preferring instead to believe that she was splitting up with him because she was ashamed of his parentage.

Deliberately she took the diamond engagement ring off her finger and tugged the matching earrings out of her ears.

'Maybe you should take these with you,' she said, her voice icy-cold. 'Just in case I don't change my mind.'

Something changed in Nikhil's face and Shweta knew that she'd done something that couldn't be easily undone. For a few seconds she stared into his eyes, her expression defiant as she held out the jewellery.

'Sell the stuff if you don't change your mind,' he said and, turning around, he strode out of the room without another word.

The rest of the day was hell for her. Unable to cry, she paced the room, replaying the things Nikhil had said over and over in her head. What he'd said had revealed a lot about the way he thought of her. Perhaps there were excuses that could be made for him—she was in no frame of mind to make them. All she could think was that she'd been right all along when she'd believed he didn't love her.

'I need a week off,' she told Deepa the next day.

She'd expected Deepa to create trouble. The sleepless night had, however, left dark circles under her eyes, and she looked only inches away from a nervous breakdown.

Deepa took one look at her and nodded briskly. 'Sure,' she said. 'Hand over your work to Faisal. He owes you for picking up the slack when he broke his wrist. Do you want to take off from tomorrow or Monday?'

'Tomorrow, please,' Shweta said.

She left the room without remembering to thank Deepa, and the other man in the room raised his eyebrows.

'Getting soft in your old age, Deepa?' he asked.

She laughed and shook her head. 'Shweta's a good resource,' she said. 'And Diwali's coming up anyway, so work is slack. Something must have happened— she's behaving very uncharacteristically.'

'Boyfriend trouble?'

'Isn't it always? And in this case the boyfriend is a hotshot type. Sometimes I feel thankful I'm middle-aged and married and beyond all this.'

Shweta would have given a lot to be beyond heartbreak, but unfortunately there wasn't a switch she could turn off to stop the hurt. Mechanically, she took Faisal through the documents on the audit she was currently handling.

'Is everything OK?' he ventured once she was done. 'You look upset.'

Shweta made an effort to pull herself together. 'Everything's fine,' she said. 'I just need a break. Now, are you sure you've got all that?'

'I think so,' Faisal said. 'You're still in town, right?

Or are you going to Pune? I might need to call you if I get stuck.'

Until he mentioned it Shweta hadn't thought of going to Pune, but now that the idea had presented itself it seemed the logical thing to do.

'I'll probably leave tomorrow,' she said. 'I haven't seen my dad in a while.'

She booked her bus tickets online before she left the office. Nikhil had tried calling her once, and she half expected him to be waiting for her when she got back home. There was no sign of his gleaming black car, though. Not sure whether she was disappointed or relieved, she climbed the stairs to her second-floor flat. It didn't take long to pack, and for the sake of something to do she clicked on the TV.

She was flipping channels when she came across a live telecast of a Bollywood awards show. Award shows were a dime a dozen now, and she vaguely remembered Nikhil talking about this particular one with her. Perhaps that was what made her stay tuned to the channel, blankly watching a lissom starlet gyrating around the stage with a troupe of bare-chested male dancers. The number came to an end and the starlet ran off the stage to thunderous applause. Anjalika Arora came onto the stage next, and Shweta sat up.

Anjalika looked stunning, in a gold sequinned sari with a halterneck blouse. She was heavily made-up, and even under the glaring lights she looked a good ten years younger than she actually was—the young debutant actor next to her was completely overshadowed. They were speaking into the microphones alternately—a carefully rehearsed but impromptu-sounding conversation, full of innuendo and Bollywood in-jokes. Anjalika announced the next set of awards and stepped off the stage. The camera followed her as she went back to her seat in the audience, and with a jolt Shweta realised who she was sitting next to. *Nikhil.* In a perfectly cut evening suit, with his hair gelled back, he looked remote and rather grim. The camera stayed focussed on him for a few seconds, and Shweta found herself hungrily taking in every detail of his appearance.

In spite of telling herself that she was being stupid, Shweta stayed glued to the TV until the programme came to an end. They didn't show Nikhil or Anjalika again, and she found herself wondering if they'd left together. Then she shook herself in annoyance. Nikhil's job entailed attending events of this sort—from what he'd said, he didn't even like them much—but they helped him build contacts that would be useful for his business. And surely it was unfair expecting him to stay home and brood when Shweta herself had been the one to split up with him.

It was five in the morning when she got out of bed after a largely sleepless night. It took her less than half an hour to bathe and change. She'd planned to have breakfast before she left, but her appetite had almost completely deserted her.

The bus route to Pune was one she had taken so often that she hardly registered the spectacular view of the Western Ghats as the bus zipped down the expressway. She couldn't stop thinking of Nikhil, of the expression on his face when she'd asked him to go. Slowly she was beginning to question her own behaviour. Shouldn't she have paused a little? Tried to understand *why* he'd come up with the ridiculous idea that she was ashamed of him? Quite likely it was something she'd said or done that had given him the impression. And instead of waiting till they'd both had a chance to calm down she'd given him back his ring.

Her father was waiting for her at the bus stop in his battered old Fiat. It was the same car he'd used for the last fifteen years, and nothing would convince him that he should upgrade.

'You needn't have come to pick me up,' Shweta said, the way she did every time.

So far it hadn't deterred Dr Mathur from driving down to the bus station whenever she was expected. He took her bag from her and put it in the boot—with a pang, Shweta noticed that his movements were slower than last time. Though in excellent health, Dr Mathur was growing old.

'How's Anita Bua doing?' Shweta's aunt never came to pick her up—instead she stayed at home, cooking up a storm to greet her niece.

'Looking forward to seeing you,' her father said. 'It's been a while since you last visited us.'

He was right—ever since Nikhil had arrived on the scene Shweta had reduced her visits to Pune. She'd told herself that it was because her father and aunt had their own fairly busy lives to lead, because she needed to get out of the habit of running to Pune every time she felt lonely. For the first time it occurred to her that they might have missed her.

'I've been busy,' she said, trying not to sound defensive. 'But I'm here for a week now.'

Her father gave her a quick look—which she missed, being lost in her own thoughts. He didn't say anything. Shweta's aunt, on the other hand, was a lot more vocal.

'Are you ill, child?' she asked, the second she set eyes on Shweta. 'You've got dark circles under your eyes and you don't look half as bouncy as you normally do.'

Shweta winced at 'bouncy'. She didn't feel as if she would even want to smile any time in the foreseeable future—being asked to bounce was almost an unforgivable insult.

'She has a demanding job,' her father said, wheeling her suitcase into the house. 'Let her relax for a while. She probably doesn't want to be bombarded with questions.' But when Shweta had left the room he raised his eyebrows enquiringly at his sister.

'Something's happened,' Anita said, unconsciously echoing Deepa's reaction when she'd seen Shweta the day before. 'I've never seen her like this before.'

Dr Mathur just grunted in response, but Anita knew him too well to be miffed. Even Shweta herself probably didn't realise how much he cared for her.

After a day or so Shweta began to look a little less distraught. Her heart still ached when she thought of Nikhil, and a couple of times she almost broke down and called him. But being around her father and aunt helped. Neither of them were demonstrative people, but they cared for her deeply, and having them around was helping to centre her and make her think more calmly.

Nikhil not having called her was proof in her mind that he'd decided a break-up was the best option. Pride stopped her from making the first move, and as the days went by she was feeling more and more resigned to the possibility that she might never get back with Nikhil.

'Dad, do you remember Mr Nair?' she asked one day, in what she hoped was a casual manner. Dr Mathur was puttering around in the garden, and he carefully finished watering his roses before he answered.

'The building contractor?'

'Yes, he…um…had a son who was in my class in school.'

'Nikhil? I remember him. Felt rather sorry for the boy—he had a lot to deal with. Got expelled from school finally, didn't he?'

Shweta gaped at him. 'Weren't you on the board then? I thought *you* decided to expel him.'

'It was a board decision,' Shweta's father said, frowning. 'He'd been caught smoking on the school premises, and there had been other disciplinary issues earlier. We didn't have much of a choice. But we did call the father down to the school and advise him to take the boy in hand. And we issued a transfer certificate instead of an expulsion letter when he told us that they were moving out of Pune. Why the sudden interest?'

He was looking right at her, and despite herself, Shweta began to blush. 'I ran into him recently,' she said. 'He's doing quite well—runs a large event management company.'

'I'm not surprised. He had a lot of potential even when he was in school.'

Dr Mathur seemed to lose interest in the subject as he examined a fat caterpillar basking on one of his roses. When Shweta went indoors, however, he looked up. There was a thoughtful look in his eyes that his sister would have recognised.

Once inside, Shweta switched on the TV and began flipping channels. It was an indication of the depths of her desperation that she actually tuned in to the channel that had been screening the awards show, in the hope that they would do a re-run. Seeing Nikhil on TV would be better than not seeing him at all. The channel, however, was running a soap of the warring in-laws variety, and she switched the TV off in disgust.

It would probably have made her feel a lot better if she'd known that Nikhil was in as bad, if not worse shape. He'd spent the days immediately after their quarrel trying to whip up his anger against Shweta. Then slowly dull resignation had begun to settle in. The more he thought about it, the more convinced he was that Shweta's hesitation in getting engaged, and her later insistence on his contacting his parents, had to do with the fact that she was ashamed of his background. Except he could no longer summon up the will to be indignant about it—at times he even found himself thinking that she was right.

The switch from anger to depression made his spirits sink completely. He was sure he still wanted Shweta— whatever else he was confused about, that fact stood out clear and incontrovertible. He'd tried visiting Shweta's apartment, to talk her around, but Priya had told him that Shweta was in Pune for a week. She didn't volunteer any further information, and Nikhil didn't ask. He wanted to approach the whole thing in a more calm and rational manner than he had hitherto—chasing after her to another city would make things worse, if anything.

Then Veena phoned. 'Nikhil, I've been trying to call Shweta but she hasn't picked up her phone. Is she all right?'

'I've no idea,' Nikhil said, his voice bleak. 'We're not engaged any more.' He waited till Veena's agitated outpourings lessened, then said, 'I don't really want to talk about it, Amma.'

'Did you fight?'

'No, we were having a wonderful time together. She just decided she didn't like the shape of my nose,' Nikhil said, his voice dripping with sarcasm. 'Of *course* we fought.'

His stepmother stayed silent long enough for Nikhil to regret his rudeness.

'I'm sorry—' he began, but Veena interrupted him.

'The fight you had with Shweta—was it something to do with your parents? Because I asked her to speak to you again. It wasn't something she would have brought up otherwise.'

'Yes, she told me that,' Nikhil said slowly. 'Why?'

'I thought she would be able to change your mind,' Veena said, sounding utterly devastated. 'I know I should have spoken to you myself, but I *had* tried, and it only made you angry.'

'It's not your fault,' Nikhil said gently. Veena in self-castigating mood could go completely out of control.

'It is. So many things are my fault—I've ruined all your lives!'

'Hang on,' Nikhil said, sounding bewildered. 'Whose lives are we talking about, here?'

There was the sound of sobbing, and then Nikhil could hear his father's voice in the background. He seemed to be trying to calm Veena down—unsuccessfully—and after a few minutes he came to the phone and said gruffly, 'Amma's too upset to talk to you now. I'll ask her to call you back when she's feeling a little better.'

Nikhil didn't reply immediately. It was a long time since he'd last spoken to his father and it felt odd to hear his voice.

'What's wrong, though? Why's she saying she's ruined my life?'

'All our lives,' his father said dryly. 'We don't agree with her, but she's going through a bad patch right now.'

Veena's voice could be heard in the background, raised in tearful and self-recriminatory protest. Nikhil could hear his own mother's soothing tones as well, and in a while Veena quietened down.

'I'm glad I've got to talk to you,' his father was saying. 'It's been a long while—the last time we spoke we both said a lot of things we didn't mean.'

'Right,' Nikhil said awkwardly.

Veena's saying that she'd ruined all their lives was making him think—Shweta had put doubts into his head already, and his father no longer seemed the villain of the piece.

'Your mother's wanted to speak to you for a long

while too,' his father said. 'But she's with your Amma right now, trying to calm her down.'

'I'll call her later,' Nikhil said. He couldn't yet bring himself to apologise for all he'd said during his last quarrel with his parents, and he knew his responses to his father sounded stilted and perhaps a little cold.

'That's all right,' his father said, and to Nikhil's surprise he added, 'Right now your priority should be making up with your young lady—from what your Amma says, she seems pretty special. And, Nikhil…?'

'Yes?' Nikhil said in neutral tones.

'Veena told Shweta a lot of things before she left Mumbai—things she's not spoken to anyone about for a long, long while. She made her swear not repeat any of it to you, but she's going to release Shweta from that promise.'

'Is this something to do with why she waited for fifteen years after I was born before she divorced you?'

'That's part of it,' Mr Nair said. 'I think it will come better from someone outside the family. All three of us have made our fair share of mistakes, and unfortunately you've been the victim of most of them.'

'Shweta and I aren't on speaking terms,' Nikhil said abruptly. 'So maybe you should tell me yourself.'

'And maybe you should try and get back on speaking terms with her,' his father said. 'If she refuses to talk to you that's different, but somehow I'm very sure she won't.'

CHAPTER TEN

THE SOUND OF a powerful car engine made Dr Mathur look up from his beloved roses. The car pulling up outside their house was black and lethal-looking, and the magnificent specimen of manhood emerging from the driver's seat looked as out of place in the little suburban street as a hawk in a chicken coop. He strode up to the little metal gate that separated the garden from the road and Dr Mathur peered up at him, suddenly feeling very old.

'Shweta's not at home,' he said. 'But you can come in.'

Nikhil hesitated. The change in Dr Mathur was disconcerting—he still remembered him as a toweringly imposing figure, and the contrast between that image and the frail, elderly man in front of him took some getting used to.

'I don't know if you remember me,' he said, hesitating a little.

Dr Mathur shot him a piercing look from under his bushy grey eyebrows. 'Nikhil Nair,' he said. 'Even if I didn't remember you I'd have guessed. Shweta's men-

tioned you a couple of times since she's got here. Have
you had lunch?'

Nikhil shook his head. He'd left Mumbai at eleven
in the morning and driven non-stop for five hours, but
he was too keyed-up to think of food.

'Will Shweta be back soon?' he asked.

Dr Mathur grunted. 'I have absolutely no idea. She's
gone to one of those shopping malls to get her aunt a
Diwali gift.'

The disgust in his voice when he said 'shopping
mall' was the kind usually reserved for words like
'cockroach farm' or 'horse manure'. Nikhil smiled involuntarily. 'Which one?'

Dr Mathur evidently thought Nikhil was clean out
of his mind, going to a shopping mall to find Shweta,
when he could wait in the garden for her and admire the
roses instead. Still, he gave him directions to the mall,
and added, 'She was planning to get some curtains as
well, for the living room—though why we need new
curtains I don't understand. These are perfectly OK.'

Glancing at the hideous flowery curtains at the windows, Nikhil grimaced—he could see why Shweta
wanted to change them.

Shweta was wandering despondently through the
mall, wishing that the Diwali decorations weren't quite
so in-your-face. Not to mention the dozens of happy
families milling around—it was enough to turn one's
stomach. But she had managed to get her father some
books he wanted, and she'd picked up a pretty cardigan
for her aunt. The last 'to-do' on her list was getting a
set of curtains for the living room of the Pune house.

Traditionally people spring-cleaned and painted their houses before Diwali—Dr Mathur would protest vigorously if she tried to get painters into the house, but there was little he could do about new curtains other than grumble.

She was comparing swatches of curtain fabric with a set of cushion covers when a shadow fell across the bales of cloth. 'Refusing to match, are they?' a deep voice said, and she looked up.

'What are you doing here?' she asked Nikhil ungraciously, though her legs felt so wobbly that she was glad she was already sitting down.

Nikhil surveyed her silently. She looked a little thinner, he thought, but perhaps that was his imagination. Her eyes were challenging as she looked at him, but her lips trembled slightly and he took heart from that. 'Leave these for a bit,' he said, taking her hands and pulling her to her feet. 'Let's take a walk.'

Like a marionette, Shweta found herself obediently trailing out of the store behind him. He took her hand and drew her into an almost deserted coffee shop.

'I've missed you,' he said softly. 'I can't tell you how much. Will you forgive me and come back to me?'

She was still looking at him, her eyes troubled. 'Do you still think that I…?' she began.

He was already shaking his head vigorously. 'No, I don't,' he said. 'I was being unreasonable and unfair, and… God, Shweta, I love you so much. I can't imagine what I was doing, letting you go like that.'

He was holding her by the shoulders now, rather tightly, and she gave a little gasp. 'I love you too,' she said, and then his lips came down on hers in a hot and hungry kiss.

It was a few moments before they realised where they were. Shweta emerged from his embrace with her hair tumbled and eyes glowing, took a look at the large and interested audience they had collected around them, and promptly buried her face in Nikhil's chest.

He laughed and swung her around, shielding her from the crowd with his body. 'Let's go,' he said, and they walked out of the mall, with Shweta hurrying a little to keep up with Nikhil's long strides.

Once they were in the parking lot, Nikhil took her into his arms again, kissing her unhurriedly and very, very thoroughly.

'I want us to get married as soon as possible,' Nikhil said.

Shweta nodded. She was in a state of deliciously blissful confusion—if Nikhil had suggested moving to the Andamans and living under a coconut tree she would have probably agreed just as willingly.

'Should I speak to your dad?' Nikhil asked, after another short interlude punctuated with kisses and little moans from Shweta. 'Ask him for your hand in marriage? Or do you want to tell him yourself?'

'I'll tell him myself,' Shweta said. 'Might as well do it now and get it over with. Somehow I don't think he'll be surprised.'

He wasn't.

'I suppose I should have guessed,' he said when they told him a little later. 'Well, both of you look happy, which is good. Shweta, did you remember to buy the *diyas* for Diwali?'

Shweta looked immediately guilty, but her aunt stepped in. 'That's all right—what a thing to ask the girl when she's telling you she's just got engaged! I'll go and buy the *diyas*. I'll also get some sweets and things, so that we can celebrate their engagement properly.'

'Why don't all of you come to Mumbai with me and Shweta?' Nikhil asked. 'We can celebrate Diwali there together—I was thinking of calling my family down as well.'

Dr Mathur thought it over for a while. 'Why don't you get your parents to come here instead?' he asked. 'They used to live in Pune. I'm sure they'd like to see the place again.'

'Just because you've turned into an old fuddy-duddy who hates travelling,' Shweta said, leaning over and giving her father an affectionate hug.

Nikhil's eyes widened. Shweta hadn't been lying when she'd said her relationship with her father had changed—right now it seemed as if Dr Mathur was the one in danger of being bossed around by a controlling daughter. He was even keeping his much talked-about opinions to himself.

'What do you think, Nikhil? Would they like to come?' Shweta asked. 'Diwali's more fun in a proper house than in a flat.'

The words were light, but there was an unspoken question in her eyes and he tried hard to reassure her.

'I'm sure they'd love to come—I'll call them and confirm.'

'Diwali's the day after tomorrow,' Dr Mathur said, getting to his feet. 'Better call them now and start booking tickets. Airfares will be sky-high.'

'You've started speaking to your parents again?' Shweta asked, once her father and aunt had gone indoors, tactfully leaving the two of them alone in the garden.

Nikhil nodded. 'Amma called me, but she broke down halfway through the conversation—when I told her that we'd split up. Well, from something she said I gathered that I've probably got the wrong idea about my dad, and when he took the phone I didn't start lashing into him right away.'

Shweta raised her eyebrows. 'Well, that's what's been happening the last few times we spoke,' he said.

'I'm sure he sees it as an improvement,' she said dryly. 'What did he tell you?'

'Not much, really—just that there's a reason why Amma feels she's ruining my life. And that you know what it is.' He looked Shweta squarely in the eyes. 'That's when I realised what a self-centred, bigoted idiot I've been. Even Amma confided in you rather than telling *me* what the real story is.'

'That's understandable,' Shweta said gently, and she went on to tell him what Veena had told her in Mumbai.

She kept the details of what had happened to a bare minimum, trying to focus on Nikhil's father and how he'd been if not blameless, then at least acting for what he thought was the best. Nikhil's lips tightened when she started speaking, but soon his eyes were moist.

'Don't blame Veena Aunty,' Shweta urged. 'It must

have been traumatic. She's a very private, conventional person, and the thought of you or anyone else knowing would have been unthinkable. It was only when she realised the extent of the harm she'd done you that she spoke to me.'

Nikhil shook his head. 'I'm done with blaming people,' he said. 'Poor Amma—to have carried this around with her all her life… And my poor parents too. They were trying to protect her, and into the bargain I turned against them.'

'But now you know,' Shweta said. 'And you can make it up to them.'

Nikhil's parents forgave him readily, and they were ecstatic to hear that he was about to get married. Air tickets at 'sky-high' fares were duly bought, and they along with Veena were on their way to Mumbai the next morning.

'I've hired a car to get them down to Pune,' Nikhil told Shweta. 'I could have gone and picked them up, of course, but I can't bear to let you out of my sight—I'm so worried you'll change your mind.'

'And you're even more worried you'll miss out on all the sweets Anita Bua's making,' Shweta said. 'She's spoiling you rotten—I need to speak to her.'

Nikhil shrugged and nicked a cashew from the bowl of dry fruits and nuts Shweta was chopping. 'What can I say? Women can't resist me.'

'Wait till she hears you. She'll chase you around the house with a broomstick,' Shweta said, slapping his hand away. 'Come and help me do the *rangoli*.'

Nikhil trailed out behind her, but he was more of a

hindrance than a help as Shweta used powdered colours to make the elaborate *rangoli* designs on the floor of the front veranda.

'You've got that line crooked,' he pointed out helpfully, after kissing her on the nape of the neck just as she began on the most complicated part of the design.

Shweta glared at him. 'Why don't you ask Anita Bua if she needs any help? Go and buy some more sweets or firecrackers or something.'

'Firecrackers—that's a good idea,' Nikhil said. 'I don't think anyone's bought any yet.'

He came back just as his parents arrived. His father shook hands with him formally, but both Veena and Ranjini burst into tears and threw themselves into his arms. He stood stock-still for a few seconds, then he hugged them back before pulling away.

'Shh, you'll frighten my brand-new fiancée away,' he said, smiling into their faces. It was the perfect distraction, and both women turned to exclaim over Shweta. Nikhil gave his father a wry look. 'I'm sorry,' he said softly. 'I wish you'd told me.'

Mr Nair's eyes were suspiciously damp as he clapped his son on the shoulder. 'If you'd known you'd have probably become a boring small-time builder like me,' he said. 'Look at you now—you're a hundred times more successful than you would have been if you hadn't rebelled so thoroughly.'

Later in the evening, when the older women were busy making plans for the wedding, Shweta wandered over to the corner of the porch where Nikhil had piled up the firecrackers. Because it was Diwali, and because she'd just got engaged, she'd allowed Anita Bua to bully her into wearing a sari. The lovely pale-gold brocade *benarasi* was draped around her slim curves in graceful folds, and the colour set off her rather elfin looks to perfection.

Nikhil watched her as she carefully opened one of the packets of firecrackers. His father and future father-in-law were discussing a rather intricate twist in state politics. Normally he would have been interested, but now he couldn't take his eyes off Shweta. The front of the house was lit up with strings of fairylights, and after she'd completed her *puja* Anita had lit the little oil *diyas* that were placed in the *rangoli* patterns on the porch. Shweta had now taken a candle out of one of the packets, and was lighting it at one of the *diyas*.

'Careful!' Nikhil exclaimed, getting to his feet as her *sari pallu* brushed the ground dangerously close to the open flame.

Shweta gave him a teasingly provocative little smile. 'Come and help,' she said imperiously, and Nikhil went to her side without even listening to the point Dr Mathur was making about populism and regional vote banks.

Dr Mathur gave a rare smile as he watched Shweta. 'She reminds me so much of her mother,' he said, and Mr Nair nodded in sympathy. He'd first met Mrs Mathur during one of those trips to the movies, long before Shweta was born, and the resemblance was striking.

'I shall light an *anaar* first,' Shweta was announcing. 'Actually, I shall light several. Six, I think. Line them up in the driveway, will you?'

'Yes, ma'am,' Nikhil said.

Shweta lit a sparkler and lightly touched it to each of the *anaars*—they went up immediately, looking like a row of fiery fountains. Shweta took out a packet of rockets next. 'Ooh, I like these,' she said, and lit several of them in quick succession, her eyes following them as they shot up and exploded in a shower of multi-coloured sparks against the night sky.

Shweta's upturned face was too much of a temptation for Nikhil to resist, and he pulled her into his arms to kiss her. Shweta cast an agonised glance towards the porch, but Dr Mathur and Mr Nair were nowhere in sight. Screened from the people in the street by the rosebushes, she went willingly into Nikhil's arms.

'Do you think they'd notice if we slipped away for a bit?' Nikhil asked, nodding towards the house.

'Not until it's dinnertime,' Shweta whispered back. 'Let's light the rest of the firecrackers, and then I'll smuggle you into my room through the back door.'

'Why don't we forget the firecrackers and go now?' Nikhil muttered, bending his head to kiss her again.

Shweta gave it due consideration. 'I suppose we can,' she said. 'Make up for the week we lost.'

And that was exactly what they did.

* * * * *

MILLS & BOON®

Why not subscribe?
Never miss a title and save money too!

Here is what's available to you if you join the exclusive **Mills & Boon® Book Club** today:

* *Titles up to a month ahead of the shops*
* *Amazing discounts*
* *Free P&P*
* *Earn Bonus Book points that can be redeemed against other titles and gifts*
* *Choose from monthly or pre-paid plans*

Still want more?
Well, if you join today we'll even give you
50% OFF your first parcel!

So visit **www.millsandboon.co.uk/subscriptions**
or call **Customer Relations on 0844 844 1351***
to be a part of this exclusive Book Club!